Books by James Ramsey Ullman

AND NOT TO YIELD

STRAIGHT UP

CARIBBEAN HERE AND NOW (with Al Dinhofer)

AMERICANS ON EVEREST

WHERE THE BONG TREE GROWS

FIA FIA

DOWN THE COLORADO

THE DAY ON FIRE

TIGER OF THE SNOWS (with Tenzing Norgay)

THE AGE OF MOUNTAINEERING

BANNER IN THE SKY (THIRD MAN ON THE MOUNTAIN)

THE SANDS OF KARAKORUM

ISLAND OF THE BLUE MACAWS

WINDOM'S WAY

RIVER OF THE SUN

THE WHITE TOWER

HIGH CONQUEST

THE OTHER SIDE OF THE MOUNTAIN

MAD SHELLEY

KINGDOM OF ADVENTURE: EVEREST (editor)

AND NOT TO YIELD

AND NOT TO YIELD

JAMES RAMSEY ULLMAN

DOUBLEDAY & COMPANY, INC.
GARDEN CITY, NEW YORK

To
SANDY RICHARDSON
who climbed it with me

. . . made weak by time and fate, but strong in will to strive, to seek, to find, and not to yield.

Tennyson: ULYSSES

AND NOT TO YIELD

1

In the beginning was the mountain. In the end was the mountain. Between were the miles and the years.

Between were places, faces, voices. Even now, at the end, there seemed to be a voice rising up through darkness, calling "Rick—Rick—"

It might have been Larry's voice. But it wasn't. Turning, he looked down the slope, and there was only white of snow, black of night. What he had heard must have been wind. But there was no wind.

He kicked steps in the snow, moving slowly up the ramp in the sky. Now there was neither wind nor voice, no sound at all but only places, and the places flickered on the snow like images on a screen.

There was the lawn of home on Desmond Street, the elms filing down toward the Texaco station on the corner, and beyond it Claremont Avenue angling off toward downtown Denver. There was a classroom in P.S. 8 (with the name ERIC VENN well gouged into a desktop); a classroom at Hughes High (with a copy of *The Epic of Everest* stashed in the drawer between *Lives of the Presidents* and *Coakley's Algebra*); a classroom at the U of Washington (on a Friday afternoon, with the jalopies waiting in the lot outside, the rows of skis on their homemade roof racks). There were the slopes and trails of the Cascades; of Camp Hale, White Valley, Chamonix, Davos. There were the cities: first Denver; beyond it Seattle, Los Angeles, Paris, Hong Kong, Calcutta, Kathmandu. (But here, except for Denver and Kathmandu, the images were blurred by time and distance.) There were the mountains, not blurred but clear and shining in their hosts: the Lookout, the greater Rockies, the Tetons, Rainier, McKinley, the Apennines, the Alps, the Himalayas.

—And Dera Zor.

In the beginning there was the Lookout. In the end there was Dera Zor. Not far above him now, where white met black, was the summit of Dera Zor.

"We're close," he said to Larry.

But Larry wasn't there. He was down in the bivouac at the foot of the slope, with Tashi and Pembol. Ken Naylor wasn't there. He was still farther down at Camp Five on the ridge. Julian Howard and Franz Harben weren't there. They were—

He wrenched at his mind. No one was there. It was an old story of the mountains that men alone at great heights thought someone was with them. He himself had experienced this before, in the stress of hypoxia, the struggle to breathe.

And yet—

They *were* there. Not places now, but faces. Larry close behind him, with Tashi and Pembol. Then Ken, Julian, Franz; and beyond them, ranged down the mountain, down the miles and years, all the others, in their boots and parkas, with their ropes and axes; and though beards and goggles masked them, he knew the faces and names. Some were near, some were far, but all were with him on the mountain. All were moving with him toward the shining top of Dera Zor.

Now, again, he heard a sound.

A voice?

No.

The wind?

No.

It was his breathing. His struggle for air where there was no air. Stopping, he leaned on his ice ax and sucked in cold drafts of emptiness. From his ramp in the sky he looked out and around him.

2

High though it was, Dera Zor had a neighboring mountain that was higher: Everest was only forty miles away. But from where he stood he could not see it, for Everest was east, he was on Dera Zor's western flank, and eastward there was only its summit, hiding the world beyond. The visible world was on the other three sides. To the north, dim under the stars, the wide miles of Tibet; to the west the white wastes of the Himalayas; to the south the hills and valleys of Nepal and, beyond them, the rim of monsoon clouds shrouding the plains of India.

There was no cloud here, though. No shroud. Only black, white and starlight. Only cold and void.

And now in the void again, faces. Now not bearded and goggled, but the faces of women. The old face of Mrs. Homer Bigelow, seamed and spectacled; the young ones of Carol Flagg, with windblown hair, green ribbon, and of Nima, brown and sloe-eyed, framed with black braid. Beyond them—at first far beyond but then closer, closer—was Kay, neither old nor young, in her beauty, looking upward, but whether at him or Larry he could not tell. And finally, of course, there was Amy—always Amy—watching, grinning; and she alone spoke to him, saying, "No sweat, baby. No sweat at all."

He wasn't sweating. He was cold. The cold of the mountain was in his bones and blood.

He hefted his ax. He climbed again.

Then another voice spoke. Not a woman's but his brother Frank's. And Frank said, "What the hell are you doing?" (That was Frank all right.) Behind him, small and dim, was their mother, saying nothing, quietly looking at Eric with desolate eyes.

He climbed away from them. He kicked steps in deep whiteness. Soon, he knew, still another would appear: not below but above him. And when next he looked up he was there.

"Come on, Rick!" called his father, beckoning.

"Are we almost there?" he asked.

"Almost."

"I'm getting tired."

His father smiled. "—And not to yield," he said.

"What's that mean?"

3

"It means not to give up. A poet called Tennyson said it. 'To strive, to seek, to find, and not to yield.' "

"I bet he never climbed the Lookout."

His father laughed. They rested a little.

"O.K. now?" his father asked.

"O.K.," said Eric.

They went on. And whether it was the rest or what his father had said, or just that the going was easier, he didn't know. But things went better now. His tiredness was gone. Snow and night and cold were gone, and in the sunlight the boulders rose gently toward the summit of the peak. A little later, at exactly noon on the third day after his tenth birthday, they were standing together on top of the Lookout.

"There's Denver," his father said.

But he couldn't see it. Not now. The night and the snow had come back, and there was only the snow sweeping up toward the stars. His father had returned to that other time, that other place. He, Eric Venn, now himself a middle-aged man, was alone on the summit dome of Dera Zor.

He had stopped again. This time, digging his ax into the snow, he rested his arms on its blade and bent his head onto his arms.

Then he looked up, listened. And yes, there was one more voice: the most remote of all, but unforgotten. And the voice called, "Ricky!" . . . Not Eric. Not Rick. But "Ricky! Ricky!"

He turned, looking down, and there close below was the one, the true one, he was waiting for. Not Larry. Not Tashi or Pembol or Ken, or anyone in parka and goggles. Not a man at all but a girl; not a grown girl but a child; and his heart sang as he saw her, saw her snub nose and pigtails, her sweatshirt and jeans, coming toward him out of the gulf of time; and now she was there, she was beside him, and he bent and kissed her and said, "Hi, Robin, you've come back."

"It's been a long way," she said.

"Yes."

"But I caught up."

"Yes."

4

"And now, now can I—oh please, Ricky—can I go on with you—all the way—us two together—?"

Through cracked, rimed lips Eric smiled at his sister. Then he put out his hand and she took it.

"Yes, together," he said.

2

In the house on Desmond Street, hers had been the room next to his (with their brother Frank on the other side); but when they were both small he had scarcely known her at all. Three years younger than he, she lived in a world of dolls, sniffles, hair-braiding, and other little girls with *their* dolls who came to the house and got underfoot. Sometimes he accidentally stepped on a doll (which meant trouble), but otherwise it was a matter of "Hi Robin" and "Bye Robin," of birthday and Christmas presents, and kissing her nose or ear when their mother forced the issue. Often he didn't think about her from one day's end to the next, and assumed it was the same with her about him; so that he could not have been more surprised at what happened during the fall when she was ten and he thirteen.

That was the year he and his father had climbed in the Tetons, and when they got home he noticed that Robin seemed somehow to be "around" more. There was an evening, with all the family in the living room, when she suddenly sat in his lap; others when she appeared in his door while he was doing his homework and stood there watching. Then came the time when, instead of just standing there, she went to him, put her arms around him and said, "I love you, Ricky."

After a swallow he said, "I love you too."

"I mean really love you. Not like my dolls or Daddy and Mommy. I mean like we'll get married when we grow up."

"I don't think we can do that, Robin," he said.

6

"Oh." She thought it over. "Well, then we can climb together."

This too was a surprise. "I didn't know you liked climbing," he said.

"I don't. I mean I never have. But please please take me next time you go."

"You'll have to ask Daddy."

"I have. He says I'm too little. He says even big girls shouldn't climb unless they know how, but how can I know how if I can't try?"

"In a few years you can try," said Eric.

"Oh, I hope so." Robin thought again. "Are there dragons on top of mountains?" she asked.

"No. No dragons."

"Kings and queens, then?"

He looked at her curiously. "Well, kings—sort of."

"No queens?"

"I don't know about queens."

"Where there's a king there must be a queen," said Robin. "Oh Ricky, that's what we'll be some day: a king and queen on top of a mountain."

A king—

It was strange that she had said that. For it had been exactly how he had felt on that day when, aged ten himself, he had stood with his father on top of the Lookout. Beyond any comparison, it was the greatest thing that had yet happened to him in his life.

They had been on the Lookout before—as far as halfway, perhaps—and the first part of the climb was on a familiar trail, up gray tumbled boulders. Then, higher up, it grew steeper. He got tired and didn't think he could make it. But his father stopped and smiled and said, "—And not to yield." And from there on it was all right. Better than all right. His heart was thumping, but not from work; from excitement. They were on the western side of the peak, and as they gained height the sun came up over its summit, turning the rock from gray to glittering gold. It seemed no longer a mountain he was climbing, but a castle—a great

7

golden castle—as he climbed up, and still up, toward its turret in the sky.

He did not look behind him. Not because he was afraid of falling, but because behind, to the west, was Longs Peak, towering above him; and Longs made the Lookout seem what it really was, a mere bump in the foothills of the Front Range of the Rockies. When he didn't see it, however, everything was all right. With Longs gone, the Lookout swelled, grew enormous. Its summit, outlined against the sky, was now the highest in all the world.

Then, at last, came the great moment. Above, there was only sky. His father had stopped and was smiling again, then shaking his hand, and they were *there*, on top, they had gone all the way. As if in a dream, he looked out to the east at the world below him, and no, there was no Longs anywhere, no peak on earth that was higher than where he stood. On this side, the Lookout fell away farther and more sharply than on its other flanks, in great cliffs and ridges to a distant valley. The woods below didn't look like woods, but like the brown-green rug in the living room at home, and a stream running through them like a thread that had fallen from his mother's sewing.

Then his father was pointing out beyond them, saying, "There's Denver." And yes, there it was all right, with no night, no snow to hide it. With a little pretending he could even see past Denver, past the plains beyond, all the way across America to the Atlantic Ocean. With a little more he could see through the blur of Denver straight to Desmond Street, into the living room where his mother was sewing, with Robin and her dolls on the floor beside her; into the upstairs room where his brother Frank was sorting his stamp collection. For a moment he wanted to wave and shout, so that they could see him too, see where *he* was. But he held himself back. He was too old for *that* much pretending.

It was enough that he was where he was: on top of a mountain: a king on a golden castle.

He was no king, though, when they got home that evening.

"Your pants are a mess," Frank said when he saw him.

And his mother: "Good Lord, you're scraped to pieces!"

"We didn't yield," he said. "And on top we—"

But his mother, not listening, was pulling his pants off and talking over her shoulder. "You can't expect the child to take care of himself," she snapped. "But for a grown man, his own father—"

She went on for a bit, with his father saying nothing. Then he went upstairs to shower, leaving Eric to the lecture and iodine.

In later years, when he thought back to it, Eric was not sure what had drawn his father to the mountains. For Arthur Venn, orthodontist, was not at all the usual outdoorsman. He was well enough built, yes, with good shoulders and little belly, and he had strong arms and legs from long hours at his dental chair. But he had been no athlete as a young man ("No time, no money"), and even now in his forties, when he had a little of both, he was neither golfer, hunter nor fisherman, as were so many men of his age and circumstances. What he loved were the forests, the trails, the streams, the high meadows, not for anything he could catch or shoot there, but for their own sakes, and most of all he loved the peaks above them. Not that he was by any means an expert mountaineer; his excursions were more hikes than climbs, on the likes of the Lookout or the "beginners' routes" on bigger peaks. But there was scarcely a summer weekend or holiday that he was not off on the rocks, the slopes, the high places of the eastern Rockies, and when he went out and returned the light in his eyes was not the same as on the other days of his life.

(At least, thought Eric, it must have been a change of pace from straightening kids' teeth.)

His mother didn't go the mountains. He could no more imagine her in the mountains than playing on the Hughes High School football team. And Frank and Robin didn't go either. Robin, of course, was too young, and a girl besides, and Frank, who was old enough to have climbed *real* mountains, didn't want to. He had gone a few times when he was younger, but hadn't liked it, and now in his early teens had not been along for years. "What for?" he said, when Eric once asked him about it. "What's it get you? A medal? Ten bucks?"

"Fun," Eric said.

9

"Fun—Jesus! Dragging your tail up a pile of rocks?"

Frank was small, like their mother, and wasn't an athlete at anything. What he was good at, and liked, was his school work, especially math, and—to Eric—queer things like being his class treasurer, selling ads for the school yearbook, running a paper and magazine route. Plus his stamp collection. Mostly he kept his stamps locked up, but now and then he let Eric look at them, and once, thumbing an album, Eric saw a set he really liked. They were from countries in Africa, and some had animals on them, others pictures of jungles, deserts, even mountains.

"Hey, these are beauts!" he said.

"No, those are junk, dime a set," Frank told him. He turned to another page, where there was a row of dull-looking stamps with only words and numbers. "Now there's a real set," he said. "Know what I paid for them? Thirty cents each. But someday, I bet you, they'll bring that many dollars."

He and Eric didn't talk much together—about stamps or anything else. Partly it was because their three years' difference in age made them interested in different things; but even when they talked about the same thing Frank usually felt another way about it than Eric.

"He's funny," Eric once said to his father.

"Funny how?"

"About stamps . . . And mountains."

His father smiled. "With mountains, Rick," he said, "I guess it's us who're funny."

They kept on being funny. The summer after the "conquest" (that was his father's word) of the Lookout, they took on several of the bigger peaks around Estes Park and, as climax, reached the top of Longs itself. The actual ascent up the well-worn Cable Route was a disappointment to Eric; less a climb than a mere hike. But the thrill of its summit outdid even the Lookout, as he realized that he was now a dizzy 14,255 feet up in the air . . . No, more than that, really 14,260 feet, he realized, while the thrill expanded, for there was not just the mountain but himself too to be counted, and in that summer he was exactly five feet tall.

The next year there was a harder route on Longs and a trek across the College Peaks. And in the next two, the Sangre de Cristos and the Tetons of Wyoming. In the Tetons there was a climbing school; and his father, after reminding him that "there's a depression on," conceded that it was less bad for orthodontists than for some others and treated him to a course of lessons. In these, for the first time, he used a rope, handled an ice ax, and at course's end he and his father, with one of the guides, went to the top of the Grand Teton, in the first "technical" climb they had ever made.

When, back home, he thumped into the house in his new nailed boots, his mother quickly made him take them off. But neither going nor coming was there the trouble there had been when he was younger. As his father put it, she had come to accept their expeditions as a "fact of life."

In terms of time, of course, climbing was just a small part of each year. Between, endlessly, was school: first at P.S. 8, then at Junior High, finally at Hughes. There was *Coakley's Algebra, Lives of the Presidents, A Tale of Two Cities, Beginners' French*. There were odd jobs, movies, sodas, secret cigarettes. There were girls—and dreams of girls—and the two were very different.

From October to June, all there was of mountains was a distant glimpse, if you walked down the street, turned at the Texaco station, and peered across a vacant lot that opened out to the west. But as a substitute, and a magical one, there was his father's shelf of mountaineering books. It was only a small collection of about a dozen titles, but in them was all the adventure, the wonder, of earth's high horizons, and closed in his room through long evenings, Eric read and reread, lived and relived them. With Edward Whymper he challenged the fierce crags of the Matterhorn. With Belmore Browne he probed the icy wastes of McKinley. With Mallory and Irvine he inched his way up the summit ridge of Everest until they disappeared forever in the mists of space. If he was sure of nothing else, he knew that someday he would climb as these men had climbed; and with that knowledge, somehow, he got through fall, winter, spring.

In his dreams he was in Alaska, Alps, Himalayas. The rest of the time he was at 512 Desmond Street with his family. And things happened in the family.

During the winter when he was thirteen he took sick with a fever. For a week he was *very* sick, with temperature so high that there was talk of taking him to the hospital. His mother, however, said no, she could care for him better than hired nurses; so he stayed home, and she did, first through the bad week, then through a second while he got his strength back.

"I've been a lot of trouble," he said to her the day before he was allowed to get up.

She came and sat beside him. "It hasn't been trouble, dear," she told him. "I've been happy to take care of you."

He knew it was true and mumbled, "Thanks, Mom," and was about to start reading when she took his hand. "It's made me feel close to you, Rick," she said. "So much of the time you're—sort of off somewhere."

"You mean when Dad and I go to the mountains?"

"Not just then; when you're home too. Even when we're all in the same room, when we're eating or talking together, you seem so often not really to be there." The hand holding his tightened. "Aren't you happy, Rick?" she asked.

"Sure, Mom," he said. "Sure I'm happy."

"I want you to be, dear. When I've said no to you about something it wasn't because I wanted to make you unhappy. It's only because I don't want you to do things that are foolish and can hurt you."

She bent and kissed him. And when she left he did not read but lay in bed thinking, and what he thought was new and strange and a little frightening; for though it was he who had been sick and she who had taken care of him, he saw now that at bottom, where it counted, his mother needed him more than he needed her.

From now on, he resolved, he would do something about it. He would try to be closer to her, talk to her, tell her his thoughts and feelings. But when he was up and around again, nothing happened. It was the same as before. Both of them lived in the same

12

house, but what they carried around inside was as different as—well—the house and a mountaintop. She had not ever *heard* of Whymper, Browne or George Leigh-Mallory.

With his brother Frank too, even as they grew older, there was little to say or share. This, he knew, was often the way with brothers, and sometimes it was worse, with the younger steadily on the receiving end of pokes and hammerlocks. At least he didn't have to put up with this. Frank had never been the poking hammerlocking kind, and even if he had he couldn't have done much about it anymore, for by the time they were sixteen and thirteen Eric was the bigger and stronger. Often it seemed to him, though, that he would rather have a whole rash of bloody noses than endure Frank's know-it-all superiority.

There were the times he needed help with homework and Frank consented to give it. Usually it was in math, for Eric was as poor at math as Frank was good; but the price he had to pay for a passing grade was almost too high. Frank had coined a private nickname for him—Hillbilly—and through the tutoring sessions it was endlessly, mockingly, "Did you get that, Hillbilly? Is it sinking in, Hillbilly?" And Hillbilly had to grind his teeth and take it.

Then there was money; always money. Eric got a weekly allowance from their father. Frank did not, because he was earning good sums from his after-school enterprises, and kept announcing that "there's a depression on. We shouldn't gouge Dad." Eric certainly didn't want to "gouge" his father. But his odd-job earnings were nothing compared to Frank's income, and even with allowance added he was hard put to find the money for sodas and movies. Sometimes, in desperation, he asked Frank for a loan. Sometimes Frank said no, sometimes yes—at a price. The biggest yes was for three dollars, so that Eric could buy something for their mother's birthday, to be paid back within a month, plus interest of a dime a week.

The gift itself went all right: a bottle of toilet water. Eric paid the ten cents weekly. But when the month was up he had returned only sixty cents of principal, at the end of two months only a dollar, and Frank was growing impatient.

"I'll pay; give me time," Eric told him. "You don't need it now."

"My needing or not needing has nothing to do with it," said Frank. "You undertook an obligation. You owe money. You should pay it."

"I can't—yet."

"You could if you had any responsibility. If you didn't throw money around."

"Around on what?"

"That dingus on your bureau, for instance."

The "dingus" was an ice ax. Eric had bought it the previous fall at Schroeder's Camp and Trail Shop, and though it hadn't been used yet, and wouldn't be until summer, it was the most precious possession he had.

"You paid more than two bucks for that," Frank said.

"What of it?"

"Return it. Schroeder's will give you at least something on it, and you can pay your honest debts."

"I *won't* return it!"

"It might be a good idea," said Frank quietly.

If he had been smarter, Eric would have taken warning and hidden the ax. But he didn't. And when he entered his room the next afternoon, it was gone. His breath came hard and his heart thumped. Running down the hall, he jerked at the knob of Frank's door, but the door was locked. "Let me in!" he yelled.

There was no answer.

"I know you're there. Let me in!"

"I'm busy," said Frank.

"You took my ax."

"That's right."

"You stole it."

"I did not steal it," Frank said in his calmest voice. "I did what any bank would do if you owed money and didn't pay. I foreclosed."

"You—bastard!"

14

"Oho, Hillbilly's foulmouthed."

"Let me in, you bastard!"

Frank began to whistle, and Eric banged on the door with fists and feet. Then there was another sound, a sort of half scream from their mother as she came up the stairs, and he ran past her to his room and locked his own door. He sat on the bed, looking at the blank place on the bureau where the ax had been, and for the first time since he was a very little boy he began to cry.

With his sister Robin there were no fights. At first there had been almost no anything, but then came the lap-sitting, the "I love you, Ricky," and from then on everything was different. She came often to his room, asking him about mountains, reading the books he had taken from their father's shelf, pulling on the boots he had brought back from the Tetons and clumping around in them. To his relief, she did not again propose marriage; but he knew, half-uncomfortably, half-pleasantly, that he was still her king, her hero. On his side, almost with surprise, he realized that she was no longer a child but a girl—and a pretty one.

In the spring of the year after the Tetons she was eleven and he going on fifteen. And one evening his father spoke to him about her.

"Robin's been begging to come with us this summer," he said. "I think she's old enough. What do you say?"

"It's fine with me," said Eric.

And that was the way it happened.

From the beginning things went just right. They rented a cabin for three weeks on the high slopes above Aspen. The weather was good. In a nearby cabin were a young teacher and two students from the university at Boulder, and after watching him on one of the practice cliffs they invited him to go along on one of their climbs. His father, after watching *them*, gave his permission, and the upshot was not one but three ascents better than anything he had yet known. Not only did he climb but he learned. Picking up where the Teton guides had left off, his companions showed him the techniques of balance and friction, of route-finding and selection of holds, of belaying, rappelling, and the other uses to which a rope could be put to protect one's partner and oneself. He was well on his way to being no longer a boy scrambling on rocks, but a mountaineer on a mountain.

Meanwhile his father took Robin on smaller climbs, to teach her "a few little tricks." And when now the three went out together, Eric saw that she had learned quickly and well. If it hadn't been for her pigtails, she would, in her sweatshirt and jeans, have seemed more a boy than a girl, as she moved easily around among the tumbled rocks; and when now and then she scraped or banged herself, there were neither tears nor complaints.

"Good girl," said Eric.

His father beamed. Indeed, so great was his confidence in them that a few days later he left them on their own, while he drove down to Aspen for marketing. "No nonsense now," was all he said as he went off. And for a while there was discussion of what was nonsense and what wasn't. Then Eric decided it was all right to go to the boulder slopes at the base of one of the nearby larger peaks. He took a coil of rope with him, slung over his shoulder, and when they got there tied them onto it and gave Robin an hour's practice on the broken rock.

"Aren't I good?" she asked as they rested.

"Not bad," he conceded.

"Then we can go higher."

"No."

"Please, Ricky."

"It's real mountain above here."

"So it's a real mountain. But we're real climbers. Just a little way up, and I promise—"

There was no boy in her now. She was all girl as she sat beside him, looking up, her eyes pleading. "I promise I'll do just what you say. And we have the rope. What could happen with me tied to the rope?"

"Well—"

"—When you climb even better than Daddy."

It was true: he was a real climber now. And the peak above them was not all that hard in its lower reaches. In a few minutes they were at the base of the solid rock, and from there they moved on quickly and easily. Eric of course went first, keeping the rope tight so as to catch even the slightest slip. But Robin didn't slip. She didn't drag. She was light, sure, agile, and when he reached a protected place and stopped, she wasn't even breathing hard as she came up to him.

"Well, how's that for today?" he asked.

Her eyes begged. "Oh Ricky, please, let's go farther."

He looked dubiously at his watch.

"Just a little farther." She looked up and pointed. "To that place that sticks out there," she said.

"That's a ledge."

"To that ledge. I bet from there we can see all the way to—everywhere."

Eric grinned. He pulled a pigtail. They went on again. And though he knew they shouldn't—knew their father would be back at the cabin before them and start worrying—he too was happy, as happy as Robin. For the first time, on a mountain, he was not following his father or another adult. He was (the word grownup was for children) an adult himself, not only a climber but a guide, a leader. He sang. He had read about yodeling, and he tried to yodel. Even when he stopped and there was no sound on the mountainside, there was a yodeling within him.

They climbed on. At the start of each new pitch he studied the mountainside, picked a route, climbed it, and then, belaying the rope, brought Robin up to him. She was still doing well, her legs steady, her eyes bright. And when at last they reached the ledge, he grinned again and said to her, "Nice going, Mrs. Whymper."

They sat on the ledge. They had no lunch with them, but he had Life Savers in his pocket and water in a canteen, and they sucked the mints and drank the water while they looked out at peaks and ranges.

"Oh Ricky," she said, "now we're king and queen on our mountain."

She didn't ask to go higher. If she had he wouldn't have taken her, for above them now was *really* real mountain, rising in cliffs and precipices to a distant summit. For a true mountaineer, though, it was climbable. Craning up, he traced the route he

17

would take: up a crack here, to a knob there, to the left, to the right, higher and higher. And then Robin had turned and was looking up with him, and she said in a small voice, "No one could climb that, could they?"

"Well—" he said.

"You mean someone could? *You* could?"

"Yes, I could," he said.

He was not boasting. It was true. He could see exactly how he could climb it, step by step, pitch by pitch. Then he was no longer looking up, but at Robin; she was looking at him; and he knew her look—he was her king, her hero.

"Ricky, could you really?" she breathed.

He felt the swelling of his heart. "I'll go a little way; I'll show you," he said. He untied the rope from both of them and coiled it neatly on the ledge. "It's nice and broad here. Stay away from the edge," he told her.

Then he began to climb.

As he had seen from below, there was a crack, a knob. He went left, then right; there were more cracks, more knobs, and he moved swiftly up them with easy balance and rhythm. It was the hardest climbing he had done—harder than anything in the Tetons or with the men from the university. But still it *wasn't* hard; he was in control all the way; he could feel strength and sureness within him, and again he yodeled in his joy and pride.

An echo seemed to come back. But in the next instant he knew it was no echo but a voice—the voice of Robin. He looked down at the ledge, but the ledge was empty, and he saw that she had followed him. She was on the mountain wall a short distance below.

"Ricky—" she called faintly.

He had no breath, no voice of his own. But he forced a voice. "Stay where you are!" he shouted. "Hold on. I'm coming!"

"I can't. I'm dizzy."

"Hold on! Look up! Hold on!"

He was maneuvering himself downward. In seconds he was close above her. With one more step he would be able to grasp her hand, hold her . . . But he never made it . . . As he reached, she swayed out. She was in space. She was falling through space, down the cliff, past the ledge, at first sideways, then spinning, legs spread, arms spread, pigtails spread, spinning about her. Then she was a blur, a dot, she was gone, and there was only the gray wall of the mountain.

Eric clung to the wall, facing outward.
Now he would let go. He would jump.
But he didn't.
Now . . . now . . . now . . .
But he couldn't.
He still clung there, still stayed there.
He would stay there until he died.

If she had cried out he had not heard her. There had been only silence, as there was silence now on the high dome of Dera Zor.

She was gone then. She was gone now. He could barely see her pigtails spinning far down in the night.

3

The year after that had been his last living full-time in Denver. For the next two he went to Winton Academy near Wichita, Kansas.

Mercifully, he had little memory of the descent from the mountain. There had been some strange men climbing up to him, one of whom had said, "Hello, son, I'm a doctor"; then a needle in his arm, some sort of sling or stretcher, and that was all. Of the funeral he remembered nothing (and it was not until later that he realized he had not been there). But then—oh God, then—there had been the world again: up and around again, back to school, sitting at meals with his father and mother. One thing he was at first grateful for was that Frank was not there: Frank was in his freshman year at Colorado State. But soon he was almost wishing he were, for at least Frank would have talked—about something, anything—while his parents simply sat in silence.

"They hate me," he thought in his agony. "They wish *I* were dead." But later he knew this was not true. If his mother hated anyone, it was not him but his father. (Once, through a closed door, he heard her sobbing, "It was *you* who took them to those terrible mountains.") And his father, he knew, was incapable of hating anyone.

Still, it was—like the mountains—terrible. The year before, his father had seemed a man in his prime: strong, hearty, with a quick smile, a warm laugh. But now he had shrunk into himself. He was stooped, slow in movement; not only his hair but face had grown grayer; and what had once been his gentleness seemed now to be only tiredness. Outwardly, his mother had changed less. She had always appeared to Eric as of no particular age, and so she continued. But inside, he knew, everything was dark and frozen, and the now-and-then outbursts, heard always from behind closed doors, only made her usual quietness the harder to bear.

The outbursts were never at him. Sometimes, indeed, she made gestures of affection, kissing him, passing a hand through his hair. And he in turn tried to make gestures to her. But it wasn't easy. Once it was awful. He had come home with a box of candy for her, but she was neither downstairs nor in her bedroom. Then he saw that for the first time in months the door of Robin's room was open, and before he could stop himself he was at the door looking in. The room was exactly as he had last seen it, with the white rug on the floor, school drawings on the wall, bright cushions and old dolls on the bed. But on the bed, now, sat his mother, holding one of the dolls. As he appeared, she looked up, but didn't seem to see him. She didn't speak. Her only movement was of her hands, caressing the doll she held: a doll with long brown pigtails.

She went to church a lot. Unlike his father (who had also been born a Lutheran but called himself a baptized heathen), she had always gone fairly regularly, but now she went not only on Sundays but weekdays. Eric had gone with her until he was thirteen and no longer made to. As his father put it, God had seemed closer in the mountains than in the Claremont Avenue Church. But now the mountains were gone, the mountain God was gone, and with his mother he again tried the God of Claremont Avenue. He heard the sermons, bowed his head, sang the hymns. When he was back in his room he tried to pray, to ask forgiveness, to find a way out of his grief and guilt. But it was no good. Prayers were words, and he could not get beyond the words.

The darkness did not begin to lift—just a little—until he was on the train bound east over the plains toward Wichita and Winton Academy.

22

The two years there were at least better than home. He studied hard. He had grown a full foot since standing on top of Longs Peak, and was now a rangy six-footer and good at sports. With waiting in the dining hall added (to earn his scholarship), he was always busy, and being busy was good. Even better was that he was in a new world, with no family, no old friends, no one at all who knew what had happened. Best of all was that he was in Kansas, and that, beyond the school grounds, the plains stretched flat and empty to the horizon.

During one summer he had a job on a wheat farm. During another he worked as a waiter at a lodge in a state park in Oklahoma; and there, as at school, he made friends and was not lonely. Among the friends—and sometimes rather more than friends—were girls. And he needed girls. For there were none at Winton, and back home he could not bring himself to go with old acquaintances who *knew*.

Home, now, added up to only a few weeks a year. And most of this time he spent reading in his room, walking the streets (of other neighborhoods) and sitting in movie houses. On the good side, simply being at 512 Desmond was no longer quite the ordeal it had been when his guilt was fresher. On the bad, his vacations coincided with those of his brother, and he and Frank still could not get on.

Subsequent to his quick, drastic aging right after *it* had happened, his father had changed little. He went to his office early, returned late, and in the evenings usually buried himself in the newspapers, now full of Hitler's impending and then raging war in Europe. It was his mother who now had done the changing, and it came from her involvement in a new religious faith. The Lutheran Church, she said, had not done enough for her in her "time of grief." She had turned to a church called the Brethren in Christ, which, as far as Eric could tell, was like Christian Science, only more so. People did not have sickness or trouble but "helped the Lord bear his load." They did not die but "moved on to the Lord." Therefore Robin had not died, merely moved on, and there was no cause for sorrow, for she was now in a state of grace that she could never have achieved on earth. In a way, all this

23

seemed good for his mother; she was at least out of her cave of frozen misery. But as time went on Eric was not so sure, for the overbright glint that now often touched her eyes became as disquieting as the dull cloud that had been there before.

And whereas, before, she had never mentioned Robin's name, she now spoke of her constantly. As he knew his father did, he tried not to listen. But it was hard; her eyes fixed on him; her voice drilled through. Then came the evening when the four of them were at table—for Frank was home too—and she was talking, talking; she was saying, "Last night Robin came to me. Not in a dream but really, she was really there, standing so pretty beside my bed, and she said, 'Don't grieve, Mommy, I'm so happy where I am.'" And suddenly Eric could stand it no longer. A wildness rushed through him and he yelled, "Stop lying! Stop your crazy lying!"

His father said gently, "Rick—"

His mother said nothing. And he yelled again:

"Robin didn't come to you and you know it. She's not flapping her wings somewhere. She fell off a mountain, right down to the bottom, and she's dead in her grave!"

He shoved back his chair, ran from the house, and walked the streets of the city. He had a few dollars. He would go to a hotel. Go to the station and take a train: any train. But he did neither. At last he went back home.

And there was more to come.

His parents had gone upstairs, but Frank was in the living room, reading, and as Eric came in he looked up coolly.

"I hope you're satisfied," he said.

"Satisfied?"

"At what you've done to her. Didn't you do enough two years ago?"

Eric said nothing. The wildness rose in him again. Crossing the room, he seized his brother by the shirt front, pulled him to his feet, and hit him in the face. As Frank went down he saw the blood dripping from his broken lip.

24

That had been in June after his first year at Winton. One night during the following Christmas vacation he was again out late, and this time when he came home it was his father who was alone in the living room.

"There are a couple of things, Rick," he said, "that I've been wanting to talk about."

Eric sat down.

"One of them's college," his father said. "Have you done some thinking about college?"

"Not much," said Eric.

"It's time to. Next fall's not far away."

"Maybe I shouldn't go. It would be a waste."

"No, it won't be a waste. And with your marks you can have a pretty wide choice."

Eric shrugged.

"I don't suppose you'd want to go to Boulder?"

"No."

"Or to State?"

"No."

"Well, there's forty-seven other states." His father paused. "What would you say to something in the northwest, like Oregon or Washington?"

"I don't know," said Eric.

"They sound like good places." There was a longer pause. "Then there's another thing," his father said. "There are mountains there."

Eric looked at him without speaking.

"You've nothing to say to that?"

"No."

"Well, I have. You should get back to the mountains."

Eric shook his head.

"Yes, Rick. Yes."

"I hate the mountains."

"No you don't. You hate something that once happened in the mountains. But not the mountains themselves. You love the mountains." Arthur Venn leaned forward in his chair. "Look, son," he said, "I've waited a long while to talk to you like this.

25

Some time had to pass, and now it has, and you're not a boy anymore but a young man."

He took a breath and went on:

"Don't think I don't know what's been going on inside you. I know, because it's been the same for me. As far as blame is concerned, we were both to blame, I as much as you. We did nothing really evil; we just used bad judgment, both of us, and to that extent we're to blame . . . But there's no use torturing ourselves. What happened happened, and it's going on three years ago now. Robin's dead. We're alive. And we have to go on living—you longer than I."

"What has that to do," said Eric, "with climbing again?"

"It has everything to do with it. Because climbing was so big a part of your life. Yes, I know we did it for only a few weeks each year, but still it meant more to you than all the rest put together. Let me tell you something, Rick: there aren't many people in the world, of any age, any sort, who care about *anything* the way you cared about climbing. And to throw it away, something as special and precious as that, is a sin and a crime."

His father was silent a while and Eric thought he had finished. But then at last he spoke again:

"There's one more thing, too," he said. "It may sound sentimental or corny or whatever you want to call it, but I'm going to say it anyhow because it's God's truth. And that's that Robin would want you to climb again, and you know it."

He got up and went toward the stairs. "That's all," he said. "No decisions now. But think about it, son. And about college too."

The next fall he became a freshman at the University of Washington in Seattle. One thing there was the same as at Winton: he still waited on tables to help pay his way. But everything else was different.

First, last and best was freedom. He could do as he liked, come and go as he liked, pick his own courses (or most of them), and choose his friends from a pool of fifteen thousand instead of three hundred. It was a freedom that at first was too heady. Within a month he had had his first drinks, first drunks, first hangovers.

26

One gray dawn he returned to his dormitory with the fuzzy awareness that, in a room on a nameless street in downtown Seattle, he had lost both his virginity and his wallet. Not long after that he sat in an office while the Dean of Freshmen spoke of "problems of adjustment."

From then on things went better. He did not work as hard as at Winton, but hard enough. Besides his dining hall chores, he took on odd jobs that kept him in pocket money. He had evenings of beer and poker, but not too many, and his dates were with co-eds, not whores. If no dreamboat with girls, he was far from a washout. In the self-consciousness of eighteen he was well aware of his liabilities: that, for instance, his ears stuck out (though so, of course, did Clark Gable's), and that his nose, broken in Winton football, was no match for John Barrymore's. Overall, though, he passed muster—tall, big-shouldered, easy and powerful in movement—and most dates seemed not averse to searching his gray-green eyes or running fingers through his thick brown hair. With them, as with most aspects of his new life, he got by, and better.

There were still times of funk, however, when he wanted the companionship of neither male nor female, and then he would put the university behind him and walk out of the city to the hills beyond. On a hilltop he would sit looking west across Puget Sound toward the forests of the Olympic Peninsula. Then he would force himself to turn to the southeast, where on clear days the dome of Mount Rainier hung white and shining in the sky. Rainier was nothing like the peaks of the Rockies. From a distance it seemed to have no rock at all, only snow and ice; to be not a solid mass but a mirage, a vision, suspended in space. It had been a long time since he had looked at a mountain. Any mountain. Looking now was not easy. But in time he was able to watch it steadily, calmly, without an aching darkness within him.

In January he joined the University Outing Club.

He learned to ski. Every weekend thereafter he was out on the slopes of the Cascades, progressing from snowplow to stem turn to christie, from novice run to intermediate to advanced, taking his bumps and lumps, learning the tricks of the trade. He took to it almost as naturally as he had to climbing, and by late spring, when the season ended, he was one of the top Outing Club skiers.

Then came June, and a hard and great decision. Summer waiting jobs were open at Paradise Inn, near Rainier's timberline. Two upperclassmen in the club, who were also mountaineers, were taking them, with the plan of climbing in their off time, and they urged him to join them. He hesitated. He struggled within himself. He wrote to his father; his father replied urging, almost begging him to do it. And he did. In late June he went to work at Paradise, and a week later, with a day and a half free, he, Ken Naylor, and Bob Koontz set off to climb Rainier.

The first half day was routine: a mere uphill slog to the twin huts of Camp Muir, where he had already been on skis. But this time it was not turn-around-and-schuss-down. The next morning at three they were out in the darkness, roped and ready, facing up toward the heights that loomed white against the stars. And there, for an instant, something happened to Eric. Bob, first on the rope, started off, and now, in his second position, it was his turn. But he could not move. Bob, feeling the pull of the rope, looked back. Ken, behind, said, "Get the lead out." And still, for another moment, he could not move, nor even speak, while panic filled and shook him. Then it passed. He was breathing deeply but steadily. "Let's go," he said. And they went on. For five hours they climbed, up snow and ice, on walls and ridges, through darkness, dawn and sunrise, and at eight o'clock in the crystal morning they stood on the summit of Rainier. By late afternoon they were back at Paradise Inn, and he had climbed his first mountain in four years.

More climbing followed. In the Colorado Rockies and Tetons there had been little snow and ice; but on Rainier that was almost all there was, and from Ken and Bob he learned the many skills of dealing with glaciers and crevasses, cornices and avalanches.

When, for a change, it was rock climbing they wanted, they went off to cliffs and spires on other Cascade peaks, and here too he practiced and perfected techniques at which, before, he had been only a fledgling. Once, mountains had been magic castles. Now they were still magical, but in themselves, their reality, as organic parts of the earth. He was learning the infinite variety of their components: of ice that was old, new, sound, rotten; snow that was powder, corn, granular, firn; rock that was granite, limestone, feldspar, schist. He was learning where safety lay, and danger; what could and could not be dared and done.

Climbing, he knew now, was not only adventure. It was knowledge too. It was a testing of skill, endurance, nerve, judgment; a conquest not of a hump of earth but of one's own self. Most of all, for him, it had been the conquest of a memory, of a grief and guilt that he had thought would torture him all the days of his life. But now he could bear it, live with it. He thought of the words of his father: "You should get back to the mountains." Then of his other words—Tennyson's words—spoken long ago, when he was a boy of ten on the crags of the Lookout . . . "And not to yield," his father had said. "To strive, to seek, to find, and not to yield" . . . Then he had smiled. And Eric smiled now, and was grateful. For his father had been right: he knew that now. Aged nineteen, no longer a boy but a man, he had come alive again on the mountains he loved.

In another way, too, he had returned to the mountains. He had begun to read again: going on from Mallory, Whymper and Browne to long shelves of books in the university library. He learned the history of the Cascades, Sierras, Rockies. He followed the great cycle of achievement in the Alps, where mountaineering was born and nurtured. He moved on to Alaska, the Andes, Africa; most eagerly, most raptly of all, to the roof of the world, the Himalayas. The Everest story he already knew as well as if he himself had written it. But now he turned to other climbers, other mountains—to K2 and Kangchenjunga, Nanga Parbat and Nanda Devi, Trisul and Jonsong and Kamet and Chomolhari—and the names were like music, distant, haunting, alluring.

These were peaks that had been explored, challenged, in some cases climbed to the top. But there were others that were little more than names, that had been seen only from distant plains and valleys, and that to the Western world were still mountains of mystery. Many of these were in Nepal, the small hermit kingdom locked in the heart of the Himalayas, which over the years had been almost totally closed to outsiders. True, Everest, to which there had now been seven expeditions, was half in Nepal, but all approaches to it had been from its northern Tibetan side. The great peaks that lay wholly in the Closed Land remained as untouched as they had been from time's beginning.

It was not quite true, however, that *no* Westerners had been to Nepal. The British Raj in India had got a few men in as envoys and agents; and there had been at least one American, a geologist named Homer Bigelow, who in the 1920s had somehow penetrated not merely to the capital city of Kathmandu but on into the ranges beyond. In an obscure stack in the library Eric had found a book by Bigelow called *Trek to Nowhere*, in which the geologist told of his journey: east from Kathmandu, then north toward a high wild region near the Tibetan frontier. Bigelow had not been a mountaineer. He had been out not to climb peaks but to discover and study them, and his prime objective had been one called Dera Zor—a mountain so shut off by lesser ones around it that almost nothing was known of its structure or height. Bigelow had succeeded in his quest. With a small group of porters he had reached the base of Dera Zor and spent a month studying the rocks and glaciers of its southern slopes. He had not had either the data or instruments to fix its exact altitude, but had estimated it as close to twenty-seven thousand feet, which would put it among the half-dozen highest summits on earth.

From the moment he read of it Eric was lost and enthralled. Bigelow was not much of a writer. He did not even try to be, for his interests were primarily scientific. But the impact of Dera Zor upon him had been so great that, for Eric, it crashed through the musty pages like an electrical charge. His first reading was in a library cubicle, where he stayed until the midnight closing time. Then he tried to take it out, and, finding it was not on the lending list, took it anyhow, under his coat, and kept it for good.

In his room, he read and reread it: following Bigelow on every step beneath the mountain, staring up with him at its awesome symmetry of rock and ice. In the book there was only one overall photograph of the peak, and not a good one. But he held it close under a light, using a magnifying glass, and time and again climbed its glaciers and precipices, choosing his routes, changing them, doubling back, traversing, climbing on again, until at last he stood triumphant on that pinnacle in the sky. As a boy, his mountain dream had been Everest. But no longer. Let the British have their Everest: they had tried it seven times and they deserved it. For him, Eric Venn, it would be Dera Zor. Some day, no matter what else happened in his life, he would get to it. He would climb it, top it. It would be his.

Its name sang in his ears: "Dera Zor—Dera Zor—"

He went home to Denver for a week in September.

His brother Frank was not there. He had graduated from Colorado State, where he had majored in economics, and was now in Los Angeles, selling for a company that made electronic equipment.

With his mother it was not too bad. She was still absorbed in the Brethren of Christ, but quieter again, more withdrawn into herself.

And with his father it was good, almost as good as in the old days. Actual climbing together was a thing of the past, but they had a not unsatisfactory substitute in the living room, while Eric talked and his father listened, eyes aglow, to his stories of skiing and mountaineering on Rainier. Then he brought out *Trek to Nowhere,* and his father read it. He told of his own dreams of Dera Zor, and his father chuckled and said, "Stick with it, son. Don't write it off. Queer things happen in the world, and some day—who can tell?—your brother Frank's going to own the state of California and you're going to be on top of that mountain of yours."

"You don't think I'm nuts then?" Eric asked.

"Sure you're nuts," said his father. "But you can't help it."

That was the last thing his father said that he remembered. A few months later Arthur Venn was dead of a heart attack, and Eric was in the army.

31

Now, on the dome of Dera Zor, he said to his father, "See, I didn't yield. I'm almost at the top."

Again he put out his hand to Robin. But this time she wasn't there.

He shook his head to clear it.

It wasn't Robin who was coming. It was Larry.

4

. . . No, not Larry either. In the time he had come to, Larry was not yet born. It was Ken Naylor coming, standing beside him, as they peered up through the night at the heights of Pizzo Rossi.

Ken, then Per Halberg, finally Harry Bushnell: the four of them. For in the war of millions there were no millions here. There were no tanks, trucks, mortars, machine guns, shells, bombs, mines. There were not even officers. Or mud. Out of the hugeness of armies and corps, a division had been created for a special purpose. Out of the division, a regiment had been assigned to a job; out of the regiment, a battalion; out of the battalion, a company; out of the company, a platoon; out of the platoon, a squad; out of the squad, four volunteers. Out of the millions, there they were: four men, four mountaineers, at the foot of a mountain.

They had come up from the mud of winter Italy, the mud of war. In the darkness they had followed mule tracks, skirted forests, crossed meadows, and now beneath their boots was no longer mud but rock and snow. Above was only rock, the rock of Pizzo Rossi—too steep for snow—rising twelve hundred feet to its hidden summit.

Their assignment was this:

To the east of Pizzo Rossi, beyond a narrow pass, was the bulk of Monte Alicia, one of the remaining German strongpoints in the northern Apennines. For American and British troops to get by it, it would have to be reduced, and this was the job of the 83rd Infantry of the Tenth Mountain Division. In the process, however, the assault force would have to contend not only with direct fire from the top of Alicia but with crossfire from a machine gun emplacement atop Rossi; and it was of the essence that this emplacement be wiped out at the critical moment. Alicia, though higher than Rossi, had long and gentle slopes. It could be stormed by troops en masse without resort to ropes and complex alpine techniques. But Rossi was something else again: a thing of cliffs and couloirs, spires and towers—at least on its southern side, which was tactically the only accessible one. This, plus the fact that it had to be scaled at night and in secrecy, made it a possibility for only a small party of experts.

There had been a few days' wait for weather. And meticulous timing, based on long study of the peak through binoculars. H-hour for arrival at the top was at first light, which on this winter morning would be a little after six. Now at the base it was not quite three.

There were stars but no moon, and they could not, of course, use flashlights.

"Christ, it's black!" said Ken Naylor.

And in the blackness they made ready. Their grenades were in bandoliers under their parkas. On their backs they carried light packs, M-1 rifles, and coils of rope, two of which they now unslung. With mittens off and fingers quickly chilling, they tied up in the predetermined teams of two: Ken with Per Halberg, Eric with Harry Bushnell. Then Halberg, who was a sergeant and in command, turned to the rock and began to climb.

Ken followed him quickly; then Eric, leading the second rope. And yes, Christ it was black, and Christ it was cold, but soon both were forgotten. With the pull of arm and thrust of leg, there came a change within him; and the change was not only a matter of straining limbs and flexing muscles, but of something deeper, that touched the rhythm of his breathing and the beat of his heart. It was not exertion—not yet. Nor was it fear, though that too might come later. Certainly there was plenty to fear in the darkness above: not only the walls of an unknown precipice, but beyond it human enemies, Germans, a machine gun. Perhaps there was death above. But this was not what he thought of. He

34

was not thinking at all, only feeling, exulting; exulting as he always had when his hands and feet touched mountain rock, as he entered again and again into his mountain home.

In the darkness he half-smiled.

Home?

Yes, home. A mountain anywhere was home, where he belonged. On the Lookout, Longs, the College Peaks, the Sangre de Cristos. On the Front Range, the Tetons, the Cascades, Rainier. On the peaks and ranges he had known in his three years in the army. Now on a bump in the Italian night called Pizzo Rossi.

It was a long way from this home to those others. And a long time. Now it was early 1945, and it had been in the fall of 1941 that he went from Seattle to Denver for his father's funeral.

His brother Frank had been there too, flying in from Los Angeles and taking charge of things: the funeral itself, the lawyer, the insurance. Their mother was, on the whole, in good control of herself. Though the service was in the Lutheran church, she was largely in the company of fellow disciples of the Brethren in Christ, from whom she seemed to receive the solace she needed. But on the second evening after the burial, when the condolence payers had left and she was alone with Frank and Eric, the control suddenly dissolved in a flood of grief and anger. "It was the mountains that killed him," she cried. "His heart would have been all right if it hadn't been for the mountains. They killed him like they killed my baby Robin—"

The next day, thanks to sedatives and the Brethren, she was calm again, and soon Frank returned to Los Angeles and Eric to Seattle. At the university he was now a sophomore and planned to major in English, for he had discovered that here—along with climbing—was what he truly cared about. Not only reading, but writing. And he had begun to write: not only for classes, but for one of the student magazines. Combining the things he loved, he wrote about mountains. His first story, which was accepted, was about a father and son (not a brother and sister) who climbed together; his second, which was not, about a fictional

35

expedition to the mountain called Dera Zor. With winter approaching, he, Ken Naylor and Bob Koontz readied their ski gear and became the joint owners of a 1935 Ford. He had met a girl called Doris Flanner, whom he liked—and who liked to ski.

Then it was a Sunday morning, and he was shaving, and out of the radio burst Pearl Harbor . . . It was two months later, and Ken burst into the room saying, "Hey, they're training mountain troops at Fort Lewis!"

Fort Lewis was only a few miles from Seattle. But the army, of course, didn't do things that way. Ken went off in one direction, Bob Koontz in a second, he in a third, and fourth, and fifth—first to California, then Texas, then Georgia, in a blur of barracks and chow lines, drills and sergeants. It was not until early 1943 that the three were back together, assigned to the 83rd Mountain Infantry at Camp Hale, Colorado.

Hale was no blur. He was there for a year, and it was a year of the hardest, toughest living he had known, or could have imagined. The camp was at ninety-five hundred feet in the Sawatch Range of the central Rockies, its site blasted out of a wilderness of boulders, its horizon rimmed by stark and savage peaks. There were still barracks, drill grounds, sergeants. There were rifles, tommy guns, machine guns, bazookas, mortars. There were five thousand mules and acres of muleshit. Added to all this, which was "regular army," was a program of training on the surrounding peaks designed either to make a man a mountaineer or break him. And many were broken. Half the men assigned to Hale dropped out and were transferred to other "softer" units of the army.

Most of this half, however, were men new to the heights. For those who were not new—the pre-army initiates of the high and the steep—the bleak, harsh, womanless life was compensated by the very fact that it was a mountain life. And Eric Venn, aged twenty, had long since been one of these. However dismal the routine of barrack and drill ground, there was always the time when these faded below. There were the white slopes of winter and spring, with skis hissing in the shining snow. There were the gray crags of summer and autumn, with boots scraping, thrusting

36

on the living rock. And this was not, as before, a thing of a day, a week, snatched from the workaday world. It was itself that world: a job, a life.

Part of the life, too, was companionship such as he had not known before. The lowlanders, the mountain draftees, came and went, but the hard-core climbers and skiers remained: a unit within a unit, bound by far more than the mere happenstance of war. Ken Naylor and Bob Koontz were still his closest friends. But there were many others of the same breed. Best of all, for youngsters like himself, there were the older men who served as NCO instructors, the pick of the country's mountain and ski professionals. Most of these were European by birth: Swiss, French, Austrian, Norwegian. But all were now American citizens, American soldiers. Out on the slopes and crags they were as tough on their trainees as any career sergeant on his drill ground. But in the off times, in bull sessions, card games, and Saturday night beer fests, they were at one with the Erics, Kens and Bobs who were their daytime pupils. The men of the 83rd Mountain Infantry were not only fellow soldiers, but companions. They were a fraternity of men doing what they knew and loved.

The world was remote beyond the circle of the peaks. But now and then the circle opened. In the late spring of his Camp Hale year Eric paid a short visit to his mother; and it was neither good nor bad but just a visit. Then in the fall came a note from Frank, in Los Angeles, saying he was going to be married. The girl's name was Kay Burden. She was from Pasadena. The wedding was to be in three weeks, and Eric was invited. As it turned out, he was unable to get away. But by mail order he sent as good a present as he could afford (he and Frank were now grown men; it was time to forget their boyhood troubles), and presently he received a thank-you from his sister-in-law, plus an invitation to visit when he could.

In November, on furlough, he went. And it was to find a few surprises. The first was Frank and Kay's home in the Santa Monica hills, with an ocean view, a swimming pool, and two cars in the carport. Frank himself was more as expected. He had put on some weight since they had last met at their father's funeral, and in clothes he had forsaken Desmond Street for Sunset Boulevard. But in fundamentals he was the same as always: cool, crisp, assured, controlled.

They spoke of their mother, who had come out for the wedding, and Frank shook his head. "She may have seemed all right to you," he said. "But she's not, of course. She hasn't been since—well, you know."

Eric knew, all right.

"At least now she can have a few more things than before."

"You're sending her money?"

"Yes. Dad's insurance wasn't much. Luckily, I've been able to help."

"I'm sorry I haven't."

Frank waved a hand. "Time enough when you're out of the army."

"What about you and the army?" Eric asked.

"I'm deferred. Essential civilian work."

"Oh?"

"Everything our firm makes now we sell to the Government. Plane components, instruments, that sort of thing."

Eric glanced around. "You seem to be getting by," he said.

"Not badly. We've expanded recently. We used to be just the Microx Company, but now we're Burden Industries."

"Burden—"

"Kay's father's the president."

That was the second surprise.

And the third was Kay herself. Just what he had expected he could not have said, but it was certainly not what she was: a stunning girl of about his own age, green-eyed and copper-haired; a girl of lightness, brightness, charm, humor; a girl he would much have liked to make his own, if she had not, inexplicably, been his brother's wife.

On an evening before Frank came home from work, she mixed them drinks and smiled quizzically over the rim of her glass. "You expected something different, didn't you?" she asked.

Eric nodded.

"Something more—formidable."

"Yes."

Kay laughed. "You expected a sort of female Frank: full of purpose, no nonsense." She laughed again. "Instead, I'm full of nonsense. I suppose it's wrong, with a war on, but I *am*. And I'm going to pump some nonsense into Frank, wait and see."

"It will take more than a hand pump," said Eric.

"Oh, he's a dear and good to me and I love him. But he does need stirring up," she said. "I don't mean in his work; God no! There are people who think when a man marries the boss's daughter it means he doesn't want to work. But that's somebody else, not Frank. Frank works like six horses. I mean stirring like this—" She raised her glass and drank. "And this—" Rising, she kissed Eric lightly. "And this—" She danced a few steps, pulled Eric to his feet, and for a moment or two they danced together. Then they were sitting again, drinking, and again she was smiling her quizzical smile.

"Me too," she said.

"What did *you* expect?"

"Something—well—" She made a large, vague gesture.

"Like King Kong."

"Shaggy and fierce."

"In the army you have to shave," he said. "But I'm fierce as hell."

"No, you're sweet. You're a big sweet domesticated indoor outdoorsman."

"Who's lost his skis."

"I love to ski," Kay said. "Oh, I'm not much good, of course, but I've done some: at Big Bear and Yosemite. When you've won the war and come back, we'll ski together and you'll teach me."

"At family rates," said Eric.

Three days later he was back at Hale. The mountains, the high horizons, closed in again. But through them now came rumors, rumors, rumors. The 83rd would be sent to this place, to that place; to San Diego to learn swimming, to the Sahara to learn desert warfare. Finally they *were* sent—to Texas. For Eric, back to Texas. Months passed, and the 83rd became part of a new

39

Tenth Mountain Division. But it was a mountain division without mountains; with only range land, sagebrush, fences, cows. The men sweated, cursed, languished in boredom.

Then they went to Italy.

After the first sight of Naples and Vesuvius, it was not much improvement. They moved up broad valleys into narrow valleys, up rutted roads and trails to ravaged meadows, empty villages, crumbled sheds. In sheds and tents they made their homes and waited. And waited. By now it was early 1945, and they were in a backwash of the war. The Italians were long since out of it, there were only a few rear-guard Germans to contend with, and the Allied Command seemed little interested in contending. The mountain troops sat. They waited. Instead of Texas dust there was Italian mud.

When action of sorts finally came for the 83rd, it was not really action at all. F Company was merely crossing a meadow on a routine deployment when a German 88 on a hill to the north got the range and lobbed a few shells. There were quick shouted orders, and to a man the company went down. A few minutes later all but three got up again. Of these, two were wounded, one was dead, and the one who was dead was Bob Koontz.

A whine, a bang. Bob dead.

As quick as that. As imbecilic as that.

In the tent the three of them had shared, Eric and Ken Naylor looked at his sleeping bag, his soap dish, his half-written letter to a girl in Tacoma. "Why him, not me?" each asked.

The next night, in the nearest village, they got drunk on grappa. What they wanted, they decided, was girls, but what they got was a fight. Eric came out of it intact; but Ken got a cracked knuckle from hitting someone—or something—too hard.

He was a tough one, Ken. Two years older than Eric, and two ahead at college, he had entered Washington on a football scholarship but had given up the game after sophomore year, when he discovered it was not football he loved but mountains. From then on he had earned his keep by running a laundry route. He had skied and climbed and majored in geology. After

40

the war and graduate school he planned to become a mining engineer, and not the least of the reasons was that this would take him to the mountains.

Through their army years he, Eric and Bob had not only climbed mountains but talked and dreamed them. Now, with Bob gone, they still did, in the mud and fog of winter Italy. They talked Alaska, the Alps, the Andes, the Himalayas; and Eric again brought out Bigelow's *Trek to Nowhere*, which he had carried with him always, and again preached the gospel of Dera Zor.

"Nowhere, for Chrissake!" Ken grunted. "That's where we are now."

"Not that sort of nowhere," said Eric.

Ken grunted again, scratched himself, fingered his cracked knuckle. "You're a romantic sonofabitch, aren't you?" he said. But for the first time since Bob died, his eyes, too, held a light.

Life—real life—was not in the present but the future. The present was nothing. It was waiting. Other divisions moved up into action, but not the Tenth. Then other regiments of the Tenth moved up, but not the 83rd. They would never move.

Then they did move: up toward the flanks of Monte Alicia and Pizzo Rossi. And now at last, on a black winter night, they had reached the place to which three long years had been leading . . .

On the lower face of Rossi the four men climbed smoothly, quickly. At first the going was over a series of ledges that formed a natural staircase. Then the stairs petered out, the true cliffs began; but the rock was sound, with good holds, and in normal conditions would have offered routine climbing. Nothing was normal now, though. In the freezing darkness they could not use flashlights. Their grenades bulged awkwardly under their parkas, and their slung rifles scraped and caught on dimly seen projections. At intervals there were pauses while Per Halberg, leading the first rope, stopped to peer upward for the most likely route. Then he would go on again, with Ken Naylor after him, and Eric and Harry Bushnell followed.

They were all, of course, good climbers; as good as any in their regiment. Halberg, who had been one of the sergeant instructors back at Hale, was no youngster, a Norwegian-American in his late thirties. But for several prewar years he had been a ski professional at White Valley in Utah, and was a lifelong all-round man of the mountains. Bushnell, about ten years younger, was a rugged Montanan who had been a ranger in Glacier National Park. And Ken, at twenty-four, and Eric, now twenty-two, were already veterans of the heights. They were a good team, a balanced team, who back at Hale had often climbed together.

After a bit the going grew harder. The cliff steepened. Up ahead, Halberg moved obliquely across the face, found a fault in the rock, and they began the ascent of a long chimney. Here there were more holds than out on the face, but also loose rocks; and on this climb these were a double menace, for a stonefall down the cliff would be surest way of alerting the Germans in their emplacement above. If they could avoid this, they were confident they could achieve the surprise that was the essence of their mission. For the enemy surely would not be expecting anyone to scale the south wall of Pizzo Rossi in the black of night. Least of all Americans, whom the Germans thought rank novices as mountaineers.

No stones fell. They wormed and levered themselves up, re-emerged onto the face, and worked their way up a series of knobs and fissures. Again the climbing was harder. There came a long pause, and another, while Halberg coped with obstacles above, and presently they were moving only one at a time. Halberg climbed fifty or sixty feet, until he found a stance where he could belay the rope while Ken came up after him. Then Eric climbed to where Ken had been and, in turn, belayed Bushnell. The process was repeated three times. Then one by one they came up over an airy bulge and found themselves all together on a narrow ledge.

"Hmm—" said Halberg, craning up.

They had now been on the wall about two hours: two thirds of their allotted time, with less than a third of the way, they judged, yet to go. But what lay ahead was obviously going to be worse than anything below. In days past, as they studied the peak through binoculars, there had seemed to be a series of gullies and ridgelets streaking the upper ramparts of the face. But that had been in daytime, with Rossi gleaming pinkly in sunlight. Now there was only blackness, blankness, steepness, with the merest wrinkles to be felt beneath searching fingers.

"Well, we try," Halberg murmured.

He untied himself from the rope that joined him to Ken Naylor and slung it over his shoulder. If he fell from above, he could not possibly be held by a belay from the tiny ledge; his belayer would only be pulled off after him. Nor could he himself use pitons for protection. They did not even have pitons with them. At the first clang of metal on rock the Germans on the summit would be alerted to their presence, and that would be the end of their mission, and themselves. All Halberg could hope for was to make the climb on his own; then find a stance from which to lower his rope to the others.

With gloves off, his fingers explored the wrinkles. Then he began to climb. What held him to the wall was invisible, but somehow he clung to it, and slowly, slowly, he ascended. Presently his feet were level with the heads of the others; then above them. Then the relief of the wrinkles must have grown sharper, for he began to move less slowly. Soon he was no longer a moving figure, but only a shadow. Then not even that; he was gone. There could, of course, be no shouting, no communication at all. The only sound in the blackness was the faint scraping of boots on the wall above.

Five minutes passed—ten—seeming like hours. Through the night the eyes of the others strained upward for the movement of the descending rope. But when at last movement came, it was not a rope. It was again Halberg's shadow, coming slowly downward. With the others' help he got his feet on the ledge and stood leaning against the rock, his breath coming in gasps.

When at last he could speak he whispered one word: "Overhang."

Then after more breaths: "No holds. Only cracks."

There was a silence. Eyes moved off to right and left, but they already knew there was no possible route to either side. It was up or down; and down, with a subsequent search for a new route,

43

meant that their arrival on top would be late, therefore useless. Their eyes went up again, and the silence lengthened. Sergeant Halberg gave no order; for they were not soldiers now but only climbers.

"I'll try it," said Ken Naylor.

Taking the rope from Halberg, he started up. Again there was the slowly moving figure, the figure becoming a shadow, the shadow nothing. There was blackness, stillness. There was waiting. For ten minutes. Fifteen. Then again there was movement; again the movement not of a rope but of a descending figure. There was Ken returning, as Halberg had returned: reaching the ledge, leaning against the wall, struggling to suck the breath of life into heaving lungs.

"Bastard rock," he muttered. "Sonofabitching bastard—"

More silence.

Harry Bushnell took a half step and stopped.

Then Eric said, "I'll climb it."

He did not mean to say that. He meant to say, as Ken had, "I'll try it." But he said, "I'll climb it."

No one else said anything.

Like the others before him, he untied himself from his rope and put it over his shoulder. He removed his gloves. He began to climb. Slowly he moved up over the granite wrinkles; then as the wrinkles became sharper, he moved more quickly. The wall, he judged, was angled at between seventy and eighty degrees. But it "went." In five minutes he was perhaps sixty feet above the ledge where he had started.

Then the trouble came. Under his hands he could feel the rock growing even steeper. Above, he could dimly see, was roughly a ten-foot band of verticality, and beyond it the overhang loomed out against the starry sky.

There were grooves and flanges in the vertical pitch, and he made it. In another few minutes he was up close beneath the overhang, his toes perched in minute niches, but his hands resting gratefully on the one true and solid knob he had found since leaving the ledge. Briefly he allowed himself the luxury of holding it with both hands. Then clinging with only one, he moved the other up, exploring. Straight overhead he found only smoothness. To the left, smoothness. To the right, still more smoothness—until, at the very limit of his reach, he could feel the beginning of a crack slanting upward. Shifting a foot into an even shallower niche and edging off from his knob, he found that it slowly widened as it ascended. If he had had a piton, and been able to use it, he could have got it in readily and provided a hold to get up and over. But without a piton, with only his fingertips . . .

He felt still farther along the crack. But what he felt he could not be sure of, for his gloveless hands were going numb. Further, his right leg, supported only by a toehold, had been seized by a tremor and was threatening to buckle. Retreating to the knob, he clung to it alternately with each hand while holding the other under his parka, in his armpit. He flexed his trembling leg and strove to control it. Then as he looked down beyond it, something else happened, something worse, that should not have happened. It was not blackness that he saw, nor his companions hidden within the blackness. It was a figure close below him, the figure of a girl, and the girl was Robin. Wrenching away, he clung to his knob and closed his eyes.

"I'm licked too," he thought. "I must go down."

But he didn't go down.

He still clung. At last he opened his eyes. This time it was not downward he looked, but upward, and he saw that the world above him was changing. The stars were paler. The gulfs between them were paler. Between him and sky, the top of Pizzo Rossi was beginning to emerge in the thin grayness of dawn.

"No, not down," he thought.

And as he thought it, he was aware of another change: a change in himself. His hands, though still cold, were no longer numb. His leg was not trembling. Control had come to it. It had come to all of him. From deep within him something had risen—the thing that had made him say, "I'll climb it"—and he would. It was not strength. It was not courage. What the exact word was he did not know. But part of it was desire; part was will; part a reserve of potential that he knew, when called on, would respond.

Again he edged from the knob to his right. First a hand, and it

45

could feel the rock; then a foot, and it held firm. There was the crack in the rock, and his fingers followed it, and this time they did not stop when he had stretched his reach to its utmost. They kept on. Simultaneously his feet moved, finding no holds but only friction. His other hand moved, leaving the knob, joining the other at the crack, and at the same instant the first hand moved farther up the widening diagonal. He did not jerk or lunge, but moved in even rhythm. He did not fight the rock, but kneaded, caressed it; not a warrior fighting an enemy, but a creature of the mountains in its natural home. For an instant his only grip on the mountain was the pressure of toes and fingertips. Then the first joints of his fingers were in the crack; the whole of them were in it; his feet below were finding leverage, swinging him on and up. He was out on the snout of the overhang. Then past it, above it. He came to a gentle slope, a level platform. He found a projection of rock on which to hitch a belay and lowered his rope to the others.

Robin was gone now. It was his father who was there. And his father smiled and said, "—And not to yield."

That was the end of the mountaineering. The rest was war.

Quickly, on easy rock, in thinning darkness, they reached the final crags of Pizzo Rossi. Unseen and unheard, they studied the low wall that formed the German emplacement. They took out their grenades, defused and lobbed them. They entered the emplacement and found two machine guns, a pot of brewing coffee, and four dead or dying Germans.

Then they sat on the peak. They drank the Germans' coffee. They watched as, far below, the rest of the 83rd Infantry moved out of a stand of woods onto the lower slopes of Monte Alicia. A little later, the sun rose. Huge and gleaming, it streamed in horizontal rays across peaks and ridges: turning the rock of Pizzo Rossi to luminous pink; glinting on the steel of the two machine guns and the blood welling from the shattered face of one of the Germans.

It was a sun of glory: as pure and radiant as any they had seen

46

on many mornings on many summits. But there was no response within them, no reflected gleam in their watching eyes. They were soldiers, and they had done their job and done it well. But they were also mountaineers who had defiled a mountaintop.

There was no defilement on the dome of Dera Zor. There was only the purity of snow and stars.

Standing in the last steps he had kicked, he looked up at the sky, and for the first time in years he thought of his Silver Star. You got a Silver Star for killing on a mountain. Or at least on some mountains. Not on the mountains of Aspen or on Dera Zor.

Ken Naylor had won a Silver Star too. Eric's eyes moved down the dome to the slant of the west ridge below it, and there on the ridge, invisible in darkness, were the tents of Camp Five, where Ken was tonight. He wished that Ken were at the snow-hole bivouac at the base of the dome; that he would be coming up this day with Larry, Tashi and Pembol.

Larry and the two Sherpas would be starting off at first light, but that was still some way off. Now in the night there was no one at all on the mountainside. Not his father. Not Robin.

There was only Julian Howard coming down the Boulevard Raspail toward the Café de la Cloche.

5

The word for Julian was *soigné*. It was not a matter of clothes; no one on the Left Bank wore anything but crummy clothes. But Julian wore them with style. He walked with style. Blond, slim and graceful, he would come down the Raspail, wave jauntily as he reached the Cloche, and take his seat at the sidewalk table. He would glance at the half-empty *bières* and *demi-bières*, cock a finger at the waiter, and order *"Pernods pour tout le monde."*

Sometimes *tout le monde* was just Eric, Eric's Nicole and himself. Sometimes it was two tablefuls of ex-GIs and their French girls. Julian occasionally had a girl of his own; occasionally a male companion. More often he was alone. Alone, that is, until he reached the Cloche; then he was the Sun King with his court.

Now and then the court moved from the Cloche to his rooms. Like all other rooms in Montparnasse, they were bare and decrepit, but things happened there that did not happen elsewhere. Instead of pernod, there was *le vrai absinthe*, rare and illegal— "direct," said Julian, "from the Rimbaud-Verlaine Distillery." One night there was Josephine Baker. Almost always, mixed in with the Montparnassians, there were Right Bank types in ties and jackets, from banks and bureaus and the U. S. Embassy.

Julian Howard, of course, had money. His family were the soap Howards of Chicago, but the only soap he himself had seen had been in bathrooms. Fresh out of Princeton, he had served through the war as a volunteer ambulance driver with the American Field

49

Service, and now, like so many other Americans, he was in no hurry to go home.

Eric, in Montparnasse, was trying to write. Everyone else in sight claimed to be either writer or painter. "And which are you?" Nicole had asked Julian on the first day they met at the Cloche and he had replaced *demi-bières* with pernods.

"Neither," he told her.

She affected astonishment. "So what do you do then?"

"I sit at cafés," he said.

"Ah, you are *philosophe*."

"Well—"

"That is nice. A writer he must be at a desk. A painter he must be at an easel. But a *philosophe* he can be all day at a café, and if he is a rich *philosophe* he can drink pernod."

She sipped hers.

"I too am *philosophe*," she said.

"I can tell that."

"I am *existentialiste*."

It was a new word then. "What's that?" said Julian.

"It is—" She took another sip, thinking it over. "It is when there is only beer you drink beer; when there is pernod you drink pernod."

That was in the fall of '45.

In May, when the war in Europe ended, the 83rd Mountain Infantry had been near Belluno in northern Italy. Then it had moved on to the Austrian Tyrol for occupation duties and beer drinking. Even more than beer, however, what everyone wanted was *out* from the army. Through the summer the Tenth Division was held together, and there were rumors that it would soon be climbing on Fujiyama; but then in their turn came The Bomb and VJ Day, and soon after, orders to return to the States. Those few of the personnel who were European-born—mostly the skiing professionals—were given the option of being discharged abroad, to visit old homes and families. And a handful of others were, on application, also separated in Europe. Among them, Eric.

It was not something long planned. Through the war he had

assumed that at its end he would go back to the University of Washington and get his degree. But when the end came he did not want to. He did not want to go home. Since leaving the States he had saved almost all his army pay and estimated he could get along for several months in Europe. As for every GI on the Continent, Europe meant, first, Paris. He went to Paris. He found the Café de la Cloche. He met Nicole Vaudrier and, a little later, Julian Howard.

Now he lived with Nicole. And happily. His past sexual experiences had been with casual tramps or nervous coeds. Now he learned what it was truly to *have* a woman: not only to lie but to sleep with her, wake with her, breakfast with her, spend the morning, the day, the evening with her, a part of the fabric of her life, and her of his. Nicole was tough. She had had a hard war, harder than most fighting men, with a brother killed, another lost, and a widowed mother who had turned collaborator. But still, with her toughness, there was tenderness, even gaiety. Her hair was touseled, and she had the face of a gamin.

They lived in a tiny box in a down-at-heel rooming house. But his doled-out savings were enough for rent and food, plus beers at the Cloche when Julian Howard was not ordering pernods. To augment the treasury Nicole worked part time at a typing bureau, and when she was away he sat alone in their room and wrote.

It was now almost four years since he tried his hand at writing, while in college at Seattle. During the war, all there had been was a monthly note to his mother and a few letters to girlfriend Doris Flanner, before she announced her engagement to a U of W assistant professor. But, throughout, he had clung to the resolve that when the war was over he would get seriously back to it; and this was the main reason he had come to Paris. He was self-conscious about Paris. He was well aware that this was the city of Hemingway, Fitzgerald, Pound, Stein and the rest, and that now, a generation later, half the Americans on the Left Bank were trying to join the club. But still, Paris was Paris, not Seattle or Denver. And he believed both that he had a talent—if he worked at it—and something true and valid to say.

51

What he had to say was about mountains. In four years he had learned about two things, war and mountains; but whereas he had little to write about war (and everyone else was writing it anyhow), his experience of climbing was another matter. The piece he was now doing was called "*Night Climb*," and it was about the ascent of Pizzo Rossi. He was not doing it in the first person; nor even as fact, but as fiction. Yet the source of it was himself, what he had learned on that night in Italy; specifically on the overhang high on the wall of Rossi which had turned back his companions but which he himself had climbed. It was not the mountain as such he was concerned with, but with men on a mountain; not with their techniques but with what was within them. He was writing about control. About reserves. About resources. Not of mere action and adventure, but of the stuff of life itself. If the stuff of life was not the living of it with one's total resources, then what the hell was it?

He wrote, crossed out, threw away, rewrote. He looked out the window, trying to see a mountain, but all that was there was the brick wall of the next house. Leaving his table, he again got out Bigelow's *Trek to Nowhere* and leafed through the faded pictures. When he and Ken Naylor had parted company in the Tyrol, they had agreed that, come hell, high water or even marriage, they would somehow, during the next few years, launch an expedition to Dera Zor. But now here he was under the chimney-pots of Paris, and Ken was back in Washington, working toward his degree in mining engineering.

Dera Zor, the Himalayas, were more remote than ever. Even the Alps were remote, in terms of money to get there. What was close was the Café de la Cloche, and he and Nicole spent more and more time there: first at the sidewalk tables and then, as winter came, in its snug interior. Over Christmas and New Year there were many Montparnassian parties. There were parties at Julian Howard's, lasting late with much to drink. Three mornings a week Nicole still got herself off to the typist bureau, but Eric found it increasingly hard to sit and stay at his writing. He paced the room, five short steps in each direction. Going out, he walked the streets. And one morning, walking the Raspail, he turned in at the Cloche.

At that hour it was almost empty. But Julian Howard was sitting alone at a corner table and waved as he entered.

"Ever been to Chamonix?" he asked, as Eric joined him.

"No," Eric said. "But I'd give my ass to."

"Come on, then."

"What?"

"I'm going down next week—for the skiing."

"Oh."

Julian looked at him thoughtfully. "You're a skier, aren't you?" he asked.

"Yes."

"So come along."

"Using what for money?" said Eric.

"Don't worry about that." Julian smiled. "I'm just a novice. You wouldn't be mooching; you could be my personal pro."

When he told Nicole about it she didn't like it. She didn't want to be left alone, for one thing, but there was something besides that, too.

"It is the Julian part that I most do not like," she told him.

"Why? Why not Julian?"

"He is a *tapette*—a queer."

Eric shook his head. "A little light on his feet, maybe," he said. "But a queer, no."

"If he is not, why then does he look like a pretty girl instead of a man? Why does he not have a girl of his own: at the Cloche, his parties—to take to Chamonix?"

"We're not going on a honeymoon. We're going skiing."

Nicole was not satisfied. There were more arguments, even tears. From the moment he had been asked, however, Eric knew he would go, that he had to go; and if Julian turned out to be what she thought, he was able to take care of himself.

"You do not love me," said Nicole, crying.

"Yes, I love you," he said.

But he loved the mountains more.

53

In that first postwar winter there were few private cars in France. For the few there were there was little gas. But Julian Howard had both. In one day, on almost empty roads, they made the run to Haute Savoie and Chamonix, and there above them in the winter sky hung the great white dome of Mont Blanc.

Chamonix, like the roads, was sparsely populated. But a few of the hotels were open, and in the best of them they took adjoining rooms. Searching the shops, Julian bought them the best that was available in skis, gear and clothing. At dinner they drank the best wine in the hotel's cellar—and after dinner, pernod.

But out on the mountainsides things were very different. The big prewar lifts were not yet back in operation; only a few small rope-tows were functioning, and for anything at a higher level it was on with the ski-skins and slog it up. Julian, however, did not complain. In the beginning he huffed and puffed (as did Eric), but as the days passed they both rounded into condition and soon were doing the long uphills in slow but steady rhythm. Downhill, of course, there were spills. As he had said, Julian was a novice. But he had natural balance, grace and timing, and learned quickly, as Eric put him through the same course of instruction he himself had had five years before on Mount Rainier. Above all, he had desire. He drove himself, made demands on himself, never wanted to quit until the sun was gone and night was settling on the long white slopes. He was a long way from the *soigné* playboy, the king surrounded by his court in the snug urban world of the Café de la Cloche.

There had been no advance talk of how long they would stay in the mountains. Eric had assumed two weeks or so; but the two passed, then three, then a month, and still there was no mention from Julian of a return to Paris. It was all right with Eric. If he had a bad conscience about Nicole, it was more than made up for by the joy of what he was doing. After the first week he wrote her and had a noncommittal postcard in reply. After the second he wrote again, with no answer. After the third, the same. He was sorry about it, even sad about it, but there was nothing he could, or would, do. No man could have everything, and he had what came first.

. . . Or at least next-to-first, he thought, as he gazed up at Mont Blanc and the Chamonix *aiguilles*. If it was the last thing he did, he would return in the summer to climb in the Alps.

They were of course not wholly alone. Other skiers came and went: a few groups of ex-service Americans, French weekenders from Grenoble, an occasional café-society sort of couple that seemed as affluent as Julian. For a few days in their second month there were two vacationing secretaries from Paris whom they took on a round of the cafés; and at night's end Eric almost, but not quite, slept with one, and what Julian did with the other he never learned.

On most nights, however, it was he and Julian alone: cocktails, dinner-and-wine, a pernod or two, then early to bed. And it was not until some six weeks had passed that the first thing, a very slight thing, happened. They were saying their usual good night in the hall outside their rooms, when Julian quietly asked:

"Are you having fun, Rick?"

"You're damn right I am," Eric said.

"So am I. Great fun."

He touched Eric's hand. He was holding it. And Eric pulled his hand away. He did not jerk it; he did not say anything. He merely withdrew his hand, opened his door, went into his room, and closed the door behind him.

He had a bad night. He dreaded the next morning. But at breakfast Julian was the same as always, and that day's skiing was the best of any they had had. They climbed higher, and on steeper slopes, than before. They came down faster, more directly, and not once did Julian fall. That night, wind- and sunbitten, tired but not too tired, they went to one of the Chamonix bars; after a while Julian drifted off to talk with one of the town girls who was there; and an hour or so later Eric left alone. It was after three when he awoke to hear Julian entering his room. But the next morning he was at breakfast as usual, ready to ski.

"I hope you know," he said some days later, "how grateful I am."

"*You're* grateful?" said Eric. "What about me?"

55

"No. You don't realize what it's meant to me, everything that we've done here."

"We've skied."

"Yes, skied. And now I'm a skier." Julian paused. Then he asked, "Have you known other people like me, Rick?"

"Not exactly," Eric said.

"Rich, I mean. Lousy-rich. With a dead millionaire father and a chairman-of-the-board uncle, all wrapped around in soapsuds and not good for a goddamned thing . . . Do you know something? I didn't just leave Princeton, I was bounced. I flunked out and tried to join the army, but even the army didn't want me, so I joined the Field Service, and that was the first thing I ever did right. I drove an ambulance, and I drove it well. I got shelled and bombed and took it the same as anyone else . . . Then the war ends and I come to Paris. Christ, Paris! And it all gets fucked up again. I'm Little Lord Gotrocks of Montparnasse, I buy friends with pernods, I buy a ski teacher; only there it switches again— you see how crazy it is—because the skiing is good, it's like the ambulance driving, I'm doing something, learning, I'm a skier by God, and the best of it all is that I don't even *feel* I've bought you."

"Shut up," said Eric.

And they skied.

They skied for another week, and another, and then one evening Julian said, "I'm seeing these trails in my sleep; let's go somewhere else." So they went to Switzerland. They skied first at Mürren, then at Grindelwald and Davos; and here, where there had been no war, there were more people, the big lifts were running; but now they went even higher than the top of the lifts, to the very base of the rock peaks, for spring had come and the high corn snow glittered.

Then all snow, even that, was receding. It was April, then May; the naked earth was emerging; and Eric realized that there would be no return to the Alps for the summer; he would already be there.

What now for Julian? he wondered.

56

And Julian answered:

"You taught me to ski," he said. "Will you teach me to climb?"

They started small. Returning to Chamonix, they worked out on the practice cliffs near the Biolet Campgrounds, and Eric taught him the fundamentals of cragsmanship, as he had been taught them himself long before. Again Julian was a good pupil. Not so good, perhaps, as in skiing; in climbing he had had no previous experience and was bothered at first by verticality. But as on the snowslopes, his balance and grace were assets, his desire was vast, and soon he was past his novitiate.

Their first full-scale climb was of Mont Blanc itself, by the *voie ordinaire*. A long snow trudge, not unlike Rainier, it was technically easier than the practice cliffs, but Eric, no less than Julian, felt a lift of the heart as they stood together on the highest point of western Europe. Then they doubled back to Switzerland: to Zermatt and the Matterhorn. And here too, though they took the "tourist route," Eric was amply rewarded, for he was climbing at last in the footsteps of Whymper, whom he had followed so often in the dreams of his boyhood.

There followed other climbs in the Pennines: Monte Rosa, the Rothorn, the Obergabelhorn. And Julian, loving it all, improved steadily. But in a single season of climbing he could not conceivably have qualified for the sort of climbs for which Eric was yearning: the faces, not the ridges, of mountains; the spires of the Chamonix *aiguilles*; the strictly "nontourist routes" that were the domain of the true Alpine masters. Now and then he spoke of such climbing. He suggested that Julian take a few days off while he teamed up with a veteran to make an ambitious try. But for the first time Julian was difficult. "Aren't I doing well?" he asked. "Let's go together. With you, I can do anything." And trouble loomed. Climbing was not skiing; if you made a mistake you paid for it not with a broken bone but with your life; and Eric was not going to gamble that high either for himself or Julian Howard.

The impasse was resolved by a cablegram. Julian's sister was about to be married in Chicago. "Oh my God, to that creep; it'll

57

last a week," he announced. But still he had to go. As they parted at the Zermatt railway station he said, "These have been the best days of my life."

If one problem had been removed, however, another had replaced it: for the first time in months Eric had to think of money. He could get by though, he figured, if he cut down on all fronts: abandoning hotels for campgrounds; eating bread, cheese and sausage; spending as many nights as possible in the high mountain refuges where shelter was free. First on his agenda were the long-dreamed-of *aiguilles*, and this time he hitchhiked to Chamonix.

The campaign was all he could have hoped for. The weather was good. At Biolet he encountered some of the best of the French guides, still languishing in postwar unemployment, and with them he climbed as companion, not client. He reached the summits of the Grépon, the Blaitière, the Fou, the Dru, exulting in their sheerness, their perfect granite, their challenge to every resource a cragsman could muster. Adding to it, enriching it, was his acceptance as an equal by the proudest professional climbers in the world.

That carried him to mid-August. Then it was back again to Zermatt—and Uli Brandel.

He heard of Brandel before he met him. The whole town was talking about two top German mountaineers who had come to climb the Matterhorn: not by the tourist route, or any of its ridges, but by the fabled North Face, one of the "impossibles" of the Alps, that had been scaled successfully no more than a half-dozen times. One of the two, however, had been called back to Germany. The other, Brandel, was looking for a partner—if a good enough one could be found. And Eric sought him out at the Zermatt campground. He was a young man of about his own age, but with a not-young face, a weathered face with bleak eyes, a wedgelike chin; and he was wearing a gray-green shirt and felt-peaked cap that Eric recognized even with their insignia removed. He had picked up some German in the Tyrol. Brandel had some English. They were able to communicate, and Eric spoke of the North Face.

Brandel measured him. "You are British?" he asked.

"American."

"Hmm. I did not know Americans were climbers."

"I was in the mountain troops in Italy," said Eric. "Like you."

The German made no comment. His eyes went on measuring. Then he said, "You are aware, I suppose, that the North Face is no child's play?"

"I've heard the rumor."

"What climbs have you made?"

Eric told him. Brandel listed his. On the next two days they did practice climbs, to get acquainted; and on the third, in pre-dawn darkness, they were at the base of the North Face, roping up.

He will take the lead without asking, Eric had thought on the way up the glacier. And he was right. After testing the rope knots and peering up the wall, Brandel started off without a word, and Eric, letting it pass, followed after. The rock of the face was rotten, but in its lower reaches not overwhelmingly steep, and they made good progress. The only delays came when Brandel, reaching the top of each pitch, took elaborate precautions with the belays that would hold Eric in case of a slip.

"You are all right?" he called down from above.

"Yes," said Eric.

And a little later: "I go too fast?"

"No."

After some two hours they rested on a small ledge. Then Brandel rose and prepared to go on.

"I'll go first now," said Eric.

The German turned in surprise.

"We'll take turns leading."

"No, it is best I lead."

"Either we take turns," Eric said, "or we go down."

Brandel thought it over. He looked up at the face. He looked at Eric. He shrugged. "We will try it," he said.

They went on, Eric leading, and progress was the same as before. Like Brandel, Eric took great care in belaying, and from one of his stances he called down, "All right?"

There was no answer.

He called louder. "All right?"

"Yes," said Brandel.

"Am I going too fast?"

"No."

Through the rest of the day they changed leads, creeping hour after hour up the vast ruin of the wall. Morning passed into afternoon, afternoon into dusk, and as dark came they found another ledge and pitoned themselves onto it for the night. They had known they would have to spend a night on the face and had brought bivouac gear and food. In the darkness it grew cold. But the stars blazed; there was no storm. They were lucky. They even managed to sleep a little, perched in their eyrie above a gulf of space.

At dawn they were off again. On the first day they had come about two thirds of the way up the mountain, but now the face was steeper, the going slower. Technically the climbing was not as hard as some that Eric had done on the needles of Chamonix. But on the rotted, crumbling rock it was far more dangerous. From their alternating lead position he and Brandel belayed each other with the utmost caution, and no longer with a barb in their shouted exchanges. Once Eric slipped. Once Brandel. If they had been alone or with an incompetent partner it would have been the end of them. But each time the other caught and held the slip. Between them there was no stronger or weaker, no leader and led. They were what men should be on a mountain: a balanced team.

They climbed, rested briefly, climbed on and on. Again morning passed into afternoon, but this time there was to be no dusk or night. As the sun sloped westward they felt the angle of ascent ease off beneath them. Raising their eyes, they saw not only rock but a ridge and sky. And at a little after four they were on the ridge, on the top of the Matterhorn; the North Face was below them; and they looked down it, and at each other, and shook hands.

Brandel's bleak eyes gleamed. His cracked lips parted to say *"Heil—"*

But he didn't say it.

He said, "*Grüss Gott.*"

"*Grüss Gott,*" said Eric.

They started down the tourist route. There had been no defilement. As evening came and the wind rose, it sang in Eric's ears like a tide of music.

Then the music was gone. In its place was rain. In Zermatt the hotels and campground closed, and the peaks were lost in autumn cloud and early snow. Hitchhiking, he returned to Paris, with the equivalent in his pocket of fourteen dollars and forty cents.

He did not expect Nicole to be waiting for him, and she wasn't. There was another couple living in their old flat, and he took a room in a cheap hotel down the street. He went to the Café de la Cloche, and she wasn't there, and he had a *demi-bière,* then another, and as he was finishing the second she came past. She was holding the arm of a big blond man who looked like a Swede, and the man was talking and she was laughing, and the gamin face under the touseled hair was alive and glowing. For a moment it seemed that they were going to stop and turn in at the Cloche, but they didn't, continuing on along the Raspail until they were out of sight.

He bought cheese and bread and ate them in his room. The next morning he sat in his room. He now had fifty-five hundred francs left, about eleven dollars. As an alien he could not take a job in France, nor could he do anything about GI benefits unless he went back home. In his one bag, with a few clothes and the copy of *Trek to Nowhere,* were the fifteen penciled pages of his unfinished "Night Climb." During the months in the mountains he had not so much as looked at them, and he was a long way from making his first dollar as a writer.

Going out, he walked the streets. He sat by the Seine and in the Luxembourg Gardens. He went again to the Cloche and had two beers and one pernod. Back in his room he again ate bread and cheese. When he awoke, after sleeping late, it was to a knock on the door, and the hotel clerk said, "*Monsieur, c'est maintenant deux nuits. Voulez vous payer, s'il vous plaît.*" When he had paid he had eighty francs left, and with this he bought coffee and a

61

brioche. Then he walked again—Left Bank, Right Bank, across the city—and in the late afternoon he came to the American Embassy off the Place de la Concorde. After a wait he saw a vice consul, and he could tell from the vice consul's face that his was not a new story.

"There is only one procedure," he said. "To send a cable to your family."

"I have no family," Eric said.

"Then a friend."

He thought of Julian. But Julian had done enough already. "Even if I had a family," he said, "I haven't the money to send a cable."

"We can take care of that," said the vice consul, "and deduct it from the remittance."

Eric shook his head and turned to leave.

"Don't let it go too long," the vice consul said. "If you get involved with the police it's much harder."

Eric went out. He walked back to Montparnasse. He sat at tables at various cafés until waiters appeared to take his order, and then he rose and left. After dark, he went to the Luxembourg Gardens, lay down on a bench and spent the night.

In the morning he walked again. He lifted a brioche from a passing baker's cart and ate it sitting by the Seine. He walked to the Tuileries, the Place de l'Opéra, Montmartre. Again toward late afternoon, he walked to the Place de la Concorde and into the Embassy and after a wait saw the vice consul.

"You've remembered some family?" the vice consul asked.

"Yes," he said.

"You want us to send a cable?"

"Yes."

The vice consul took a form from a drawer. "To whom?" he asked.

"To Frank Venn, 2120 Seaview Drive, Santa Monica, California."

Frank was hard to see from a mountain. He had nothing to do
with mountains.

But even on the dome of Dera Zor he could hear Frank's voice,
cool and even. And Frank was saying, "What the hell are you
doing?"

"I've just been to Denver," he said.

6

From plane to plane Denver had been only three hours. First he had phoned home from the airport and been told there was no such number. Then he had taken a bus and walked and stood on the sidewalk of Desmond Street looking at the for sale sign. His first impulse had been to ring at either the Blacks or the Pownalls next door, but he didn't. He returned to the airport, boarded the first plane for Los Angeles, and bussed and walked to the offices of Burden Industries in Culver City.

"Mr. Venn is very busy today," a secretary told him. But when she learned who he was she said, "Oh," and when after a while two men emerged from an office, she led him in. It was not a corner office, but it was large, carpeted, air-conditioned. Frank himself had more middle and more forehead than before, and his cool gray eyes were now framed by glasses. As Eric entered, he shook hands and gestured him to a seat. Then his phone rang.

"Wilson of Lockheed? Put him on," he said. And for the next several minutes he discussed invoices and bills of lading, calling his secretary onto the line to take down pertinent figures.

"Sorry," he said as he hung up.

And Eric said, "When did Mother die?"

"Die? She didn't."

"Where is she then?"

"She's had a breakdown. She's here in Los Angeles."

"With you and Kay?"

Frank shook his head. "It wasn't anything sudden, of course;

it had been coming a long time. But this year it got worse. More hysteria, more hallucinations, to the point where she couldn't take care of herself anymore. Dr. Farrelly called me from Denver, and I went there and brought her on. Here at least she's away from those damn Brethren, and Kay and I can visit her more often."

"Visit her where?"

The phone rang again. "Yes . . . Yes," said Frank. "You and Tom better come in and we'll talk it over."

He hung up and said, "Sorry."

"Where *is* Mother?" Eric asked.

"She's at a home."

"What home? Where is it?"

Frank considered his words before he spoke. "I'm not going to tell you that," he said.

"Not tell me?"

"I'll give it to you straight, Rick. I don't think you should see Mother. More important, the doctors don't think so."

"What doctors?"

"At the home. I've told them you were coming back, and they feel strongly about it."

"Why, for God's sake?"

"Can't *you* figure out why?"

Eric got up, went to the window, and looked out at a parking lot blaze of sun, chrome and concrete. When he turned back Frank had left the room, but he returned in a few moments and said, "Sorry."

"The hallucinations," said Eric. "They're all Robin?"

Frank nodded.

"She thinks she still sees her?"

"She thinks she's alive."

"And me?"

"You're dead."

"She knows damn well I'm not dead. I've written her once a month all along."

"Not that kind of dead," Frank said.

Eric was silent. He tried to feel grief, but there was only a void.

If he was dead to his mother, it was no more than she was, and long had been, to him.

The phone rang. "Tell him I'll call back," Frank said. "And don't put any more calls through unless it's Mr. Burden."

"You might have let me know," said Eric.

"Let you know what?"

"What happened with Mother."

"How? Care of General Delivery, Europe?"

Eric said nothing.

"I gather you've been getting around since the war ended."

"Some."

"Doing what?"

"Skiing. Climbing."

"In Paris?"

"In Paris I was—writing."

"For a paper? A magazine?"

"No, just feeling my way."

"And living on handouts?"

Eric drew a breath. "Thanks for the money," he said.

"That's all right," said Frank.

"I'll pay it back."

"What are your plans?"

"I don't know yet."

"Where are you living?"

"I just got in. My bag's outside."

"Hmm." Frank thought about it. "Kay and I would be glad to have you at the house, but—"

"How is Kay?"

"She's fine. But with the two kids—"

"Two?"

"There's Joyce, you know about her; she's almost two now. And Sheila: she's six months."

"Congratulations."

"Thanks. You might pull for a nephew next time."

"I'll do what I can."

"Anyhow, with four we're pretty crowded. But there's a motel just down the hill from us." Frank paused, then asked, "How much money have you left?"

"Sixty dollars," said Eric.

Frank lifted his phone. "Make out a check on my personal book, Miss Swenson. To the order of Eric Venn for five hundred dollars."

Eric started to speak, but his brother waved him down. "With what I cabled, that's a thousand," he said. "From here on you're on your own."

"It's damn good of you, Frank. I'll pay it all back."

"I'm not worrying. Compared to what Mother's costing you're a bargain. But it's got to be understood: a thousand is it."

The thanks froze in Eric's throat. It was Desmond Street all over again.

"I'm no moocher, Frank," he said.

"No one's calling you a moocher."

"What then?"

Frank gave him his cool level look. "All right, you ask me and I'll tell you," he said. "You're a child, that's what."

"I'm almost twenty-four, for God's sake."

"All right, a child of twenty-four."

"With three and a half years in the army."

"You did fine in the army. I'm talking about since."

"What's wrong with since?"

"You know damn well what's wrong. Eighteen months adding up to zero. What the hell are you doing with your life?"

"God damn it, Frank—"

"Well, what *have* you been doing? Besides running away from a day's work."

"I've told you—"

"Yes, I know. The Alps, Paris; seeing life and the world and all that . . . Well, now it's my turn to say God damn it." Frank slapped his desk. "God damn it, that's not life and the world; that's being a bum. This is the world: this office. That plant out there. Stores, factories, machines, salesmen; people doing a job, earning a living, going home to their wives and kids—that's the world, that's what it's about—not all this crap of yours chasing around after rainbows. And I'm telling you, if you don't realize it soon you're going to make a mess of your life."

Frank did not raise his voice, even while swearing. It remained as cool and level as his eyes. Now the door opened, his secretary came in with the check, and in the same tone he said, "Thank you, Miss Swenson."

"Mr. Matson and Mr. Richardson are outside," she said.

"I'll see them in a minute."

Frank signed the check and pushed it across his desk. But Eric ignored it and stood up.

"Don't be a fool," his brother said. "Sixty bucks won't get you far in Los Angeles, and the police take a dim view of sleeping in parks."

Eric said nothing.

"And don't work yourself up into taking a punch at me." Frank stood up too. "You can't play the kid brother all your life," he said, not unkindly. "Take a deep breath, Rick. Take this check. Stop being a kid right now."

He held out the check. There was a pause. Eric took it.

Then the phone rang.

"Hello. Oh—yes, Dad," Frank said. "It's the Lockheed thing; I thought you should know about it." He listened. "Right . . . Right . . . I'll get the General Dynamics file too. Tom and Fred are here. We'll thrash them out a bit, then come up to your office."

He hung up. "There's a branch of the Bank of America on the corner," he said. "I'll have Miss Swenson call and say you'll be in to cash a check. Then go to that motel near us—it's called La Quinta—and we'll expect you for dinner at seven."

The evening was different.

The house on Seaview Drive was the same he had visited from Camp Hale, but it had been newly furnished. There was a maid. There were martinis and canapes and his two nieces, whom he held briefly on his lap. What there wasn't was Frank. He had phoned, said Kay, that he had to fly to San Francisco for a breakfast meeting, and had sent a company car for an overnight bag.

"He's away a lot?" Eric asked.

Kay nodded, then smiled. "But I don't always have such a good stand-in," she said.

Three years and two babies, Eric noted, had done no harm to her figure. Copper-haired and green-eyed, she was still a stunning girl. And still easy to talk to. With the children put to bed, she plied him with questions about the war and after—but mostly after—and the green eyes brightened as he talked of skiing in the Alps.

"You made a promise," she reminded him.

"Which I'll keep," he told her.

"And I want you just the way Julian Howard had you: as my private pro."

She herself, she said, had skied only once or twice since she had seen him. "First there was the war and gas coupons. Now the babies. And besides, Frank doesn't care for it."

"He's not Mr. Outdoors," said Eric.

They had two martinis; then dinner by a picture window overlooking the Pacific. The maid brought a bottle of wine, Eric opened and poured it, and Kay said, "You learned things in Paris."

"A few," he conceded.

"Tell me about them."

He did his best. He talked of Montparnasse and the Cloche, of beer and pernods and Nicole and trying to write; then somehow got back to the war and Pizzo Rossi, from there to the Matterhorn, from there back to Paris; and Kay sipped her wine and listened, and still her green eyes glowed.

"You've had a lot of living, Rick," she said. "A lot of doing."

"At least a lot of moving."

"No, more than that. Not just outside—inside. The kid brother takes off, but someone else comes back."

Eric smiled. "Your husband begs to differ," he said.

"Did he give you a hard time?"

"He gave me five hundred dollars. Now I owe him a thousand."

"You know what I mean."

"Frank was—Frank."

"No nonsense."

"No." He smiled again. "What happened to that pump of yours?" he asked.

Kay looked puzzled, then remembered and laughed. "The nonsense pump, the stirrer-upper . . . No," she said, "no big success there. Frank was born no-nonsense and I guess he'll stay that way."

There was a pause, not an easy one, but she did not veer away. "Are you still surprised, Rick?" she asked. "At me. That I'm Frank's wife."

"Yes," he said.

"So am I, sometimes. But there are reasons, of course." They had now finished dinner and were back in the living room, with coffee and brandy, and Kay tasted her brandy before speaking again. "One of them that you wouldn't know," she said, "is that Frank's a good husband. He's kind and considerate. He loves the children. He doesn't get angry or drunk or mess around with other women."

She took another sip. "But that's not all of it," she said. "You've not met my father, have you?"

"No," said Eric.

"Well, I'll tell you a funny thing. Part of the reason I married Frank was Daddy. Not because he was so like him, but *un*like him. Daddy inherited money, you see, and the family business, and that's how he ran it, as a sort of comfortable fuddy-duddy little family thing. I don't mean he's stupid, or even lazy; he just isn't ambitious. What he's really interested in is his golf and his bridge and going to Hawaii every winter. When Frank came into the business it was as if a cyclone had hit it. He came in just as a salesman, but soon everything started to jump and grow and come alive. I'd never met a man who worked so hard, who cared so much about what he was doing, and I found it an exciting thing. In fact I still do—sometimes."

She had finished her brandy and refilled Eric's glass and her own.

"Now I'll tell you another funny thing," she said. "Frank and my father are so very different, but you and Frank aren't."

"We both have two arms and two legs," said Eric.

"You both care so much. About very different things, but still you care."

He thought it over.

"What you want you want terribly, don't you?"

"Yes," he said.

"What Frank wants is money and power. What is it you want most, Rick?"

"I want to climb a mountain called Dera Zor."

She repeated the name. "It's beautiful," she said. "Where is it?"

He told her about it, about Bigelow and *Trek to Nowhere*, and again she listened with glowing eyes.

"You'll get there," she said. "I know it; I know you. You'll get there."

"It will take some doing."

"And meanwhile?"

"I don't know," he said.

"Has Frank offered you a job?"

The question took him by surprise. "No," he said. Then, "I doubt if he's thought of it."

"He's thought of it," Kay said. "If he offers it will you take it?"

"No."

"I'm glad, Rick."

He smiled. "One Venn's enough for you and your father."

"It's not that. Oh no—" Her voice trailed off. Then her hand moved swiftly out and rested on his. "Don't let him tame you, Rick," she said. "Not now. Not ever."

A while later he rose to go, and she went with him to the door. "It's ridiculous that you don't stay here," she protested.

"My bag's at La Quinta," he said.

"You could use some of Frank's things. And I can—"

"It's better this way."

"Then I'll walk you down."

"Ridiculous."

"Worse than that, it's illegal; that's why I like it. Walking at night in L.A. is worse than rape or arson."

Kay took his arm and they walked the five minutes down the hill to the motel.

"Now I walk you back," said Eric.

And it was ten minutes up.

"This is nice and crazy," she told him. "We could do this forever."

"I wouldn't mind," he said.

He sat in his room at La Quinta. Leaving it, he went to the nearby beach to walk on the hard winter sand, and on the way back he ate at a hamburger place. He had thinking to do and decisions to make.

The first was about his mother. If he forced the issue with Frank or, better, Kay, he could learn where she was, go to see her. But to what purpose? If she didn't recognize him it would be useless, and if she did, probably worse. Frank was right, and the doctors. She was gone from his life. As gone as his father. Or Robin.

He turned from past to future. To what now? He could go back to the U of W, or some other college, and get a degree, and GI benefits would pay for it. But again to what purpose? What help was college toward Dera Zor? Or for that matter, toward writing? Self-respecting writers didn't hang around colleges; they got thrown out of them.

All right then: if you're a writer, write. He took out the fifteen pages of "Night Climb" and read and reread them. He sat for an hour before a fresh page with a sharpened pencil, and nothing happened. Pizzo Rossi was as remote as Mars.

He took out Bigelow and began to read of Dera Zor. It was as remote as Betelgeuse.

The next morning he bought the Los Angeles *Times* and read the want ads . . . Physicist, chemist, shipping clerk, dishwasher . . . His old friends from the Tenth Mountain (except Bob Koontz) had picked up their careers where they had left off when they went to war: Ken Naylor as a graduate engineering student in Seattle; Harry Bushnell with the National Park Service; Per

Halberg as head of the ski school at White Valley, Utah. Only he had left off nowhere—and was back there.

Frank called and asked how things were going.

"All right," he said.

"Something lined up?"

"No."

"But prospects?"

"Yes."

"You might try the Bank of America," Frank said. "I was talking to one of their v.p.'s today. He said there are openings in one of their trainee programs where a college degree isn't required."

"Thanks," said Eric, "I'll keep it in mind."

Then there was a knock, and it was Kay, and she said, "Remember me? I'm your sister-in-law."

"I'm sorry," he said. "I've been sort of fighting things out."

"I know. I'm not here to pester." She put a paper bag on the table. "Brownies—Mother Venn's finest. To ward off malnutrition."

Beside the bag on the table were his sheets of manuscript, and she looked at him questioningly.

"Not yet," he said.

"But soon."

"First I need a job."

She nodded; then looked around the bare cubicle of his room. "I'll tell you another thing you need, Rick," she said. "A girl."

He smiled. "Second things second."

"I can scare some up for you, if you like. Brownie types, martini types; anything but ski types. For skiing I'm your girl and don't forget it."

Later, when she had kissed him and left, it seemed to him it was this that started everything under way. But still later, he knew that it wasn't; that it was only the catalyst. Ever since he had been in Los Angeles, since he had left the Alps, perhaps since the war had ended, he had known what he wanted to do; what was the only conceivable thing for him to do if his life were to be anything more than a dismal acceptance of defeat. The difference was that now he *knew* he knew it. It was plain and clear: as clear as a snow peak against a winter sky.

That evening he phoned Per Halberg at White Valley, Utah.

There was no more Frank now; only mountain and snow.

There was no more darkness, but sunlight. He was not on Dera Zor but on Crystal Peak. His skis were pointed, ready, and his poles were poised.

Through his goggles he peered down the gleaming slope of the Hermit Trail, and at its end, far below, were the clustered buildings of White Valley. He could see the Lodge, the chalets, the ski shop, and the squat chimneyed shape of the Sitzmark Bar.

He smiled through cracked lips and aimed his skis at the bar.

7

He pushed off. The steepness took him. For a few seconds there was a thrusting, a straining; then speed without effort, flight free as wind. There was no scraping and sawing of skis, as on the packed surfaces lower down; no adhesion of snow, as even on the heights of the Alps, where the climate was damper. Here on the rooftop of Utah the powder was dry, pure, soft as gossamer. Pouring in billows from below, it rose to meet the ski tips, crested over, engulfed them; but in the engulfing there was no pressure, no slowing. The powder flowed as if it were not snow at all, but white cloud, and spumed out in great fans to the sides and the rear. This was not descending a mountain. It was soaring through space.

There were several runs down the flank of Crystal Peak, and he had skied them all. But this, the Hermit, was the best. In that year of 1947 there was still no lift to its high takeoff point; and it was well named, for there were few skiers either expert enough to schuss it or tough enough for the long grind to its top. For the few wild minutes it took to come down, you were out of the world and in another beyond it.

It was only a sometimes world, however: a bonus on days off. Through the rest of the week, through winter and spring, he earned his living as a teacher in a less rarefied realm of practice slopes, rope tows, snowplows and tottering pupils. As the most junior instructor, he worked largely with novice classes. The "carriage trade" of better skiers and those who could afford private lessons went to the more established pros; and he was also not unaware that the Europeans who comprised the bulk of the staff had a higher glamour quotient than a next-door type from Denver. Nevertheless, he was content with his job. For the first time in his life he was making reasonable money—to the point where he began paying off his debt to Frank. Days on the slopes and trails, nights in the Lodge or Sitzmark Bar, made for a pleasant if repetitive pattern; and Per Halberg was a good boss. As in the mountain troops, he was in a fraternity of men bound in interest and spirit. And if, as at Camp Hale, it was a tight, circumscribed world, it was at least a world that he knew and loved—and that, unlike Hale, was far from womanless.

"Skis + shes = no complaints," he wrote Ken Naylor in early April. "But I'm counting the days until summer."

It was going on two years now since he had seen Ken. But he had written him in Seattle; Ken had replied; and presently there had come a letter saying that during the following summer he was going to the Wyoming Tetons as an instructor-guide at the climbing school . . . "Interested?" he had asked. "Damn right," was Eric's reply . . . With the days counted and summer at last at hand, he returned to the Tetons after eleven years' absence and did his first climbing with Ken since Pizzo Rossi.

At first, Ken seemed to have aged five rather than two years in the interval. His hair had begun to recede, his face was jowly, and his bodily heft had turned, if not to fat, to still more heft, which he carried ponderously. His mining engineering studies had allowed him little skiing during the winter past. The previous summer he had done field work in Montana, involving much out-of-doors but no climbing. "I'm a goddamn mess," he announced to Eric when they met; on their initial outings he was slow, deliberate, almost awkward. But this was a phase that, happily, was soon over. Quickly, his bulk slimmed and hardened. His coordination and confidence returned, and it was again like the old days.

Most of their climbing, of course, was with clients. As with White Valley skiing, most was routine. But here too there were days off, with climbs done not for pay but for their own sake. And though the Tetons were no Alps either in size or variety—

77

in summer they were almost void of ice and snow—they were nonetheless good mountains, climbers' mountains, with form, texture and sound soaring rock.

Eric loved the Teton rock. He loved it even more than the snow of Crystal Peak. Or perhaps it was not a matter of rock versus snow, but of climbing versus skiing. True, there was nothing in mountaineering to compare in speed and razzle-dazzle with a steep schuss on skis. Skiing was the fastest means of movement known to man, unaided by machinery. Climbing was probably the slowest. But in that very slowness lay, for him, the quality that made the difference. On skis there was thrill and glitter, but these were outward things, the products of sensation. On skis you were not part of a mountain; the mountain was a mere means to an end, the end of speed. Whereas in climbing, the mountain was more than that. Yes, the summit was an end, a goal, but that was secondary, almost superficial. It was the climbing *in itself* that was the true end, the matching of man and peak, the struggle of leg, arm, breath, mind, spirit, not against the mountain—oh no, never against it; the mountain was no enemy—but against your own inadequacy and fear. Skiing without speed was nothing. Climbing without a summit gained was still climbing. It depended on no reward beyond itself. It was a oneness, a communion with a mountain, and therefore with the earth, the life, of which you both were a part.

Climbers, of course, did not talk this way. They said, "On belay . . . off belay . . . bear right now . . . get the lead out." Even with pencil and paper (as Eric well knew) the meanings beneath were hard to unravel; for communion was one thing, communication another. With skiing, on the other hand, it was easy. Skiing was—or had begun to be, since the building of lifts—in the mainstream of American experience and understanding. Speed without effort was "fun"; therefore skiing was "fun." But climbing a mountain was perhaps the hardest sustained effort of body and will that a man could impose on himself, and one who did so freely and gladly was, in the majority opinion, weak in the head. At White Valley, none of the nonskiers (of whom there were few) asked the skiers, "Why do you ski?" But in the Tetons, all the nonclimbers (of whom there were many) asked the climbers, "Why do you climb?" Eric's answers varied, but he carefully stayed clear of "communion." "For penance," he would say. Or "for thirty bucks roundtrip." Or—borrowing from Mallory of Everest—"because it is there."

He had said that last once (with a small grin) to Nicole in Paris. And she had answered, "Then you too, *chéri*, are *existentialist*."

"How come?" he had asked.

"Because with *existentialisme* there does not have to be a reason for everything. Life is there: you live it. A mountain is there: you climb it."

Now he grinned again, remembering.

The Tetons were there, and he climbed them.

Something else was there too, far beyond them: higher, wilder. In their bunkhouse in the Tetons, as they had in the cowsheds of the Apennines, he and Ken talked through the nights of the Himalayas, and of a vast and hidden peak called Dera Zor.

It was he, Eric, of course, who began it, and in the beginning Ken seemed skeptical, even indifferent. "So you've still got that bug for Christ's sake?" he said.

Yes, said Eric, he still had it. He would never lose it. And neither would Ken, he added, though he might have grown absent-minded about it. Again, as so often before, he pulled out Bigelow's *Trek to Nowhere*, following it up and up in text and picture; and again, as in the hills of Italy, he could see the light begin to kindle in Ken's eyes.

"And what am I supposed to do about mining engineering?" asked Ken. "Just chuck it, like that?"

"You know damn well you won't have to chuck it. You take time off. If you want something enough, there's always a way to it."

Soon they were *on* the way: deep in detailed and practical discussions of how an expedition could be mounted. Three basic elements were involved—men, money and political permission—and of these only men posed no major problem. True, they had to be carefully selected: four besides themselves, they decided, to make a team of six. But there were plenty to choose from; they were acquainted, at least by name, with almost all the top climbers in the country; and they knew that, like themselves, most would give body and soul for a chance at a great Himalayan peak. Money, on the other hand, was a very high hurdle. It would take plenty of doing to raise the fifty thousand dollars they figured was needed. And permission, too, was a sticky affair, for Nepal was still a notoriously hard place to get into. Nevertheless, they resolved, they would give it the big try, and carefully, minutely, they laid out their campaign.

It was now the summer of 1947.

"We'll shoot for the spring of forty-nine," said Eric.

The Teton climbing season ended in early September. Ken returned to Seattle and he to White Valley, where, through the fall, he helped in the construction of a new aerial lift. In his spare time he wrote Dera Zor letters in many directions. Then came waiting . . . and hoping . . .

In December, White Valley turned white and the skiing season began. Again there were the slopes and trails, the classes and "clinics," the schusses and pratfalls; in the evenings the luxury of the Lodge and the Sitzmark Bar; on days off the long climb and wild descent on the high stillness of the Hermit. Professionally he had moved up a few notches, for some old instructors had left, with new ones replacing them, and he had acquired a year's seniority. He was assigned fewer novices, more intermediate classes, and also more private clients, which was where the real money came from. By the time the season was half over he had paid off the last of his debt to brother Frank.

A letter came from Kay. She was planning a visit of two weeks, and those much-talked-of ski lessons would begin at last. But a week before scheduled arrival she sent a wire saying the children had measles and she couldn't come. Whether he was disappointed or not Eric could not quite have said; and in any case, even without Kay, there was no lack of women in the Valley. Many of them were unattached, some attractive, some rich or near-rich. Among them were new divorcees from across the line in Nevada and Idaho, social types from San Francisco and Denver, members or quasi members of the film world of Hollywood. They were a gay and glossy breed, a predatory breed, and they knew what they wanted—which was often a ski pro of their very own. Among their trophies had been one of the nonreturning instructors from the previous year, who had been carried off by a starlet to Sunset Boulevard, where he was now doing God knows what.

For Eric it did not come to that, but he had his share of big evenings in the Lodge and Sitzmark. At first he had found it hard to accept tips from his female clients and let them sign checks for meals and drinks. ("I'm no skier, I'm a goddamn gigolo," he had written to Ken.) But he had learned that this was s.o.p. in his profession, and a large part of the gravy too; for the tips (of twenty, fifty, up to a hundred dollars) made all the difference between tight and easy living. Sometimes he drank too much, and he knew it. Several times he came to his early morning novice class with a hangover, twice he missed it entirely, and once, having tooled off for a night in Provo with a new Reno divorcee, he missed a whole day of appointments.

It was after this that he was hauled, gently but firmly, onto the carpet by Per Halberg and told that, though his night life was his own, he had better be on hand in the mornings, or else.

"You are restless, yes?" Per asked, appraising him. "You think of this mountain of yours. Of this Dera Zor."

He admitted as much.

"It does not go well? The plans, the money?"

"It's too early to tell," Eric said.

But each week, each month, it was less early. As he and Ken had foreseen, assembling a tentative team had been easy: a few letters to top prospects had drawn the same number of enthusiastic replies. But on the two other fronts there had been a total blank. For political permission, first he and then Ken had written to the Foreign Ministry of Nepal, but now five months had passed since the first letter, three since the second, with no answer. In their financing efforts, on the other hand, they received answers, but no good ones. They had written to the American

81

Alpine Club and the National Geographic Society, to other clubs and societies, to government agencies, private foundations, indeed to anyone they could think of who might conceivably put money into a Himalayan expedition. But the replies, with varying degree of regret, were all to the same effect that no funds were available for such a purpose.

"What now?" they asked each other.

And they had no answer.

As spring came on, Ken was no longer even able to help search for one; all his time was taken by preparation for exams for his engineering degree. For his part, Eric looked past the end of the skiing season to a prospect of nothingness. But in the end it was not to be as bad as that. Dera Zor remained a remote, apparently impossible dream. But in April he was invited to join a summer expedition to Mount McKinley, in Alaska.

The bid came from one of the other men who had guided in the Tetons the year past. He was a first-rate climber, the rest of the team no less so; and the expedition was a success. Inevitably, McKinley threw its storms at them, and its arctic cold, but in a six weeks' campaign they fought their way up a new and demanding route to its summit. Eric was one of four who reached it, and its 20,320-foot altitude was by far his "highest yet." But even as he set foot on it, there was an irony, a shadow, on the moment of victory; for he knew that where McKinley ended was where the hard climbing on Dera Zor barely began.

This fall there was no construction work at White Valley. The inn and its facilities were closed for off-season. But he nevertheless took a room for three months at a nearby motel, for the Valley was the closest he came to having a home.

He was resolved to write again—really to work at writing—and he did. First he set down the story of the McKinley climb. Then he returned yet again to Pizzo Rossi, and at last moved on from his broken-down eight pages to a finished piece. Next came Uli Brandel and the north wall of the Matterhorn; but not so much in its climbing aspects as in his strange partner-enemy relationship with the unreconstructed Nazi. And finally he got away from

82

the mountains entirely with a vignette, half memoir, half short story, about a girl called Nicole in postwar Paris. He wrote and rewrote, tinkered and polished, until he was satisfied that the work was the very best of which he was capable; then sent the four pieces off to four different magazines.

Fall passed into winter, and it was time to ski again. There were the classes, the private clients, the days off on the Hermit. There were the evenings in the Lodge and Sitzmark; but he watched his step with drinking and women and did not again get into trouble with Per Halberg. On the face of it, it was a good life—in a place he liked, doing what he liked—but beneath the face, in his inwardness, it was something else, and the else was close to a zero. What he wanted most in the world, what for years he had dreamed and planned and struggled to bring to fruition, was as remote as when he had first found *Trek to Nowhere* on a shelf in the library of the University of Washington.

Even Ken was remote now. After graduation he had taken a job with Cerro de Pasco and gone off to their copper mines in the Andes of Peru. On his own, Eric still followed every lead, every hint of a hope he could think of. He wrote again to Nepal. He tried new financing prospects: societies, corporations, individuals. He corresponded with the alpine clubs of England, France, and Switzerland, which had had more experience with Himalayan ventures than their American counterpart. But still he drew a blank. Back in the Tetons with Ken, he had set the spring of 1949 as the target date for the great adventure. But now that spring was upon him, and he had moved not so much as a step toward Dera Zor.

Then out of nowhere, in mid-March, came the day when everything changed. He had come down off the slopes in the late afternoon, and in the ski shop Per Halberg said to him, "There is a new guest, just arrived, who is looking for you. A man," he added, and glanced at a note. "His name is Julian Howard."

Soigné was still the word for Julian. Time had not touched his blondness, his slimness, his light grace of movement, and he wore his ski clothes as if he had been modeling them for *Esquire*.

83

"I thought you'd dropped into a crevasse somewhere," he said to Eric. "Then last month I ran into Mimi Falconer down at Hobe Sound. She'd just come from here and started talking about her yummy ski pro, and he sounded familiar and I asked the name and here I am."

They had pernods in the Sitzmark. The next day they skied together. And Julian's skiing was about what it had been in the Alps: on the borderline between an advanced intermediate and a not-quite-up-to-scratch expert. "I went back to Chamonix the next winter," he said, "but it wasn't as good. Here in the States I've been to Sun Valley and Stowe. But none of it's been up to those days we had together."

"How about climbing?" Eric asked him.

He had had some of that too, said Julian. Again in the Alps. Once around Mount Whitney in the California Sierras. "But the big deal with mountains," he added, "wasn't climbing—just looking."

"At what?"

"Have you been to the Himalayas?"

"No," said Eric.

"Neither have I, really. But last year I was out in India—on shikar mostly, hunting for tiger—and I had a look at them from Garhwal and Kashmir."

They were drinking pernods in the Sitzmark and he ordered two more. "My God!" he said. "That's all I can say: my God! . . . You should see them, Rick . . . I'd have given anything to get really near them, on them, to have a crack at even one of the smaller ones. But you can't do anything, of course, without a real expedition."

"Yes, I know," said Eric.

That was on Julian's second night at White Valley. All the next day they skied. And that evening, again over the pernods, Eric told him of Dera Zor. He told of it from the beginning: from Bigelow on the library shelf, through the years of dreaming and hoping, through the planning with Ken Naylor, the correspondence, the disappointments, the dead end of the present. And

Julian heard him through, raptly, without a comment, without a word.

"You've raised no money at all?" he asked at last, when Eric had finished.

"No," said Eric.

"How much do you need?"

"About fifty thousand."

"Hmm—"

"Then on top of that there's the Nepal thing. Permission. We can't get a peep out of them."

Julian smiled a little. "That part's easy," he said.

"Easy?"

"On that shikar in India I was with the Maharajah of Nepal. The top one. They've a king there, but he's a figurehead, and this is the man who runs the country. We became pretty good friends, and he said that any time I wanted to come to Nepal he'd lay out the carpet."

Eric said nothing. He reached for his glass and it was empty.

"Two more pernods," said Julian, beckoning to the waiter.

He stayed two weeks in White Valley. When he left it was almost April, the ski season was ending, and Eric left with him. For the rest of the year he was all over the map.

First stop was Chicago, seat of the Howard family and its empire of soap. Other than drawing money from it, Julian had no connection with the empire, and like Eric, though on the grand scale, he was basically homeless. There was an empty house on Lake Shore Drive, however, that belonged to his sister, now on the Riviera. ("You remember, the one who got married," said Julian. "I said it would last a week, but I was wrong; it was three months.") And in a small part of its vastness they set up their headquarters. Julian called his lawyer and formed a DZ Corporation. He opened a bank account. He cabled the Maharajah of Nepal. Eric turned to the thousand other items that in the end would add up to an expedition.

Number one was an exultant cable to Ken, followed by a detailed letter. And in due time a letter came back, and it was what he had hoped for. Yes, said Ken, he would be available for the spring of 1950; come hell, high water or a pink slip from Cerro de Pasco, he would still be available. Further, he had another man, and a topflight one, to recommend for the team: a C de P doctor named Gilbert McLeod, with whom he had done some hard climbs in the Cordillera Blanca, and who was that rare and much-sought combination of mountaineer and M.D. With Eric, himself and Howard, he wrote, that left only two more to get; and they must of course be the best. Howard he hadn't heard of, but he assumed he was that, or Eric wouldn't be involved with him.

That Ken was aboard was the big thing for Eric. And he was pleased, too, to have climber-doctor McLeod. Presently, by correspondence and phone calls, he lined up the fifth and sixth men: Franz Harben, an Austrian-born member of the ski staff at White Valley, with whom he had often talked Dera Zor during the past two years; and Ted Lassiter, a Stanford geologist, who had been his summit ropemate on the climb of McKinley. Both were what Ken, and he too, wanted—the best—especially on snow and ice, which was what Dera Zor would largely consist of. With Ken, and himself and these two as hard core, plus McLeod in reserve, they would have as strong a team as could be assembled from among American climbers.

And Julian?

"Julian will be all right," he wrote to Ken.

He *had* to be all right, he told himself. He would *make* him all right. When summer came he would take him out to Rainier and give him a crash course in snow-and-ice mountaineering. He did not tell Ken or the others that he had never climbed without a guide, let alone led a rope, nor that his only ascents had been by standard tourist routes. By the time the others met and climbed with him, he, Eric, would have brought him along, coached and trained him. Julian had balance and grace. For a slight man, he had strength and endurance. He had guts. He had desire. He would learn and improve . . . "Face the facts, you liar,"

86

said a voice from somewhere. "He's no Himalayan climber; he's the money man" . . . And it was the truth. But not all the truth. For he admired Julian Howard. In a way he admired him as much as anyone he knew; for both guts and desire had come to him the hard way, against the very grain of the life he had been born to. It was not happenstance but his own need, his own will, that had brought him to war, to mountains, to the world of hardness and hazard—out of richness and softness, out of his cocoon of soapsuds—to be and make and prove himself a man.

Yes, Julian would be all right, he told himself, almost fiercely.

And the rest was so all right as to be unbelievable. Magically, a cable came from Nepal saying that the expedition would be welcome. Money was in the bank. And he began to spend it.

First there were lists, lists, lists. Of food, clothing, climbing gear, living gear. Of ropes, axes, crampons, boots, parkas, mittens, helmets, socks, tents, pots (and pans), knives (and forks and spoons), meats, soups, sweets, juices, sugar, salt (and pepper), rucksacks, flashlights, matches, sleeping bags, air mattresses, goggles, soap, skin cream (thank God, McLeod was handling the drugs), packboards, shovels, pressure cookers, photographic supplies, toilet paper. After listing, there was getting. And it was not easy; for Himalayan mountaineering was not big business in the United States, and many things had to be specially designed and made to order. On his corporate expense account he went to New York, Boston, Philadelphia, St. Louis. For climbing hardware he wrote to France; for high altitude boots to Switzerland. For the lining up of Sherpas and other porters he corresponded with the British—for there was no American—Legation in Nepal.

Julian helped to the extent of his limited experience. Franz Harben took care of things in the Far West. But with Ken and McLeod in Peru and Lassiter busy at Stanford, most of the job was his own. He was far from minding, though. Indeed, he reveled in it, as item by item, checkmark by checkmark, his lists became accomplished facts, and slowly the whole complex organism drew together. The gear from France and Switzerland was to be sent direct to Nepal. The rest began accumulating in the basement of Ted Lassiter's home in Palo Alto, close by San Francisco, from where it would presently be shipped.

It was not all smooth sailing. As summer came, and he was about to take off for Rainier with Julian, the company supplying parkas and other clothing ran into labor trouble, and he had to chase around for another source. Then came a depressed phone call from Harben that his wife (of less than a year's standing) was becoming increasingly unhappy about his going on the expedition, and it took several more calls, plus a visit to Utah, to straighten that out. Finally it developed that Eric could not get to Rainier at all. Julian went by himself and climbed for three weeks with a local guide . . . "How did it go?" Eric asked on his return. "Marvelous!" said Julian . . . And it had to be let go at that.

Then it was fall, and the two of them and Harben joined Lassiter in Palo Alto. For weeks they worked on the accumulated food and gear—checking, sorting, packing, repacking—until at last it was ready and went off to the San Francisco docks. Except for odds and ends, the preparations were over. It was now late November. Ken and McLeod would be up from Peru by Christmas, and in mid-February they would all be on their way to the far side of the earth. As Eric emerged for the last time from the now empty Lassiter basement, he gave forth with a joyous yodel that startled Palo Alto for blocks around.

There was even a dividend to his happiness. Not only was he on his way to Dera Zor but to becoming a writer. A published writer. After long silences and a few rejections, three of the pieces he had written the previous fall in White Valley had been accepted by magazines: McKinley by the *American Alpine Journal*, Pizzo Rossi by a small "man's" publication called *Outdoors*, and the Matterhorn-Brandel story, to cap the climax, by no less than the *Saturday Evening Post*—leaving only his Nicole-and-Paris story still without a taker. Adding more to the brimming cup, the *Post* expressed interest in his future projects; he told them of Dera Zor; and the reply came that one of the editors would soon be in Los Angeles and would like to talk with him about it. In early December he flew down, met the editor, and accepted an offer of a fifteen-hundred-dollar advance.

He called Burden Industries and asked to speak to his brother Frank. It would be a pleasant change of pace, he thought, to see Frank when he was up, not down. But his secretary, Miss Swenson, said he was away on a business trip.

He called the house in Santa Monica, and Kay answered. "I'm mixing martinis," she said.

They drank them. His two nieces kissed him, then stared at him. When Angela the maid had put them to bed, he and Kay dined again at the table by the picture window, and Kay's green eyes and copper hair glowed softly in candlelight.

"Forty-three, forty-six, forty-nine," she said musingly.

"Next comes fifty-two," he offered.

"Will it be that long again?"

"Will what?"

"Until I next see you. You're my every-three-year brother-in-law, you know. This is only the third time I've seen you since I married Frank."

"I haven't been in L.A.," said Eric.

"You could have come."

"You could have come to White Valley. You were going to."

"That was when the girls had measles."

"There were other times."

Kay didn't answer at once. Then she said, "Yes. But also no." She looked away for a moment, out toward the dark Pacific. "It didn't seem to work out, Rick. I—well—I just couldn't."

"Have you had any skiing?" he asked.

"A little."

"And trips? Other trips?"

"We went to Hawaii last winter. Then Frank still gets around a lot on business, and sometimes I go along."

"Where is he now?"

"At a convention in Miami. Then Washington, New York, Chicago. I've done it with him two or three times." Her voice was dull and flat; then abruptly it changed. "Let's stop talking about me, I want to know about you," she said. "What are you doing here? Why aren't you in White Valley? Things are happening; I can tell by looking at you."

Yes, things were happening, he said. He told her about Dera Zor. And as he spoke she listened as she had listened three years earlier, when he had first told her of the mountain: raptly, all dullness gone, her eyes shining, never leaving his face.

"Oh Rick, I'm so happy for you," she said. "I told you it would happen, that you would make it happen. Remember?"

"I remember," he said.

"And the writing? Is that happening too?"

He told her about that. And this time, when he had finished, she rose and came to him and kissed him; then, with dinner ended, led him back to the living room and brandies.

"And now?" she asked. "Before you leave for Nepal—what will you do?"

"I'll be here and there," he said.

"Can't it be here for a while? You said most of your work is done." Kay paused, started to speak, stopped herself. Then it came out. "Can't we go skiing, Rick?"

"Skiing?"

"I don't mean at White Valley. I mean closer, in California. They've had the first snows up in the Sierras and it must be beautiful. We could go for a week, Rick. Frank won't be back for two and Angela's wonderful with the children." She had become excited; her words came tumbling out. "Please take me," she said. "I've been looking forward to it so long. Before I just couldn't— but I'm ready now. We could have such fun together, you know that. Oh please, Rick—please—"

Eric smiled. "At family rates?" he said.

Two days later they drove up into the Sierras. It was not yet full winter season; but the resorts were open, with their lifts and tows, and they found a good inn called High Crest and took adjoining rooms. The surrounding slopes and trails were on a modest scale, with nothing approaching White Valley's Crystal Peak, let alone the majesty of the Hermit. But for Kay's skiing talents modesty was in order, and from the beginning her enjoyment was huge. She listened carefully to Eric's instructions. She watched him demonstrate. She tried to follow him. Though she had her share of falls, they were happy laughing falls, and she rose from them with her face glowing under its plastering of snow.

"I'm improving," she announced after three days of it. "But I want you to say it. Say I'm improving."

"You're improving," said Eric dutifully. "But don't count on making the Olympics."

"There aren't any Olympics for three years. I'll be ready by then." They had racked their skis at the ski hut and were walking back to the inn, when suddenly she squeezed his mittened hand in hers. "I'm having such fun, Rick," she said. "It's just what I hoped it would be."

In the evenings they had drinks at the High Crest bar—not martinis here but whisky or mulled wine. They had dinner. And one night, afterwards, they drove a few miles down to a road-house and danced.

"Do you give lessons in this too?" she asked as they circled the floor.

"On the night shift," he said.

"You had lots of practice at White Valley?"

"Some."

"More than some. I'll bet you were fighting off snow bunnies every night."

They danced on a while. Then she said:

"You still don't have one, do you?"

"Have a what?" he asked.

"A female. A girl."

"Plural, yes."

"I mean singular. Someone you're really involved with."

"No."

"Do you remember, three years ago when you came back from Europe—so alone, so lost—I said what you needed most of all was a girl?" He nodded, and she thought it over. Then she said, "I don't think so now. Now you have so much else: your mountain, your writing: all that you want there ahead of you, and the freedom to take it. When you're involved with a woman, freedom comes harder."

"One of the men on the expedition," said Eric, "has been finding that out."

But Kay's thoughts led her elsewhere.

"Are you ever lonely, Rick?" she asked.

"Sometimes," he said.

"There's always a price, isn't there? You have your freedom, a wonderful freedom, but also loneliness. For me it's the opposite. I'm never lonely, but I'm never free."

She fell silent then. The band played slowly, softly, while they gave themselves to its music. They moved through patterns of light and shadow, and once, in the shadow, he raised her eyes and held his.

"Except now," she said.

Later, with a few more drinks, she lost her pensiveness. They laughed a lot. They laughed at breakfast. During the next few days, on the ski runs, the sun seemed to shine more brightly than ever, and so did her face, her eyes, as she followed him, now faster and steadier, down the glittering slopes. The evenings, both at inn and roadhouse, were the gayest they had had.

But the sixth night—the last—was different. Like all the others, it started at the bar after they had changed from their ski clothes and progressed through drinks and dinner. But from the beginning he felt in her a constraint, a withdrawnness, and later, when they were again at the roadhouse, she was quiet, almost abstracted, as she sat watching the play of light and shadow on the dance floor.

Then suddenly she turned to him and said softly, "It's not what you're thinking, Rick."

"I'm not sure what I'm thinking," he said.

"It's not that I don't want to go home. I do want to go. Home is where I belong. With Frank; with Joyce and Sheila."

He nodded.

"Frank's my husband," she said. "He's a good husband, a good father." She paused, not looking at Eric, looking out at the dance floor. "And do you know something?" she went on. "Frank will stay my husband. I'm sure you've wondered about that. So did I, for a while. But now I know. I'm a wife and mother. The rest is—"

"Silence."

"Well, almost silence." She smiled at last. "Except once in a while—like this past week."

The band, which had been playing in fast tempo, reached a pause with a riffle of drums, then continued in a slow murmuring beat. "Come on," she said, and they danced. They danced slowly and close, without speaking, without looking at each other, and when the music ended they returned to their table.

"Once in a while," she said, as if there had been no interval, "it's different. It has to be different, or I couldn't be what I am the rest of the time. Sometimes, just that little once in a while, there has to be something besides Frank, children, home. Even for me—oh I know it sounds ridiculous, but it's true, Rick, it's true!—even for me there has to be something beyond them, something to reach out to—like your Dera Zor—"

When after midnight they arrived back at the inn, the stars hung huge and silver in the black-and-whiteness of the night. It was cold, but there was no wind; the chill did not penetrate their coats and gloves; and instead of going in, they walked from the parking lot back along the packed snow of the driveway. For a short distance there were dim lights along the drive. Then they were gone, and there were only the stars, only white earth, black sky, and their eyes moved up with the rising earth toward the high Sierras, across a night world frozen in stillness and space. They did not speak; the only sound was the soft crunch of snow beneath their feet; and when they had gone perhaps half a mile they turned and walked back to the inn. Entering, they crossed the empty lobby, went up the stairs and along the corridor to their adjoining rooms. At her door, on other evenings, Kay had stopped, they had said good night, and Eric had gone on to his own. But this time he stopped too, for she was holding his hand. There was an instant, a wild instant, when an old image crossed his mind: the image of Julian Howard holding his hand in the corridor of the inn at Chamonix. Then it was gone, there was only Kay, and her face was raised to him.

He kissed her. Her face was cold. Her lips were cold. But the cold was a flame. After a moment she drew back, took out a key and opened her door; and then she took his hand again and led him in and closed the door behind them.

There had been the dream of the door. The punishing dream . . .

In the first moment Kay was there, and in the next she was gone. It was no longer a door in the High Crest Inn in the Sierras, but the door of Frank's room in the house on Desmond Street, and he was beating and kicking it because Frank had taken his ice ax. This time his mother did not come running up the stairs. He beat and kicked until the door gave way, and there was Frank inside, and he hit him. It wasn't with his fist, as before, but with his retrieved ax, and when Frank fell he stayed fallen. He lay fallen and still, and blood came not just from his lips but from his nose and mouth, it welled up from his eyes, until his whole face glittered with blood, like the face of the German in the sunrise on Pizzo Rossi.

Had Kay dreamt too? He didn't know, for she was gone. But he had his ax, and it had taken him far. Whatever the door and the dream, he had passed through them, through the miles and the years, from the house in Denver to the summit dome of Dera Zor.

In the end. Now . . . But he was not yet at *now* . . . He was still twenty years in the past; not on a summit dome but in a glacial valley. He was not alone, as now, but with Ken and Julian and Tashi and the others. He was not looking down but upward; staring at last at the mountain called Dera Zor, in the moment for which, so long, he had been waiting . . .

8

It was on an afternoon in early spring, and for hours they had been threading the gorge of the Amun River, now following the banks of its glacial torrent, now moving high along the ledges of its containing walls. All the way their course had been east to west. But now at last the gorge bent to the north. The walls fell away into the sweep of boulder-strewn valley.

And there it was.

It was the Sherpa Tashi who saw it first. As for much of the approach march, he had been at the head of the column, picking his way through the rock masses of the gorge's mouth. Then he came to an open place and stopped, and though he neither pointed nor called out, Eric, some yards behind him, knew instantly what it was. As swiftly as he could, he came out into the open place and raised his eyes with Tashi's.

Through the days and miles of the approach there had been no glimpse of Dera Zor. Always, as they moved on through the hills and valleys of Nepal, there had been the white wave of the Himalayas looming to the north: a wave that, as they drew nearer, became a host of subwaves, a myriad of peaks cleaving the sky. But the one of the myriad they sought remained invisible behind a rampart of its lesser neighbors. Indeed, the closer they came to it, the more improbable it seemed that it truly existed; for as they breached the rampart through the gorge of the Amun, the sensation was not of approaching a height but of entering the gate of a subterranean world. Their horizon was no longer measured in miles but in yards and feet. The sky was a mere strip between the cliff rims above, and they moved through a dim realm of gray rock and roaring water.

When the change came, it was a crash of music, an explosion of space and light . . .

For the opening of the gorge was sudden. From confinement they stepped into openness, from shadow into a dazzle of brightness, and all at once, in its vastness, its wholeness, there was the south face of Dera Zor. For Eric Venn, it was simultaneously a moment of recognition and revelation. From the photographs in Bigelow's *Trek to Nowhere* he had for years been familiar with what his own eyes were now seeing: the sweep of bouldered wasteland in the foreground; above it a coil of glaciers; above this, in turn, the peak itself leaping upward, in wall and buttress, ridge and tower, to the far white dome that seemed to light the sky. But whereas in the pictures it had been only a shape, an image, it was now a mass as well; and the mass was solid, palpable, overwhelming. Here was not only a vision, bright in afternoon sunshine. Here, too, was a *thing*: immanent, monstrous. An organic, living thing: living and on guard.

One by one the others came out of the gorge and stood beside him and Tashi: Ken Naylor, Julian Howard, Franz Harben, Ted Lassiter, Gil McLeod. Beside them, the file of low-level porters moved past, and on into the field of boulders, scarcely glancing at what lay ahead. Their only interest was in depositing their loads at Base Camp, collecting their pay, and getting back to their valley homes. But the Sherpas, who would go on to the mountain itself, stopped and stared, as did the men from the West, until there was a group of twenty at the mouth of the gorge. For several minutes all stood motionless, silent, before the impact of the mountain, but when at last someone spoke it was not of a vision.

"So there's the bastard at last," said Ken Naylor.

Two months and half a world lay behind them in their pilgrimage. From their gathering point in San Francisco they had flown the Pacific and across southeast Asia to Calcutta. There had

97

been the classic ordeal of Indian customs. There had been a broken journey by rail, truck and pack train through northern India, across Himalayan foothills, to Nepal's capital, Kathmandu. There had been a welcome by Julian Howard's maharajah, one of the great family of Ranas, who for years had ruled Nepal as a feudal fief. He had tried to dissuade them from mountaineering in favor of a tiger shoot on his private preserve. ("The wilds are pleasanter, gentlemen, on the back of an elephant.") But in the end, switching to French, he said, *"Chacun à son goût,"* and provided them with documents for safe conduct through the country.

In the week that followed, in Kathmandu, they picked up their fourteen Sherpas and two hundred approach march porters, repacked and distributed their loads of food and gear. Then in the last week in March they began the trek in to their goal. Kathmandu, its gates newly and barely ajar to the outside world, had itself been more a medieval than a modern city; but beyond it the twentieth century was wholly gone and lost. Up and down, down and up they went, following a foot trail that had not changed in millennia, toward the white waves of the mountain ocean that notched the sky to the north.

During the first days, the trail passed through many settlements, between terraced and cultivated fields; but as they moved on farther, the land became wilder and inhabitants fewer. Such people as they saw were different, too, for the lowlands had been Hindu country and this was Buddhist. Sacred mani walls and chortens rose by the path outside the villages. From lamaseries came the sounds of horns and gongs, and prayer flags fluttered on the ridges against a stainless sky. "Here is a magical world, a secret world," Eric wrote in his diary. "Some day, if I am lucky, I may learn a few of its secrets." But now it could not be; their mountain waited. They had only until mid-June, at the latest, to make their bid for it; for then the summer monsoon would close in, turning the whole of the eastern Himalayas into a deathtrap of melting, avalanching snow.

In the world that surrounded them, they were a transient, self-contained little world of their own. They trudged through the days. They stopped, pitched camp, ate, slept, trudged on again.

"Is it we or the poles of the prayer flags," wrote Eric, "who carry the banner with the strange device?"

Their Kathmandu-to-Base Camp porters were Nepalese Hindus, and a sorry lot. Ignorant, spiritless, steeped in the poverty of ancient Asia, they were the scrapings from towns and villages of the lowlands, lifetime carriers of loads in a land where there were no other beasts of burden. The fourteen Sherpas, however, were of a different breed. They were Tibetan in stock. They were Buddhists. Their homeland was in the northeastern highlands of Nepal, an area called Solu Khumbu, south of Everest and Dera Zor; and though materially they possessed little more than the rank-and-file porters, they had a drive of will, a glow of spirit, that were unique and priceless. They were an elite and knew it. For years they had gone out with expeditions to earth's greatest mountains—not only to their bases but to their heights; not only for pay but for the adventure itself—and there was scarcely a record of a Himalayan climb in the twentieth century that did pay tribute to their contribution.

There were, of course, grades and ranks among them. Headman, or sirdar, of the group now moving toward Dera Zor was Ang Pemba, a small but powerful man of middle age, who had been twice with the British to Everest in the 1930s and since then, like many Everest "Tigers," had made his home in Darjeeling, India. So too had five of the other men, and all, as a result, had at least a smattering of English and the ways of the outside world. The remaining eight, mostly the younger ones, were, on the other hand, from Solu Khumbu. None had been farther afield than Kathmandu, and this was their first expedition. What they lacked in experience, however, they made up for in energy, goodwill, and pride in the thought that they would soon be Tigers themselves.

Meanwhile, the pride of all was in taking care of their *sahibs*. For the climbers, each day began with a brown face at the tent flap, a white-toothed grin, and a cheery "tea, sah'b" or "coffee, sah'b." Then they got breakfast. They struck the tents. They slung on their loads (of sixty to seventy pounds, though they were mostly short, slight men who weighed no more than twice that

99

themselves); and after the day's march they pitched the next camp, laid out the sleeping bags, prepared dinner. "Like a traveling Ritz," said Julian Howard, "but the service is better." The British Raj was now gone from India and the Himalayas, but its vestiges remained.

Tashi, Eric's "personal" Sherpa, was one of the Solu Khumbu group; and though he lacked the prestige of the Darjeeling veterans, he was the prize of the lot. Even among the clan of little men, he was among the smallest: no more than five-foot-two or three in height, with a slight, wiry frame. His wizened face and bright eyes were those of a weatherbeaten monkey. But it was what was behind them that set him apart as special, a blend of drive and intelligence that would have been rare in a back-country illiterate from anywhere in the world. His desire to climb was enormous. In the late 1930s, a boy in his teens, he had been about to take off for Darjeeling to become an Everest Tiger. But then the war had come, and all expeditions were off. After the war, a few years back, he had twice accompanied British surveying teams in the Nepal Himalayas, and though he climbed no actual peaks, he had had much experience on the heights. Also, he had picked up English, to the point where he could speak it as well as the Darjeeling men; and in the camps on the long march he would often talk, with a light in his eyes, of what lay ahead.

"Am not yet Tiger," he said, "but will be one, Rick Sah'b . . . Will go to top with you, yes. You will see, Rick Sah'b" . . . In the mornings, he would shoulder a pack that seemed bigger than he was and, more often than not, was first off on the march.

Eric, too, carried a heavy pack. During the past year, involved in organizing the expedition, he had had no climbing at all, and needed conditioning. Through the hours and the miles he trudged up and down, down and up, across the rugged warp and woof of Nepal. At night, in the tent he shared with Ken Naylor, he talked plans and problems, wrote in his diary and, healthily tired, fell asleep.

Sleep itself, though, was not good. This was the time of the dream, the dream of the door. Of Kay—and Frank. With the years, the old guilt, the guilt of Robin, had faded; the spinning pigtails were almost gone. But now, instead, there were the door, Kay's hand, Kay's lips, Frank's bloody face. From behind the dream a voice asked, "Are you satisfied? Are you even with him now?" Outside the tent, thrust upright into the earth, stood his ice ax, and in the dream, in the moonlight, its blade gleamed with blood.

Did Kay dream?

There was no answer.

On the drive back from the Sierras to Santa Monica she had been her usual self: on the quiet side, perhaps, but not tense, not distraught. At the door of the house on Seaview Drive she had asked him in, but he had said no, that he had to be going. "Going where?" she had asked. "Back to Palo Alto," he had said. And she had not tried to stop him. She raised her face again; he kissed her; she said, "Climb your mountain, Rick." And that was that.

—Except the dream.

Then came another voice. Not a dream voice, but Tashi's. It said, "Coffee, sah'b." And he was drinking his coffee. He was up and out, eating breakfast, giving orders to Ang Pemba, shouldering his pack, hefting his ax, swinging off down the trail. He was doing what Kay had told him to do—what he wanted to do—going to climb his mountain; and each day he was closer to the white wave in the north.

During most of the march he was, in effect, alone. The trail was too narrow for two abreast; and further, it had been found best for the climbers to spread themselves out along the column and keep an eye on the porters' progress. It was in the evenings that they were together, around the cook fires between the tents: reviewing the day's progress, planning the next, learning the ins and outs of one another's natures. Most of them had been acquainted with most of the others before the expedition began, but there still remained the complex process of building six individuals into a team.

Ken Naylor had come back from the Andes with his hairline receding ominously; but all traces of overweight were gone and, from forehead down, he looked again the old football linesman, finely trained, hard as iron. Officially, there was no "leader" of the expedition. In practice, however, Eric, as organizer and prime mover, was recognized as such; and he in turn considered Ken his deputy and chief consultant. They did not always agree on everything. Or, rather, they reached eventual agreement by widely differing routes: Eric usually by quick instinctive judgment of "this is right, that is wrong"; Ken by a slower, deliberate weighing process, as if he were involved in a problem of engineering. But as old partners, old friends, there was far more that bound than divided them. Over many years they had climbed together, strongly, amicably: in the Cascades, at Camp Hale, in the Apennines and the Tetons. Now at last it would be on the mountain they had talked of so long and so longingly; and if it was granted him to reach the top, Eric hoped it would be with Ken as his ropemate.

Of the others, he had climbed with Ted Lassiter on McKinley. And Ted, too, was a mountaineer to be reckoned with. At Palo Alto and Stanford, Eric had been close to forgetting it; he had been every inch the assistant professor—tweedy, soft-spoken, a club member of academe. But now, on the trail, he was transformed back to the man he had known on the heights of Alaska. He was hard. He was tough. Though smaller than Ken, he was almost as powerful, and propelled himself along like a compact locomotive. How good he was on steep rock, Eric did not know from direct experience. On snow and ice he was magnificent, and that was what Dera Zor would mostly consist of.

As a professional skier, Franz Harben was also basically a snow-and-ice man; but he had done difficult rock climbs both in his native Austria and the States, and rated full marks as an all-around mountaineer. What rated considerably lower, however, was his new status as a husband. Back at White Valley he had been one of the Golden Boys of the staff: gay, debonair, blondly handsome, the day- and nighttime darling of a horde of female clients. But now one of that horde was his wife; a pink-and-white, debutantish girl from San Francisco called Jill Edwards. And though, with an assist from Eric, Franz had talked his way to the Himalayas, she was apparently not happy about it—nor was he. In the camps, he sat in his tent by the hour, writing letters, to be sent back with the approach march porters when they returned from Base Camp. Beside the evening campfires, while the others talked, planned and joked, he was often glum and abstracted.

"You'll work it out in a week when you get home," Eric told him. "Stop stewing now; it does no good."

"*Ja, ist dumm*," said Franz (who sometimes lapsed into German when talking more to himself than to others). "When we are climbing the mountain I will forget it."

Dr. Gilbert McLeod, who had come up from Peru with Ken Naylor, was the only one of the team Eric had not known before. But his credentials were the best; Ken's recommendation had been glowing; and from every indication during the days on the trail, both were amply justified. Physically, he was tall and lean, with a crooked, humorous face. Temperamentally, he was calm and unflappable. Like Franz, he was married—with not only a wife but two children (now all in Texas)—but if there had been familial strains in his leaving them for the Himalayas, they were strictly invisible. On the march-in, there were far greater demands on him than on any of the others. Not only was he trudging the miles, carrying his load, but also treating the assorted ailments of climbers, Sherpas, and porters. Yet he never seemed to tire, never lost his quiet good humor. On the trail, in camp, in whatever circumstances arose, he took everything in stride, and the stride was long and easy.

. . . McLeod, Harben, Lassiter: a strong threesome. Plus Ken and Eric: a strong five. But there were six of them on the way to the mountain. And the sixth was Julian Howard.

"*Who?*" Ken had asked from Peru when he first heard his name. "What's his record? What has he climbed?"

And after meeting Julian in Palo Alto: "What is he, for Christ's sake? A faggot?"

"He'll be all right," Eric had said.

"You mean his money's all right."

"I've climbed with him, skied with him. Leave him to me; he'll get by."

Ken had remained dubious. The others were dubious. But once on the trail, he had surprised them all. On the rough road to the Himalayas, as in the Alps and White Valley, his maleness surfaced, flourished. He carried his load. He kept up the pace. During the first week he suffered a bad case of blistered feet without complaint, and never, by word or act, did he remind them that it was he whose money was paying for the expedition. Gradually the doubt of the others became openmindedness. Then came liking, even admiration.

"He'll be all right. Wait and see," said Eric.

"Could be," Ken now conceded.

And that was progress.

So was their daily mileage. Using Bigelow's old *Trek to Nowhere* as guide and timetable, they had set three weeks as an estimate for the march from Kathmandu to the mountain; and they kept to schedule. Two thirds of the way in they came to the Sherpa homeland of Solu Khumbu, a place of steep pastures and stone villages, close under the walls of the main Himalayas, at a height of ten to twelve thousand feet; and here they paused for a day of rest (for themselves) and festivity (for their own Sherpas). When they moved on again, it was through humankind's last outposts. Above the highest village, on a hillside spur, was an ancient lamasery; beyond it, grazing yaks and their herders. Then man's domain was gone. Growth and greenness were gone. The mountains that had so long been a distant wave in the sky closed in around them, and they entered a mineral world of rock and ice and rushing waters.

There came a moment one morning when a long valley opened out to the northeast, and at its head, beyond glacier and precipice, barely emergent above the shoulder of a nearer peak, they saw the snow-plumed crest of Everest. But their route was not that way. It was now north-by-northwest. Later the same day they came to the torrent of the Amun River and camped close by its bank. They followed it the next day, and the next. They came to the Amun Gorge and threaded it, moving deep through its roaring shadows. And then finally the shadow lightened; the gorge bent and opened; in their long file they came out of it into an open place, into a glare of brilliance, and in midafternoon of their twenty-first day on the march they stood silently staring at what lay ahead.

. . . At the vision, the thing, the bastard that was Dera Zor.

They made camp that night in a wasteland of boulders and the next morning took stock of their position. It proved to be at the end of a long, narrow valley, running east to west, rimmed by mountain ramparts in which the only deep break was the gorge by which they had entered it. Dominating the scene, of course, was Dera Zor itself, towering skyward to its height of twenty-seven-thousand-odd feet. East of it, and closer to them—for they had come from the east—was a peak of about twenty-four thousand feet that they knew from their maps was named Malu, and to the west, at the far end of the valley, another of similar height called Kalpurtha. These were the major trinity; the half-dozen peaks that angled back from Kalpurtha to the Amun Gorge, along the valley's southern flank, were slightly lower. But only slightly. For it was these that formed the screen which hid Dera Zor from everywhere southward, and it seemed doubtful that there was any point of less than twenty-one thousand feet along its jagged skyline of crests and notches.

At the heart of this double uplift, the gash of the valley was perhaps five miles in length, one mile wide, at an altitude, they estimated, of sixteen thousand to eighteen thousand feet. Only a small lower section of it was floored with boulders. Filling the rest was glacier—the Kalpurtha Glacier, Bigelow had named it—originating on the slopes of the mountain Kalpurtha and augmenting itself, as it flowed downward, by subsidiary glaciers from the flanks of Dera Zor and the other peaks. One of these (they knew from Bigelow, though they could not yet see it) descended from a gap between Kalpurtha and Dera Zor: so steep and tumbled that it was less a glacier than an icefall. Yet in Bigelow's opinion it was the key to the heights of both mountains; and from long study of his text and pictures, Eric agreed. To be sure, Dera Zor had other sides: most importantly, a vast northern flank rising close along the Tibetan border. But Bigelow had not seen this. In the early days of planning, Eric and Ken Naylor had talked of investigating it; indeed, of making a whole circuit of the peak in search of the best route. But such a reconnaissance, they had soon realized, would be an expedition in itself, with no time left for high climbing. They would throw in their lot with Bigelow, they had decided; it would be the south side or nothing. So now the long file moved up the valley toward the foot of the icefall.

For a short distance they were still among boulders, moving close beside the milky torrent of the Amun River. Then they reached the snout of the Kalpurtha Glacier, and the torrent vanished, its roar diminishing to a faint gurgle in ice caverns far below. As they came up over the snout onto the bed of the glacier, they entered a world frozen in silence and immobility. They trudged, in their twisting column, across ancient ice, past humped moraines and mazed crevasses, through forests of twisted towers, over mounds and ridges, furrows and trenches, and slowly they gained height on the gleaming causeway.

It was nothing, however, to the heights still above them. Eric and Ted Lassiter had been on McKinley, Ken and Gil McLeod in the Andes, but these had barely hinted at the scale of the High Himalayas. To their right—the north—the south face of Dera Zor rose, monolithic, ice-sheathed, for two vertical miles, its upper reaches lost in distance above them. Malu filled the horizon behind, Kalpurtha ahead. Even the lower peaks to the south were giants, now shutting out everything beyond, as from the far side they had shut out their higher neighbors. Here was a world to itself: sealed, hermetic; a world in which man was dwarfed, silenced, an interloper, suffered merely to creep through unhuman immensities. Throughout the approach march, in however wild country, there had always been greenness, growth, living creatures, other men. There had been the trail twisting back behind them to the lives they had come from. But here, now, the trail was gone; all they had come from was gone; all was lost and hidden behind mountain walls.

On their second night in the valley they camped about halfway up the glacier, and in the morning even Dera Zor was gone. There was no full storm. High above, there probably was—they could hear the wail of the wind—but in the valley there was only mist, and through the mist a gentle fall of snow. Extra care now had to be taken because of concealed crevasses, and the porters were instructed to follow exactly in the footsteps of the climbers. But progress was still possible, and through the day the long file moved on in a procession of ghosts. Now and then, to right and left, they heard the rumble of avalanches plunging unseen from unseen heights; but by holding to the middle of the glacier they kept them at a distance. That was all they could see: the glacier. Nothing else existed.

The night before, in his tent, Eric had written in his diary: "We have followed the *Trek to Nowhere*, and now we are here, and the two are the same. Now-here equals no-where: you just move the hyphen." And he had smiled at the conceit.

Now, in the snow and mist, he thought of it again. And yes, they were nowhere all right; in the very auricle and ventricle of the heart of nowhere. In the whiteout, the vast nothingness, it was inconceivable that other human beings had been here before them. Once a mastodon, perhaps, or a snow leopard, lost and dying. But men, no. A man called Bigelow—no, it was beyond belief.

Then he was listening, looking up; and there ahead was the Sherpa Tashi, calling, pointing. "See something, sah'b," he said as Eric came up. He pointed again. "There—you see too?" And following him off to the right, Eric stood looking at the remains of a camp.

There was not much of it left: no more than some bits of rubbish locked in the ice and half-covered with snow. There were a few old tin cans, a tent peg, bits of cloth and rope. Then another object caught Eric's eye—a knife—and, bending, he freed it from the ice with the point of his ax. It was of course battered and rusted, less an implement now than a mere lump of metal. But it was nevertheless recognizable for what it once had been, an old-style, multibladed American Boy Scout knife, and it was obvious that it once had been none other's than Homer Bigelow's. Instinctively Eric tried to open the blades, but they would not budge.

Then he put the knife in his parka pocket. Perhaps when he got back home he would be able to find Bigelow—or if he was dead, a widow or children—and present it as a souvenir. As he and Tashi moved on up the glacier, he smiled again. In the desolation of that lifeless world, it was a small, a warm, a pleasing thought.

Toward afternoon the snow stopped, the mist lifted, the glacier glared in the sun. Close ahead, the icefall between Dera Zor and Kalpurtha swung into view. It was hereabouts, near its foot, that they wanted to establish their Base Camp; and after some search they found a good site on a medial moraine, a patch of rock and rubble that would provide a firmer and less chilling foundation than the surrounding ice. Here the long centipede of the approach march column ended its final crawl. The loads were dumped. During the rest of the day the ground was cleared and leveled, tents were pitched, food and gear were checked and stowed. And the next morning the brigade of low-level porters was paid off and left. At the threshold of the mountain there remained a community of twenty men: the six expedition members and fourteen Sherpas.

Here, at about eighteen thousand feet, they had planned a layover for acclimatization. But even without the plan they would have had to take it, for all six were now feeling the altitude. Eric had a hacking cough. The others, in varying degrees and combinations, had coughs, sore throats, headaches, insomnia and fits of nausea. Gil McLeod, himself with a headache-cum-nausea problem, did what he could with pill and powder, but warned that time was the only effective dosage; and they spent hours in their sleeping bags or puttering restlessly about the camp. Only the Sherpas, to a man, were unaffected, and they did what they could to help their ailing sahibs. "Here—what my mother makes for cough," said Tashi, bringing Eric a cup of something warm and muddy. And though, after it, Eric's cough was as bad as ever, he tried to suppress it in front of his benefactor.

Then, to the ills of the flesh, something further was added. During their third night at base they awoke to a wailing of wind, a drumming of tent walls, and in the morning the world around them had again disappeared—this time in a full-blown storm. It raged through the day, the next night, the next day, in a white caldron of blizzard: so violently they could barely make the few yards between tents; so loudly they had to shout to one another to make themselves heard. They spent even more time in the sack. They tried to read, to sleep, to count the hours away, and when they shouted it was increasingly in annoyance or anger. Eric and Ken had bitter words about dried apricots. That was all they could remember later: it was about apricots. Ted said to Franz: "You're out of your mind to smoke with a cough like that." And Franz said in return, "Wipe that *gottverdammt* snot from your nose." Only Gil and Julian, despite storm and ailments, kept their peace and their tempers. "Doctor Kildare and the Cub Scout," said Ken in disgust, before going out to vomit in the blizzard.

Then, in quick succession, the storm stopped, their ailments subsided. In the white radiance of a new morning they even found one another endurable again. With the help of the Sherpas, they dug out and cleaned the shambles of the camp. They sorted and repacked loads. Through binoculars, they studied the chaos of the great icefall that rose before them, trying to select at least a tentative way through its labyrinth. From base to top, they estimated, it was about three thousand feet high, ending at the gap between Dera Zor and Kalpurtha that the Sherpas called the Nup La, or West Pass. From this gap in turn, the West Ridge of Dera Zor rose massively skyward, and this, if anything, would be their route to the heights. But from so far below, balked by distance and foreshortening, they could see few of its details.

The ridge would come later. First came the icefall. By the evening of May 1 the snow brought by the storm had consolidated; the roar of avalanches had eased; their gear was ready, and they themselves were at least temporarily acclimatized. After months of preparing, weeks of trekking, days of waiting at Base Camp, they were ready at last to set foot on their mountain.

Eric was not one of those who had previously been plagued by insomnia, but on this last night at Base he found that sleep would not come. In the darkness, at last, he rose and, putting on boots and parka, left his tent. Passing beyond the radius of the camp, he walked out among the rocks of the surrounding moraine and stood looking upward into the night. It was clear and still. A sickle moon rode the sky, the stars were huge and brilliant, and Dera Zor seemed to tier up among them until it lost itself in blackness beyond. His eyes followed it, followed rock and snow, wall and ridge, until he too was lost and could follow no farther. But here and now this did not matter, for he was not searching a way or planning a route. He was simply looking at what he had come to through the miles and the years.

Then he realized that he was not alone in the darkness. Another figure had come from the tents, was standing, watching; and the figure was Julian Howard.

"Big," said Eric.

Julian nodded.

"Too big?"

"We'll find out."

There was a silence. Then Eric said, "You don't have to, you know."

"Have to?"

"You could stay here at Base. The five of us can manage, with the Sherpas. You could work on sending up the loads."

"No. Oh no," said Julian.

"It's not the Matterhorn. Or Crystal Peak."

"I know."

"Still you want to come?"

"Yes," said Julian. "Oh please—yes."

There was another silence.

"All right," Eric said.

"There's just one thing—" Julian hesitated; then he said it. "Can I—in the beginning at least—be with you on a rope?"

"That's what I've been planning," said Eric.

He felt for the rope at his waist, but no rope was there. He looked back toward Julian, and there was no Julian. There was only the white dome of the mountain slanting off into space.

He sat down in the snow. He waited. Pushing back the cuff of a gauntlet, he looked at his watch, and it was after four. He looked at the sky: soon the night should be paling, the stars receding. At first light, Larry, Tashi, and Pembol would be leaving the bivouac and starting up after him.

He sat in the darkness, the stillness. And again there was a sound in the stillness, the sound of his breathing. Even sitting, he had to fight for breath, for air. He had to fight for clearness, in his eyes, his mind.

"Come on, Larry— Come on Tashi, Pembol—"

No.

"Come on, Julian—"

It was still Julian he was waiting for. Julian, who had been on the rope but was there no longer; who was, somehow, still down at the Base, in the icefall, far below.

He got to his feet. He would go down and get him. He would have to climb the mountain all over again.

9

They were ten days in the maw of the icefall. Unlike the approach march, it was not an affair of continuous progress, but of back and forth, up and down, for a way had to be found and a route established before the loads could be brought up to their next highest camp. Each night, for the first several days, they returned to sleep at Base Camp; each morning they set off again to push the route farther.

The icefall was at the same time both frozen and alive. Angled far more steeply than the main glacier below, its billion-tonned mass was forever rumbling, shifting, settling, as gravity pulled it down from the heights to the flatness of the valley. Also, it was tightly contained and squeezed between mountain walls on either side. Gigantic pressures had convulsed its surface into a chaos of rises and falls, towers and chasms, like the wreckage of a hundred bombed cities; and the wreckage moved downward, toppling, splintering, in an eternal tide of ancient ice.

They were now beyond "Bigelow country." Since earth's beginning, no man, no living thing, had ever breasted this tide. With each step, each reach of an arm, each stroke of an ax, they were that much farther into an unknown world.

For the work involved, they split into two teams. The first did the pathfinding: trying one way and another, searching for passages around crevasses, past crumbling towers, up the cliffs and clefts and ridges of the labyrinth. The second, following, improved the route selected: hacking steps and stringing fixed ropes that would be used for later ascent with the loads. Taking turns, three of the five experienced climbers comprised the advance group, and the other two, with Howard and the Sherpas, were in the follow-up. On the first two days, Eric was one of the rear guard, staying with Julian as he had promised. Julian did well, however; Eric was needed above; and on the third day and others thereafter he went up with the leaders. Julian was content. Indeed he urged him to go and, to Eric's relief, did not ask to come with him. It was, instead, Tashi the Sherpa who kept pleading to go forward, his tiny frame poised as if for a takeoff, his monkey face pleading.

"You take me with, Rick Sah'b. I climb good—you will see."

Eric grinned. "Later, Tashi," he told him.

"Now—please. With you today, Rick Sah'b."

"No, later—when the loads are up. Then you'll go high. I promise."

Axes swung, crampons scraped, ropes inched upward. In the whiteness figures moved: hooded, goggled, bearded. In the stillness voices called:

"Ready above?"

"Ready."

"Below?"

"Ready."

"On belay."

"Climbing."

And so it went. Up, around, across, up. At day's end, down. The next day, up: farther, higher.

At grips with the ice, there was no breadth, no horizon. Not only the world was gone, but the mountain as well, its peak remote and hidden beyond containing walls. Eyes were on the knot in a rope; on the crystals flying from a step hacked in a cliff; on the light and shadow on a patch of snow that might tell if beneath it there was solidity or an abyss. There was only the icefall. The next step, the next belay, the next rope-length. The next decision.

Even at night, in tent and sleeping bag, there was nothing beyond. For Eric, Kay was gone, and Frank, and the dream of the door. For Franz Harben, his new wife was gone: there were no more letters, no brooding. In the world they had left, they were both ski professionals. The others were engineer, doctor, geologist and . . . What? Was playboy the word? That was what Julian Howard was called in gossip columns . . . But he was no playboy now. He was a mountaineer. That was what they all were —mountaineers—and nothing else.

On the fourth day in the icefall, at roughly its midway point, they found, among towers and chasms, a stable spot for their next campsite. The rest of the day was spent cutting steps and stringing ropes up the last stretch below it; and on the next, eight of the Sherpas came up with loads, and Camp Two was established. Later, there were more carries. Two became, for the time, both base and staging post for further progress, and the climbing spearhead moved on into the upper icefall.

Here it was compressed into an even tighter slot between the flanks of Dera Zor and Kalpurtha. The jumble of towers and chasms was wilder, and threading the defiles between them, they seemed to be in a deep white-walled cave rather than at twenty thousand feet on a mountainside. One consequent advantage was that there was no wind. But they would almost have preferred its fresh blasting to the cold stale air that, in spite of its thinness, pressed down on them like a palpable weight. "I've had all kinds of things happen on mountains," said Ken Naylor, "but this is the first goddamn time I've had claustrophobia."

Still, bit by bit, they gained height . . .

And at last came the day when the stillness was broken. Close above was the Nup La, the high gap between the mountains above them, and they could hear the wind keening across it, wild and free. Beneath it, however, forming the upper extremity of the icefall, was the most formidable barrier they had yet encountered: an almost vertical wall, perhaps a hundred feet high, that swept unbroken across their line of advance. Here, for most of a day, Eric, Ken and Franz labored to forge a way up. Virtually every step had to be clawed out of underlying ice and sheathing

snow. Hanging from rope slings or supported by toes and fingertips, they wielded axes, drove pitons, attached snaprings to the
pitons, threaded rope through the rings, wormed themselves up
to new stances, and clung, hacked and hammered, again and
again. Their steel hardware clanked heavily at their waists; arms
and legs ached; after a bout with ax or hammer breath came in
short harsh gasps, and they had to rest, stiffly spread-eagled against
the wall. But foot by foot they gained height. The whiteness
slowly glided away into depths beneath them. And at last, in the
late afternoon, they cut their way through a final cornice, pried
themselves up on the points of their crampons, and stood no
longer on precarious footholds but on level ground.

The whole of the icefall was below them. They were on the
Nup La—the Gap—twenty-one thousand feet up on the western
flank of Dera Zor.

There was no claustrophobia here. There was space. There was
wind. The Gap itself consisted of rock and rubble, scoured bare
of all but a few patches of frozen snow. Extending for about fifty
yards, it then fell away on the far side of the mountain, and beyond its rim, vast and distant, were two things and two only—the
blue of sky, the brown of featureless earth—and they knew that
the earth was the plateau of Tibet. Framing the miles on either
side were two arcs rising steeply, two ramps of rock and snow: the
one on their left the east ridge of Kalpurtha, the one on the right
the west ridge of Dera Zor. And it was to the right that their eyes
moved during the days that followed; to the right and up—and
up—over rock and snow, past cliff and tower, past slope and cornice and bulge and buttress, to a battlement of snow, a fortress
of rock, and beyond this to snow again, a dome of snow, rising,
soaring, until their vision blurred in a white dazzle in the sky.

Reaching the Gap, however, was one thing; occupying it another.
The next job was to set up Camp Three on its desolate sweep,
and for this the focus was still on the upper icefall. First, the
whole route was worked over. Deep steps were cut and ropes
slung on the final cliff. Then up from Camp Two came the
Sherpas, led by the climbers, carrying the loads for the Base in the

Gap. On May 12 the first tent went up, pinioned tightly between boulders that broke the tide of the wind, and that night it was occupied by Eric and Franz Harben. Then it was down again, up again, until four tents were in place. On his final ascent, leaving the guidance of the Sherpas to the others, Eric led Julian Howard up for the first time; and Julian did well. On the night of the fifteenth, the tents were occupied by all the climbers plus four Sherpas, and they were ready for the first move onto the west ridge of Dera Zor.

For long hours they had studied the ridge, and in its lower reaches at least it seemed potentially climbable. It would be no straightaway slog, however, for its steepness was unrelenting, and it was further broken by towers and clefts that might well necessitate detours on the adjoining southern and northwest faces of the peak. Just what these would involve could not be determined from below, and the whole upper section of the ridge, beyond them, would remain a question mark until reached. The first objective was the lower section: specifically the finding of a site, some two thousand feet above the Gap, where it would be possible to pitch the first of their two proposed higher camps.

Meanwhile, there were still food and gear at the camp in the icefall, plus ten Sherpas, headed by the sirdar Ang Pemba. The next day, it was decided, Franz Harben and Gil McLeod, with the other four Sherpas, would go down and lead them up to the Gap in the final big carry. Eric and Ken would go up the ridge on reconnaissance. Julian and Ted Lassiter would stay at the Gap for a day of R & R.

"I'd like to go up too," said Ted to Eric.

And Eric looked at Gil, the doctor.

"A day off would be good for you, Ted," said Gil.

"I'm all right. I can climb."

"You've been coughing a lot."

It was true. After his first altitude trouble at Base Camp—which had been shared by everyone—Lassiter had gone strongly in the icefall, again a small locomotive in his thrust and drive. But as soon as he had reached the Gap he had begun to cough. In spite of dosages by McLeod, the cough had persisted, grown worse;

and even now, as he tried to argue, he was suddenly racked by a paroxysm.

"Take a day," Gil said gently. "It'll be the best thing for you."

It was a while before Ted could speak again; then he reluctantly agreed. "But then I'll be all right," he added.

"Sure you will," Gil told him.

They dispersed to their tents and sleeping bags, and in the tent they shared Eric and Ken prepared their gear for the next morning. Their hopes were high. Through the past several days the weather had held clear; now even the wind had dropped. During the night it was no more than a thin whispering across the waste of the Gap, through which at intervals came the sound of Ted Lassiter's hacking and retching.

In the morning, again, the sun beamed in glory.

It had barely cleared the eastern horizon when the two details set off: Franz and Gil, with the four Sherpas, down into the icefall; Eric and Ken toward the arc of the west ridge. At the last minute there was another applicant to go with them. Tashi (who had been the first of the Sherpas to reach the Gap) asked to go up rather than down; but again Eric had to disappoint him, saying there was greater need for him below.

"But soon, sah'b?" the little man persisted. "You take me soon with you? High—high—"

"Yes, soon," Eric told him. And leaving a disconsolate monkey face behind, he and Ken moved off.

By previous decision they did not approach the ridge head on. In its initial rise from the Gap it presented a sheer, almost overhanging cliff; so veering off to the right, they worked toward it on its southern flank, up a deep gully that cut through the face of the rock. The gully was diagonal, the going not hard, and though roped, they were able to move simultaneously. But they were now above twenty-one thousand feet—higher than the top of Mc-Kinley, higher than Ken had climbed in the Andes—and their progress was slow. Every twenty steps or so they rested, breathing deeply; and so it went, through an hour, into another, until, as the second hour neared its midpoint, they had their first reward.

117

For now the gully flared open. It leveled off and ended. At eight in the morning they were standing on the crest of Dera Zor's west ridge.

Again, as when they had emerged from the icefall, the world leapt at them—but now with even more impact than before. For whereas, then, they had come to a notch between rising ridges, they were now on a high catwalk between gulfs of space. Looking down, past where the ridge fell away into cliffs, they could see the Gap and, in it, four green dots that were the tents of Camp Three, now some seven or eight hundred feet below. But this was nothing to the drop on either side of the ridge: to the south, down four thousand feet to the white ribbon of the Kalpurtha Glacier; to the north, even farther, to another glacier, unknown to them, that spread long fingers out toward the plains of Tibet. Nothing to the north rose remotely to the height at which they now stood. Southward, the ridge line of the peaks beyond the Kalpurtha Valley was already, at many points, lower than they. Only to the west, before them, on their own mountain, did the earth still rise: an arc of ridge, gray and white, twisting, soaring, climbing another vertical mile into the blue of the sky.

They sat and rested. They peered up in silence. Then Eric shattered the silence with a yodel—high, wild and exultant.

Ken grinned. They rose and moved on. And for a while the going, though different, was no harder than in the gully. The spine of the ridge was largely rock, and steep; but the rock was sound, it gave good holds and stances, and it was broad enough between its bordering gulfs to allow room for maneuvering. As before, they climbed simultaneously, taking turns in the lead, and they were still able to take twenty-odd steps between pauses for breath.

Ahead, however, they could see there was a change. And in another hour they reached it: a point at which the ridge sprang up in a smooth and precipitous tower. It might, just might, they agreed, be climbable at sea level or near it, but not at the height they now were at; so they searched for a way around it. To the left there was nothing, only more sheer wall and space. But to the right it was different: the mountainside was not vertical. It was no longer rock but frozen snow, and the snow, though steep—at an angle of perhaps sixty degrees—was not so steep as to be impassable. By following it obliquely upward for some two hundred feet, they could regain the ridge beyond the obstructing tower.

They put on their crampons. But their steel points would not be enough; the tilt of the snow was too great and its texture too hard. They would have to cut steps as well, and, going first, Eric went to work with his ax. It was hard work: first a dozen or more whacks with the pointed end of the blade; then a scraping with the flat end; then a tentative step, a full step, more whacking, more scraping, another step, repeated over and over, while through it all keeping the body in exact balance on the delicate footing. Ken followed, belaying the rope that joined them with hitches around his own ax; then further clearing and deepening the steps, which would again be used on their way down and on subsequent ascents. On this first passage, however, it was Eric who bore the burden. And it was a heavy burden, a labor for which a man, at such a height, needed more oxygen than he could get from the air. But there was no oxygen. Back home there had been talk of bringing a supply, but the decision had been against it, except for a few bottles for possible medical use. If they were going to get to the top of their mountain, it would be on such fuel as their own lungs could extract from substratospheric space.

Eric crept on. After each bout of chopping he rested, bent over his ax; then moved on to the next step, the next ten, the next twenty. Each movement was slow, but it was measured, controlled, rhythmic; and as the line of steps moved on and up he was still able to keep going. Indeed, he was not just holding his own, but feeling better, stronger. He was not only enduring but enjoying his labor. He heard the crisp bite of his ax in the crusted snow, watched the crystals rise and glitter in windless sunlight, felt the firm tread of his feet in each succeeding step. Beneath each step the mountain wall fell to an abyss below. But he ignored the abyss. He was used to height, he was a mountaineer, and for a mountaineer an abyss was no more than background, like sun and sky. Besides, there was a rope around him, a rope going back to Ken Naylor, whom, of all men on earth, he would choose to be his companion and belayer. Reaching a new step, he waved his ax at Ken, and Ken waved back. And then he chopped again, he climbed again. He saw that the tower blocking the ridge was now below him, that another ten steps would bring him back to the ridge above the tower; and as he cut the steps the last vestiges of tiredness left him; within him there was only will and strength that swelled to another ululating yodel as at last he stood upon the ridge and belayed Ken up after him.

His watch showed ten minutes before noon, the altimeter 22,600 feet.

Beyond the tower, the ridge again offered straightforward going, with only a few pitches that required selective climbing. Altimeter and watch showed that they were averaging a vertical gain of a hundred feet every twenty minutes, and by one-thirty they were at twenty-three thousand, about two thousand above the Gap, where they had hoped to find a place for Camp Four. Here, however, there was nothing approaching a campsite; so they climbed on. They searched the ridge ahead for another break in its gradient. And in a half hour more they found it: a sharp rise and beyond it a hollow, broad and saucer-like, offering both protection and a base for the pitching of three or four tents. Dropping their packs, they grinned through beards and goggles. Their next-to-last camp on the mountain would be a good one hundred and fifty feet higher than they had planned.

The day was still windless: pure and gleaming. On top of the rock that rimmed the hollow, they sprawled in comfort, munched cheese and chocolate, and poured great drafts of fruit juice into their dehydrated bodies. Unlimbering cameras, they took pictures. Later, in the almost warm sunshine, they closed their eyes, half-dozing; then opening them, studied the mountain above.

"Still a few hops to go," Ken said.

"Not as far as before," said Eric.

"From Base, for instance."

"Or Camp Hale. Or Italy."

"Italy—that's where we first planned it. Five years ago, in the mud."

Eric nodded. "Five years." But for him it was more than that—almost twice that—since he had walked from the library in Seattle with Bigelow's book under his coat.

"Ken—" he said.

"What?"

"I shouldn't say this, it's against the rules; but I'm going to anyhow. We're going to make it, Ken."

"Let's hope," Ken said.

"No, we *will*. Four or five of us, maybe, but you and I for sure. I feel it. I know it."

"But does the mountain know it?"

Eric was peering up again. "It does today," he said.

"Mountains have lousy memories."

Eric didn't answer. He was looking long and steadily at the white radiance in the sky.

"But *I*," said Ken, "have a good memory. I remember what I called you five years ago—a romantic sonofabitch."

He grinned again through his beard.

"You still are," he said.

It had been their best day thus far on the mountain; and when, in the late afternoon, they got back to the Gap, it was to learn that things also had gone well in the icefall. Franz and Gil were already back, with all the Sherpas. All the loads were now up, and Camp Three had been augmented by three new tents.

So far, so good. But there were also two things that were not so good. One was that Ted Lassiter had got no better during the day: indeed his coughing was worse, his retching more frequent. The second was that, as night fell, the wind, which for three days had been benignly absent, began to hum and whistle through the keyhole of the Gap.

It was inevitable that it should rise again; they had expected it. And if it did not rise too far they would still be able to function. As, later, Eric lay in his sleeping bag listening to its cadence, it did not seem too menacing, and he still had hope for the morning. Awakening toward midnight, however, he could tell at once that

121

there had been a change for the worse, for the tent walls were drumming, and when he put his head out through the sleeve it was into a torrent of blackness without moon or stars. Through the rest of the night he listened, sleepless, while the torrent grew even wilder, and at dawn, when he looked out again, the world had vanished in a tide of spume and snow. It was not only wind that was now lashing the mountain, but their second all-out storm.

At least they now had all their food, gear and manpower together; and there was nothing to do but weather it out. As the day wore on the gale held to its pitch of violence, a howling unremitting blast that numbed ears and mind. Fortunately, the rim of boulders around the campsite broke at least some of the wind's force, and it was only occasionally that they had to cope with whipping canvas and loose guy ropes. But the din was so great that there was little communication; for the most part they stayed in their sleeping bags, among the welter of clothing, food, utensils and climbing gear. Originally, Eric and Ken had shared one tent, Franz and Ted a second, Julian and Gil a third. But now Franz and Gil had changed places so that the doctor could be with the ailing Ted. The Sherpas were distributed in the four new tents that had been brought up from the icefall.

They struggled to keep warm, to keep the snow out, to pump up pressure cookers for the brewing of warm drinks; and at intervals Eric or Ken crept to the other tents to see how the rest were doing. The Sherpas were mostly asleep—with the exception of the indefatigable Tashi, who also kept crawling about seeing what he could do for his sahibs. Franz, hunched in his sleeping bag, was back to writing his wife, and Julian, taking things well in stride, lay quietly reading. Only in the Ted-Gil tent was there manifest trouble—in the person of Ted—for he was still coughing, still retching, and the strain of it was making him steadily weaker. Gil was doing all he could for him: keeping him warm and dry, giving medication, preparing food and drink. But Ted could keep nothing down. Each time he tried, he coughed, gagged, vomited, then sank back exhausted. Toward midday, Gil gave him an injection that put him to sleep for a few hours, but when he awoke he was no better than before.

Back in his own tent, Eric brought out his diary. Or rather diary plus notebook, for he was keeping both—one a day-to-day log of progress and happenings, the other a jotting of thoughts for eventual use in his writing. Even in the thrust and grind of the mountain assault he had not forgotten about writing. Indeed, he had resolved that when the expedition was over he would write not only the magazine story he had contracted for, but a book as well. Not a mere we-did-this, we-did-that book. A book of inwardness, of meanings; of why, as well as how, some men climbed mountains.

Now, in his diary, he wrote:

May 15 (Tues?)—All-day storm. Wind from NW, c 60mph, with gusts to 100. Temp +5F. All well but T.L.

And in the notebook:

—Well, yes. But cold, cramped, miserable. Question: Why do we do this, voluntarily, willingly? Answer(s): 1 crazy, 2 masochists, 3 death wish, 4 phallic symbolism, 5 inflation of ego . . . Ego does not feel greatly inflated just now.

It was something else that was inflated. Muttering, he freed himself from his sleeping bag, put on parka and hood, and, dragging a shovel, crept through the tent sleeve into the storm.

"Still got 'em?" asked Ken when he returned.

They took half an hour to start a pressure cooker. They opened a can of stew and spilled it. The tent shook. The wind howled.

The storm continued all night. Through the next morning. And Ted Lassiter continued to be sick. On the previous day Gil McLeod had refrained from giving him oxygen from their medical stores, in the hope that he would start to acclimatize. But it hadn't happened; it didn't now; and Gil began administering small amounts of the gas, to relieve his misery. The effect was immediate and remarkable. During the time that Ted breathed oxygen he became, in appearance and manner, almost a well man. But when it was withdrawn—as it had to be, for the supply was small—he relapsed at once into weakness and nausea.

This cycle went on for hours. And the hours dragged. From the Gil-Ted tent, Eric went to Franz and Julian's, then to the Sherpas'—not that there was anything to do there, but from sheer restlessness. Cooped in his own again, he dozed, fidgeted, listened to the storm, and kept creeping through the tent sleeve to look outside. Finally he was rewarded, for in late afternoon the storm began to break up. It was the snow that stopped first. Where before there had been boiling whiteness, there was a thinning, a lifting. The Gap came into view, the west ridge, the sky beyond it, and the sky was red with sunset, then purple with dusk, then black with night and pricked with shining stars. Meanwhile, though more slowly, the wind fell. Its howl became a moan, the moan a wail, the wail no more than a whisper brushing the snow-shrouded boulders of the Gap; and in the darkness the men of the expedition came slowly, stiffly from their tents, like a troop of bears out of hibernation.

The storm was over, but another problem was not. And later, crowded into one of the tents, the five functioning members of the team discussed the case of Ted Lassiter. After his acclimatization trouble at Base Camp, shared with the rest of them, he had done as well as anyone in the icefall. Two years ago, with Eric, he had reached the 20,320-foot top of McKinley in good shape. But from the moment he reached the Gap, a mere seven hundred feet higher, he had been in trouble, and now, after five days, there was still no improvement.

"In fact, he's getting worse," said Gil McLeod. "If he stays much longer, deterioration may be serious. There's nothing to do but get him down off the mountain."

The others were silent. It would be a bitter pill for Ted, plus a setback to plans and hopes; but Gil was the doctor and what he said went.

"He acclimatized at Base before, and he will again," he said. "I'll take him down tomorrow."

"*We'll* take him down," said Ken Naylor.

Gil shook his head. "No, that's not necessary. Ted will feel better when he's just a short way down, and all he needs is an

124

escort. If any more of you come, it will foul up the whole climb to no purpose."

They talked it over, and it was decided that no other team members would go. But for Gil to get Ted down and then re-ascend alone was no good either; so he would take four Sherpas with him. One would be the sirdar, Ang Pemba, who also had not been doing well at the Gap, and he and another of the older men would stay with Ted at Base, while the other two would come back up the icefall with Gil. The round trip, it was estimated, should take one day down, one at Base, two up, for a total of four. Meanwhile the others would set up Camp Four on the west ridge.

In the unhappy circumstances, it was the best they could do; and later, in their own tent, Eric and Ken discussed new tactics and logistics. The next day they and Franz Harben would work on the route to the ridge camp. Then would come two or three Sherpa carries, and by the time Gil reappeared they should be established at Four. Above that, they would need one more camp, Five, as high as possible, from which to launch their summit tries. Or rather try, now—one try—for without Ted things would be different. What they had planned, as the climb developed, was that two teams of two men each would go for the top, themselves on one attempt, Franz and Ted on another. But now at best there would be themselves and Franz in one team of three. From the beginning, Gil McLeod had been considered a support rather than a summit man, and now, with his long descent and reascent, there was no question about it.

"He'll be doing damn well if he gets up to Four," said Ken. "With him there and Julian here at the Gap, we'll be strung out thin, but with enough to get by."

"Julian's hoping to make Four too," said Eric.

"Oh?"

"We could bring him up after the route's in—with the Sherpas."

"Are you sure you want to?"

"He's been doing all right."

"So far. But now the real thing starts."

"The route will be in. I'd take him on my own rope."

They had crept into their sleeping bags, the light was out, and Ken lay silent.

"You're against it?" Eric said.

"I didn't say so," said Ken.

"What do you say, then?"

"That I hope you're thinking straight. That you won't do this because you owe him something."

"Such as fifty thousand bucks?"

"Such as fifty thousand bucks."

Eric thought it over. "No, it's not that," he said. "Not the money . . . But still, yes, I *do* owe him something . . . He's trying so hard; he wants to go on so goddamn much; I can't just dump him until he shows he can't do it."

There was another silence.

"Well?" he said.

"You put this show together," Ken said. "You've got to do what you think best."

"You'll go along with that?"

"Yes, I'll go along. But watch him, Rick. For Christ's sake, watch him."

In the morning the sun was golden in a cobalt sky. The mountain blazed white in its cloak of new snow, as they readied Ted Lassiter for his descent of the icefall. Ted did not have to be carried; once out of his tent he stood on his own. But his legs were shaky, and his body, even in its thick clothing, appeared angular and wasted. There was no trace left of the man who, a few days before, had resembled a small locomotive, full of power and drive. Those he was leaving—Eric, Ken, Franz, Julian—shook his hand and embraced him, and though his face was all but hidden by beard and goggles, they knew that behind the goggles there were tears.

"Happy landings—get well quick—see you soon," they told him.

"Climb the bastard for me," he told them back.

Then he coughed. He retched and vomited his breakfast on the snow. When he straightened, Gil McLeod tied him onto a rope between himself and the Sherpa sirdar, Ang Pemba, and they started off slowly, Ted supporting himself by the taut rope in one hand and his ax in the other. The other three Sherpas who were going with them followed on a second rope, and soon they had all disappeared over the lip of the icefall.

Ten minutes later, Eric, Ken and Franz began the ascent of the gully that led to the base of the west ridge.

Ascent? . . . No, descent.

He had started down to get Julian, to bring him up. But there was something wrong. He was not in the gully but on the dome, a mile higher, and the dome was steep, the night was dark, and he could not find the steps he had kicked in the snow on the way up.

He slipped, lost his balance. The dome reeled; the stars reeled; he was about to fall. Digging in with his ax, he clung to the snow, steadying himself, struggling for clearness. What he needed, he knew, was oxygen. But there was no oxygen. There was only himself. If he was to find clearness, it must come from within himself.

For a while he remained motionless, eyes closed. He willed clearness; with all his strength he willed it; and when he opened his eyes his will had won. The reeling had stopped. Mountain and stars were in place. Below, now plain in the snow, was the long chain of steps he had kicked up the summit dome; above, the few steps he had tried to descend, and, beyond them, untouched snow, still rising.

Turning, he began to climb again. He reached the highest step and went on.

It was not down but up that he was going.

Still up . . .

10

On the ridge, as in the icefall, it was up and down, down and up. Said Ken: "If a man and a half lugs a load and a half for a day and a half, how the hell far is it from Camp Three to Kamchatka?"

At first it was mostly a snow-clearing job: in the gully, on the ridge above, finally on the slope flanking the tower on the ridge, where the steps cut by Eric and Ken before the storm had virtually to be dug all over again. The next day they strung ropes on the slope, as well as on other steep pitches, and cleared the track all the way to the selected spot for Camp Four. On the third, they led up a squad of Sherpas—headed, as usual, by Tashi —and dumped the first loads at the new campsite. That night, Ken and Franz stayed over in the single tent that had been pitched there, while Eric escorted the Sherpas back to the Gap. And the next morning he reascended with another convoy, plus Julian Howard. Again, as on the lower mountain, Julian did all right. Roped to Eric, he followed instructions, suffered no slips, maintained the same pace as the others. On arrival at the twenty-four-thousand-plus altitude of Camp Four he was breathing hard, but so was everyone else.

No further storms struck. But in the sea of space through which they moved, the weather varied day by day, almost hour by hour. The sun beamed, then paled. Clouds massed and dissolved. Wind rose and subsided. One morning, as they climbed, it beat in with sudden fury, churning the snow on the ridge into a seething white-out, forcing them to stop and huddle blindly in their tracks. Another morning, windless, was spectral with gray mist. Then both mist and wind were gone; there was only sunlight; and even from behind dark goggles the brilliance of sky and snow were an explosion in the eyes.

As the weather changed, so too did the mountain. Now that they were upon it, it was as when they had first seen it: part vision, part *thing*. There were times when it rose above them in exquisite, almost delicate grace. Its white arcs gleamed, its rock glowed warmly pink; its thrust seemed a benign and soaring force, newborn and pure. Then with a change of light, of mood, it was utterly different. Gleam became glare. Rock walls became dark and savage. The mountain was warped, desolate, brutish and evil, Ken Naylor's bastard incarnate.

By now, however, Ken had another name and another sex for it: "Dera Zor, the big white whore." And so it was.

—When it was not the Faerie Queene.

On the day Eric brought Julian and the Sherpas up from the Gap, Ken and Franz reconnoitered for a way above Camp Four, and on their return reported that, though some of the going had been hard, there was nothing insuperable. They had cut steps in two steep snow slopes, strung lengths of rope, and got to about twenty-four thousand feet in altitude before turning back. Towers above had blocked off much view beyond their highest point. But from Base Camp observations it was known that another ten to twelve hundred feet higher the west ridge leveled off into a massive shoulder, and it was there that it was hoped to put the fifth and final camp.

The next day, climbing alone and light, Eric and Franz would get as close to it as they could. Meanwhile, it would be Ken's turn to descend to the Gap, taking with him seven of the eight Sherpas now at Camp Four. If the planned timing held, Gil McLeod, coming up from below, would also reach the Gap that evening, and the following day he, Ken and a final Sherpa caravan would ascend the ridge to Four and stay there, making it the new advance base of the expedition. With one task force above, and one below, Julian Howard and the Sherpa Tashi would stay at the ridge camp, putting it in order and preparing to receive its increased population.

"We have whole city—high city," declared Tashi. "Look, I show how high." Enthusiastically he hurled a rock into space toward the distant Kalpurtha Glacier. Then he grinned. "No hit now, just fly," he said. "Tomorrow morning we listen, it go bang."

Night came. The walls of the tents glowed faintly in blackness.

Then another day—and the glow was the sun's. In its slanting rays, Ken and the Sherpas began the trek downward; Eric and Franz set off up the ridge.

They climbed in the tempo that had now become routine on the upper mountain. Twenty steps—a pause. Twenty steps—a pause. Franz, who had been over the ground the previous day, did the leading, with Eric on the rope behind; but there was small need for the rope, for the going, though steep, was straightforward, and the stiffer pitches had already been eased by hacked steps and fixed lines. Then, toward midmorning, they passed the high point reached by Franz and Ken, and progress grew slower. Sometimes they were on snow and ice, sometimes on rock. For perhaps an hour they found themselves on a band of rotten rock that demanded careful testing of each hand- and foothold. Then there was snow and ice again, in a long angled pitch of laborious step cutting.

The day was not quite so perfect as the one on which Eric and Ken had made their first ascent to the site of Camp Four. A thin, bitter wind fingered the mountainside. But the ridge above them rose into a flawless sky; and to west and north, too, above the sweep of the Himalayas and the plains of Tibet, there was crystalline clearness. Only to the south were there clouds, a swollen tide of them, dark and purple, banding the horizon. But they were distant: beyond the ranges, beyond Nepal, over the lowlands of India. They were the clouds of another world. There was no menace in them for Dera Zor. At least not yet. But as they took their rests the climbers watched and assayed them, knowing that in the long run they were the ultimate menace. For they were the clouds of the monsoon. It was now late in May; and each day they would move closer, across northern India, across the hills

131

of Nepal, until they reached and engulfed the eastern Himalayas. When other storms struck, they came and went. When the monsoon came, it stayed—for the whole of the summer. They would either climb their mountain before it arrived, or not at all.

They dismissed cloud, distance, future. They turned to the ridge. They climbed. Above them, the spine of rock narrowed to a knife edge, and they had to work their way off onto the south face and ascend by a series of broken ledges. Then beyond the ledges came a deep gully, or couloir, that in itself offered easy going. But it proved to be a chute for rocks falling from higher up on the ridge, and they quickly abandoned it in favor of a steep flange that rimmed it to the left. For a way it involved real technical climbing. As they advanced, they hammered in pitons, both for their own protection and for the stringing of ropes to be used on later ascents. The process took an hour or more, and it was past noon by the time they were off the rim of the couloir and back on the ridge.

Here, however, they had a reward. Ahead, the ridge now rose in a long concave arc, and for the first time they could see, projecting against the sky, the shoulder of the mountain that was their objective for that day. At an estimate, it was some five to six hundred feet above them, and as seen from below it seemed broad and level enough to hold the two small tents that would be needed for their highest camp. Eric, now in the lead, stopped and pointed with his ax. Franz, joining him, nodded. That was all. They didn't speak. Now, at almost twenty-five thousand feet, it was enough to ask of their lungs that they keep them in motion, heaving their leaden bodies up step after step.

Still, Eric was pleased, for they were doing all right: both he and Franz. Indeed, Franz, since he had simultaneously acclimatized and stopped fretting about his wife, had been doing magnificently, and today he seemed almost to be getting stronger as they went higher. Back on the ridge again, they gained another fifty feet. A hundred. Each time they looked up, the shoulder was encouragingly closer.

Then, abruptly, things were not all right. At least abruptly for

Eric. At one moment they were moving at their usual pace, the rope slack but not dragging between them; and in the next it *was* dragging; there was a pull and a jerk as it caught on the rocks of the ridge, and looking back, he saw that Franz had dropped behind and was limping.

He went back to him. Had he twisted an ankle? Franz shook his head and, bending, flexed and rubbed his left leg. How long had it been bothering him? Eric asked. It had just begun, Franz told him. "A stupid cramp, that's all." He rubbed and flexed some more, then straightened. "It's nothing," he said. And they went on.

But it wasn't nothing. He continued to limp, to drag, and after a few steps Eric again went back to him.

"*Verdammt!*" said Franz angrily.

"We'll go down," Eric told him.

"No."

"Yes, it's the only thing."

When Franz still protested, he pointed out that it would be no great setback if they didn't reach the shoulder that day. They had spotted the site for Camp Five, the route to it was plain, and they were carrying no loads to be dumped there. The next day they would come back in force—themselves plus Ken, Gil McLeod and a team of Sherpas—and Five would be established on schedule anyhow. The effort of talking this much left him struggling for breath, and for a while both of them rested. Then Franz made still another try at climbing. But it was no go.

"*Verdammt! Gottverdammt!*" he swore.

And giving in, he started down.

Even on descent they moved slowly. Franz could put little weight on the bad leg, he hobbled and stumbled, and Eric, following him in anchor position, belayed the rope carefully against the chance of a serious slip. They rested often. By the time they reached the previous day's high point it was already midafternoon, and when the sun set they were still well above Camp Four. Though it grew colder, however, the weather held. And there was enough snow on the ridge so that, even in dusk and then darkness, they could see their way in reflected starlight. Then at last, toward

133

eight o'clock, there were lights that were not stars. There were flashlights beaming from below. There were shouts, which they answered, and dark figures ascending the ridge, and soon Ken, Julian and Tashi appeared and led them down to camp.

But where was Gil McLeod?

Gil, said Ken, had not come up.

—No, he added, it had nothing to do with Ted Lassiter. Gil had reappeared at the Gap on schedule the evening before and reported that Ted was safely at Base Camp. As he had predicted, Ted felt better as soon as he was at lower altitudes; so he had felt no qualms at leaving him at Base with Ang Pemba and a second Sherpa, and himself had come back up with the other two Sherpas. He had been in good shape, spent the night at the Gap, and this morning had been ready to move on to Camp Four with Ken and a platoon of carriers. But now the Sherpas decided it was their turn for ailments. "Decided" was the word, Ken and Gil had agreed, for the complaints were both wholesale and vague. But no one, of course, could be forced to climb, and Gil, as a doctor, felt he could not walk out on men who, however dubiously, claimed to be ill. Ken, therefore, had come up with three Sherpas, which was all they could talk into going. And Gil, after a day of dosing and morale building, would ascend the next morning with as many of the remaining eight as could be stirred to action.

Though no major crisis, it was an unfortunate development. Gil was needed at Four not only as a support climber, but also as a doctor to have a look at Franz's leg. And with only Tashi and three other Sherpas on hand, they would be badly undermanned the next morning for the carry to the shoulder. Nevertheless, weather permitting, the carry would be made, for they were now too high on the mountain, and time too much of the essence, to waste a good climbing day. Those taking part in it would be Eric, Ken, Franz (if his leg was all right) and the four Sherpas. Julian Howard (plus Franz, if he needed a day's rest) would stay at Four to await the arrival of Gil and the remaining Sherpas. Since the small advance party would be able to carry only a limited amount of tentage and food, just two of its members, one climber and one Sherpa, would stay at the shoulder that night to put the new Camp Five in order. The rest would return to Four; the following day there would be a bigger carry; and at its end the whole summit contingent would be in position at Five.

Now that he was in camp and at rest, Franz's leg seemed better. All he had had was a cramp, he repeated; he would be fit in the morning. The loads for the high camp were ready and neatly ranged outside the tents. The night was quiet and starry. "We're still in business," said Eric to Ken.

In the morning one thing continued right: the weather. But immediately two other things went wrong. Franz Harben crept from his tent, took a few steps, and began to limp. It was obvious that on this day he could not make a long climb with a heavy pack. Then, when Eric, Ken and Tashi slung on their loads, the other three Sherpas stood by glum and silent, making no move to join them.

"Oh Christ," said Ken, "now *they*'ve decided to be sick."

But it wasn't that, it developed. Since they were all Solu Khumbu men with almost no English, Eric called on Tashi to talk with them, and after some back-and-forth in the Sherpa language Tashi explained what was wrong.

"They say it bad day," he reported.

"Bad? It's beautiful."

"They no mean here. They mean high." Tashi pointed.

Eric looked up the ridge. "It's fine there too."

"They no like wind."

Eric had heard no wind. But now he listened and, yes, there was a wind sound, a faint, thin keening from the heights above. "So there's wind up there," he said. "It's no storm wind. Not bad."

"They say it bad, Rick Sah'b. They say it godwind."

"What?"

"When god of Dera Zor is angry, he blow godwind. When man come high on mountain into godwind, he die."

There was a pause.

"Do you believe that?" Eric asked.

Tashi hesitated. "Sherpas believe," he said.

135

"Do *you*?"

"Sometimes I believe. When I am boy I believe."

"And now?"

Again Tashi hesitated. Then he said, "No, now I not believe. Not afraid. I believe with sah'bs godwind can no hurt. That we climb mountain, do not die."

"Have you told them that?"

"Yes, I tell."

"Tell them again."

There was more talk in Sherpa, but it was no use; the three porters would not budge. That left only Eric, Ken and Tashi for the climbing party, and a minimum of four was needed to carry enough to stock a two-man camp.

Eric stared at the ground. Ken said, "Shit." Then a new voice spoke:

"I'm an old hand with godwinds," it said.

Eric looked at Julian Howard.

"What?"

"I said I'm pretty good with godwinds. We have a lot of them in Chicago."

Eric looked at Ken but got no response. He thought for a bit. "We're getting high now," he said.

"I know that," said Julian.

"And this is with loads."

"I know that too."

Julian went to where the packs that the three Sherpas were to have carried still stood untouched between the tents. He slung one onto his back. "Are we ready?" he asked.

Ken seemed about to speak, but didn't. Eric thought it over for another long moment, then uncoiled an end of the length of rope he held and handed it to Julian. Both tied themselves onto it. Ken and Tashi roped up. Franz Harben sat on a rock kneading his leg and watched them disconsolately.

"You'll be coming tomorrow," Eric told him.

"You're damn right," Franz said.

"Gil will fix you up when he gets here. And for God's sake, between the two of you, get the Sherps unbugged."

"Them and me both," said Franz grimly.

Then he was gone below. Camp Four was gone. There was only the ridge soaring above them. Eric led the first rope, with Julian behind him; then came Ken with Tashi; all goggled, mittened, their axes probing, bent forward to the rise under the weight of their loads. They climbed twenty steps and rested. Another twenty, twice twenty, ten and fifty times twenty, hour upon hour, up the spine of rock, ice and snow. After the loss of Ted, Gil, Franz and Sherpas, Eric was almost superstitiously prepared for still more to go wrong; for Julian or Tashi, or even Ken or himself, to break down or start sliding into space. But they moved on steadily, uneventfully. With each of them carrying fifty pounds or more, progress was hardly swift, but it was not *too* slow. The rests were not too long. They used the steps and the fixed lines that he and Franz had put in the previous day. Julian and Tashi followed carefully where he and Ken led, and there were no slips, no faltering. In spite of the Sherpa trouble they had had an early start, and by noon they were in sight of the shoulder of the mountain that was to be the site of Camp Five.

Another of his grins split Tashi's monkey face as he peered up at it. "We go good, sah'bs," he announced happily. "Whoosh—we go like birds!"

Julian did not grin. Under goggles and beard his face was tight and strained, and his breathing was labored. But when Eric asked, "All right?" he silently nodded. And he still moved on, still kept the pace.

A little before one they passed the point where Eric and Franz had turned back. Beyond it, along the concave arc of the ridge, the going was not technically hard; there was only an occasional pitch where they had to climb one at a time, with Eric and Ken moving ahead on their ropes, then bringing Julian and Tashi up after them. But they were high now—at twenty-five thousand feet or more. With each rope's length gained, their movements were slower, their loads heavier, their rests longer. Another hour passed before the ridge at last eased off and they were standing together on a platform in the sky.

For a while no one spoke; not even Tashi. Unslinging the loads, they sat on them, motionless, and the only sound was the suck and hiss of their measured breathing. Again, however, there was a reward for labor. As they had judged from below, the shoulder was broad enough for a small campsite. It was fairly level. Once occupied and stocked, it would be as good a base as they could have hoped for on the final summit push for Dera Zor.

First, however—in fact immediately—there was a decision to be made. In their reduced group of four they had been able to bring up only one tent, two sleeping bags, and a limited amount of gear and provisions. Only two men could stay here tonight; two others would have to go back down to Camp Four . . . But who would do which? . . . If the four of them had been roughly equal as mountaineers, it would have been a matter of choices, or if choices conflicted, of drawing lots. But they were not equal. Though they had done well, Julian and Tashi were too inexperienced to be allowed to team together, either to stay or go down. As on the ascent, it would be Tashi with Ken, Julian with Eric ("He's your baby," thought Eric, "and he'll stay your baby") . . . But again: who up? who down? . . . He looked at Julian, bent over his ice ax, head resting on its blade, chest and shoulders still heaving in his struggle to breathe. Then at Tashi; and the little Sherpa was no longer even sitting. He was at the rim of the platform, again scaling rocks into space, and as he saw Eric watching he grinned and said, "These no go bang till next week." Obviously he was in better shape than Julian for the long descent. But if he went, it meant that Ken would go too. And was that fair to Ken? He didn't want to make a decision that would favor himself at Ken's expense.

He didn't have to. Ken, too, had been watching, weighing. And now he rose.

"Let's go, Tashi," he said. "We want to get down before dark." And when Eric half-protested, he would have none of it. "No, we'll go. You stay. We'll be back up with the others tomorrow."

Julian had risen, as if to show that he could. But he didn't speak. Tashi, after a moment of disappointment, got his grin back and said, "Yes, tomorrow, sah'bs. Tomorrow we many here, and next day go whoosh to top."

Now loadless, he and Ken moved down off the shoulder and soon were receding specks on the ridge below. Telling Julian to go on resting, Eric set about the job of getting their camp pitched. But Julian, now breathing more easily, insisted on helping, and they worked together in silence. After an hour the tent was up and secure, the things they needed inside. Then came the pumping of their pressure cooker and a long wait while food and drink came to a tepid boil. Neither was hungry, but they forced themselves to eat. What they craved was drink, and they poured great drafts of tea and fruit juice into their dehydrated bodies. By the time they had finished, the sun was down. Dusk deepened into dark. There was no wind on the shoulder, but the air, black and icy, nevertheless penetrated the walls of the tent, fingering their flesh, probing for blood and bone.

Soon they were in their sleeping bags. For the night they would keep on all their clothing except boots, and these they would take into the bags too, to keep them from freezing stiff. For once, when dawn came, they would not have to be up and on their way, but could stay in the sack as long as they chose. The next day would be one of rest and acclimatization, waiting for the others to join them.

And then—

Lying warm and quiet in his bag, Eric thought of the *then;* of the day, the event, that was now so close. On the following night there would not be just two of them at the high camp, but a whole task force. And in the morning, if the weather held (please God, make it hold), there would be the final setting out. Himself and Ken together. Hopefully, Franz too; perhaps even Gil. (Four would be the ideal party, if Franz and Gil were up to it.) But he and Ken surely: the two of them roped together as so often before: moving slowly, steadily upward, over rock, over ice, into the void of space, until they stood at last in that ultimate place of which he had dreamed through the years of his life.

He was half-dreaming now. He was sinking toward sleep.

"Ken—" he murmured.

"You wish it were, don't you?" said Julian.

"I—I—" Eric came awake. "You're doing all right, boy," he said.

"I know I'm no Ken. Or Franz or Gil either. But I've not let you down, have I?"

"I said—you're doing damn well."

There was a silence.

Then Julian said, "Remember the Alps, Rick? First the skiing, then the climbing: how much it meant to me." He paused. "Well, this means more. This means more than anything in my life."

In the darkness, Eric heard him moving. Then something touched his sleeping bag, his shoulder, and it was Julian's hand. For a moment he was no longer in a tent on a Himalayan mountain peak but in the corridor of a hotel in Chamonix, and the gilded soapsud heir of Montparnasse whom Nicole Vaudrier called a *tapette* had taken his hand and was holding it.

Now the hand moved no farther than his shoulder.

"Rick—" Julian said.

"What?"

"Thanks, Rick."

Then the hand was gone. There was only darkness, stillness. Then sleep.

In the morning the sun shone. It was still quiet on the shoulder. But the sound of wind again came from above, and they could see white spume churning out against the sky. What they could not see was the upper mountain itself. The west ridge, climbing on steeply overhead, shut out not only wind but view, and what lay beyond the next fifty feet or so they could not tell.

"I'm going up a bit and have a look," said Eric.

"*We'll* have a look," Julian said.

Eric studied him. During the night Julian had had several bouts of coughing and strangled breathing, but so had he himself. Now in bright sunlight his face was worn and haggard under its growth of blond beard; but no man who had climbed to more than twenty-five thousand feet and without oxygen would have looked much better.

"I'm all right, Rick," he pleaded.

Like Eric, he was goggled and helmeted. His crampons were on his boots, his ax in his hand, and now he tied on a rope and held out the other end.

"I won't hold you up."

Eric hesitated another moment. Then he took the rope.

"Step where I step," he said. "Stop when I stop. If you start feeling wrong let me know right away."

Julian nodded.

"We're high now—damned high," said Eric. "We're close to the edge of what men can do."

They started up. And above the bulge of the shoulder there was a change in the composition of the ridge. Below, for four thousand feet up from the Gap, it had been a patchwork of alternating snow and rock. But now the rock was gone, it was deeply buried, and under the surface snow was a sheath of blue ice. It was hard, hard as iron; blows of the ax barely dented it. The only way up was on the sharp points of crampons, and thus Eric climbed, clawing, grating, trying meanwhile to keep the rope taut as support for Julian below. Not far above the shoulder the ice burst out from its snow covering in a series of towers, like tall stalagmites, and as they threaded between them it seemed as if they were again moving through the white forest of an icefall. It was a brief illusion, however, for this was a forest in the sky. Soon it had fallen away and there was only sky. Only a bareness of ice between two seas of space.

There was wind here. They could not only hear it; they were in it. And it was now clear how they had been screened from it at their campsite. The shoulder projected northward from the main spine of the west ridge. The flare of the ridge above it shut it off from the south. And the wind was a south wind. The monsoon wind. Hunched over his ax, Eric peered through it into distance, across glaciers, peaks, valleys, across the breadth of Nepal toward the plains of India; and the purple band of cloud was measurably closer than before. It would be only a matter of days before the monsoon storms reached the eastern Himalayas—and Dera Zor.

He turned back to the ridge. He moved up again: slowly,

slowly. For the way was unrelentingly steep; there was wind but no air; and though today they were without packs, his body seemed not his own self but a huge burden he was carrying. It was no longer twenty steps between rests. It was ten—then five. And the rests were longer.

Resting, he crouched in the wind. He listened to it. And in its sound there was a cadence and timbre he had never before heard in wind on a mountain. It was not close around him; it came from above; and he recognized it as the same sound that had frightened the Sherpas into refusing to climb up the ridge from Camp Four. Now it was nearer, though, and louder, and wilder. It was a wild keening. Then no longer that; it had changed. From a keen it descended in pitch to a wail, a howl, a full-throated moan; then rose again through all the spectrum of sound, like music piped from a gigantic organ. What caused the music he could not tell. Above, he could see only a steep ramp of ice rising to a crest, and what was beyond the crest was hidden. Perhaps when he reached it he would learn the answer.

He glanced down at Julian.

"All right?" he called.

"All right," came back.

And they went on.

At this point they had been gone from Camp Five about two hours and had gained, according to the altimeter, three hundred feet. At the crest ahead it would be, say four hundred, and they would be at a height of 25,600, about fourteen hundred short of the best estimate for Dera Zor's summit. Today, with Julian, Eric had decided, the crest would be as far as he would go. From it, he hoped he would be able to see the final reaches of the peak; and if so, the reconnaissance would be successful, for he would then be able to plot out tomorrow's try for the top. He labored on up the snow-covered ice, and Julian followed. In fifteen minutes they were halfway to the crest . . . In fifteen more, almost there . . . Then they *were* there. And his hope was fulfilled. For above them, against a cobalt sky, loomed the whole top of the mountain.

They had seen it from below, of course: from the Kalpurtha Glacier and Base Camp. But it had then been so distant, the intervening mountainsides so foreshortened and distorted, that it seemed merely a white gleaming without detail or substance. Now, too, it was the gleaming that first caught the eye; the topmost dome of the peak ablaze in morning sunlight. But the dome did not begin immediately before them. It was only the roof, the superstructure of what lay ahead, and beneath it, supporting it, was something totally different.

First, in the foreground, there was a short, almost level stretch of ridge. Then it rose again, but not straight up before them. Instead, it curved off to the north, rising in a great arc of ice and snow to a point, perhaps halfway to the summit, where it reached and was absorbed into the final dome. It was not a balanced arc, for it was corniced. Throughout its sweep, wind-carved eaves of snow projected out still farther to the north, and beneath the eaves was nothing, ten thousand feet of nothing, ending at last in the glaciers at the mountain's base. To the south of the ridge, on the other hand, there were no cornices. No snow at all. No ice. There was dark bare rock: the south face of the mountain. It, too, fell ten thousand feet, to the Kalpurtha Glacier, and above, like the ridge, it rose—but not slantingly, almost vertically —several hundred feet more to the summit dome. Even in its blaze of whiteness Eric could see that it *was* a dome. Not a spire. Not a tower. Once it was reached, there would remain only a few-hundred-foot slope of snow to its ultimate point in the sky.

Once it was reached . . .

His gaze moved along the ridge; up the precipice. And now Julian, too, was eyeing the sweep of rock.

"The Wailing Wall—" he said.

And it was true, the name was right: it was the wall of rock that was the organ of the wind. The wall was pillared, fluted, funneled. Facing the south, it caught the southern wind and drew it into itself, sucking it into grooves and channels, into clefts and honeycombs, and piped it out again in eerie torrents. It was no longer simply wind, a thing of air and space. It was an emanation of the mountain itself; of its height, its mass, its lonely grandeur. The godwind, the Sherpas had called it. And the god's name was Dera Zor.

The two men listened; they looked. And the voice of the mountain was wild, its face of rock dark and murderous. Then they looked again at the ridge, and it too was Dera Zor, but wholly different: an arc of grace, of brightness, shining in sunlight.

Julian spoke again. "It'll go, Rick," he said. "The ridge is easy. It'll go."

But Eric shook his head. His face, in the reflected brightness, was somber, grim, for he knew that the ridge would not go. The cornices would not go. Once on the way, it would be impossible to tell what was solid ridge, what was unsupported cornice. Inevitably, somewhere along its rise, a climber would move a foot, an inch, too far out onto a cornice; the cornice would crumble, fall; and whatever was on it would fall with it, ten thousand feet to a glacier.

No, no ridge. Not possibly the ridge.

He turned back to the wall. The Wailing Wall—

But he heard no organ now; no godwind. He saw it not with the eyes of emotion or imagination, but of a mountaineer, studying it as a geographer might study a map, or a mathematician an equation. One could begin its ascent at point A, here on the ridge. He could follow crack B to ledge C, traverse bulge D to another ledge, and from there climb one of the "organ pipes" to . . . No, it petered out. He moved down, made another traverse, found a deep cleft between two other pipes, and moved up again, up, up . . . Technically, the wall was climbable for an expert cragsman. Franz Harben and Gil McLeod might have trouble with it; they were more experienced on snow and ice than on sheer rock. But for himself and Ken—yes, it would go. It was no harder than some of the faces they had climbed in the Tetons, or than the wall of Pizzo Rossi . . . Except that there they had not been at almost twenty-seven thousand feet of altitude. They had not been at the edge of where men could breathe and live . . .

Julian was watching him. "The wall," he said. "You think the wall is possible?"

"It damn well has to be," said Eric. Then he turned to go down.

It was about noon when they got back to Camp Five. They forced down some food, gulped juices and tea; then prepared food and drink for the others who would be arriving from below. How many there would be they of course did not know. Ken surely. Either Franz or Gil or both. Tashi surely, and hopefully a few other Sherpas, if the godwind phobia had not become too rampant. A good guess was a total of five or six.

The previous day, arrival at the shoulder had been at about three o'clock, and at two-thirty they were out on its rim looking downward. They saw no one. At three they saw no one.

At three-thirty and four and four-thirty they saw no one.

Between five and five-thirty there was movement below; but it was only a sea of shadow flowing up the mountainside as the sun sank toward Mount Kalpurtha in the west.

They shouted, but there was no answer.

They remained on the rim, shouting, and there was no answer. There was no movement but the flowing shadow.

And about six the shadow reached them.

At seven it was night.

In the darkness they still stood on the rim, beaming flashlights downward to guide anyone who might be climbing toward them. Again, at intervals, they shouted. But now in the night it was too cold to stand motionless on the edge of space; and besides, a wind had risen, ramming the shouts back into their throats.

It was not the south wind, the monsoon wind. On the shoulder they were protected from that. The tide of air had shifted, it was now coming from the west, and for this there was no shield on the jutting platform. Soon their little tent was trembling and flapping, and they had to crawl into it, both for shelter and as ballast.

The wind grew louder, stronger.

It became a gale.

Lying in their sleeping bags, head to foot, they held on to the frame of the tent. The din of drumming canvas was so great they could not talk, and even if they could have, Eric would not have known what to say, as his mind groped blindly for what could have happened below.

An hour passed.

Another.

Then suddenly, in their bags, both were sitting bolt upright, for at the entrance of the tent there was a sound, a movement that was not the wind. In the darkness a hooded head pushed through the sleeve, then a body, and a moment later, in the beam of Eric's flashlight, there was the brown, wizened face of the Sherpa Tashi. In the tininess of the tent, even his small body could barely squeeze between Eric and Julian. As he lay panting for breath, Eric beamed the light at the sleeve, but there was no further movement; no one else appeared.

"The others—where are the others?" he shouted over the howl of the wind.

"No others, Rick Sah'b," said Tashi. "Just me."

Tashi—

There was no Dera Zor without Tashi.

Twenty years ago, at Camp Five, it had been Tashi with himself and Julian. One night ago it had been Tashi and himself with Larry and Pembol. There had been no storm for them this second time. The storm had come and gone, and it had been quiet on the shoulder. It was not until the next morning when they started up that they heard the sound of the wind on the Wailing Wall.

Now, on the summit dome, he was above the wall; it was hidden below. But he could still hear it, see it, as he had heard and seen it yesterday—exactly as it had been twenty years before. Again his eyes had moved up over the dark rock: from A to B to C to D. He saw the cracks and ledges, the bulges and hollows, the tall fluted pillars, the "organ pipes." Atop a pipe was the resting place. Above it the overhang. And so on, detail by detail, up and across, across and up again, seven hundred feet up from the ridge, ten thousand from the Kalpurtha Glacier, to where the snows of the summit dome shone white and radiant against the sky.

All was the same. In the life of a man, twenty years took some time in passing. In the life of a mountain, they were the flick of an instant.

Now, after that instant, the climb would begin again.

The wall waited. The wall wailed.

11

On that night at Camp Five, however, it was not the Wailing Wall that they heard but the howl of the west wind. Now the three of them—Eric, Julian, Tashi—clung to the frame of the tent and pinioned its corners to keep it from being lifted and carried off into space.

During the first lull Tashi took a penciled note from his parka pocket, and in the yellow beam of his flashlight Eric read it:

Rick—Franz's leg is bad. Gil, here at Four now, says he has thrombo-phlebitis, clots in the veins of his calf. At this altitude they aren't apt to dissolve—more likely to break off and go to lungs or heart, which would probably be fatal. He'll be all right though, Gil thinks, if we get him lower, so he and I, with Sherpas, will start carrying him down at once. That means, of course, we can't give you support up there, so come down too and we'll see if we can reorganize.

Ken

In the next lulls, Tashi, to the extent that he was able, filled in the rest. When Ken and Gil, with Franz, had headed down for the Gap that morning, they had sent Tashi with two other Sherpas up toward Five with the message; but halfway up the two had said they heard the godwind and refused to go farther. "I tell them no godwind at Five, O.K. at Five," Tashi said. But they had said no and gone back down, and he had continued alone. "Then real wind, real storm comes," he said, "and is hard, I go slow, am late. You tell me often, Rick Sah'b, I not should climb alone. But if I not come, no one come."

Eric put a hand on his shoulder.

"I not do wrong, Rick Sah'b?"

"No, not wrong," Eric said.

It had not only been the storm that interrupted Tashi's story. He was obviously close to exhaustion and could barely croak out the words. With a sustained effort, Eric got the stove going, brewed tea, and made him drink it. Then he unrolled the sleeping bag Tashi had brought with him, laid it out, and got him in. Tashi was small—the smallest man on the expedition—but even so, the three of them with provisions and gear jammed the tent almost to bursting.

That was from inside. On the outside the gale did its best. Unlike the storms that had struck at Base Camp and the Gap, it brought no actual snowfall. But it was a snowstorm nonetheless, a whirlwind of snow, as its blast ripped the white covering from the mountainside and spewed it, seething, against thin canvas walls. Every half hour or so, booted and hooded, Eric or Julian went out on hands and knees to check the guy ropes, held by pitons in the rock and ice of the shoulder; and, as they emerged and returned through the entrance sleeve, clouds of snow billowed in. There was no getting it out. Reopening the sleeve would mean more snow, not less, and letting it lie, they crawled back into their sleeping bags. Whatever else happened, they had to maintain at least a semblance of warmth, or they were finished.

Once, for a few wild minutes, it seemed they were finished anyhow. The wind shrieked. The tent rocked, jerked, and began to slide. Heavily, clumsily, they tore themselves from their bags, lurched through the sleeve, and, outside, found that two of the pitons holding the guys had broken loose from their anchorage. They hammered them back in. They checked the other pitons and the ropes. And they held. The tent held. Presently they were back in it: in more snow, black chaos. They were back in their bags, holding the tent frames, panting for breath; but the sound of their panting was drowned in the howl of the wind.

Midnight passed.

It was one o'clock . . . two . . .

His hands still holding the tent frame, Julian had fallen asleep. Tashi lay motionless, face hidden, in his bag. For perhaps the tenth time that night Eric crept out into the storm, examined pitons and ropes, and returned to his own bag; then lay there in the roaring darkness, struggling to think. It was a struggle, however, that he was not up to. In his brain there was only the sound of the storm. In his body, coldness, tiredness. Then even these were gone, and he too slept.

When he awoke it was to the instant awareness of change. It was still dark in the tent; the dial of his watch showed about half past four. But the roaring was gone. The wind on the shoulder had not merely lessened but stopped entirely, and the only sound in the tent came from Julian and Tashi as they rasped for breath in their sleep. Eric lay still for a while. Then he could lie still no longer. Unzipping his bag, he pulled on his boots, groped past the bodies of his two companions, and crawled out of the tent. The difference of outside from inside was startling, as if he had moved suddenly from night into day. In the tent the darkness had been blackly opaque, but here it was white, shining. Around him, the snow gleamed; above, the stars in their galaxies; and the details of the ridge, up and down, were almost as clear as with a sky full of sunlight.

He looked down for only a moment. Then up . . . at the leap of the ridge as it climbed from the shoulder . . . at the forest of ice towers that rose from it, like ghostly beacons lighted from within. He saw that the snow was no longer deeply drifted on the ridge line that led toward them. The gale had not merely brought no new snow, but had blown away much of what was already there, leaving a less obstructed route than had existed before.

There was now no breath of wind. Was there above? . . . He listened . . . Yes, he could hear it faintly. It was no longer the west wind but the south, the godwind, touching the organ pipes of the Wailing Wall.

He crept back into the tent. Julian still lay motionless in his bag, but Tashi was half-sitting up, coughing and, retching, and when he was able to speak he said, "I make tea now, Rick Sah'b."

"No, rest," Eric said. "I'll make it."

He got the cooker lighted, filled a pot with snow and waited. In the blue glow of the flame he reread the note from Ken that Tashi had brought with him.

Poor Franz, he thought.

First Ted Lassiter. Then Franz Harben. But Franz's trouble was obviously more serious than Ted's.

. . . so come down too, he read, *and we'll see if we can reorganize . . .*

Reorganize, how? Two of the team were out. The Sherpas were afraid of the godwind. In a few days the monsoon storms would arrive . . . Reorganize where? At the Gap? Base Camp? Chicago?

After a while, tepid water bubbled in the pot. Julian had not yet stirred, but Eric made tea for Tashi and brought out crackers and jam. The Sherpa took a few swallows, then gagged and threw up in the now empty pot. When he had himself eaten and drunk a little, Eric took the pot from the tent and dumped it.

Now there was still another change outside: the night was ending. To the east, beyond the slant of the ridge, the stars were fading, the sky paling, and the ice towers above stood transfixed in the stillness of dawn. Watching, Eric too was transfixed, for it was a daybreak such as mountaineers dream of. And in the dream— no, the reality—he could feel tiredness and weakness, the wrack and strain of the night, draining out and away from him, gone and forgotten. Suddenly his heart was pounding; but not from exertion, not from altitude. It was pounding as it had when, as a boy of ten with his father beside him, he had stared up at the Lookout in the Front Range of the Rockies.

There was no father beside him now. No anyone. "We're going to make it, Ken," he had said to his oldest friend days before, as the two of them looked up from the site of Camp Four on the ridge below. But where was Ken now? Even lower. Going down, down, with Franz Harben and Gil McLeod, as the heights of Dera Zor receded in distance.

. . . so come down too, he had said . . .

151

But he couldn't have meant it. He wouldn't mean it, wouldn't say it, if he could see where Eric was now: so close to the summit in that perfect dawn. If their positions had been reversed, he, Eric, would have wanted Ken to go on. A day's delay in descending could not make a great difference, and up here it would give a much-needed rest to Julian and Tashi.

He looked down at the long spine of the ridge . . . Then up again . . . But now his heart was quiet, for he knew what he must do.

With a handful of snow he cleaned the pot that Tashi had been sick in. Then he re-entered the tent.

"Tashi—" he said.

"Yes, sah'b?"

"Are you all right?"

"Yes, sah'b."

The Sherpa's voice was weak, but again he sat up in his bag.

"No, stay where you are," Eric said.

Tashi looked at him, uncomprehending.

"You and Julian Sahib stay here today and rest. Tomorrow you'll be all right and we'll go down."

"All right now, sah'b."

"No—rest."

In the still dusky tent Eric groped for the things he needed. Into a small pack he put pitons, a piton hammer, carabiners, a length of rope; then chocolate, raisins, a canteen of juice. He assembled mittens and gauntlets, wind and sun goggles, crampons and ax.

Then he turned to Tashi.

"I'm going up," he said "—as far as I can. I may be gone all day."

Tashi was trying to get out of his bag. "I come too," he said.

"No. You stay here with Julian Sahib. I'll be back by evening."

The Sherpa tried to protest, but again broke down in a seizure of coughing.

"Easy. Easy does it," said Eric. He looked at Julian in his sleeping bag, but Julian still had not moved. "Both of you rest," he repeated. "Eat and drink all you can. I'll see you tonight."

Again he left the tent. Outside, he laced on his crampons,

slung on pack and rope, and hefted his ax. Then he started up the ridge toward the ice towers that rose tall and white against the brightening dawn.

As he had anticipated, the going was easier than on the previous day. Soon the towers were behind him, and he was on the bare ice of the ridge above them, cramponing steadily upward. Even after an almost sleepless night, he was not conscious of tiredness. With steps already cut in the steeper pitches, and with no Julian behind him to guide and belay, his progress was almost twice as fast as before.

No Julian . . . No Tashi . . .

Briefly he turned; but the camp on the shoulder was hidden behind the towers below.

No Ken . . .

He was hidden even more deeply.

All was hidden now, except the world of the mountaintop into which, step by step, he was now entering. That, and the world beyond it, spreading out to horizons in the brightening dawnlight. He had climbed through many dawns on many mountains, but none had been like this. On other peaks the coming of light had revealed the earth roundabout: slopes, valleys, forests, other peaks, foothills, plains. But now such detail was too far below to have individual identity; it was seen though a gulf, an abyss, like an ocean bottom. The eye was drawn out from it, into distance, into dimensions that were continental, almost global. Beyond the march of the miles—beyond the Himalayas, Tibet, Nepal, India—it could see the curvature of the globe.

To the south, the monsoon clouds still lowered: purple, swollen. The south wind was still bringing them closer. But to east, north and west the sky was stainlessly clear. Straight up it was clear, and so too was the hump in the ridge that now rose against it. Still moving steadily, he climbed the hump, reached its crest, and there before him, frozen in space, was the top of the mountain. On the left, the final curve of the corniced ridge. On the right, the Wailing Wall. Both were gray, somber, touched only by the dawn. But above them the summit snow dome, lighted from behind, gleamed like a prism against the rising sun.

Moving on from the crest, he reached the level stretch close beneath the wall, and here he rested. Again, as on the reconnaissance of the day before, he stared at the gentle arc of the continuing ridge; and again he rejected it out of hand, for he knew it was murderous. A climber might take one step, or ten, or a hundred, along its projecting snowy eaves, but sooner or later would come the last step, the step of crumbling, plunging death . . . No: no gentle ridge. It was the wall, the route that *looked* murderous, that was the only hope . . . Once more he studied it, his eyes moving up the dark precipitous rock: from A to B, thence to C, to D: and yes, technically it would go, he had climbed rock as hard as this. But not at five miles high, without oxygen.

He breathed slowly, deeply, sucking air from the wind. For now, again, there was wind: not west but south: not strong and wild but thin and keening. Above him the wall wailed in the pipes of its organ.

Removing his outer gloves, he unlaced his crampons. They would be a nuisance to carry up the wall, and so too would his ax; but both would be needed on the final snow dome, and he therefore tied them on around his waist. Added to pitons, carabiners and other gear, they made a cumbersome deadweight, but there was nothing for it. He slung them in a position where they would least interfere with his movements. He checked his pack and rope; then, edging off the crest of the ridge, moved out onto the base of the Wailing Wall. It was no true base, of course. Only a base for him. Beneath his feet, beneath the angle where it met the ridge, it fell ten thousand sheer feet to the Kalpurtha Glacier.

It was not down that he looked, but up. At A, B, C, and beyond. As near as he could estimate, there was about six hundred feet of rock above him, to the base of the summit snow dome. If he could average one hundred and twenty feet an hour he would reach the dome by noon. And then—

And then would come later. Now there was the wall.

He began to climb it.

At first, the going was almost routine, for he knew in advance every move he was going to make. From his starting point he wedged up a diagonal crack, reached a ledge, eased around a bulge to a second ledge, and went straight up from there along a narrow chimney. His rate of progress was all right. It was no more than half what it would have been at lower altitude—but still all right—and though he had continually to fight for breath, there were no slips, no fumblings. In a half hour he gained what he estimated to be a full hundred vertical feet, which was far better than he had dared hope for.

Now, however, the going grew slower. He had come to a level which he had not been able to see in detail from below, and there was therefore more trial and error, more groping and testing. Also, he had now reached the zone of the wall's "organ pipes," the tall fluted pillars with fissures between them that sucked in the wind and spewed it out, wailing; and on the rounded bulge of the pipes the rock was weathered and smooth. When he could, he maneuvered himself into the fissures, elbowing and kneeing his way up through tall caves of the wind. When he could not, he moved out onto the pipes, climbing either by friction or, when the steepness was great, with the help of pitons that he drove into cracks in the rock.

Seen tilt-headed from their bases, the pillars seemed to soar up, monolithic, to the very top of the wall. But fortunately this was not so. Most were, at intervals, warped and broken, and at the points of breakage were platforms and embrasures with sound stances, some of them even broad enough for sitting down. On one of these, resting, Eric brought out his canteen and half-drank, half-ate its semi-frozen fruit juice. He forced down a few raisins and bits of chocolate, not from hunger but to give him strength.

Meanwhile he looked out from his eyrie. While climbing, faced in to the mountain, he had been conscious only of dark rock slipping past, but now the vastness of earth and sky struck with an impact that almost stunned the mind. Beneath his dangling legs, the wall—the south face of Dera Zor—fell in its thousands of feet to the Kalpurtha Glacier, no more than a grayish white ribbon in the gulf below. At the glacier's head was Mount Kalpurtha, beyond its snout Mount Malu, their twenty-four-thousand-foot summits falling far short of the level of his platform; and on the far side of the ice stream the line of lesser peaks that were Dera Zor's outer bastion seemed no more than a puckering on the face of the earth. South of these were hills, valleys, rivers, plains, spread through miles beyond measuring, and in a great band above them, blotting out the horizon, the dark approaching clouds of the monsoon. They were still, however, three or four days away. The Himalayan sky was clear, the morning sun a bright flame in its blueness. Through the untinted goggles that Eric had been using on the snowless rock wall, it struck into his eyes with blinding spears.

He turned them back to the glacier, which was still in shadow. Base Camp was there, though he could not find it. Ted Lassiter was there. Doing what? Besides waiting . . . And the others: Ken, Franz, Gil, the Sherpas. Where were they? At the Gap, also waiting? Already descending the icefall? And how was Franz? Poor Franz . . . He tried to force his mind down; to be with them, to feel their presence. But it was impossible. They were remote and lost beneath the sweep of mountainside. Even Julian and Tashi, only a few hundred feet down at Camp Five, might as well have been on the other side of the earth. Here on the final heights of Dera Zor, he had entered a world beyond the world: apart, sealed, hermetic.

He came back to that world. He heard the wail of the wall. He felt the breath of the wind, and even in the flooding sunlight he was growing cold. He looked at his watch and it was a little past nine. That was all right. Peering up that wall, he estimated that he had already come about a third of the way to its top; and that, too, was all right. He got up and turned to the mountain. Again there was only the mountain.

For a way, above the resting place, the going was fairly easy. First, the route led up a deep and rough-walled crevice between two organ-pipe pillars, in which the only trouble was the frequent jamming of his useless ax against projecting rock. Then the pillars ended; above was a steep pitch of jumbled slabs. But here too the rock was rough, it gave holds and stances, and in fifteen minutes he gained some fifty feet. Then, ahead, loomed trouble, for at its upper rim the patchwork of slabs buckled outward. They became vertical; more than vertical. They overhung. Maneuvering to the side, he could see that above them the wall again eased off into fairly straightaway going; but where the eye could go the body could not follow, for on both flanks of the bulge the rock rose sheer and holdless. It was up and over or nothing.

The next hour saw a struggle such as he had never before experienced on a mountain: a sequence of advances, halts, retreats, new advances, repeated over and over. He had dealt with overhangs before. This one, indeed, was not greatly different from that on Pizzo Rossi, on which, five years before, he had fought and won after Per Halberg and Ken Naylor had failed. But he was now twenty thousand feet higher than on Rossi, gasping for breath with every slightest movement. And no belaying rope went down to companions below. On that Wailing Wall of the mountain called Dera Zor he was as alone as a man could be on the face of the earth.

He hammered a piton and levered himself up on it. Above was a niche big enough to hold his fingers, then the toe of a boot. Beyond it, he drove a second piton, gained another few feet. But above, now, there was neither hold for hand nor crack for piton; only smooth rock angling out to the farthest bulge of the overhang. Standing on his higher piton, he stretched to his utmost, inching his right arm up over the bulge to its hidden upper slope; and at the final limit of reach touched a patch of roughness, a few wrinkles, in the rock above. Would the wrinkles hold him? He did not know, but he thought so, for he needed only a tiny grip, the slightest leverage, to start him up over the bulge, and then the friction of his body against its upper slope would do the rest. If he could hold on only until he got his shoulders and chest up and over, he would be all right. If not—if his fingers slipped—

They weren't going to slip.

He went for it. First with one foot, then with both, he left the stance of the piton, his fingers clawing the wrinkles above with tip and nail. His body moved up—and out. The bulge pushed it out. Relentlessly the rock pushed at his chest, as if it were a living thing, expanding, swelling, trying to thrust him off into space. His legs and feet were useless now, merely scraping against steep smoothness, and he was held only by his right hand on the hidden wrinkles. He was squirming, heaving. He was trying to get his left hand up over the bulge so that it too could grasp the wrinkle, and the movement thrust him still farther out, to the last possible point of balance. Another nudge from the rock, another shift of so much as a pound of his weight, would have overbalanced him, sent him into a fall. But the equilibrium held. His left hand moved on, up, over the bulge. It reached the wrinkles, grasped them, pulled. And now both hands were pulling. His head was past the bulge. His shoulders, his chest were past it. His chest was flat against the slope of its upper surface, and friction held him; he was supported not only by his fingertips but by the rock itself; and still he wormed on, with his waist now up over the bulge, and then his hips, his legs, his feet. He was lying prone on the slope above, gasping and heaving, like a great fish that had been cast up on a rock in the sea.

There was a moment when the sea seemed to rise, to cover him. He blacked out. Then the blackness was gone, sky and mountain returned, and for long minutes he lay sprawled on the tilted roof of the overhang, fighting for breath and strength. At last he raised himself to a sitting position. He was on his knees. He was standing. His knees buckled and he went down; then rose again, swaying, but this time stayed upright. More minutes passed while he clung to the mountain wall, motionless except for the rise and fall of his chest; and gradually the rise and fall became slower, more rhythmic. The breath that was life itself was returning.

He raised a hand, a foot. He was climbing again.

Compared to the overhang, the going was not hard: first up a deep fissure that held him in from space, then up a buttress with adequate holds. But even after his rest he was not functioning properly. With every movement, his breathing again became convulsive. His legs were alternately leaden and rubbery. And something was wrong with his eyes, too, for the rock close before them seemed no longer solid and static but to be slowly undulating in a vast gray tide. Stopping, he closed his eyes. He laid his hands on the rock, feeling its hardness and mass, willing it to be still; willing his body to obey his commands. At first, nothing changed. As he went on, the mountain still swayed, and he himself swayed with it. He was stopping after every step, and after each one faced the prospect that the next would be the last . . . But it wasn't. There was still another. Another . . . He stumbled and fumbled, he gasped and lurched, but still he went on. And slowly, through his pain and weakness, he became aware that something strange and wonderful was happening.

It began with a dim impression that the steepness of the rock was relenting. Then he looked up, and yes, the impression was true: it was. Whereas before, endlessly, the wall had risen sheer above him, it was now easing off; a vista was opening up ahead; a vista that comprised the whole remainder of the wall to the summit snow dome that rose above it. More than this, the dome was close—no more than, say, two hundred feet above. Its snow shone clear and blazing against the deep blue of the sky.

Yes, clear: that was the wonder of it. The undulation of the mountain had stopped. It was still and clear. His eyes and mind were clear; it was as if the clarity of the mountain were communicating itself to him, filling him, strengthening him, as he moved on, more quickly now, up the easing wall. His legs ached, but he scarcely noticed it. His breathing was still labored and stertorous, but now it was only sound, a minor sound, unimportant, impersonal, in the greater sound of the wind. It was the wind he was listening to, the music of the godwind, of the Wailing Wall, and, like the clarity of the peak, the music filled him, lifted him, seeming to pour great drafts of oxygen into every cell of his body. His weakness and agony were gone. In their place were strength, resolve, will. Out of the past, out of the miles and years, an image flashed into his mind: the image of his father on the crags of the Lookout, turning, smiling: the voice of his father saying, "—And not to yield" . . . "What does that mean?" he had asked then. But he knew now what it meant. And his will was a flame, an engine of power, as still, step by step, he forced his lump of flesh still farther, higher; as he moved to the very edge, and past the edge, of what a man could do.

It was then that he saw a movement.

With a steep, holdless pitch blocking the way straight ahead, he had borne off to the left, when suddenly, farther to the left, where the Wailing Wall met the west ridge of the mountain, there was a flicker of motion on the angled skyline . . . It was a falling rock, he thought. But rocks did not fall upward. It was imagination, then, a delusion of hypoxia. But if so, it was a delusion that continued, grew clearer . . . Perhaps a hundred yards to his left and a hundred feet below him, a human figure was ascending the ramp of the west ridge.

His eye moved upward—downward. There was no other figure: only the one. He tried to shout, but his voice came out as no more than a croak:

"Julian! Julian!"

For he knew at once who it was. All the others, except Tashi, had been too far down the mountain to come so high in a few hours; and Tashi, apart from his exhaustion, would not have disobeyed his instructions to stay at Camp Five.

"Julian!" he called again, as strongly as he could. And this time his voice must have carried, for the moving figure stopped.

"Get off the ridge!" he called, once, twice, a third time. But now, still on the ridge, the figure moved on.

Then Eric was moving too: no longer upward but sideways, traversing the Wailing Wall toward the skyline slope of the ridge. He did not move quickly; that was impossible. But at least progress was easier than when he had been climbing straight up, and he was able to find adequate holds and stances.

As he moved, and the first shock of surprise wore off, he tried to picture what had happened below. Julian must have awakened soon after he himself had left the high camp, feeling stronger than had seemed possible the night before. He had decided to come up too, and there was nothing the ailing Tashi could have done to stop him. The ridge, to the point where it met the wall, was, except for altitude, routine going; and above the junction, Julian had obviously preferred its continuation to the all but vertical wall. "It's easy," he had said the previous day as he and Eric looked up at it. And so it was: in gradient, in lack of obstacles—

in everything except its cornices of unsupported snow. It was astonishing that none had yet given way under Julian's tread. And with each passing hour, each minute, as the sun beat down on them, it became more certain that one would break and fall.

Eric himself was now nearing the ridge. He did not shout again, for at such close range even a loud sound could trigger an avalanche. But he was near enough to see Julian plainly, and when the goggled, blond-bearded face turned toward him he gestured to him to leave the ridge for the wall. Whether Julian did not understand or simply chose not to comply, he could not tell. But he stayed on the ridge, plodding slowly but steadily up the snowy cornice. Eric, too, moved on, and in another few minutes reached a point on the wall perhaps fifty feet diagonally above him.

He could speak quietly now.

"Get off the ridge," he said.

Julian made no reply.

"Get off onto rock. There's nothing under the snow."

Julian stopped and looked up. "I've been doing all right," he said.

"For Christ's sake, stop arguing and get on the rock."

"I'm not arguing. I'm climbing a mountain."

"Come up here on the wall, and we'll climb it together."

"You don't want to climb with me. You walked out on me. You don't think I'm man enough."

"Look, you fool—"

"I'll see you at the top," said Julian.

He began to climb again. He took a step, a second, a third. But that was all he took, for in that same instant the snow directly in front of him disappeared. It did not seem to fall or break away. It was simply no longer there. In the place where Julian Howard had been about to set his foot were two vertical miles of blue air.

"Don't move! Not an inch!" Eric called.

Simultaneously he was unslinging his pack. He brought out his rope, uncoiled one end and tied it around his waist. With the rest held in his hand, he maneuvered his way to the best belaying position he could find; but short of going out onto the ridge himself, there was no way of getting directly above Julian.

He called again: "I can't throw the whole rope. Too much impact. I'll swing the end out toward you."

Even as he spoke, however, he realized that the rope's end, unweighted, could not perform a pendulum swing. So, working as quickly as he could with half-numbed hands, he attached to it four of his steel pitons. Then he lowered the rope. He began to swing it.

"Don't lunge for it," he said. "Don't move. I'll get it to you."

On the first swing the weighted line came within perhaps ten feet of Julian. On the second it was closer. On the third it nudged against him and Julian held it.

"Tie on," said Eric.

First Julian had to get the pitons off. He tugged and fumbled while seconds passed into minutes.

"I can't—" His voice came up, barely audible.

"Leave them then. I'm giving you more rope. Tie on beyond them."

Eric paid out the line. There was more fumbling.

"All right?"

After what seemed an endless wait there came a faint "All right" from below.

Meanwhile Eric had braced himself as well as he could behind a small projection of rock, passing his end of the rope around his back and shoulder in a body belay. "Come on now," he said. "Straight toward me. Get off the snow onto rock as fast as you can. If the snow breaks, I've got you."

The effort of so much speech left him gasping for breath. He drew in great drafts of nothingness, braced himself, held the rope taut in his mittened hands.

"Come on."

Below, Julian half-turned—away from the gaping hole in the snow. Again he took a step. But this time there was no second or third, for as soon as his foot descended into a new position the snow beneath it gave way too. There was another hole in the ridge. There was thin air, a falling body; a body swinging down and in toward the mountain wall, out of Eric's sight. The rope was straining, holding. Then it slipped. It ripped the outer gloves

162

from Eric's hands, and he felt the fire of pain beneath their semi-numbness. It jackknifed his legs and slammed him into the protective outcrop of rock, cutting into his back and snapping his neck sidewise onto his shoulder. Then, as suddenly as it had started, the slipping stopped. He had held it. From below there came the sound of a thud, as the far end of the rope, with its burden, struck the rock of the mountain wall. There was a swinging out, a second lighter thud. Then the straining rope was still.

Julian had made no sound. There was no sound now except the creak of the rope and the wail of the wind.

The rest was a blur, a half-remembered nightmare.

A blur of hours. Of rock and wind. Of labor. Of pain.

But first there was the blur of shock. Eric lay sprawled, motionless. Men have lived and died in the time he lay motionless; in the timelessness of the few seconds before he was able to rise, to heave on the rope, to run it around a projection of rock, so that some of its pull was off himself.

Then, edging out, he peered down the wall. And Julian was hanging there. He was revolving slowly at rope's end, about forty feet down, his shoulder almost brushing the vertical rock as he turned; but he was making no movement of his own, and Eric could not tell if he was alive or dead. Another fifteen feet or so below, the verticality was broken by a jutting ledge that would hold him, and Eric lowered him to it. Then, looping the rope around the nearby projection of rock, so that he could pull it after him, he rappelled himself down.

Julian was alive. His eyes were open, his lips moving, but he could not speak intelligibly. Fumbling with his layers of clothing, Eric tried to examine him. That some ribs were broken was almost a certainty, but his arms and legs seemed all right. It was not for a few moments that he saw the thin, dark streak extending from beneath Julian's hood to the rim of his goggles, and then, removing the hood and wool helmet beneath, found the deep head wound that had obviously been inflicted when he swung against the mountain wall. Little blood had flowed, and what there was had already clotted. There was nothing to do but replace helmet and hood.

Suddenly, to his astonishment, Julian moved. He got to his knees, his feet, made as if to start climbing. "I'm man enough—" he said thickly.

Eric held him. "No, this way," he said.

Directly below them was only an abyss; so, holding Julian on a foot's length of rope, he led him, lurching and stumbling, back across the wall to the line of his original ascent. On his way toward the ridge the traverse had taken him perhaps ten minutes. Now it took half an hour. But at last they reached his turnoff point, and here, briefly, they stopped. Julian slumped, half-standing, half-sitting, in a niche in the rock. And Eric, once again, looked up at the short remaining stretch of wall above them; at the gentle snow dome above it, white and shining against the sky.

Then he turned away.

"Now down," he said.

Julian seemed to have fallen asleep, but responded to his voice and, with Eric now behind him on the rope, allowed himself to be maneuvered downward. Below them was the section of the wall with a relatively easy gradient, and again they were moving, slowly, painfully. But moving . . .

Down. Down.

For how long Eric did not know. An hour, perhaps? Then there was steepness again.

There was the overhang.

Descending, he was able to detour it by affixing a piton and carabiner to the rock and lowering Julian down the smooth but nearly vertical wall that bordered it. Then, using the same anchorage, he rappelled down himself. On the ledge below he rested. He drove in another piton. He lowered Julian again. Himself again . . . And again . . . And again . . . Julian was able to hold onto the rope, thus taking some of the pressure of his own weight off his waist and broken ribs; but he could not follow Eric's instructions to guide his descent by the movement of his feet against the wall. For each lowering Eric had to play a grim game of marksmanship, finding a roping-down point directly above a ledge or outcrop below, so that Julian would land on it and not be left dangling in space.

He did three without missing . . . Four. Five . . . He lost count . . . On and on it went: pitoning, lowering, rappelling, down the vast face of the Wailing Wall.

Julian had begun to talk. But not to Eric, not about the descent. Once, looking down, he shouted, "Track!" and brandished imaginary ski poles. Later, he seemed to think himself back at the Café de la Cloche in Paris, ordering *"pernods pour tout le monde"*; then in the great house on Lake Shore Drive in Chicago. He did not seem to know Eric was there. Or the mountain. But he neither resisted nor collapsed, as still they moved down.

Down. Down.

It was his own collapse, as much as Julian's, that now seemed imminent to Eric. Even with the braking aid of piton and carabiner, the lowering of the almost helpless man was, with each repetition, a more killing task; and rappelling after him was scarcely easier. Far from numb, his hands now ached and burned. His arms, his shoulders, his back ached, and legs were again an ill-mixed blend of rubber and lead. The rock of the wall seemed to lunge and tear at him with a life of its own. The wind lunged and tore. It was growing stronger. Its wail grew so loud that he could no longer hear Julian as he wandered, shouting, murmuring, through the maze of the past.

Dimly he recognized the features of the wall as they slipped by: the "organ pipes," the vents between them, the bulges and buttresses, ledges and gullies. He knew that the hours were passing; that behind his back, to the south, the sun was moving across the sky. It had been high above his left shoulder. Then close above it. Beneath it. It was gone. In its place was grayness, darkening, thickening, and below the grayness, the glint of the glacier two miles down.

His hands slipped, and Julian jerked on the rope below. His foot slipped, and he himself almost fell. He could, he told himself, manage just one more lowering, one more rappel; and he did them. He did a second. A third. Again he lost count. And then at last came the time, beyond count, beyond number, when he roped down to join Julian—this time not on still another ledge or outcrop, but on the level section of the west ridge at the point where it joined the Wailing Wall. It was not quite seven-thirty in the evening. He had been on the wall for twelve hours.

As he looked up from his watch, he swayed. His knees buckled and he fell. Julian was already down, sprawled on the ice-crusted ridge, and for minutes they lay as they had fallen, two humps of flesh among the humps of rocks. At last he raised his head. He struggled to his knees. Hunched against the blast of the wind, he peered about him in the lowering dusk.

There was no question, no possibility, of continuing on down to Camp Five. They would have to bivouac . . . But how? where? Here on the exposed ridge they would be finished in an hour . . . His eyes moved down the slope to his left: the north flank of the ridge, in the lee of the wind. It was a bouldered slope, not steep at this point, and a short way down was a hollow among the rocks big enough for two men. Still on his knees, he crawled down toward it, pulling Julian after him.

Then they were in the hollow. The stars came out. Dusk turned to night, and through the night the wind wailed across the frozen mountain. Julian lay on his back, unmoving except for the labored rise and fall of his chest, and at intervals Eric rubbed his hands, kicked his feet, and pummeled him weakly. Once he lifted Julian's head and tried to pour fruit juice from a canteen into his mouth. But the juice was frozen. When he pried some out, it simply lay in yellow blobs on Julian's lips and beard.

He too wanted to lie flat, but fought against it. Sitting hunched and huddled, he fought against sleep. But sleep came nevertheless, and for a while he too was back in the past, in the house in Denver, pounding on a door that his brother Frank had locked against him. When he awoke, he was pounding the rocks of the hollow with his hands and feet, but could barely feel them.

Later, as he lay still, Julian spoke. "I'm man enough," he said clearly. Then, a few minutes later, he moved. He moved toward Eric, lay beside him, close against him. "I'm cold—hold me," he murmured. And Eric held him. "Hold me, Mother," Julian said.

In Eric's next sleep there was only blackness. In the next wakings, blackness and stars. Then at last came the time when he opened his eyes and there was a difference. Night and stars were gone. In their place was grayness; in the east, redness, and behind the redness, soon, the rising sun.

In the eye of the sun, above him, stood a figure. Julian seemed to have risen, and with a monstrous effort he rose and stood beside him.

But no, it wasn't Julian. Julian was not big, but bigger than this man. This was the Sherpa Tashi, and Tashi said, "I find you. Oh, Rick Sah'b, I find you—"

In the sun's red glare Eric could see him only faintly. He was doing something with a rope. He was pulling it gently, firmly. They were coming up out of the hollow toward the ridge; and Eric stumbled and fell and got up again; and then they had reached the ridge, and again he fell, again he rose; and then they were going down the ridge—slowly, slowly—with Tashi holding the rope close and tight behind him.

Suddenly he remembered. He turned. "Julian!" he cried. "Julian—we must bring Julian—"

But Tashi shook his head.

"No, Rick Sah'b," he said. "Cannot bring. Cannot help."

Now, twenty years later, he stood on the slope of the dome above the Wailing Wall and looked down at the ridge. His eyes followed its descent. And then he too was following it—he and Tashi, long ago—stumbling down the long ramp between sky and earth.

It took them until midafternoon to reach Camp Five, and he could go no farther. They spent the night there; the next morning moved down again, and halfway to Camp Four met Ken Naylor and two Sherpas, who were coming up to look for them.

"Julian's dead. I killed him," he told Ken.

Ken, in turn, told him that Gil McLeod was at Camp Three, at the Gap, taking care of Franz Harben. Gil had wanted to get Franz, with his blood clots, off the mountain as quickly as possible; but he had also not wanted to go lower than the Gap while others who might need help were high on the peak. So he was waiting at Camp Three, doing what he could for Franz, while Ken came up to see what had happened.

They spent that night at Camp Four, and the next morning descended toward the Gap. This time it was Gil, with two Sherpas, who came up to meet them, and he told them that Franz had died early that morning.

12

All that had been in ten weeks in the spring of 1950.

Next, there were not weeks but years. Years of fragments.

There was the fragment of Kathmandu.

. . . Of taking leave of the others. For he did not go with the others. He stood at the door of the Government guesthouse in the ancient city while Ken Naylor, Gil McLeod and Ted Lassiter, with bag and baggage, climbed into an old slat-sided truck. McLeod did not say goodbye. Throughout the return march from the mountain he had spoken to Eric only when necessary; and now he neither spoke nor looked at him but simply turned away. Lassiter murmured a word and was gone. Ken alone shook hands, and for a brief, bitter moment the two old friends stood face to face. "Take care, Rick," he said. Then he too was in the truck, and the truck moved off.

It would carry them only a few miles to the southern rim of the Valley of Nepal. From there they would travel on foot over roadless, wooded ranges to the plains of northern India. From Patna, their first Indian city, Ken would send cables to Julian Howard's mother in Chicago and Franz Harben's bride-widow at White Valley, Utah. When he reached the States he would go to see them.

That, Eric could not do. Of all things on earth, that, most of all, he could not do.

He closed the door of the guesthouse against the dust of the

departed truck. He closed it against homecoming, against Howards and Jill Harben, against the shame and bitterness to which
his dream had led him. In his box of a room he lay on the straw
mattress of the cot, eyes to the wall. But it was not this wall that
he saw. It was that other one, tall and savage, tiering up
through the wind into the Himalayan sky. It was Julian, hooded
and bearded, lying in his arms at the foot of the wall. It was
Franz—as he had not seen him, but could see him now—lying
stiff in his sleeping bag on the bouldered waste of the Gap. After
a while he rose. Kneeling, he bent his head to the straw mattress
and tried to pray. He tried as he had tried years before in his room
at home in Denver, next to the empty room of his dead sister
Robin. But now, as then, it was no good. There were only words.
Beyond the words he could still hear his mother sobbing in her
room down the hall.

He lay down again. He may have slept. When he next opened
his eyes it was to a knock on the door, and the woman called Amy
Bulwinkle appeared. She was a big disheveled woman of about
thirty, with dark eyes in a white face and a mop of streaked
blondish hair, and in her hands she held a bottle and two
tumblers.

"It's not Haig Pinch," she said. "Just rotgut arak. But you look
like you could use some."

There was no bar in the guesthouse; no liquor for sale at all.
An antique red-brick structure, like most of the buildings of
Kathmandu, it was a confused three-story warren of tiny cubicles,
with a communal latrine out back, a sparsely furnished dining
room (which served no beef), and an impenetrably dark and
odoriferous kitchen. Through the maze, dimly visible in the glow
of fat-burning lamps, moved a procession of Nepalese merchants
and officials in skullcaps and tight white trousers, Tibetan traders
in robes of yak wool and fur-trimmed boots, and hordes of ragged
barefoot unidentifiables who might have been guests, servants or
strays from the street. There were no women—except Amy Bulwinkle; no Westerners except Eric, Amy and her husband Cecil.

The Bulwinkles were not guests. They were, incongruously, the

170

managers. Apparently they had got to Nepal in the same fashion as the Dera Zor expedition: like Julian Howard, they had met the top maharajah somewhere on the outside and been invited to come. But the rest of the hows and whys were obscure. Cecil Bulwinkle was, at a guess, British, but it was hard to tell, for his presence was marginal. He spent most of his time in their so-called "suite" on the top floor of the guesthouse labyrinth, and when occasionally he appeared in public, tall, bony and spectral, he was so drunk as to be, in effect, absent even though present. In contrast, his wife was very much there indeed; in fact ubiquitous. And though she too was no teetotaler, liquor seemed to help rather than hinder in the discharge of her duties. She not only ran the hotel; she was on top of it, forever issuing orders, confronting crises, shouting loudly and profanely for tatterdemalion servants. Roughly half her conversation was in Nepalese, or her own version thereof; the rest in English that, unlike her husband's left no doubt about her national origin. She was unmistakably, if mystifyingly, American.

She supplied no information, invited no questions. Nor, with Eric, did she ask questions of her own. It was common knowledge that the expedition had met with defeat and disaster. She had seen with her own eyes that a team of six had become a team of four. But not once had she spoken of Dera Zor. She spoke of cockroaches. ("We used to spray 'em but they lapped it up like mother's milk.") Of the dining room menu. ("I've smuggled in some beef for you. It's from before the flood and'll break your jaws, but still it's beef.") And now in Eric's room, pouring arak, she said, "I brought two glasses. Hope you don't mind."

Eric had sat up, and now he took a glass.

"Drinking alone's no good," she said. "Bulwinkle drinks alone; look at him." She raised a half-filled tumbler. "Here's to company," she said and drank it down.

Eric took his own drink more slowly. Arak, the homebrew hard liquor of the East, was raw and fiery, and it burned his throat; but once down it did good where good needed doing.

"I drink alone too, sort of," said Amy Bulwinkle. "But only sort of. I sit in that goddamn dining room and drink by myself, because Bulwinkle's passed out upstairs and the wogs around here won't touch it. They watch me, though. Oh boy, do they watch me! At first it used to get me mad, but now I like it; it's good, really. If someone's even just watching you, it beats drinking alone."

She refilled their tumblers and grinned.

"So watch me," she said.

He watched her: as she drank, as she set her glass down. And perhaps it was his own drink, perhaps her ease and friendliness, but now she seemed more attractive than she had before. She was a big woman, yes, but not fat. Though there were bulges under her tight skirt and low-cut orange blouse, they were in the right places; and though there was much that was slatternly in her, there was also strength. Her neck and shoulders were strong, and the bones of her face, with only a hint of blurring and bloating in the white flesh of her cheeks. Her mouth was big and red, and even minus the grin there was humor in it. Her mop of hair, though carelessly done, was lustrous and alive. Her dark eyes were alive. They were smiling.

. . . Then in the next instant not smiling but angry, flashing, as abruptly she leapt to her feet and threw open the door. From beyond it, down the maze of hallways, there had risen a cacophony of banging, thumping, yelling, and now to it, stridently, was added the yelling of Amy Bulwinkle. "Shut up, jerks!" she screamed from the doorway. Then switching to Nepalese, she charged off down the hall.

For the first time in weeks, Eric smiled. She was a hardboiled one all right. But he was grateful to her, *for* the smile—not to mention the arak. When she didn't come back he finished the bottle she had left, and with the liquor in him, he slept. In the morning she scolded him for drinking alone. "I wouldn't have been alone if you hadn't left," he pointed out. "And if I hadn't left," she said, "there wouldn't be any more goddamn guesthouse." That day, later, she came to his room with a second bottle; in the days that followed, with others. Each time there was an interruptive crisis of some sort, to which she made off in a gale of bilingual swearing. And each time he finished off what was left in the bottle. He got no lift from the drinking. Once she was gone, it was a grim mechanical business. But at least, in the end, Dera Zor receded. Julian and Franz receded. There was a dimming, a thickening. And he slept.

For days he did not leave the guesthouse. Then followed days when, on each one, he walked the streets of Kathmandu. The monsoon had come; he walked in rain and muck, but scarcely noticed it. He walked under the eyes of Buddha and the arms of Krishna; past temple and pagoda, bazaar and palace, turban and nose ring, rajah and beggar; through the glitter and stench of the heart of Asia. But all this, too, he scarcely noticed. He walked with head down, eyes unseeing, as he had walked years before in the streets of Denver, of Paris, and on the bare winter beach of Santa Monica. When he could walk no more he returned to the guesthouse and waited in his room for Amy Bulwinkle and her bottle.

Once, twice, a half-dozen times he brought out pen and paper and tried to write two letters.

Dear Mrs. Howard . . . Dear Jill Harben . . . I can't tell you . . .

No, he couldn't tell them.

By now, Ken had already told them.

From his pack he pulled other papers, his diary and notes, and tore them up.

Dear Saturday Evening Post . . . I am sorry . . .

Lying on his cot, he remained unmoving until Amy Bulwinkle appeared. "Rise and shine," she said cheerfully as she opened the bottle.

The weeks had become a month. A month became two. One problem he still did not have was money; for at expedition's end, thanks to his Howard-financed expense account, he had had more than five hundred dollars, and his outlay at the guesthouse (with arak courtesy of his landlady) came to three dollars a day. What was a problem, however, was his Nepalese visa; for it was now about to expire. Abandoning his random walking, he went to

Government offices trying to renew it. But without success. The visa, it was pointed out, was specifically for entry into Nepal on an expedition to Dera Zor; and it was obvious that he was already suspect for staying on after the others had left.

Perhaps if he stayed away he would be forgotten, he thought. But he wasn't forgotten. A week after his last visit to a Government office he received notice that in three more days he must be on his way.

He packed his few belongings. He drank arak with Amy Bulwinkle. And on the morning of the third day, in the monsoon rain, he climbed into the same truck that had taken his companions off ten weeks before.

Unmindful of the rain, Amy came out of the guesthouse entrance and handed him a bottle. "Might as well be wet inside too," she told him.

He stowed the bottle in his pack, and when he turned back to her she had suddenly changed: her face and eyes were different.

"How about me too?" she said.

"You too, what?"

"Going with you."

He stared at her. She meant it.

"Where?" he asked.

"Anywhere."

"I'm not going anywhere."

There was a pause. The rain drummed on the truck, and the strange look drained from her face. "I was kidding," she said. The red lips smiled. "Goodbye now."

"Goodbye. And thanks," he said.

"Come back sometime."

"Who knows?"

The truck's gears ground and it lurched forward. "If you come back," she said, "we won't drink arak. It'll be Haig Pinch on the house."

There was the fragment of New Delhi.

. . . Of airport, hotel, hotel bar. In the bar, on the first night, he drank Haig Pinch-bottle scotch. On the second and third nights he drank more. On the fourth morning he counted his money and found it was considerably less than when he had left Kathmandu.

He went to the American Embassy and asked for a job. All American personnel, he was told, was sent out from the States. Only Indian personnel was hired locally.

He went to Pan American Airways, the National City Bank, General Motors, Ford, General Electric, Coca-Cola. Four had no jobs. Two did, but required experience.

He went to the office of an American construction company that was building a dam on the Gogra River in Uttar Pradesh. They needed a foreman to supervise Indian work crews, but he had to speak Hindi. Could he speak Hindi? Yes, he said. Then he bought a dictionary, went to the Gogra, and lasted a week.

There was the fragment of Calcutta.

. . . Of railway station, hotel (a cheaper one), and the bar (not cheap) of Scoreby's Palm Club. Outside, on Chowringhee Street, men, women and children lay in the gutter and privileged cows in the shopping arcade; but inside there was mahogany, damask, crystal and Haig Pinch. When his check came it was twelve rupees more than he had in his pocket. Presently Mr. Scoreby appeared. He was a short, plump Englishman with white hair and red jowls, and considering the circumstances he was not unpleasant.

"What's wrong, lad?" he asked.

"Plenty," said Eric. "But the part you're interested in is that I'm broke."

"What are you doing in Calcutta?"

"Nothing."

"Where do you come from?"

"A lot of places."

"Such as?"

"Denver, Paris, Kathmandu—"

"Ah, Kathmandu!" Scoreby was interested; he sat down, "How long were you there?" he asked.

"A while," Eric said.

"You must know old Cess, then?"

"Cess?"

"Cecil Bulwinkle. Runs the Ritz-Plaza up there."

"I've seen him," said Eric.

"Just seen him?"

"Even that takes some doing."

"Oh?" Scoreby eyed him. "He's on the sauce, you mean?" He shook his pink head. "Poor Cess, he could never stick to just selling it. And up there it's worse, I guess, with no one even to sell it *to*."

After a moment he brightened. "And Amy?" he asked. "You saw Amy? How's Amy?"

Eric thought it over. "She's getting by," he said.

"Getting by, eh? Yes, that would be Amy all right. There was the greatest little getter-byer I ever saw in my life.

"—Except that I guess she's not so little anymore," Scoreby added.

"Well—"

"She was always fighting weight, poor kid. While she was dancing she could keep it down; had a hell of a neat figure. But up there now, I guess—"

He went on about the Bulwinkles. For two years, until some eighteen months before, they had worked for him here at the Palm Club: he as manager of the cabaret part of it, she as a featured dancer. One of the big-spending on-and-off customers had been the Maharajah of Nepal—"and he took a big shine to them. Not just to Amy, that's the queer part. To Cess too. He kept after them to go to Kathmandu and run this Ritz-Plaza of his. One fine day, by God, they did: just like that, the damn fools. And I haven't had a decent cabaret manager since."

He talked on, told stories, asked questions.

"What's your drink?" he asked after a while. And there was Haig Pinch on the house.

Later there was dinner on the house. And the next day Eric was back at Scoreby's Palm Club to begin his apprenticeship as its first decent cabaret manager since Cecil Bulwinkle. How well he succeeded was perhaps open to question.

But he stayed for six months.

There was the fragment of Palembang.

. . . And it began with snow. It was snow in a dream, the steep snow of a ski run, and he was schussing down it swift and sure, with the white powder streaming out from beneath the rushing boards. This did not last, however, for soon it turned warm and the snow began to melt. It was no longer white and powdered but gray and wet; he could not hold his course but slipped and wobbled; then fell, sprawling in wetness, and awoke soaked in sweat on the bed in his room in Calcutta.

Later, still sweating, he walked down Chowringhee Street. He sat sweating in his office cubicle at the Palm Club. And he thought, "I am not a cabaret manager. I am a skiing instructor. I am no longer a mountain climber, but I am still a skier. A ski instructor, for Christ's sake, in Calcutta, India."

Soon after that he left the Palm Club, and he knew where he was going. It was not home—he had no home—but to New Zealand. It was the nearest place to Calcutta where there was skiing, and he would go there, to the mountains, and find a job at a resort. On a steaming day in late April, which would be mid-autumn in New Zealand, he took a ship bound for Auckland by way of Jakarta and Sydney.

He did not get there, however; for the night before the ship reached Jakarta, in Java, he had another dream. Again it was of snow and skis, and this time the snow stayed good. But there was another change too, for before he had been alone and now he was not. There was a client with him, close beside him, never leaving; it was Julian Howard; and together, inseparable, they schussed the white slopes of the New Zealand Alps. In the morning, shaken, he had a few drinks at the ship's bar, and, that afternoon and night, many more in the bars of Jakarta. When the night had passed and it was day again, he was on a bed in a seaman's rooming house and his ship was gone.

It was all right, however, for Julian was gone too. For a few more days he drank and slept and drank; then took a smaller boat to the town of Palembang, on the island of Sumatra, where he had heard there were jobs in an oil refinery.

In Palembang, as in Calcutta, he sweated. But sweating was better than skiing with a ghost. Though there was no Haig Pinch on hand, there was Holland gin, when he could afford it, and when he couldn't, various homebrews that were not notably different from arak. After several weeks he had a bout of amoebic dysentery, after several more, dengue fever, but the oil company doctor got him through both. When, a few months later, he moved on, he was in no worse shape than when he had arrived. If no better.

There were the ships at sea.

But now not as passenger. As crew.

There was Jakarta again. There were Singapore, Sydney, Auckland (for two days), Yokohama, Penang, Manila.

More than a year passed this way. Then there was Hong Kong.

There were the harbor, the peaks, the streets, the manswarm. In the swarm he lost himself: one speck in three million.

For a while he lived on what he had saved from sailoring. He ate, drank, slept, walked. He walked the steep streets of Victoria and the flat streets of Kowloon; along the sea-girt road around Hong Kong Island and through the fields of the New Territories to the frontier of Red China. He walked on Nathan Road, past the hotels and restaurants, tailors and jewelers, camera and perfume shops. On Queen's Road Central, past the banks and trading houses. On Ladder and Cat streets, under forests of laundry, past whole skinned pigs, pickled snakes, scarlet coffins, and crones in doorways playing mah-jongg. In all the myriad city the only place he did not walk was up the roads and paths to the island peaks.

He lived in a cheap rooming house in Kowloon, with a clientele part Westernized Chinese, part seedy European. His meals were usually Cantonese, his liquor British (though rarely Haig Pinch). Sometimes in bar or restaurant he struck up conversations: with Chinese, local British, tourists, whatever. Sometimes at night he took a Chinese girl to his room. But mostly he ate, drank and slept alone; and with this he was satisfied, for he was not lonely. To be lonely was to want companionship and not have it. And he did not want it. He had had too much of it crewing on ships; of close quarters, unwanted intimacies, prying questions. In the swarm of Hong Kong there were no questions, and he was grateful.

When his money ran low he had to get work; and he found it. Or, rather, devised it. From his far-ranging walks he knew the city well, and he became a self-employed guide, picking up tourists at the airport, on the docks, in the lobbies of the Peninsula and Miramar hotels. The fact that he was young and American had an attraction for certain types of visitors—especially women. And besides fees from his clients he was soon collecting commissions from the local merchants to whom he steered them.

There were also other ways, he had early discovered, of making a living. Smuggling was one of the colony's major industries; there were brisk trades in narcotics and women. But something out of the past—perhaps the Claremont Avenue Lutheran Church?—kept him away from these. Now and then he himself smoked opium, with unsatisfactory results. Sometimes he would produce a girl for a male tourist or traveling businessman, but never with a fee from the professional end. Always it stopped at thus-far-but-no-farther. He was a tout, yes. A pimp and pusher, no.

One problem with the tourist business was that it was seasonal. During the more or less dry winters the visitors came in tides, but from April on through the hot, wet summers they stayed away, and he became a guide-tout without clients. By the time it was late May of 1953, however, this was all right with him, for he was tired of the endless rounds. Of Nathan Road, Ladder Street, the Star Ferry, the Tiger Balm Garden, the Tai Pak Floating Restaurant; of widows from Santa Barbara, divorcees from New York and Chicago, retired couples from Dallas, Burlingame and Shaker Heights; of Wang Li the Tailor, Chok Sing Cameras, Ho Fong Perfumes, and the Jade Palace Emporium of Oriental Gem Stones. He withdrew into himself. Into his room. Into the Blue Dragon Bar and Grill.

The Blue Dragon was a good place—two blocks from his rooming house in the old section of Kowloon. Knowing that he would pay up when he was working, they gave him credit when he wasn't; so he ate and drank there; with no clients to meet in the morning, he sometimes drank through the night, but still they let him sign the chits, and when he no longer could they signed for him. It was good in other ways, too. The tourists gabbed, asked personal questions, but here no one moved in on him. There was a Chinese girl called Lily who sat with him when he wanted her and went away when he didn't. There were the other customers, mostly seamen, with whom he could talk or not, as he chose. On some nights there were fights, but he didn't get into them. He sat, watched, drank. Often, when he drank until late, Lily took him home to his room.

That was all there was now—room, Dragon, the street that joined them—and in the rains of late May the street was a slit between dripping walls. The swarm and glitter of the city were hidden; harbor and peaks, ships and planes were hidden, with all the world beyond dim and remote. The only intimations of it were at the Dragon, in the talk of the seamen, the blare of the radio, the occasional newspaper left behind by a customer. Now and then, as he drank, Eric glanced at a paper, trying to force his mind out past the lacquered walls of his refuge. But the refuge remained reality, with the rest mere words on sheets of paper. Back home—home?—Eisenhower had succeeded Truman as President. (Good or bad?) Stalin was dead. (Presumably good.) In Africa, something called the Mau Mau was raising bloody hell. (There was always bloody hell somewhere.) And in the Pacific they had exploded something called a hydrogen bomb. (Apparently the atomic one wasn't bloody hellish enough.) As of the moment, only the British—for a change—seemed to have something to cheer about, with the Commonwealth in a global dither over the imminent coronation of Queen Elizabeth; and the English-language Hong Kong papers were awash with news of it. With glazed eyes, in his corner of the Blue Dragon, Eric noted the parade route through London, the seating in Westminster, what Queen, Queen Mother and Princess Margaret would wear.

And then—

It was late one night; the Dragon was almost empty; and there on the floor, among the butts and spilled beer, was the tattered front page of the Hong Kong *Times*. He looked down at it. He bent and picked it up. He read the headlines:

Coronation Gift for Queen
BRITISH CLIMB EVEREST

He finished his drink. It was his tenth or twelfth of the night, and his eyes were no good for reading. He pushed the paper away, off the table, and his glass fell with it. He ordered another drink; then two or three more. He broke another glass. Stooping to pick up the *Times* again, he fell himself, and Lily came and said, "We go home now, Elic—"

He was ready to go. Now, suddenly, he *had* to go. The tight lacquered box of the Blue Dragon was no longer a refuge, but a prison. He had to break out of it: through the door, a window, a wall—any way. He found the door, or Lily found it, and they were out in the street. In the dark, the rain. Lily was leading him, and once or twice he stumbled, but did not fall again, and then they came to his rooming house and she was trying to lead him in. But he would not go; for his room, too, was a prison. He pulled away, looked up and down the dark slit of the street. And the street was still another prison. He must break out of it too; out of all the prisons. He began to run. Lily called after him, but he did not stop.

He turned a corner. Another. Then he was out of the old city, out of the slit streets, on the broadness of Nathan Road. And he was no longer running but walking. Nathan Road was the main thoroughfare of Kowloon: the street of the tailors, jewelers, camera and perfume shops. But now the shops were dark and shuttered. The manswarm was gone, and he walked alone under the yellow street lights, in the rain.

Then, ahead, there were more lights: not merely of a street but of a whole city: for he had come to the foot of Nathan Road, to the harbor. There were the lights of sampans, junks, freighters, liners; the lights of the Kowloon waterfront sweeping off to either side; the lights of Victoria across the half mile of intervening water; great tiers and arcs of light, constellations in the wet darkness. But it was not at the lights that he looked. As he stood alone on the harbor's rim, his eyes moved up past the blaze of Victoria's center, past the straggles of brightness that climbed the slopes behind it, to the peaks of Hong Kong Island rising black into rain and mist. He watched them for a long time. Then a cluster of lights that was the Star Ferry slid across the water to a nearby wharf.

He boarded it. Soon a gate clanked; the ferry moved. Then it clanked again and was behind him. He was walking through Victoria: first on level streets past banks and offices, then up the steepness of the streets beyond, through alleys and lanes, from pavement onto gravel and mud. The last of the street lamps were now below him. All the lights of Hong Kong were below him, spread out in their constellations as if in an upside-down sky, and ahead, above, were only darkness and rain. The path he was following wound through a scattering of shacks, past the moving shadows of tethered goats; then twisting and steepening, bore up long slopes of shale and brush.

He climbed slowly but steadily. Though he was drunk, he knew he was drunk, and placed his feet carefully, without stumbling or lurching. Nor had he hallucinations. He did not think he was climbing Everest. Or Dera Zor. Or the Lookout or Rainier or an Alp or Teton. There was no one with him: neither his father nor Robin nor Ken Naylor no Julian Howard. He was alone. He was climbing Victoria Peak, eighteen hundred feet high, on Hong Kong Island, and a few yards to his right were the tracks of the Peak Tram, on which, with his tourists, he had ridden a hundred times to the top. He was on no tram now, however. He was climbing. For the first time in three years he was climbing more than a flight of stairs or a city street; and if it was a drunken thing, a crazy mindless thing, it was nevertheless a thing that he had to do.

At last, again, he was climbing a mountain. Any mountain. And it was joy, it was freedom, it was life itself.

The path angled over toward the tram tracks, and he did not

want the tracks. He left the path. He moved up the steepening slope, his feet kicking into the wet brush, his hands grasping it and pulling. Then the brush ended and there was rock ahead. He began to climb the rock. It was not sheer: nothing like the rock face of the Matterhorn or Pizzo Rossi: nor like the Wailing Wall of Dera Zor. But it was slick with rain. His fingers, groping for holds, found mud and slime, and his leather-soled shoes slipped on smoothness below. Still he kept on. When he looked up he could see almost nothing: the rain beat into his eyes, and beyond the rain was only darkness. But he continued by groping, by climber's instinct. He found a hold, a stance, moved up, slipped, and held it. Moved up again, slipped, held it. Again—slipped—and did not hold it. His fingers came loose. He slipped farther. He was falling, his fingers still groping, clawing, but finding nothing; his legs yawing, his body turning, the lights of Hong Kong spinning below.

They spun away. There was darkness—

Later, whiteness.

A ward. A nurse. A doctor. There was a bandage on his head, a splint on his arm, a cast on his foot.

"You were lucky," the doctor said.

Ah yes, lucky.

There was a man who was not a doctor. He was an American vice consul. (Again.) And the vice consul said, "Your passport has expired."

Eric said nothing.

"Your Hong Kong visa has also expired. Immigration here says you've been working illegally as a guide, and they refuse to renew it."

He still said nothing.

"Have you money?" the vice consul asked.

"No," he said.

"We can send a cable for funds to your family."

"I have no family."

"Then to a friend."

"I have no friends."

183

"No one who will send money to get you home?"

"No," Eric said.

And this time he stuck to it.

"In extreme cases," the vice consul said, "the State Department can supply funds for the repatriation of American citizens. But they must sign an affidavit of destitution."

There was a pause.

"Do I understand that you claim destitution?" he asked.

There was another pause.

"I must have an answer. Are you destitute?"

"Yes," Eric said.

Out from Victoria Peak there had been the lights of Hong Kong. Out from the summit dome of Dera Zor was only darkness.

But he could see beyond the darkness.

He could see Hong Kong itself: first close and swarming, then receding. He could see the broad Pacific. He could see all the way across the Pacific to Kent Street in San Francisco.

13

On Kent Street, as in Kowloon, there were shabby rooming houses, and in one of the houses a shabby room. In the room, on a hot plate, he cooked the food he had bought with his relief check. When he had eaten he read the back pages of the San Francisco *Chronicle*.

WANTED, he read: *mechanical engineers, electrical engineers, thermal engineers, test engineers, electronic engineers, aeronautical engineers.* WANTED: *chemist, physicist, tool designer, systems analyst, office manager, dental technician, veterinarian.* WANTED: *draftsman (experienced), accountant (experienced), claims examiner (experienced), pipefitter (experienced), teletype operator (experienced).* WANTED: *dishwashers: hotels, clubs, restaurants. Apply Acme Agency, 715 Mkt.*

For three weeks he worked in the kitchen of the St. Francis Hotel. For two months he filled gas tanks at a service station in Sausalito.

Then he found North Beach. He found the Phriendly Phoenix. In Paris there had been the Café de la Cloche, in Calcutta the Palm Club, in Hong Kong the Blue Dragon. Here, in a narrow street behind the fish wharves, was the PP, and it became, like the others, a protective pocket in the night. At first he was alone, anonymous. He drank coffee and Coke. Then came a night when he pushed a Coke away and drank a whisky, the first since Hong Kong, and after that there were more whiskies and the aloneness was gone. In its place were smoke and voices, trumpet and drums. Around him were sweaters and jeans, beards and bangles. He was at a crowded table; at the crowded bar. He was behind the bar—for the old barman had quit and they had taken him on—and for every six drinks he sold he poured one for himself.

He had even acquired a name. He was Ricky-O.

Across the bar, often, was a girl called Thalia. Like Nicole, of long ago, she drank pernod and was an existentialist. But whereas Nicole looked like a gamin, Thalia looked like the Charles Addams lady in *The New Yorker*; and whereas Nicole had talked French, Thalia spoke a language called Beat. In fact, she *was* beat. She was also Hip, Cool and a Cat, and when she was sober enough to pronounce the words, Nonjudgmental and Disaffiliated. "It's the squares who're iliated," she announced. "Yammering at what everything's all about." She studied her drink, then finished it. "We cats don't dig that, huh, Ricky-O? We know the answer."

"Sure as hell," said Eric.

"It's not *about* anything. It just is. It's there."

"Because it's there."

"That's Sartre."

"No."

"Camus? Kerouac?"

"Mallory."

"Who?"

"A cat called Mallory. He climbed mountains. He's dead."

"Because it's there. That's cool; I dig it." Thalia began to sing: *"It's there because it's there because it's . . ."*

For a while longer *she* was there. Then she wasn't. Two fags were there. Ten fags were there. Booze was there. It was the next night, the next week, the next month, and still it was there. It was in his mouth and throat and stomach; it was in his eyes and hair and toenails; it was in a glass on the bar, and behind the glass was Muffs the trumpeter, and Muffs said, "Hey, Ricky-O, you look shot to hell."

"No, I'm fine," said Ricky-O.

"The shit you are, man. Come with me; I got medicine."

Then the bar was gone. The john was there. He and Muffs

were there, a fix was there, and Muffs fixed the fix, fixed himself, and told Eric to roll up his sleeve. Eric rolled it, and the needle went in, and Eric jerked away. Then blood was there; a broken needle was there; a spilled syringe was there on the dirty tiles of the floor. Muffs was swearing, and Eric was running. His arm still bare and bleeding, he ran from the john into the main room of the Phriendly Phoenix. The bar was there, but he ran past it. The street door was there, and he ran through.

He returned to Squaresville. He drank coffee and Cokes. He sold pots and pans door to door in the San Joaquin Valley.

Then it was December. On the valley's eastern rim a band of white appeared against the winter sky, and swinging the wheel of his company car, he climbed up out of the valley toward the High Sierra. That evening he was in snow country. The next day he found a job as assistant ski instructor at a small resort called Pine Hill Lodge. And two days after that, before meeting his first class, he stood, for the first time in five years, at the top of a snow slope and pushed off for a practice run.

It was no Hermit Trail he was on—only an intermediate slope. And at first it seemed as if there had been no five years, for it was all familiar, routine, and he moved with balance and rhythm. For a time after his fall in Hong Kong he had suffered occasional headaches and dizziness, but these were long since gone. His broken arm and ankle had mended and were things of the past . . . Or so he had thought, until now, a third of the way down the run, the ankle began to ache and quiver . . . Stopping, he rested and flexed it. Then pushed off again. But as soon as he gained speed the pain and trembling returned; and when he shifted weight to his other foot, he overbalanced, sideslipped, almost fell. He would have to stop again, he thought. But he didn't stop. Either he could ski or he couldn't. And for ten seconds—fifteen—twenty—he did ski: not stemming and angling, but schussing straight down as fast as the slope would take him.

The aching swelled. The quivering became so violent that he thought it would shake the ski from his foot. But he held on; he managed. As long as it was straight down with no turns he *could* manage. But now he was approaching the foot of the slope; the lodge, the crowds around it, were rushing up at him; he had to turn, to slow and stop—if he could. In any case he had to try. And he did. And he couldn't. As he made his swing and the skis turned, the lateral strain was too much for the ankle, and no effort of will could hold it. The ankle buckled. He swayed and fell in a tangle of arms and legs, skis and poles. From the door of the nearby ski shop Pine Hill's senior instructor was watching him silently. A group of children who were to be his pupils were watching and laughing.

Eight miles down Route U.S. 40, near the town of Cisco, was the Big Bend Motel. For two days he was there as a paying guest; thereafter as clerk and general handyman.

It was an undemanding job. The proprietress, an elderly widow called Mrs. Nucker, was easygoing and absent-minded, and the guests, mostly one-nighters, checked in, paid their bills (usually), and were scarcely visible otherwise. Eric occupied a room in an older building behind the motel that had once been the Nucker farmhouse. Mrs. Nucker fed him. Two girls from Cisco appeared daily to work as motel chambermaids, and one of them, a small blonde named Charlayne, sometimes came to his room when her work was done. She was not a bright girl, and their talk was rudimentary. But she was better than fair in bed and, like his job, undemanding.

He did not drink. He walked a lot. (No ankle trouble there.) While the snow remained deep it was along the highway; later on forest trails; and once a week or so he went in to Cisco. There he borrowed books from the library or bought paperbacks at the drugstore. He read in his room. He read at the desk in the motel lobby. The choice of books in Cisco was not great, and he read what he could get. At the library it ranged from Dickens to Gertrude Atherton. At the drugstore it was Gardner and Spillane.

He did not buy newspapers. But sometimes guests left them and he looked at them. Not at HELP WANTED. At the news. One day he read in the *Chronicle* that an Italian expedition had climbed K2 in the Karakoram Himalayas, the second highest mountain in the world. But it did not send him out into the night to scale a peak of the Sierras. A while later there was a story in the Los Angeles *Times* that an American team had returned home after a near miss on Makalu, earth's fifth highest summit. The names of the team members (all of whom had returned) were listed, and most were familiar to him. One was more familiar than the others: Ken Naylor's.

He had lost track of Ken—as of everyone. He did not know if he was still with Cerro de Pasco, still based in Peru; or where, or what. One night, a few weeks later, he was seized with the desire, the need, to re-establish contact. He could write him in care of the American Alpine Club; not only could but would. At the desk in the motel office he put pen to paper and wrote *Dear Ken*—

Then stopped.

Dear Ken—what?

Dear Mrs. Howard—*Dear Jill Harben*—what?

There was another letter he might write, that he thought often of writing. To his mother. But he didn't write that either, for anything to her would have to go by way of his brother Frank.

No thanks, no Frank.

No Ken. No anyone.

He was as alone, as sealed off from the world, as when he had been high on the Wailing Wall of Dera Zor. More so; for then Julian Howard had been following him.

Summer passed. Autumn. It was winter again. Cars went by on Route 40 with skis on their roof racks, and sometimes their occupants stopped at the Big Bend for the night. But his only contact with them was to sign them in and take their money. He averaged perhaps five hours a day at the motel desk, another three or four at odd jobs. He walked. He read. For a year Charlayne had come to his room about once a week, but now she had left, and the woman who took her place was both middle-aged and married.

It was all right with him.

In the spring and early summer there were again newspaper reports of expeditions to the Himalayas. The British had climbed Kangchenjunga, the French Makalu (too bad for Ken & Co.), and several teams had been involved with slightly lesser ones in central Nepal. Obviously Nepal had opened up since the days when the only way to get in had been by invitation of the maharajah.

He thought increasingly of Nepal. Not of Dera Zor; he had at last closed that off in a deep pocket of his mind. Nor of the weeks, numbed with grief and arak, in the frowsy guesthouse in Kathmandu. He thought of Nepal's shining skies, its emerald valleys, its high horizon of the Great Himalayas, beside which the Sierras of California were the mountains of Lilliput. He thought of the Sherpas of Solu Khumbu: small, brown, laughing. He thought of Tashi. Tashi had not only saved his life—which was a doubtful service. During the dreadful days of the march back to Kathmandu he had been virtually his only companion. A wall of grief and guilt had stood, implacable, between him and his surviving teammates: Gil McLeod, Ted Lassiter, even Ken Naylor. But with Tashi it had been different. There had been no laughter then, of course, but there had been no wall either. No judgment and estrangement. In Kathmandu, before the Sherpas had left for their return trip to Solu Khumbu, Tashi's last words to him had been, "You come back, Rick Sah'b. You come back Dera Zor; we climb sonabitch together."

He had planned to write about the Sherpas. About Tashi. Even after the disaster, once in Calcutta, once in Hong Kong, he had tried to, but couldn't.

Could he now?

He tried again.

And no, he couldn't.

It was not a matter of the writing itself; of memories, events, images, and the words to evoke them. It was that in the heart, the core of him, he did not want to; did not even *want* to want to; to want anything. All his earlier life he had wanted too much, too strongly, blindly, and it had brought him in the end to the Wailing Wall of Dera Zor.

Now he did without wanting.

He did his job. He ate and slept. He walked and read. One autumn afternoon, when he had been at Big Bend almost two years, he was alone in the office reading Perry Mason, when a car pulled up outside, and a few moments later a woman opened the door. At first, with the light behind her, he could not see her features; just a woman's figure. Then she closed the door behind her, and it was his sister-in-law Kay.

She stopped when she saw him, and neither spoke. Then, as he rose, she came across the little room, stood before him, and raised a hand to his face.

"It is," she said. "*It is*. Oh Rick, it's you—"

He still could find no words.

"I really didn't believe it. I couldn't. But I had to find out."

He looked at her, uncomprehending.

"This isn't an accident," she said. "Do you remember a couple called Farnham?"

He shook his head.

"Bill and Sally Farnham; she's an old friend of mine. They stopped over here one night a few weeks ago on their way down from Tahoe. Somehow they heard your name, and she told me, and after all, there aren't so many Eric Venns.

"—So I came to see," Kay said.

Eric glanced at the door. "And Frank?" he asked.

"No, Frank's not here. I had to come north for a few days anyhow, so I drove up from San Francisco."

There was silence.

"I—I hope you don't mind," she said, almost shyly.

Mrs. Nucker came in then, and he introduced them. From his employer's expression, it was clear that Kay was not what she would have expected of the sister-in-law of her clerk-handyman; but she rose well to the occasion. "Take the rest of the day off," she told Eric. "I can mind the store."

He led Kay to his room in the old house behind the motel. She sat down in a chair by the window, and the slanting sunlight gleamed on her fresh skin and copper hair. She had changed little. Not as he had changed. But her green eyes that had so often smiled at him were not smiling now, as they searched his face.

"We tried to reach you, Rick," she said.

"Reach me?"

"We read in the papers about the expedition. Then later your friend Ken Naylor came to see us. I wrote you in Kathmandu, where he said you were staying, but the letter came back. Then afterward, when your mother died—"

"Died—"

"About three years ago. I'd have written you then too, if I'd known where you were."

Eric's eyes were on the window behind her. He was trying to visualize his mother as she might have been in her last years, but all he could see were trees, a hillside and the setting sun.

Kay spoke again softly. "I'm sorry, Rick."

"It doesn't—"

"I don't mean just about your mother. I mean my coming—out of nowhere—bringing back old things."

"That's all right," said Eric.

He sat down too, and looked at her, and yes, she was as young and lovely as ever. He wanted to say more, but no words came. In the old days she had been so easy to talk to; the easiest of anyone. But not now.

The best he could think of was "How's Frank?"

"Frank's fine, the same as always," she said; then smiled. "No, more so. Now he's executive vice president of Burden Industries."

"And the girls?"

"Fine too. Joyce is in sixth grade and crazy about horses. Sheila's in fifth and prefers mice."

There was a pause.

"Then there's Larry," she said.

"Larry?"

"Lawrence Burden Venn, aged not quite seven. Also known as Superboy."

"Like Daddy."

"No, not so much. He has his own ways. He's—"

Kay broke off, rose, and looked around the room. But there wasn't much to look at.

"You're the motel man in my life," she said. "Remember when

you stayed in La Quinta, down the hill from us in Santa Monica?"

Eric nodded.

"You were writing then."

"Trying to."

"Not now?"

"No."

"I'd been so much hoping—"

Again she broke off. She smiled. "There's another not-now too," she said. "This time I don't have brownies. But I bet we can find some nice martinis if we set our minds to it."

He had risen too, and she took his hand. She led him out of the house and around to the front of the motel, where her car, a Thunderbird, was parked. They got in, and she drove out to the highway and then asked, "Uphill or down?"

He thought.

"Up," he said.

And they drove the eight miles to Pine Hill Lodge. He had not been there since the day he had come and left, almost two years before. But it would be all right now, in autumn. The hills would be green, not white. There would be no skiers, just people. When they got there, as it turned out, there were not even many of those, and in the bar of the Lodge they were alone in a corner.

The martinis came, with rocks and twists, and his was his first since the last one with Kay. Meanwhile there had been an ocean of drinks: arak, Haig Pinch, pernod, rotgut, the gamut. Then no drinks. Now there was a martini again. Kay again. He tasted his, and it was better than arak.

"This is a ski place in winter?" Kay asked.

"Yes," he said.

"Are you here often?"

He shook his head. "I don't ski anymore."

"You just work at the motel?"

"Yes."

"For how long now?"

"Going on two years."

194

He sipped his drink. She sipped hers. Then her hand moved out across the table and came to rest on his.

"I'm not here to ask questions, Rick," she said. "Just to listen—if you want to talk. You used to like to talk to me, remember?"

For a long moment their eyes met. Kay said nothing more. Then he said:

"You read about the expedition."

"Yes."

"Ken came to see you."

"Yes."

"What more is there to tell?"

She was silent.

"I killed two men," he said. "I killed two friends."

"No, Rick, no! The mountain killed them."

"As a boy," he went on quietly, almost dispassionately, "I killed my sister Robin. As a man I killed Julian Howard and Franz Harben. I killed them because I was selfish. Because I wanted so much to climb a mountain that I thought of no one, nothing, but myself."

She started to speak but he stopped her. "What the papers told, what Ken told, doesn't matter," he said. "That's the way it was. That's the truth."

Kay protested no further. After a while she said, "Even if it is, Rick, aren't there other truths too?"

"Other?"

"That it's in the past now. That what happened happened. That you yourself still have a life to live."

He smiled thinly. "That's what I've been doing," he said.

"Where? How? Would you tell me about it?"

He looked into his glass. He drank from it. Then he began to tell her.

"First there was Kathmandu," he said. But he made that brief. He moved on to New Delhi, Calcutta, Palembang. After Palembang their glasses were empty; he ordered two more drinks; and perhaps it was the drinks—no, he thought, not the drinks, it was Kay—for still he talked on, while she listened, as he had not talked to anyone since their last time together. He told her of his year at sea, of Hong Kong and Victoria Peak, finally of his return to California and the devious route to the Big Bend Motel. And when he had finished she sat for a while as if still listening, and then she smiled and said, "Venn's Ventures—"

"To nowhere."

"No, to here. To now."

Their second drinks were gone, but they did not have a third. Going to the dining room, they again found a corner, and ordered, and Kay said, "Now tell me the important part."

He looked at her questioningly.

"We've had what's been. Now what's going to be?"

He was silent.

"You can't ski? Teach skiing?"

"No."

"But you can climb."

"I don't want to climb."

"That isn't true, Rick. It can't be. Time changes people, but not that much." Again her hand touched his. "You have to climb again," she said. "*You have to*. Don't you see that? No matter what happened, you can't turn your back on something that was your very life."

Suddenly, as she spoke, there was a shifting for him of time and place. He was no longer with his sister-in-law in the dining room of a lodge in the California Sierras, but back in the house on Desmond Street in Denver, and his father was saying to him, "You should get back to the mountains."

Now Kay said, "You cared so much. You had so much to give, to live for. You can't throw it all away."

"I lived one sort of life," he said. "Now I'm living another."

"No you're not. You're not living at all. You're trying to turn yourself into a vegetable." For the first time her voice changed. Not to loudness; it was still low. But it was tight and tense. It was pleading. "You've got to get out of here—out of that motel," she said. "You've got to breathe again, climb again."

Her eyes held his.

"And write again—"

"I've tried to write," he said. "I can't."

196

"The hell you can't. After everywhere you've been, all you've done." A brief smile broke through. "I've even given you a title for a book: *Venn's Ventures.*"

He did not smile back.

"You've done so much, Rick. Experienced so much." She paused. "Of all the places you've been, which did you like—no that's the wrong word—which meant the most to you? Which do you think of—dream of?"

Another pause.

"You haven't talked of Nepal, but Ken Naylor said you loved it. Not just the climbing, the mountains, but all of it. The land, the people. He said you loved the Sherpas."

Kay thought a moment.

"Then I remembered," she said, "how you had loved Nepal even before you went there. I remember now that book you had, that you carried everywhere; it was about Dera Zor, yes, but about Nepal too—about its towns, valleys, skies, horizons—and you loved them too; you wanted so much to know and possess them.

"The name of the book was *Trip*—no, *Trek to Nowhere.*" Her smile returned, then passed. "That's where you just said you are: nowhere. But not the right nowhere. Your nowhere's out there, Rick. It was then; it is now. It's where you belong."

Again there was a change. In her voice, her eyes.

"Do you have money?" she asked.

"Some."

"You can't earn much."

"More than I spend."

"I can give you money—lend it—invest it: as you like."

He shook his head.

"But whichever way, go. Please go. Start living again, Rick. Please—"

Their dinner had come and gone. They drank their coffee. Again time and place shifted, and they were no longer at Pine Hill Lodge but at another mountain inn called High Crest, three hundred miles to the south. Now he would order liqueurs, a cognac for him, a green mint for her, and then they would get in the car and drive down to a roadhouse, and there they would dance.

This time, no liqueurs. Down the road was the Big Bend Motel. He asked for the check, and when it came Kay looked at him questioningly; but he shook his head and paid it.

"Thanks. It was lovely," she said.

Then they went out, got into her car, and drove down the hill toward the motel.

"Will you stay over?" he asked. "There are plenty of rooms."

She shook her head. "I have to be in San Francisco early tomorrow. Then back home Thursday for Larry's birthday."

"Larry?"

Then he remembered.

"He'll be seven years old," Kay said.

"Seven—"

"On September twentieth."

The car lights shone on the pines and firs along the curving road. They had shone, too, on that other road leading from the roadhouse where they had danced, back to the High Crest Inn. But then it had been January, with the trees streaked and flecked with white. Now it was September and they were green and brown . . . September, seven years and nine months later.

He was no longer looking at trees but at Kay as she drove. Her eyes were on the road, her face in profile, dimly lit by the glow of the dashboard.

The face told him nothing.

Then he spoke her name.

"Yes?" she said.

"Is he—?"

She spoke very quietly. "It's possible, Rick."

She swung the wheel of the car.

"That's all I know," she said. "It's possible."

"You're not sure?"

"No. I was with Frank before and after."

"And"—he groped—"and the doctor, later—what did he say?"

"I didn't tell the doctor. I've told no one." Kay paused. "I didn't mean to tell you either. Just that there *was* a Larry: I somehow

198

had to do that. But then the birthday came out and—well—there we are."

She swung the wheel again, slowed for a dip, resumed speed.

"Does he know about me?" Eric asked.

"Know—?"

"That I exist?"

"Yes, he knows he has an uncle. He calls you Uncle Gone."

"Are you going to tell him you've seen me?"

Kay thought. "I don't think so. If I do, Frank of course will find out too, and I don't think I want that. Frank and I don't exactly agree when we talk about you."

"I'll still be Uncle Gone."

"For a while, yes."

The lights of the Big Bend Motel appeared ahead, and she drove to its entrance and stopped. Then she turned to him.

"But not the same kind of gone, Rick. Please . . . I don't mean you should write—unless you want to. I mean, think of what I've said; don't reject it. Don't go on through your life rejecting yourself."

It was lighter in the car now. The neon motel sign glowed through the windshield, and he could see her face, her eyes. It was not easy to look into her eyes. He opened the car door.

"Will you stop off for a bit?"

She shook her head. "No, I'll keep going." Again her hand sought his. "Goodbye, Rick."

"Goodbye . . . And thanks."

He started to get out of the car, but her hand held him.

"Rick—"

"Yes?"

"Kiss me."

He hesitated.

"Do you want to?"

"Yes," he said.

Then he kissed her; at first gently, then less gently; not with force or passion, but with something deeper than passion. He held her close, and she held him, and for long moments that was all there was, the kiss, the holding. Then it was over, done; they had moved apart; her hands were back on the wheel, and he got out of the car and closed the door, and she drove away.

A week later he received a letter, the first in his almost two years at Big Bend. It contained a check for two thousand dollars and a scrap of paper with one word: *Please—*

He returned the check, explaining that he had saved almost that much during his time at Big Bend.

The next week came a second letter. *All right, do it yourself,* it said. *But please—*

The week after that there was a third one that read:

Please—

I am going to do this every week, until a letter comes back undelivered like the one to Kathmandu.

The next two letters contained the one word: *Please—*

It was late autumn now, and the first snows showed on the ridge lines of the Sierras. On the day when the first skiers stopped off at Big Bend he gave his notice to Mrs. Nucker. A few days later he withdrew his savings from the bank in Cisco. The day after the new clerk-handyman had arrived, before going again to Cisco to catch the San Francisco bus, he said goodbye to Mrs. Nucker and asked her to return to the sender a letter that would arrive for him the next week.

"I can send it to you," she said, "if you'll give me an address."

"No, return it to the sender," he told her.

"It's important," he added.

He was sitting, resting again, sucking the thin night air into his laboring lungs. He had found a rounded hollow in the high snow cone of Dera Zor and, perched in it, looked down toward the bivouac above the Wailing Wall, from which his three companions would soon be coming:

Tashi, Pembol, Larry. Alias Lawrence Burden Venn . . .

14

Larry . . . Kay . . .

They faded. They were in the past. The future.

Again a door had closed. Another opened. Beyond it lay the land of Nepal, and he walked the land under shining skies.

It was not to the east that he went; not toward Solu Khumbu and Dera Zor. He walked through the central Valley of Nepal and the low ranges around it: along the age-old trails, past towns and temples, skirting the flat pale green of rice paddies and the steep emerald green of terraced hills. Beyond the hills, always, there were higher hills; beyond these, mountains. When he was in the trough of a valley, the mountains vanished and there was only greenness. As he climbed a ridge they reappeared, gleaming in a white wave against the northern sky.

He turned to the north. And the valleys narrowed, the ridges steepened. The trail led down, down, and at each final down was a rushing stream, a spidery bridge. It led up, up, and at the utmost up there were the mountains again, but closer now, and a thin wind blowing from the Himalayan snowfields.

He was not alone on the trails. Each day he had with him two or three porters, whom he picked up at one village and dropped at another. Nor were he-plus-porters alone; for they were traveling the turnpikes and Main Streets of rural Nepal, and along them, from dawn to dusk, moved other processions of travelers. There were no beasts of burden; each man was his own; and on and on they went, up and down, down and up, backs deeply bent beneath the weight of loads, faces thrust forward, straining, against the pull of headstraps. Usually, on the way south, it was produce that was carried; on the way north, the manufactured goods of Kathmandu and the world beyond. But now and then there came bearers of special burdens. A wedding party passed: the bride, in crimson sari, riding a palanquin borne by four men: behind her the groom, attendants, and a band of horn, drum and cymbals. Another day it was a funeral: the body wrapped in a sheet hung from a long wooden pole, the mourners following, and behind the mourners, again, a band, but bigger, louder, gayer than the band for the wedding.

For the outlander passing among them, there were stares, there were smiles, sometimes both together. In the evenings, in villages or wayside shelters, the stares could become unsettling, but a gift of cigarettes or bits of chocolate would usually dissolve them into smiles. Once the price was higher. At a Government checkpost outside a village he was stopped and asked for his permit to travel beyond Kathmandu. Having none, he was told he must turn back, but in the end twenty rupees proved an acceptable substitute.

As he went north, the land changed. It grew wilder, steeper; the trail snaked its way above sheer cliffs and roaring torrents, and ahead the snow peaks of the Langtang Himal shut out half the sky. He was close to Tibet now, and as the land changed so did the people. In the lowlands most had been Indo-Nepalese: slim of body, soft in feature, dressed in the ragtag cotton clothing of the semitropics. Here the faces were Mongoloid; bodies were broad and sturdy, clad in thick homespun wool, and feet were shod with boots of yak hide. Along the trail, Hindu temples and shrines were gone, and in their place were Buddhist chortens and sacred mani walls. Many travelers now held prayer wheels in their hands, and on the heights were prayer flags streaming against the sky.

"It is a magical world, a secret world," Eric Venn had once written in his diary. "Someday I may learn a few of its secrets."

203

He had not learned any yet. But now that did not matter. He had plenty of time.

He veered off from the trail that led on to Tibet and traversed the southern rim of the Langtang. Here man was gone altogether, except for a few scattered herders and their grazing yaks. High meadows gleamed with primula and gentian. Then the meadows were gone; he walked through forests, and in the dimness was the glow of orchid and rhododendron. When the forest fell away there was a white glare as of an explosion. There was the Langtang again, its snows afire under the mountain sun.

He did not climb up into the mountains. He was content to see, to contemplate . . . as he had once done on a hill in Seattle, gazing out across the miles at Mount Rainier. And yes, he could look again at mountains. He could bear it. Moving on westward, he came to still greater ones: to Dhaulagiri, the Annapurnas, the horn of Machupuchare cleaving the sky. In the valleys to the south he passed through Gurkha country. He coud now distinguish the peoples of Nepal, one from another: the Gurkhas, Sherpas, Tamangs, Newari. He swung back into the Valley of Nepal, and now he knew the roads, the lanes, the streams, the bridges.

Out from Kathmandu were the two ancient towns of Bhadgaon and Patan, and he walked through their squares and alleys, past pagodas, temples, bazaars. In the city's outskirts there was now a primitive airstrip; he himself had arrived there on a flight from India two months before. He passed it. He entered the city. Six years ago he had walked the streets of Kathmandu, but blindly, unperceiving. Now he saw them. He sat for hours in its broad sunlit maidan. He threaded its warrens. Here the bazaars were vast, the pagodas tall; in the crowds he was a speck, a midge, journeying through miles, through centuries. The colors, the sounds, the stenches of time enveloped him. Lean pi-dogs followed him, monkeys scampered, an elephant lumbered past. Following the Bagmati River, high feeder of the Ganges, he came to the holy Hindu temple of Pashupatinath. On hills beyond he climbed to the Buddhist shrines of Bodhnath and Swayambunath. The prayer wheels turned. The long flags fluttered. From tall towers the painted eyes of Buddha asked, "Who are you? Why are you here? Where are you going?"

He knew where he was going.

In the heart of the city he came to the Government guesthouse but did not go in. With the new planes had come tourists, with the tourists, hotels; there were now three of them in Kathmandu —the Royal, Snowview and Himalayan Palace. He passed the first two and came to the Palace. He entered his room, dropped his pack, and presently Amy Bulwinkle appeared with a bottle of Haig Pinch-bottle scotch.

"I keep my promises," she said.

The Himalayan Palace *was* a palace. Or had been. Until a few years before it had served as residence of a branch of the vast and potent family called the Ranas, who for more than a century had ruled Nepal. Throughout, there had been a king, but a powerless one, with the Ranas in charge. Julian Howard's hunting friend had been a Rana, the top one, with the title of both maharajah and prime minister, and he and his multitudinous kinsmen had virtually owned the country outright. On its gates, in effect, had been a sign, PRIVATE PROPERTY, KEEP OUT. It had been only for an occasional Julian Howard that the bars had been lowered.

Then change had come. In the same year as the expedition to Dera Zor, the puppet king, Tribhuvan, had fled to India; the Indians had taken up his cause; and presently he was back in Nepal, a king in power, with the Ranas deposed. Soon after, he died, but his son Mahendra, as new king, held the power. Now it was the Ranas—some of them—who left the country. Others stayed on, but with clipped wings. One who stayed was Osmun Shumsher Jung Bahadur Rana, aged seventy-plus, elder cousin to the late prime minister and proprietor-of-sorts of what had once been his private home and was now the Himalayan Palace Hotel. The proprietor-in-fact was Amy Bulwinkle—at the price of an occasional night (when he felt up to it) in the bed of O.S.J.B. Rana.

And her husband Cecil? Old Cess, quondam ghost of the Government guesthouse?

"He's gone," she told Eric.

"Gone?"

"Dead. He used to pass out every night, remember? One night he stayed out . . . Poor slob," she added.

"Then you moved here?"

"Two years ago. That old fleabag gave me the meemies. This is a fleabag too, of course—the whole country's a fleabag—but at least the fleas are higher class."

Her name for O.S.J.B. Rana was "Gramps," and he had apparently been in the picture for some time. "When the king thing happened," she said, "Gramps, like the rest of his outfit, had to take his paw out of the till. He still kept this place, though, and with tourists starting to come in I told him he should turn it into a hotel. He said O.K., if I'd run it. I said O.K. by me. He wanted his little price of course, but that's O.K. too and no sweat. If Gramps gets it up once a month he thinks he's going great."

O.S.J.B.R. was seldom to be seen. With three wives and assorted hangers-on he occupied an upstairs wing of the sprawling building, and the rest was Amy Bulwinkle's domain. It was big, ornate and strictly non-Nepalese: a Rana version of a ducal villa on Lake Como or the Grande Corniche. It had galleries, terraces, curved stairways, frescoed ceilings, and acres of brown paintings in vast gilded frames. It also had peeling paint, cracked windows, spavined beds, nonlightable lamp bulbs, nonflushable toilets. It had—Amy was right—fleas. It had ants, roaches, mice, rats and lizards, and, for their convenience, small bored holes in the bedroom ceilings designed for the passage of good and evil spirits.

"Which way the spirits go I'm still working on," said Amy. "But the beasties just go one way, and it sure as hell isn't out."

If her setting had changed, she herself was much the same as before. Big of breast and buttock, she still wore tight skirts and low-cut blouses, and her blond hair, blonder than before, was almost platinum. ("Gramps likes it that way.") Her dark eyes were as alive as ever, her mouth as big and red, and often grinning—when it was not wide open shouting for nonvisible, nonserving servants.

"I'm a slob at heart, baby," she told Eric. "As bad as old Cess. But if I didn't keep after these jerks the place would fold in a week."

On the day of his arrival she had come with her Haig Pinch to his room. But the Palace, unlike the guesthouse, had a bar, and thereafter most of their encounters were there. When other guests were present she was professional and circumspect, making the drinks but drinking little herself. Then, as it grew late and the place cleared out, she got to work on her own.

Eric took only one drink to her two or three.

"So what's wrong?" she asked him.

"Nothing."

"Maybe you don't like Pinch?" She grinned. "I still got arak too," she said.

"No—thanks."

"There've been some changes, huh?"

She looked at him curiously, but, as before, she asked no questions. He might have been gone a week, not years. But one night she brought two objects into the bar with her and put them before him. "I kept these for you," she said.

One object was a book: Bigelow's *Trek to Nowhere*. The other was Bigelow's scout knife that he had found on the Kalpurtha Glacier.

"They're just junk," said Amy. "I guess you left them on purpose, but I kept them."

He did not open the book or touch the knife, but left them lying on the bar while he finished his drink. When his glass was empty Amy refilled it, along with her own, and later, at intervals, she refilled them again.

"That's more like it, baby," she said.

As he tramped the land of Nepal the sun had shone in splendor. Now it withdrew, clouds came from the south, and the first monsoon rains fell on Kathmandu. The ranks of tourists thinned out. From north, east and west mountaineering expeditions marched in, their ventures over, and flew off to their homelands. This year there were no American parties. There were British, French,

Swiss, Austrian, and though some of the members' names were familiar to Eric, he did not know them. The French and Austrians stayed briefly at the Palace in orgies of eating, sleeping, bathing, demobilizing. But he met them only casually, and his role was a tourist's.

Then one day he was in town, in the old bazaar. Around him were the now familiar colors, sounds, stenches, the familiar crowds —Hindu and Buddhist, Newari, Tamang, Gurkha, Tibetan—and then from out of the crowd, out of nowhere, suddenly, a known face, a monkey face, brown and wizened. There was a shout, a small figure running, a tight embrace, and he was looking down into the bright eyes of the Sherpa Tashi.

"Rick Sah'b! Rick Sah'b!" said Tashi over and over. And Eric too, at first, could find no other word, no action, but to speak the Sherpa's name and hold him close.

Then they were walking together. They came to the Palace and went in and had beers and a meal. And Tashi talked. His English was better now. In six years he had been on six expeditions, three of them British or American—"and each time, Rick Sah'b," he said, "I hear, I learn" . . . He had been to Makalu with Ken Naylor, and the next year with the French. He had been to Everest with the British—"yes, to South Col, still more higher. If no Tenzing there, is me who go with Hillary to top." Now, in this early summer, he was just back with a Swiss group from Dhaulagiri, and the next day was heading off for Solu Khumbu to his wife and yaks and new potato crop.

"Is fine mountain, Dhaulagiri," Tashi said, "and the Swiss they climb good. But still more, Rick Sah'b, I like be with you on our Dera Zor."

Eric was silent.

"You come now from Dera Zor?" asked Tashi.

"No," Eric said.

"What mountain, then?"

"No mountain. I took a walking tour in the spring. Now I'm here in Kathmandu."

"You do not climb at all, when in the spring is time for climbing?" Tashi shook his head, uncomprehending. Then he brightened. "But next year yes, Rick Sah'b? Next year you have again expedition. You go again Dera Zor, and I go with, and you and I we climb to top."

Again Eric said nothing.

"Of all mountains I know," said Tashi, "Dera Zor is greatest, finest. Is more fine than Everest—more steep, more beautiful—but other climbers they do not know it. Is hidden; is our secret. Next year we go back, we climb. I climb more better now, can climb Wailing Wall. You, me, we climb it, big sonabitch. With you, Rick Sah'b, can climb anything. Many climbers I have gone with— American, English, Français, Schweiz, I go with all—but you are best. You try most, want most." Tashi paused and tapped his chest. "Me, I want too, Rick Sah'b," he said. "With you. *With you* . . ."

From the Palace they walked back through the town to the old streets, the bazaar, the Government guesthouse, where Tashi was staying. And there they said goodbye.

"Next year you come. Yes, please, you come, we climb," he said.

They embraced. He grinned. He was gone.

Eric walked back to the Palace and into the bar, and there was Amy behind it. She brought out her bottle of Pinch and poured a drink, and as the hours passed she poured others.

For some time thereafter he did not go to the bar. Except at mealtimes, he stayed in his room and wrote. Using pencil and yellow paper, then transcribing on the hotel's one vintage typewriter, he wrote the story of his Nepalese walking tour, titled it "Skylines," and sent it airmail to the *Saturday Evening Post*. Six years before, the *Post* had paid him a fifteen-hundred-dollar advance for the story of Dera Zor he had never written; but he did not mention that, and hoped they wouldn't either. Perhaps by now they had forgotten—or there were new editors.

He wrote a piece on Kathmandu, called it "Kathmopolis," and sent it to the *Atlantic Monthly*.

He wrote a piece about Tashi—called "Tashi"—and sent it to *Esquire*.

A month passed.

Another.

He began work on a book, a novel about a man like his father; wrote two chapters, destroyed them, began again.

Then his script came back from the *Post*. There was no mention of the fifteen-hundred-dollar advance. Simply a rejection slip.

The script came back from the *Atlantic*. An accompanying note said, "There is much good observation and writing here, but unfortunately it does not fit in with our present editorial needs."

From *Esquire*, he did not hear at all.

He sent "Skylines" to *Collier's* and "Kathmopolis" to *Harper's*. The young Nepalese bearer Amar, who cleaned his room, threw out the first fifty-seven handwritten pages of his novel. Leaving the room, he walked down the hotel's long corridors to the bar, and Amy Bulwinkle said, "Well, whaddya know, the ghost walks!"

She brought out the Haig Pinch, but he shook his head.

"No, arak," he said.

"Arak?"

"I can't afford whisky."

"Afford? Who's paying?"

"That's the point—"

"You're not. I'm not. Gramps is. He can afford it."

"It's not just drinks," said Eric. "I haven't paid you anything in two months."

Amy shrugged. "No sweat, baby."

"I will, soon."

"Soon schmoon: there's no such word in this man's country. Besides, you're my pet welfare case."

She started to pour the scotch, but he stopped her.

"Arak," he said. "Straight rotgut arak."

She studied him, then shrugged again and from beneath the bar produced what once had been a gallon jug of detergent.

"Like the old days," she said.

"Like the old days."

She poured out two tumblers neat.

"I haven't had one of these since hell-and-gone," she said. "But don't say I'm not chummy."

They drank.

"Jesus!" she said.

But she poured two more.

"If you can take it," she said, "so can I."

The only American Government enterprise in Nepal was a branch of AID, and the man in charge was an agronomist from South Dakota named Eklund.

"The main thing we're doing here," said Eklund, "is trying to teach the farmers new methods, and for that, of course, you have to *know* the methods. We've got a few men in Nepalese Government bureaus; they're auditors, CPAs. And a few building bridges; they're engineers. Besides, I'm not authorized to hire any U.S. citizens. They're all sent from the States."

The director for the International Red Cross was a Swiss named Kurtl.

"Our vork," said Kurtl, "is mostly wiz ze Tibetan refugees from Communist China, and zere are only four of us, all Sviss, here in Nepal. Ve could use more, of course, but any furzer appointment vould have to come from Geneva."

The head of the mission hospital in the outskirts of Kathmandu was Dr. Lakeford, an Englishman.

"The Lord knows," said the doctor, "we need everything here. Doctors, nurses, technicians. You've had no laboratory experience, I suppose?" He spread his hands. "In any case, we have no funds for hiring."

Principal of St. Joseph's Academy, the only English language school in Nepal, was a Jesuit, Father Mulcahy, once of Chicago.

"From the outside," said Father Mulcahy, "there are only two other priests and myself. The rest of the staff are young Nepalese whom we train as they teach. From the home diocese we get barely enough to feed and house them."

In the monsoon rains Eric walked the streets. Beyond the city he walked through wet emerald meadows. He came again to the

Buddhist shrines of Bodhnath and Swayambunath, and the eyes of Buddha asked, "What now?" He came to the Hindu temple of Pashupatinath and watched the pilgrims, the Brahmin priests, the untouchable bearers and sweepers.

He was learning something about untouchables.

Back in his room he sat again at a table and re-began the novel about the man who was like his father. This time he got to the fifth chapter. But now it was time for the man to get married, and if it was to be to a woman like his mother, he, Eric could not write it.

He put the novel away. Bringing out the handwritten draft of his story about Tashi that he had sent to *Esquire*, he retyped it and sent it to *True*.

He stood at the window.

From the window, when he had first come to the Himalayan Palace, he had been able to see past the city, past the fields and hills beyond, to the wave of white mountains that gleamed in the north. Now there were no mountains. There was mist and rain. There was an old man in rags picking through the hotel garbage.

He went down the halls to the bar, and there was Amy.

He pushed back the cuff of his gauntlet to see his watch, and it was past four o'clock. He looked at the sky, and it was still black. But it would not be black much longer.

He looked down the long slope of snow toward the snow-hole bivouac at its foot. Soon the others would be coming. He would see movement.

But there was no movement yet. There was only Amy behind the bar. And Amy said, "No sweat, baby. No sweat at all."

15

Fall came. The rains stopped. Tourists returned—but not enough to satisfy Amy. Too many, she said, were going to the Royal Hotel, run by Kathmandu's celebrated White Russian, Boris Lissanevitch.

"He's got more fleas than here. Worse food. More ceilings falling down. But the travel agents he's got trussed up like chickens. Russian grand dukavitch, they tell the customers: once of the Whosis Ballet, toast of Paris, outhoofed Nijinsky. And they run to his dump like it was the Taj Mahal."

"He's not the only dancer around," said Eric. "So were you."

She eyed him curiously.

"What makes you think that?"

"I worked at the Palm Club in Calcutta."

"Hmm. You got around."

She had said no more then. But later, in bits and pieces, her *curriculum vitae* emerged. Born in the small-town Midwest, she had left home in her teens, gone to Chicago, and found work in nightclubs. Later there had been other cities, other clubs, too many to count, leading up—or down—to Los Angeles. There she had of course made a bid for the movies, but with no luck ("lots of couches," she said, "but no cameras"); only more nightclubs, a few roadshows, finally a job with a troupe that was going to Australia. In Sydney she had met Cecil Bulwinkle, half dancer himself, half manager-promoter. They had danced together, lived together, got married. "Cess was always full of bullshit," she said.

"Almost as full as of booze. Any minute, for two years, we were gonna take off for London, Paris, New York, and knock 'em all dead; but when finally we went that wasn't quite it." They had gone to Singapore, Manila, Saigon. They had gone to Calcutta and Scoreby's Palm Club. "And if you worked for Scoreby," she said, "you know the rest."

Eric nodded.

"On to Endsville," said Amy.

"For how long now?"

She counted. "Ten years."

"Without ever leaving?"

"Leaving—ha!"

"You haven't wanted to?"

She looked at him levelly. "You know damn well I've wanted to. I asked you to take me."

"You picked the wrong man, the wrong time. You might as well have asked a corpse."

"That's what I seem to go for," she said. "The Widow Bulwinkle—"

The tourists were mostly middle-aged or older. There were more women than men. They asked:

"Can you see Mount Everest?"

"Can you see the Matterhorn?"

"What about the Abominable Snowman?"

"We call him the yeti here," said Eric. "He takes care of the plumbing and electricity."

That was after some araks. (He was staying with arak.) In the daytime, sans drinks, he fielded questions too, and presently found himself back in his old Hong Kong profession of guide. He took guests at the Himalayan Palace on tours of Kathmandu, Bhadgaon, Patan. He led them through the alleys, bazaars, shrines, temples; showed them beggars and pilgrims, bathing ghats and prayer wheels. He threaded the maze of carved walls, gates and doorways: to the eyes of Buddha, the myriad-visaged Krishna, the elephant god Ganesh, the monkey god Hanuman. With Mr.

215

and Mrs. Virgil Houck of Muncie, Indiana, he stood before an ancient but well-preserved frieze in which an acrobatic god and goddess demonstrated fifteen classic positions for sexual intercourse . . . until Mrs. Houck, through rigid lips, said, "Take us to the hotel, please," and they returned to the Palace in stony silence.

The next day, while she shopped, Mr. Houck asked to go back ("that was sort of quick yesterday") and paid Eric fifty rupees. Some paid more, some less. When he had accumulated the equivalent of about a hundred dollars he gave it to Ashkar, the Palace cashier (who also doubled as day clerk, night clerk, complaint receiver and head roach hunter). And that night, when he entered the bar, Amy said, "Well, it's Solvent Sam, the big lingam-and-yoni man—"

He set down a glass of arak, untouched. He left the bar and again, for several weeks, did not go back. By day he met his hotel expenses by guiding. At night, in his room, he wrote. He had again taken out the novel about the man who was like his father (before finishing he would have to read up on dentistry) (where?) and this time forced himself to face the woman who was like his mother. When the time came, he would face Frank, Robin. Yes, even Robin. "I love you, Ricky." Then the spinning pigtails . . . His three short pieces—"Skylines," "Kathmopolis," "Tashi"— came back from *Collier's, Harper's, True*. And he wondered why. Years before—before Dera Zor—he had written and sold. Again why? He had been little more than a boy then, but a boy on the crest, with wings. He had been mountaineer, skier, writer. He had had momentum, power.

And now?

He did not send the pieces off again. It was not selling that mattered, but the writing itself. And he wrote. Partly, he knew, it was a confrontation, an exorcising of old ghosts. (Perhaps the day would come when he could even face Julian Howard.) But even more it was a matter of simply writing. Of—functioning. He had been skier and mountaineer, but now no longer. What was left was writer. (Perhaps.) What was left, beyond that, was the bar of the Himalayan Palace. And whisky and arak.

And Amy.

He did not think of Amy.

He thought of Kay.

"You must write," Kay had said.

He was writing.

"And climb," she had said.

He pushed the thought away.

"Larry will be seven years old," she had said, "on September twentieth."

He pushed that away too.

There was to be a party—a party for Osmun Shumsher Jung Bahadur Rana on his seventy-second birthday—and Amy asked him to tend bar.

"Me, I've got to be Queen of the May," she said. "You know, li'l ole Perle Mesta of Slobsville, and no one else knows how to make a drink."

Eric hesitated, then agreed.

"But just make 'em," she added. "Don't drink 'em."

"I haven't been drinking," he told her.

"I know that. That's why I'm telling you. When you fall off that wagon it's gonna be with a crunch."

From somewhere she produced a mildewed red jacket with brass buttons. He found a white shirt. He shaved. And on the designated evening he stepped behind a bar for the first time since at the Phriendly Phoenix in North Beach, San Francisco. Here, however, there were no beats, no Thalia the Existentialist or Muffs the Mainliner. There was O.S.J.B. Rana, white-maned and cadaverous, in long black coat and tight white jodhpurs, who sipped dry sherry. There were his three wives, thin and silent, who sipped lemon squash. There were other Ranas and semi-Ranas, Government officials, hotel guests—about eighty in all. Cocktails were served before dinner, wine during it, and liqueurs after, while a three-piece ensemble of horn, drum, and sitar

217

played music for dancing. But no one drank much—except a tourist named Mr. Sutherland ("call me Jock") from Ridgewood, New Jersey, whose wife soon got him off to bed. The dancing was sedate. By midnight Eric was back in his room, working on Chapter Eight of the novel.

Then the door opened. Amy came in.

"Jesus, that's over!" she said.

She was wearing the same clothes she had at the party—her usual low-cut blouse (sort of magenta) and short tight skirt (this one black)—but she had taken off her shoes, and her mop of platinum hair was rumpled.

"I thought this would be one of your nights with Gramps," said Eric.

"It was. I go up to his pad, and he says, 'My ranee,' and messes my hair. Then he says, 'Excuse it, please,' goes to the john, comes back and falls asleep."

Amy set down the bottle of Pinch she was carrying. "Jesus!" she said again. Then, brightening: "You were a good boy tonight. I was a good girl. I've brought our reward."

Going to the washbasin in the corner, she took his toothbrush from a glass and looked for another.

"That's it," Eric said.

"What a dump. I'd complain to the management." She brought the one glass back. "Well, cozy-like then." She filled it full of whisky and half-emptied it at one draft. "Now you," she said, handing it over.

He held it.

"Come on," she said.

He sipped.

"*Come on!*"

He drank it down.

"That's better, baby."

She refilled the glass, drank, and looked around the room. There was only one chair, and he was in it, and she sat down on the bed. She looked at him over her glass, handed it to him, and looked at the papers spread on the table.

"You're really some kind of nut, aren't you, baby?" she said.

218

"Some kind," he agreed.

"This stuff you're doing. Half the day, every night, all alone."

"I'm writing."

"What for?"

"I'm a writer."

"I thought you were a mountain climber."

"I was once. No more."

"That shows some sense, anyhow. But this—" She had taken the glass back from him and now waved it at the table. "Do you *do* something with it?"

"Sometimes."

"Do you sell it?"

"No."

"Then for Christ's sake lay off it, baby. Why bug yourself, beat yourself?"

"Because I have to, I guess."

"Have to?"

"For you," said Eric, "hasn't there ever been anything for you that you *had* to do?"

"Like what?"

"Like dancing."

She thought it over. She took a drink.

"That was the hell-and-gone," she said. "I haven't danced in ninety years."

"You danced tonight."

"Tonight? Ha! You call that dancing? Doing the dead march with Gramps and those other zombies." She took another drink, re-refilled the glass and passed it to Eric. "When I say dancing, baby, I mean *dancing*. Old Scoreby must of told you. When li'l ol Amy danced, it was with pizazz."

She slapped her knees.

> "—yeah, piz*azz*, piz*azz*,
> piz*azz* and razma*tazz*—
> 'cause that's what she *has*,
> that old razma*tazz*—"

The words came in rhythm. Then there were no words, only rhythm, as her hands slapped knees and thighs, faster now, harder, and her bare feet slapped the floor. Abruptly she jumped up. She was dancing. She was dancing with feet and legs, with arms and body. She spun and weaved, whirled and kicked, and the kick caught against her short, tight skirt and almost upended her.

"Damn!" she said.

She kicked again.

"Goddamn!"

With a quick movement she unhooked the skirt, stepped out of it and flung it in a corner. Her thighs were white and strong, a dancer's thighs, topped by black panties. And now, with legs free, she kicked higher.

"Yeah, man!" she cried.

Still higher.

"*Yeah—man—*"

Her red lips grinned. Then stopped grinning. Her face changed, and her body. She had been moving faster, faster . . . but now no longer . . . now it was slower, slower. She no longer danced with her feet—her feet barely moved—but with her thighs, her hips, her belly, her shoulders. Her white shoulders twisted, jerked. They were out of her blouse. Then all of her was out of it. It was in the corner with her skirt, and there had been nothing beneath it. She was bare to the hips, to the waist; her breasts were bare; and they were big but firm, they were firm, white, tipped with rosy pink, as still she danced slowly around the small sleazy room.

Now she smiled again. But the smile was different, slower.

"All right for an old widow woman?" she asked.

She danced closer to Eric. She took his hands, pulled him up.

"Ten easy lessons," she said, "from Madame Pizazz."

Then the two were dancing. Or rather, she was still dancing, with him close against her, and she was holding him and he was holding her. He felt the flesh of her back; he felt her breasts, her belly, her thighs tight against him; and they were moving slowly, in rhythm . . . then less slowly (or so it seemed) . . . not slowly at all but now swiftly, wildly . . . and then they seemed to be spinning, the room and his head were spinning . . . and then (another change) no longer spinning, no longer dancing, but on the bed, locked tight, entangled . . .

Still her body moved. Her hands moved. For a while the only sound was her breathing.

Then she said, "What gives, baby?"

He didn't answer.

"What's wrong, baby?"

There was another silence.

"Look, Amy—" he said.

"Amy baby."

"Look, Amy—"

"I don't want to look," she said. "You know what I want."

"Yes."

"Well?"

"I can't," he said.

"Can't?"

"It's—no good—that's all—"

"No good for who?"

"For us. For me."

He disentangled himself and sat up on the bed. She lay looking up at him, her eyes dark and angry.

"I'm sorry," he told her.

"Sorry—ha!"

"Really."

"Ha!"

Now it was she who rose, thrusting herself up and off the bed. Going to the corner where she had thrown her skirt and blouse, she picked them up and jerked them on. She went to the door, then turned back to him.

"A fine lot of nothing I picked out," she said.

He sat with elbows on knees and eyes on the floor.

"Did you hear me?" she said.

"Yes, I heard you."

"Well?"

"You're right," he said. "That's what I am."

"The big lingam-and-yoni man—"

She laughed harshly, and he bent his head into his hands. After a few moments he heard her move again and thought she was leaving, but when he looked up she was still there, watching him.

"You're spooked, aren't you?" she said.

Her voice had changed. It was no longer harsh.

"Real spooked, I mean. Like with screaming meemies, without the screams."

She came across the room and stood before him. "Is it still that damn mountain?" she asked. "If it is, forget it; that's the hell-and-gone. Or if it's something since, forget that too. It's gone, finished. You're here now. Right here in Room 42, Himalayan Palace Hotel, Endsville, Nepal, Amy Bulwinkle prop."

She sat down beside him.

"And the prop's here too," she said.

Eric looked at the floor.

"I've had a thing about you from the beginning. You damn well know that," she said. "When you were here before, in the old dump, I tried to help you. I think I *did* help you . . . Didn't I?"

"Yes," he said.

"So why can't I now? Why don't you take what I have to give?"

She put her hand on his, and he raised his eyes. It was a while before he spoke. Then he said: "You can't just take if you can't give back too."

"So—why can't you?"

"Because—" He thought about it. "Because," he said, "I don't know what's left of me, but whatever it is I've got to hang on to it."

She looked at him for a moment. "What the hell are you talking about?" she asked.

"About us, I guess."

"What about us?"

He thought again.

"Shall I tell you the truth?" he said.

"Yes."

"I'm afraid of you."

"Afraid?"

"Of what will happen to me, to what's left of me, if we get—involved."

"If we—" Her eyes were still fixed on him, and the eyes were changing. Her anger returned and she jerked her hand away. "Oh, for Chrissake!" she said.

"I mean—"

"You mean I'm an old bag, is that it? That I'll give you the clap or something?" She leapt to her feet again. "Why you jerk! You crummy impotent sonofabitching jerk! . . . You get out of this hotel, you hear me? I'm sending Ashkar in here at the crack of dawn to put you out—out! You jerk, you punk, you mountain-climbing pansy—"

Wheeling, she swept his papers from the table and kicked at them as they fell. Seizing the bottle of Haig Pinch, she made for the door, then suddenly turned and threw it. It sailed past his head, shattered against a wall, and fell in shards of glass and gobbets of whisky onto the bare floor.

Then she was gone. From the next room came a woman's voice crying, "Henry, Henry, wake up! It's the Abominable Snowman!"

Ashkar did not appear at the crack of dawn. He did not appear during the morning. In the afternoon, by appointment, Eric took two elderly ladies sightseeing, then ate supper alone at the Government guesthouse. When he returned to his room at the Palace nothing had been touched.

Later, however, when he was at work at his table, there was a knock at the door and Ashkar came in. With him was a boy of perhaps fifteen, slim of build, fine of feature, with the dark liquid eyes of a Newari.

"This is Babul," said Ashkar. "He is nice and clean, and also experienced." Then, with a little bow, he left.

The boy looked at Eric, and Eric looked at the boy. Then the boy said in Nepalese, "I shall make ready, sahib."

Moving swiftly and gracefully, he went to a corner and, with back turned, stripped down to a cotton loincloth. Then, at the basin, he washed his face and body and dried himself with a towel.

223

When he had finished he turned and asked, "Shall I dance, sahib?"

"No, I think not," said Eric.

"You would like a massage?"

"No, thanks."

The boy seemed perplexed. He looked at Eric as if awaiting instructions, and, receiving none, lay down on the bed. Eric took from his pocket one of the two ten-rupee notes he had received earlier in the day from the elderly ladies; then went to the bed and held it out to him.

"Here, Babul," he said.

The boy's perplexity deepened. Then he giggled. "I have no place to put it, sahib."

"When you get your clothes on you'll have a place."

"Yes, later."

"Not later. Now."

"Now?"

"Yes, now."

Babul stared in incomprehension. A flicker of fear touched his eyes.

"I have done something wrong, sahib?" he asked.

"No."

"There is something you want me to do?"

"Yes. I want you to get out of here and find a girl—"

"A girl, sahib?"

"Yes, a girl, a pretty girl, and take her to the movies. There's a good movie in town this week—Clark Gable in something—and I want you to watch what Mr. Gable does with his girl in the movie and do the same with your girl when you take her home."

The boy's eyes were now all fear. He jumped from the bed and stood rigid.

"I should dress now, sahib?" he asked.

"Yes, dress now."

He all but leapt into his things.

"I should go now, sahib?"

224

"Yes, go now . . . Here's your movie money . . . And don't forget to watch Mr. Gable."

Babul nodded.

Then ran.

"Was it fun, Queenie?" asked Amy, as she passed next day in the hall.

Winter came. There were fewer tourists. During the fall he had both paid his back bills at the Himalayan Palace and kept up with the current ones, but now he could keep up no longer. From day to day he expected Amy to throw him out. But she didn't.

On his own, he groped for a solution, a way out. But found none. The Royal Hotel and the Snowview, he knew, would not take him on credit, and at the Government guesthouse, too, there would be a weekly nondeferrable bill. Other than his seasonal guiding, there was no way for him to earn a living in Kathmandu. (Even the guiding, as in Hong Kong, was illegal, but here he had not been caught.) As for clearing out entirely, he had not even the money to get to Delhi or Patna.

—If he had wanted to go.

He again sent out his three articles, to three new magazines. Turning from the novel, he wrote two new short pieces and sent them off—with Ashkar advancing the postage.

Weeks passed. Nothing happened.

By midwinter he knew that Amy was not going to put him out. That she was waiting: waiting for him to break: to come to her, drink with her, sleep with her. But that he would not—could not—do. What he had told her that night in his room had been said in despair, but also in truth. She had been good to him. He was grateful. He liked her. But to become Amy's man was to become Amy's creature.

With Amy, he would not write. He would not even try. And beyond this, deeper than this, there was yet another thing he would not do. It was not for writing alone that he had returned to Nepal; he could have done that, tried that, anywhere. It was for Nepal itself, for its mountains, the Great Himalayas, towering high and pure above the rubble of the earth. As a boy, a young man, he had known them in dream and desire. He had had a vision, and it too was high and pure; then he had soiled it, fouled it; in revulsion he had turned from it, he thought forever . . . Until Kay had turned him back. And now here he was again . . . Already, in the very beginning, he had gone out to the mountains; at least *toward* the mountains. Next time he would go farther, higher . . . If (the big IF) he could remain his own man, become again the man that, he now knew, was still alive within him . . . Not if he became entangled with Amy Bulwinkle. With bar and bed. With arak and Pinch. As he sat at the table in his room, he could see the scar on the wall where the Pinch bottle had crashed and shattered.

Late winter came. The new year's expeditions came. During early March there were Americans and French at the Royal, Norwegians at the Snowview, British and Germans at the Palace, and a half dozen teams, on tighter budgets, in small encampments outside the city.

He did not go to the Americans. But on their second day at the Palace he spoke to the leader of the British. He did not present himself as a mountaineer; simply as a man who knew Nepal, plus something of its language, and could perhaps help with transport and logistics on the march to Base Camp. The reply, polite but firm, was a "Sorry, old chap, all our arrangements are made."

It was the same, in assorted languages and accents, with the Germans, French and Norwegians. In the camps outside the town he tried Italians, Poles and Japanese, but they could not even understand what he was saying.

The city swarmed with Sherpas, in from Solu Khumbu to accompany the various teams to their mountains. And one day in the compound of the Palace, where the Germans were sorting their gear, he saw the short slight figure, the wizened face of Tashi. He made toward him; then stopped; then turned away.

"You no go climb, Rick Sah'b?"

"No, no climb, Tashi."

He wanted none of that.

The expeditions set out. Spring came. Tourists came. For several weeks he worked at guiding and began again to catch up with his hotel bills. (These he *had* to pay, as the price of freedom.) Then one morning, at the desk, Ashkar handed him a letter—and this time it was not a magazine rejection slip. It was from a Government bureau, stating that his visa had expired and that he would be required to leave the country within a week.

Again, as years before, he went to the Government offices.

"I would like to extend my visa," he said.

The official shook his head. "It has already had three extensions."

"I would like a fourth."

"No, three is the maximum. You must leave"—the official consulted a calendar—"by next Monday, April twenty-eighth."

Eric argued, pleaded—futilely. At last he said, "But I can't leave. I have no plane ticket."

"You can buy one," said the official.

"I have no money."

"None?"

"What little I have I owe to my hotel."

The official frowned. He picked up his phone, but it didn't work. Rising, he left the office for some time, and when he returned he said, "I have arranged transportation for you to the Indian border. An army truck will pick you up at the Himalayan Palace next Monday morning at seven o'clock."

That was it.

He went back to the hotel. To his room. He sat at the table, but he did not write. He walked in the city, then returned to room, table, bed. Perhaps twice each day, during the next four days, he decided to seek out Amy; to tell her what had happened, or at least say goodbye. But he did not do it. He kept to himself.

On Sunday evening at sunset he stood at the window of his room and looked out to the north. It was a clear evening, clear and still, and beyond a fringe of city, a scallop of hills and ridges, he could see the Himalayas looming vast in the sky. By day they were blinding white, but now they were pink, then mauve, then lavender and purple; they were a spectrum of all color glowing, glittering on the horizon. Then the sun went down and they were white again: not blinding now, but ghostly, cold. As the dusk thickened, they faded, receded, their shapes dissolving until they were no more than a faint luminescence in the distance. There was a glint here, a gleam there, in seeping darkness. Then it was night, full night, and they were gone.

He had two pieces of luggage—a suitcase and a rucksack—and he packed them both. Into the suitcase he put his manuscripts and most other possessions; into the rucksack the few things he would need most in the days ahead. When he had finished he went to the dining room and ate alone; and he ate a lot, for he did not know when or where the next meal would be. Amy was at a table on the far side of the room, with a group of tourists. They were younger than most, drinking wine and laughing, and Amy too was laughing, drinking, talking, and if she was conscious of him she gave no sign of it. When he had finished his meal he returned to his room and went to bed.

He got up at four and dressed. Closing the suitcase, he placed it in the center of the room and slung on the rucksack. Then he left the room, followed the hall to the hotel entrance, and went out. The streets of the city were still dark and empty; but he knew his way through them, and by the time the sky grayed they were already behind him. He was on a trail, an old familiar trail, leading northeast. Ahead, as he walked, the Himalayas emerged from the night.

Amy was gone now. There was only the dome of Dera Zor; only snow and sky.

But the sky—he peered up—yes, the sky at last was changing. The stars were paler. He could not see off to the east beyond the bulk of the mountaintop, but here too, he knew, the dawn was coming.

Again he looked at his watch, and it was going on five. In his high perch in the snow he had slept for more than half an hour.

He stood up, and he was stiff and cold. As he climbed again, kicking steps, the snow seemed deeper, steeper than before, and he cursed it. But this was his job: to break trail for the others who would follow.

His breath rasped in the stillness.

He plodded on.

16

   . . . He plodded on.

   Up, down, across the grain of the land.

   He knew now where the Government checkposts were located, and having no money for bribes, he had to avoid them. This he did successfully. But it involved frequent detours from the beaten trail, cross-country through bush and forest, over hill and stream; and the going was hard. After the months of Kathmandu, his body was slack, untempered, and except for a few basic items he had filched from the larder of the Himalayan Palace, he had no food supply. For the most part he had to live off the country, and the living was meager.

   Still he kept on. His pace was slow, but he made progress—for a week, a second week—and gradually the land grew higher, steeper. It was not the trail to the Langtang he was following now. It was the trail of years before: to the northeast, toward Solu Khumbu and beyond. How far he would go he did not know; he did not think about it. He would go as far as he could, and then . . . He did not think about that either. He plodded on . . . The air was clear. The earth was green. Ahead, the mountains shone in sunlight.

   That was for a week. A second week.

   Then change came.

   It came from the south, from India. It came in cloud and rain. "It will last only a day," he thought. Then "—only a few days."

But it came and stayed. Though it was only mid-May, the monsoon had come, wrapping the world in a caul of rain and mist.

Still he went on. The mountains were gone; the sky was gone; everything beyond the radius of a few scant yards was gone, and he moved through a lost drenched world that was like the bottom of a sea. Underfoot was a sea too—a sea of mud—and he was able to make no more than three or four miles a day. When the paths steepened he slipped and fell. Soon his face and hands and clothing were permanently caked with mud, and the contents of his pack were soaked and rotting. At night, in wayside shelters (when he could find a shelter), there was no respite from the damp, the cold, the mud.

The morning came when he awoke with fever.

"I should turn back," he thought.

Turn back—to what?

He went on. The next evening he came to a small village and a family took him in. He was not yet in Sherpa country, nor did they speak the Nepalese of Kathmandu; so there was small communication between them. They did what they could to help, but it was not much. His fever continued, grew worse.

He would have to go back.

But he didn't. Another few days, he estimated, would bring him to Solu Khumbu, the land of Sherpas; and he struggled toward it. Still he pushed through fog, rain, mud, still slipping, falling, picking himself up . . . until the time came when, on a steep rise, he fell once more, rolled down the slope, and when he tried to rise had not the strength to do so. Later he tried again, but his legs buckled, his head spun. He sank back. Sprawled on the path, he felt the rain in his face, the mud beneath him. The mud and fever together seemed to rise, to envelop him—and he felt nothing.

When he awoke, it was to faces, voices. There were many of them. Some of the faces seemed to be Sherpa, some white, and one of the white ones, burned and bearded, was bent close above him. He heard a word that sounded like *Polonski*. He felt himself being lifted. He was lying on some sort of litter and being carried downhill.

Now and then, in the days that followed, his fever ebbed. He knew he was with the Polish expedition that had been camped a few months before outside Kathmandu, and had now been driven back from its mountain by the early monsoon. Then the fever rose again, and the Poles receded. They were there but not there: distant, disembodied. Then not there at all. There was only the swing and jolt of the litter. There was mud and water, mud and fire, the fire of fever, and at last, beyond the fire, a voice that spoke to him. It was not a man's voice now, nor Polish. It was a woman's voice, a voice he knew: his mother's, perhaps—or Kay's —or Amy's. He could not tell.

It was Amy's.

"No sweat," she said. "No sweat at all."

And later:

"I got you out of that crummy mission hospital as soon as I could. It's crummy here too, of course, but more your kind of crummy."

And still later:

"I was wrong, baby. You're not a jerk. You're just a goddamn fool."

He was not in his old room, but in hers—or one that made sort of a suite next to hers. She brought him his meals, washed him, gave him medicines. One evening, when he was still in bed, but with the fever gone, she appeared with a bottle of Pinch and announced, "New medicine." Then she stayed and drank with him until he fell asleep.

As he grew stronger, he moved about. He stood at the window, looking out. But there were no mountains; only monsoon. One day, as he watched, a convoy of army trucks rolled down the street, and when Amy appeared he asked, "Have they been after me?"

"They?"

"The Government. My visa expired. They were going to put me out."

"Oh, that," said Amy. "Yeah, they were here once or twice—but no sweat."

"Why no sweat?"

"I talked to Gramps. Gramps ain't what he used to be, but he still can do a little fixing."

"I can stay, then?"

"Till you rot."

She poured them two whiskies. Then she said, "You could have come to me about it back when and saved yourself all that mud bath. But you're a dope, aren't you, baby? Just don't know your ass from first base."

After a drink she added, "For you, I'm first base, baby; haven't you found that out yet?" She thought it over, then amended: "First base hell. Home plate."

That time, after a while, she left. But a few nights later, without preamble or discussion, she took off her clothes and got into bed.

"You can't play it alone, baby, don't you see that?" she said. "No one can play the goddamn game all alone."

He did not argue. No bottle crashed against the wall. For a long time, then, there was no talk between them, and when at last she spoke it was with a purr of contentment.

She was no romantic, though: not Amy. What she said was, "Baby, that's the first good lay I've had since li'l ole Sydney Austrylia."

Thus began the time of Amy.

The weeks.

The months.

Then the years.

He lived with her, worked for her, drank with her, belonged to her. And seasons, monsoons, tourists came and went. As before, he took visitors on tours of Kathmandu and environs (and became expert at distinguishing the Grundys from the lingam-and-yoni crowd), but now as an employee of the Himalayan Palace, with the clients paying the fee as part of their hotel bill. In the evenings he tended bar. He took turns with Ashkar at the lobby

233

desk. He fended off complaints about electricity (intermittent), hot water (schizophrenic), roaches (omnipresent). And he answered questions.

"Where's Everest?"

"Up to the northeast. You can't see it from here."

"But our agent told us—"

"I'm sorry, he was wrong."

"Oh." (Disappointment. Sometimes anger.) "Where's the Matterhorn, then?"

"You can't see that either."

"The Abominable Snowman?"

"He's on leave right now."

Seasons, monsoons, tourists came and went. But his own life was enclosed, tight, hermetic. When he took out his tours, it was by schedule and rote. When he went to a window, it was to look no farther than the road beyond it. When he went to his room, it was also to Amy's room, Amy's world. On the table, instead of papers, were cosmetics, cigarettes, a bottle and glasses. His manuscripts (according to Ashkar) were in his old suitcase in a cellar storeroom.

For months he did not think of them. Then one night he did. As usual, he had been in the bar with Amy and others—this time including the venerable Osmun S.J.B. Rana—and when the old man left to go off to his suite, Amy had gone with him. Later, Eric closed the bar and went up to his and Amy's room. He waited for her, and when, by midnight, she hadn't come, he began to drink from the bottle on the table. By one, she still had not appeared, the bottle was empty, and he sat looking at it on the table, beside the glasses, cigarettes and cosmetics. With a swing of the arm he swept them all to the floor. Then, with a flashlight, he groped his way down halls and stairways to the cellar storeroom and began searching for his suitcase. It took him a long while: fumbling about among boxes and crates, baskets and bales, choking on dust, pulling, pushing, kicking, overturning, with frantic intensity that swelled to desperation. But at last he found it. Pulling it out, he hauled and jerked at its rusty fastenings; then saw, in the beam of his light, that he didn't need to, for almost half one side of the case had been ripped away . . . No, not ripped. Gnawed, chewed. It was an abandoned rats' nest . . . Pulling the rest of the fabric away, he saw the whole of the inside, saw his manuscripts in tatters, shredded by teeth and fouled by droppings. Squatting and holding the flashlight, he looked at them for some time. Then slowly, almost thoughtfully, he rose, unbuttoned his trousers, and urinated into the suitcase. Pushing it into a corner, he piled boxes and bales onto it, groped his way back upstairs to his room, opened another bottle, and waited for Amy.

He had been drunk then, of course. He was often, increasingly drunk; every night and half the days he was drunk. But seldom alone. He held to the Gospel according to St. Amy—*don't play it alone*—and when he was with others he managed.

With Amy he managed.

With Amy, often, he was almost content.

The other women in his life had been come-and-go. To begin with, his mother, Robin. (Why did he count them?—they weren't *women*.) There had been Doris Flanner in Seattle, Nicole in Paris, Lily in Hong Kong, Charlayne (was that it?) at the Big Bend Motel. There had been Kay. (No, Kay didn't count either; she was—) Anyhow, they had been briefly part of him; then not, then gone. But Amy stayed. He was with her by day and night, by week and month. They lived together, drank together, slept and fought and laughed together. He laughed more than he had thought he could. She made him laugh. (Or was it the liquor?) Then she made him angry. But she did not leave. She was *there*.

"—like a bloody mountain," he told her.

"Like *what?*"

"A mountain." He waved his glass at her and sang off key: "*You're there because you're there because you're there because—*"

"You're a looney," she said.

"I'm an existentialist."

"Come again?"

"A philosopher. A student of the thereness of the there."

"Shut up and come to bed," she said.

He nodded. "Because you're there."

235

"I'm here all right. But are you?" She pulled him to her. "You're stoned again, baby."

She herself could drink astonishingly: by night and day; by glass and bottle. Yet never did it interfere with her running of the hotel. As back at the Government guesthouse, she seemed to be everywhere simultaneously: in bar, dining room, kitchen; at the desk and the ledgers; joking with contented guests, placating irate ones, storming eternally through hallways shouting for waiters, bearers, sweepers. From Chicago to Kathmandu she had had her knocks and bruises, and they showed in her voice, her words, the line of her lip, the glint in her eye. But never in tiredness. Never in funk. Her vitality was boundless, awesome. The more she cursed her life, the more intensely she lived it.

Sexually, liquor made Eric—like most men—unpredictable. But not Amy. After the long-term feeble performances, first of "Old Cess," then of "Gramps," sex was number-one what she wanted —and gave. An aficionado of the fifteen positions in the "lingam-and-yoni" frieze in the old city, she delighted, with Eric, in testing their own ingenuities. They made love not only in bed, but on the floor, in the bathtub; once, late at night, on the bar in the barroom, while glassware crashed about them onto the bare stone floor. She liked crashes, he had learned—however they were made. She liked to claw and bite and spit out four-letter words. She liked him to rip her clothes, piece by piece, from her body, and in the morning did not complain of the resultant ruin.

Sometimes he could keep up with her; sometimes not. "I thought you were the 'no sweat' girl," he protested after one of the nots.

"No sweat for some things," she said. "Pizazz for others."

"And razmatazz."

"Yeah, pizazz-razmatazz . . . Which you sure don't have tonight, baby," she added.

But she rarely got angry when he failed her. There was usually the "baby"; usually a joke, a laugh, a grin. She grinned now as she rumpled his hair, poured them each a drink, and got back into bed.

"Down with them," she said.

They downed them.

"Now close your eyes."

He closed them. His head spun.

"You called me a mountain. Okay, I'm a mountain. Start climbing."

The bed spun.

"Hey, you're falling off!"

She laughed.

Then, later, stopped laughing.

"You made it right to the top," she said.

She was the only mountain. He no longer thought of mountains. He no longer thought of the rat's nest in the cellar storeroom.

It was winter again.

(The winter of what? It didn't matter.)

The tourist tide had swelled. The Himalayan Palace was full up; so were the Royal and Snowview, and there was talk that one, or even two, new hotels might soon be built. Kathmandu's airstrip, until now a pasture, was being enlarged and paved. "Nepal is now firmly on the travel map," declared a Government official in the bar of the Palace.

It was also on the map between India and China, and the Chinese in Tibet were looking menacingly southward. They had opened an embassy in Kathmandu, and so, too, in counterploy, did Russia and the United States. An American ambassador arrived, plus a staff; a headquarters was opened; a party was given. Amy attended it, in high heels and new coiffure, with Osmun S.J.B. Rana and two of his three wives. But Eric did not go. Nor did he visit the embassy afterward. Like his Nepalese visa, his American passport had long since expired. But he had no need of it. He kept away.

Except for his guiding tours, he went nowhere, and even these —in spite of the increase in tourists—were becoming less frequent.

He missed some of his morning appointments because he overslept, some of the afternoon ones because he had drunk too much at lunch. Once, he had drunk too much, but still went, and it was a mistake. Just what he had said at the lingam-and-yoni frieze he later couldn't remember; but his three lady clients had apparently not cared for it and complained in outrage to Amy—who, in turn, had not cared for the complaint. "Are you trying to put me out of business, you jerk?" she snapped at him that evening. And he, for the first time, snapped angrily back. No glassware flew, but their words crashed almost as loudly, and no "baby" was to be heard until they were safe in bed.

Increasingly, he confined himself to bartending. Here, for some reason, he was able to make drinks for hours, nip himself for hours, and still retain the requisite control of hand and tongue. When late at night he would begin slipping over the edge, Amy would ease him out, and he would go to their room, drink there, and wait for her. Sometimes, when she herself arrived, there was a scene; more often not. If he went on drinking with her, then made love with her, she had what she wanted.

The only trouble was that she could take more of both.

It was spring.

(Or several springs; they tended to merge.)

And with spring, again, the expeditions.

This time (or times) he did not seek them out. They came and went. An American team, bound for the Dhaulagiri region, stopped briefly at the Palace and sorted their gear in its compound. But being in training, they did not come to the bar ("Boy Scout deadheads," said Amy), and in dining room and hallway he saw no face that was familiar.

Nor any sign of Tashi.

It was summer.

The expeditions had returned and gone home. Most of the tourists were gone. What was left was the monsoon—and Amy.

Things were going downhill with Amy.

Not in a rush, an avalanche. They still lived, drank, slept together, and some of the time it was the same as always. But increasingly, now, there were frictions, rough edges: from her fewer "baby's," more "jerks" and "slobs"; for him, fewer times when he got a lift from liquor, and more when he was unable to satisfy her sexually.

"You don't want a woman," she told him. "You want that pansy kid I sent you."

"He had pizazz," said Eric.

"I'll have Ashkar bring him again . . . Or maybe you'd like Ashkar; he's nice and juicy."

One thing led to another. One drink to two, three, six, ten. Words to more words, to shouts, yells, flying glassware. Once a tumbler, half-filled with whisky, caught him on the cheek, broke, and cut him. Once when he pushed her she fell and bruised her hip. Always they made up afterwards; sometimes within five minutes of a brawl they were laughing, joking, rolling in bed. But still the brawls continued: more frequent, more ugly.

He tried to ease up on drinking. But it was no good; it was worse than before. No less than in sex, Amy demanded that he keep pace with her. When he didn't, she sulked or taunted him. And within himself it was even more intolerable. With liquor, full rations of liquor, there was at least a swing of the pendulum, a back and forth, up and down. Without it—even with some but not enough of it—there was only down. Only grayness and funk. Through the grayness, lying sleepless in bed, he began to see distant mountains that dissolved and crumbled as he watched them. When at last he fell asleep, it was to dream that he was locked in a rotting suitcase filled with shredded paper and rat shit.

He resumed drinking—full-scale drinking—and the same night, for the first time, he hit Amy with his fist.

Then he found hashish. It was not hard to come by in Kathmandu; indeed, half the hotel's waiters and bearers used it in some form or other, and Ashkar, at the desk, was an off-hours dealer. He had his first try at it in a shed in the hotel compound, with indifferent results. But the second try went better, the third better yet. So well, in fact, that, that same evening in their room, Amy looked him over and asked, "So how's junkie-boy tonight?"

As it turned out, he was all right, better than for quite a while ("that's my baby," she said), and thereafter he smoked in their room, with no protest from her. She didn't join him, however. She had, she said, tried hashish, opium, the whole lot of them, when she first came to the East, and they had done nothing for her; she had stuck with booze. But if hashish was what the doctor ordered for him, she was all for it. "You've been getting spooked again, baby," she told him. "God knows you need *something*."

With hashish, he did not want liquor. He did not need it. With practice and experimentation, he arrived at the right amount of smoking, at the right times, and the rough, raw edges of drunkenness were replaced by a smooth and rounded peace. Amy's voice, when angry, seemed less harsh and strident; and she was angry less often. Her face seemed younger, softer. Everything was softer. The bed, the light, the very air. The monsoon rains no longer fell on the roof with a clamorous drumbeat, but with a gentle whisper. The rain was green. "You're hopped up," said Amy. But still it was green. "It falleth," he told her, "like the gentle green from heaven."

It was fall.

No monsoon. No rain.

Now it was the sun that was green in a yellow Gauguin sky.

The letter he held in his hand was green too. Then it changed to blue, to pink, to a color that had no name. It had been brought to the Palace (after stops at the Royal and Snowview) by a messenger from the American Embassy, asking, "Have you a guest called Venn?" And Amy, handing it to him, said, "Whaddya know? Someone thinks you're alive."

Now in their room—with Amy elsewhere—he sat down with it. By an effort of will he made the envelope turn to white and the typing to black. His name was there, all right. The postmark, which he could only partly decipher, was Something, Texas.

He opened it and read (or half-read):

. . . *called your sister-in-law, Kay, who said she thinks you're*

240

in Nepal, but has no address, so I'm making this stab through the embassy . . . It's been a long time, but . . . putting together a team to go out early next year for another try at . . . The paper was green again. The typing rolled and billowed . . . *at Dera Zor,* it said . . . *As I'm sure you know, it's one of the big ones still unclimbed, and . . . and* (etc.) . . . *I'm hoping you can . . .* The type billowed again. Then . . . *no bygones . . . Ken Naylor.*

A while later, Amy came in, sniffed the air, and saw the cigarette in his hand.

"For Chrissake, in the morning—" she said.

When she had gone again he rolled more hashish and smoked it slowly, deeply. Then he left the room, went downstairs, left the hotel, and for the rest of the day wandered the streets of Kathmandu. Back at the hotel, in the evening, he told one of the waiters to tend bar and returned to the room. There he smoked again, dropping cigarettes because his hands were shaking. He looked for the letter, but couldn't find it . . . He had to find it. He still had not read it all, and all he could remember of Ken's address was Something, Texas . . . He searched the room. He turned it upside down. He could not find the letter. He smoked again, fell on the bed, and when he awoke Amy was back.

"What the hell goes on?" she asked.

Her face and figure were wavering before him.

"The letter—" he mumbled.

"What about the letter?"

"It's gone."

"So what?"

"It's important."

"Important—ha! Someone leave you a million?"

"Yes."

"Goody! I'll make a list in the morning of how we'll spend it."

She poured herself a drink. He rolled and lighted cigarettes and dropped them on the floor. He prowled the room, and Amy was talking, but he wasn't listening. He was digging, burrowing into his mind, through the fumes of hashish, through green and yellow caves, toward the place that would remember where the letter was . . .

241

Then he found it. He *did* remember.

He ran to the door.

"Hey!" said Amy.

He dashed from the room, down halls and stairs, to the cellar. There he realized he had no flashlight and dashed back up again.

"Hey!" Amy said.

He dashed down again, tripping, stumbling. He came to the storeroom. On hands and knees he clawed through boxes and bales, through piles of rubbish, until he came to his suitcase. He pulled it out, got it open, plunged his hands in, and came out with shreds of paper. Placing the flashlight on a nearby box so that he could see what he was doing, he began piecing the shreds together, while the rat droppings rolled and crumbled in his shaking hands.

It was winter.

(It must have been winter; there were so many tourists.)

"Where's the hot water?" they asked.

"Where's Everest?"

"Where's the Matterhorn?"

"Where's the Abominable Snowman?"

"We *have* a Snowman," Amy told them. "He does his tricks every Saturday night."

For some time she had been plotting ways to lure guests from the Royal and Snowview, and had struck on the idea of a weekly dance show. She did not dance herself. It was a strictly Nepalese affair, performed by a haphazardly assembled troupe of locals, including several employees of the hotel. Some of the dances were Hindu in origin, some Buddhist, some a mixture of both. All were derived, in one way or another, from folklore and mythology; and notable among the weirdly garbed performers, in a costume that had once seen service as a gorilla in a traveling circus, was a facsimile of the yeti, alias Snowman.

The show was a success from the start. Staged after dinner in the Palace compound, by the light of big bonfires, it attracted even larger crowds than Amy had hoped for, and both dining room and bar did a booming business. Hit of the performance was always the yeti, who appeared toward the end to a great thumping of drums, chased other members of the troupe about the premises, and ended by seizing a brand from a bonfire, waving it wildly, and disappearing over the compound wall. He was played by one of the hotel waiters, a man from the north country called Dorje, who in his usual profession seemed barely able to trudge from kitchen to dining room, but as yeti raced and leapt like a madman.

Then came the Saturday night—in early March, at the height of the season—when Dorje took ill. He groaned on his cot; he was, he said, about to die. And Amy could find no one to replace him.

"We got the biggest crowd ever," she wailed. "A busload from the Royal, another from the Snowview. Two whole expeditions are coming—one with each—and without a yeti there's no damn show."

She paced the room, drink in hand. Eric smoked, and the world was pleasantly green. Since the night in the cellar he had taken great care to keep it green.

Now he pointed at Amy.

"You," he said.

"Me, what?"

"You're a dancer. Toast of ten continents. *You* be the yeti."

"Very funny."

"Lady yeti: great change of pace."

"Ha!" She barked it out.

"You're chicken."

"Ha, ha, ha!"

He lit another cigarette. Things got still greener. He stood up. "*I*, on the other hand, am not chicken," he announced. "My name, madam, is Eric Sir Edmund Hillary Errol Flynn Venn: climber, skier, soldier, sailor and gentleman adventurer, at your service. And *I*, goddamn it, will play the yeti!"

Her "ha!" was the loudest yet.

"You heard me," he said.

"You're a loony."

"I am not a loony. I am what the poet calls a man for all seasons."

"You're a cotton-picking hophead, and you'll fall on your face."

"Then you'll come out as the Good Fairy and pick me up and bind my wounds. It will make a touching climax to the night's revels."

He went to the door—a little unsteadily. She yelled after him, but he didn't stop. As he went down the hall her voice followed him: "If you louse things up, I'll—"

He kept going. First he went to the not-yet-open bar, where he kept an auxiliary supply of hashish and cigarette papers, and in the pantry behind the bar he had another smoke. Then he went to the nearby room where the dancing troupe's costumes were kept, found the yeti outfit, and examined it. It was heavy, black, hairy, and it stank. The head, which was attached to the rest at the back of the neck, like the lid of a box, was that of a huge lopsided ape, with two long yellow fangs added. Holding up the skin—or whatever it was—he clambered into it. There were hooks up the belly and chest, and he fastened them; then brought the gorilla head down over his own. A cracked mirror hung on the wall, and he peered at himself through the head's eye slits. Two bulbous bloodshot eyes stared back at him malevolently. One of the cardboard fangs was loose and swung slowly when he moved.

The stench was now awful. Returning to the bar, he got more cigarette makings, raised the head partway, and lighted up. It took some doing with his ape paws, but he managed. A lady guest of the hotel appeared in the door, stared, screamed and ran. Taking more hashish and papers with him, he returned to the costume room and sat on a bench. As he went on smoking, the stench was gradually neutralized.

Presently he could hear the bar coming alive. Three of the hotel waiters were tending it, and the evening crowd was arriving. For an hour it was full, noisy; then it was dinner time and the noise shifted to the dining room. Outside it grew dark. Members of the dance troupe came in and began putting on their costumes. On arrival, they were an indiscriminate crowd of local men and boys —there were no women or girls—but soon they had become a colorful, if seedy, assemblage of gods, goddesses, devils, warriors, monks, pilgrims, peasants and yaks. He himself, having got used

244

to the stink, kept his yeti head on, and found it was still possible to smoke by inserting paw and cigarette between his cardboard fangs. His fellow performers seemed to take the smell of hashish for granted. And if they knew he was not Dorje, they said nothing about it.

Finally, dinner was over. The crowd moved out to the verandah and compound, where rows of chairs had been placed for them. Simultaneously the bonfires were lighted, and the blackness outside turned to an orange glare. There was a sound of drums and horns. The dancers piled out into the compound. The only one left in the dressing room was Eric the yeti; for the yeti did not make his appearance until the finale and, for dramatic effect, was not supposed to show himself until he was officially "on."

The dances started, and he watched from the window. But the routines were familiar; he would know his cue from the music; the flames of the bonfires glared dizzyingly in his eyes. Turning away, he prowled about the room. But the glare seemed to follow him, the heat of the fires to press in through the window. He was hot now and sweating, dripping with sweat (though no sweat, said Amy, was the First and Great Commandment), and the stench of his ape suit was almost overpowering. Again he tilted the head back. Again he smoked. He tried to suck into himself the anodyne, the green softness and gentleness, of hashish. But now there was too much going against it; it didn't work. It only made him hotter, made him pant for air, gave raw searing edges to the blaze of fire, the din of horns and drums.

Still he smoked.

He prowled.

("No sweat, baby.")

Then the horns blared to a climax and abruptly stopped. There were only drums now: louder—louder. It was his cue. He clamped down his yeti head. He flung himself from the room, crossed the verandah and bounded down into the compound.

At the first step he stumbled, almost fell. Amy had said he would fall . . . To hell with Amy . . . He caught himself, ran on. The yeti was not supposed to dance, merely to run; to chase gods, goddesses, pilgrims, peasants, yaks—whatever appeared before him. They appeared, and he chased. He was not supposed actually to catch anyone, but at the last moment to veer off in pursuit of another. He veered and pursued. He crouched, sprang, whirled, raced off again. He raised hairy arms skyward and shook them in rage. He beat his hairy chest with hairy paws.

The drums rolled and thundered, and the compound reeled around him. The dancers reeled. And the bonfires. He was now in the very midst of the fires, and it was they that seemed to leap and lunge at him. If he had been hot before, it was nothing compared to now. He was swimming, drowning in sweat. Drowning, and simultaneously on fire. The heat of the flames was in his bones and blood. Their glare exploded in his eyes and brain.

A bonfire lunged and almost caught him. But again he veered; he was past it, angling off. He was chasing a dancer—a yak, a something—and it fled to the rim of the compound; it was running along the edge of the watching crowd; and he followed. Through his eye-slits, the glaze of sweat, the blur of movement, he saw figures, faces. He saw Amy (with a glass). He saw Osmun S.J.B. Rana (with wives). He saw others he knew, from the hotel, the town, streaking by him, their faces red, glinting, flickering in the glare of the fires. He saw a row of young men—Japanese —an expedition?—and cameras flashed as he passed. Then another row—white, British perhaps?—he couldn't tell; they streamed too fast. Their faces raced, blurred, flickered, like a strip of film in a projector gone wild . . .

Then locked, froze, stopped.

He had stopped.

There was no longer a blur but frozen clarity; no longer a row but one face in the row. A brown, craggy face above a powerful body, below receding hair.

He looked at Ken Naylor.

And Ken looked at him.

Ken, too, had a camera; he raised it, there was a flash; and Ken smiled and said, "Thanks."

There were other flashes.

246

There was the glare of the fires, the beat of the drums. Through the drums, there was Amy's voice yelling, "Hey, get going!" There was Ken: Ken glowing in firelight.

Then no more Ken.

He had turned, lunged off. The film was racing again. *He* was racing. He was leaping, bounding: no longer after the yak or whatever—he had lost the yak, lost all the dancers—but straight at one of the bonfires. He would plunge into the fire. It would burn away the yeti skin and Ken would see who he was.

Yes . . . Yes . . .

He was almost there now.

Then, at the last instant . . . no.

There was a better way to show Ken. To show them all.

For the last time, he veered. He followed the script. As Dorje had used to do at the end, he snatched a brand from the fire and waved it wildly. He ran on across the compound. But whereas Dorje had made for the low compound wall and vanished over it, he went in the other direction, toward the hotel building. Thrusting himself through startled spectators, he reached the verandah. He clambered onto its railing and up a post that supported the roof above it. He reached the roof and looked up at the remaining three stories of the hotel that rose beyond. Turning, he threw his torch, in a great arc, down into the compound. He beat his hairy chest. He began to climb.

The wall was vertical, of course. But it was made of stucco, with bumps and hollows, and somehow he held on. He came to a window, used its sill, then the moulding on its side and top, and moved on beyond. As he went, he was conscious of a change behind and beneath him. The drums were louder, he thought. Then —no, it was opposite—they had stopped, they were silent. The crowd was silent. The only sound now was the crackling of the bonfires, and their light glowed orange-red on the stucco wall.

He could see only the wall. But he felt the crowd's eyes watching. Ken's eyes watching.

"How'm I doing, Ken?" he asked aloud, within his ape's head. "Mind the ropes. Drive a piton."

But there was no rope, no piton. No Ken—just Ken's eyes. There was another window—except that it wasn't a window—it was a ledge, a pillar, another ledge—then bare wall. It was the Wailing Wall. And he climbed it. Foot by foot, clinging with finger and toe, he moved upward. He had passed his previous high point—and Julian's—and still he moved—and now the top of the wall was close above him.

"See, Ken! See!" he exulted. "It goes—we've made it—we can climb the bastard!"

He reached, stretched. All that was left was the ultimate cornice, and he grasped it. He pulled up. And it gave. There was a crumpling of rock. No, of metal. The gutter that rimmed the hotel roof buckled under his hand, ripped away, and fell clattering, banging, to the roof of the verandah below. He swayed, lurched. But he did not fall with it. He had reached again, stretched, swung sideways. There was a drainpipe, and he grasped it, and it held him. There was a rib of rock, above it the cornice; and he climbed it. He was *at* the cornice. His arms were over, then his shoulders, his chest; the whole of him was over; he was up, off the rock, off the wall; the Wailing Wall was at last below him, and he rose and stood in the shining snow of the summit dome of Dera Zor.

"Ken—Ken—come on!" he cried into his ape's head.

He stepped forward. Pitched forward. Firelight flamed in his brain, and he fell. Into the softness of snow. Onto the hardness of tar and gravel. For a moment there seemed to be an explosion of light, of clearness, around him. Then the darkness and stench of the yeti skin closed in and extinguished it.

It was later. Much later. It was light, and he was somewhere else.

Again he called Ken's name.

"Who's Ken?" Amy asked.

"My friend—with the climbers. Where is he? *Where is he?*"

"The climbers have gone. They took off yesterday."

"Yesterday?"

He tried to rise from the bed—or whatever he was on—but his head spun, his legs crumpled.

"They liked your show, though," said Amy. "They left you ten rupees and a Polaroid picture."

"Ken!"

He had actually called it out—croaked it out.

But it was not Ken who was coming. It was Larry, Tashi, Pembol.

Again he turned, looked down the slope toward the snow hole. But there was no sign of them. It was dawn now, true dawn; the stars were gone; blackness was grayness. But there was still no sign.

What the hell were they doing?

He struggled on in the snow. Up steepness. Through deepness. His breath rasped, his chest heaved with the labor; his head spun, as it had spun that night, years ago, when, dressed as an Abominable Snowman, he had climbed the wall of the Himalayan Palace Hotel.

Something that was half rasp, half laugh rattled in his throat . . . Well, he was a Snowman again all right, on a different sort of Himalayan Palace.

"Ha! Ha!"

His throat had actually said it.

No, it was Amy who said it.

"Amy!" he called.

He shook his head. He had to get control, stop its spinning. Back there, back then, it had been hashish that spun it. Now it was the air, the no-air, and he heaved, he fought for it . . . Christ, they should have brought oxygen . . . No. No, they shouldn't

250

. . . That was one of the things this was all about. Dera Zor was not only the highest unclimbed mountain on earth; it would be, if they made it, the highest ever to be climbed without oxygen.

The hell with oxygen!

He floundered on.

—But oh God, he needed it—

His mind spun back, past Amy, to another time, another place; to this same mountain years ago. As they left Camp Five for what lay beyond it, he had said to Julian Howard, "We're close to the edge of what men can do."

He was higher now. That had been below the Wailing Wall. Now he was above it, on the summit dome, a scant few hundred feet from the top of the mountain.

He was twenty years older.

The gray dawn spun around him.

He was again close to that edge. Very close.

17

There had been a time back then when he had been close too: to a different edge. And if it was Amy, life with Amy, that had got him there, it was also Amy who helped pull him back.

"You're climbing walls, baby—but for real," she said.

He didn't answer.

"You're spooked again. You've got the meemies."

"I need a smoke," he said.

"No."

He got up, began to search the room.

"I've thrown the stuff out," Amy told him.

He started for the door.

"And I've told Ashkar not to give you any."

He stopped. She poured two drinks and came to him, holding a glass in each hand. "This is our kind of poison," she said. "The other's for gooks."

"I—I need—"

"You need this." She made him take a glass. "It's Pinch."

The glass shook in his hand.

"Come on," she said.

He raised it, still shaking.

"Come on."

He drank.

"That's it, baby," she said. "No sweat. No sweat at all."

There was plenty of sweat. His body dripped with it, as if still enclosed in the ape skin. His hands went on shaking, his head ached, and the corpuscles of his blood seemed to grind like gravel in his veins. The day came when he could stand it no longer. With money taken from the till in the bar, he went down to the old city and bought hashish. Almost at a run, he returned with it to the hotel. Going to the shed in the compound where he had first tried smoking, he rolled a cigarette, lighted it—and with a sudden movement hurled it away. He threw all the hashish away. He went to his room and sat there shaking and sweating, until Amy came and gave him a drink and pulled him down with her onto the bed.

She was patient with him. Sometimes almost gentle. Tough and hard-bitten, she was still a woman; she responded because he needed her—as she needed him. And gradually, with her help, he got the monkey off his back. His shaking stopped. His sweating stopped. He was able to tend bar again, and occasionally, as before, he took hotel guests out on tours of the city. He was able again to make love to Amy as she wanted to be made love to.

Instead of hashish, of course, there was liquor. He was drunk every night, half-drunk most of the days. But in this, at least, he had company, for so was Amy; and he, like her, had by now reached a point where he could take it in stride. There was no crack-up, no climbing of walls. They had their fights, and there were again nights when shouts and glassware filled the air. But by morning everything was as before; everything was routine. All of living—even the fights—were routine, as the days blurred into weeks and the weeks into months.

Dorje the waiter had not died on the night he had said he was going to. The next Saturday night he had been back playing the yeti. Then spring had ended, and with it the tourist season and the dances. In their place was monsoon and rain. The rain was gray now. Eric could scarcely remember it as green. He could scarcely remember the night of the dance, the climb, the apparition of Ken Naylor. The rain shut them out. Time and drinks shut them out. In the early days of the monsoon he heard from someone (Amy? a visitor?) that the American expedition of that year had returned to Kathmandu. It had been to a mountain with a peculiar name (the someone said) and hadn't made it. High up, they had come to some sort of wall and had to turn back. But no one had been lost; all had returned. And now they were gone.

Gone . . .

Behind them, at the Royal Himalayan Hotel, they had left a ten-rupee note and a snapshot of a man in an ape suit in front of a bonfire.

In the Buddhist calendar it was the Year of the Rat . . . Then the Year of the Cow.

In the calendar of the West it was something else.

It didn't matter.

Then in the year, the month, the week of something, came the second day in all the hundreds when he held a letter in his hand. This one was not hashish green, but white. His name and address —again the American Embassy—was not typed but handwritten, and the writing was a child's. The postmark—this time wholly legible—was Santa Monica, California.

He opened it and read:

Dear Uncle Rick,

Mother says your real name is Uncle Eric but I should call you Uncle Rick. Also that she isnt sure of your adress but I should try it like this.

Anyway I am eleven years old now. I climb some mountains in the San Benadinos with my Junior Scout Troop and it is fun. They are not big mountains but they and me will get bigger. Mother says you have climbed lots of big ones and will like to know this.

Some day Uncle Rick I hope I can climb with you. I will be good and carefull, realy. Please let me know when I am big will you climb with me.

Truly yours your nephew

Larry Venn

"Another million?" asked Amy.

He reached for the Pinch.

"It looks like a kid's writing."

He poured the drink, raised it. Then set it down . . . No. No drink. Today, in all the hundreds of days: no drink.

"What kid?" asked Amy.

"Jackie Coogan," he said.

"Jackie Coogan's an old man now."

"The mail's slow here."

He stood up and put the letter in the pocket of his shirt. This one he was not going to lose. Amy was still talking, but he did not hear her. He went to the door and out, and out of the hotel, and as so many times before, he walked the streets of Kathmandu. This time, though, it was without a drink, without a smoke. When he stopped, it was to take out the letter, reread it, and put it carefully back in his pocket. He continued walking through the day until it began to get dark. Then he returned to the hotel; to his room. He knew that, by now, Amy would be in the bar. The room was empty. He found pen and paper and sat down at the table.

Dear Larry, he wrote—

It was so long since he had held a pen that he could scarcely manage it. His writing was as awkward as Larry's. Worse. Destroying the first sheet of paper, he tried again.

Dear Larry,

(It was a little better.)

It's fine to have your letter, and I'm glad you've been climbing and like it. Yes, I'd like very much to climb with you—even now—but I'm afraid we can't because we're so far apart.

Maybe later I can come where you are, or you can come here. There are fine mountains here. Yes, that's it—in nine or ten years, when you're grown up, you come here, Larry, and we'll climb together.

(He sat for a while.)

Say hello for me to your mother, he wrote.

With love,

Your—

(There was another pause.)

—Uncle Rick

At the desk in the lobby, he stamped the letter and put it in the mailbox. Then he went to the bar and had his first drink of the day. Later he had his second, fourth, sixth, and eighth. If he had nine or ten years to wait until he again went to a mountain, the bar of the Himalayan Palace was as good a place for it as any.

The wait was shorter than that.

The Year of the Cow became the Year of the Tiger. Spring became summer, and summer fall. On an early fall evening he was alone behind the bar when an elderly woman he had not seen before appeared in the doorway. On his night in the yeti skin, now long past, another female guest had made a similar solo appearance; then stared, screamed and ran. But this one looked as if she would have held her ground even then. Though old—perhaps seventy or more—she was tall, lean, big-boned, and moved with a purposeful stride. Her face, beneath short frizzed hair, was strong and angular, and from steel-rimmed glasses to flat-heeled brogues she was strictly no-nonsense.

"I am looking for Mrs. Bulwinkle," she announced briskly.

"She's not down from her room yet," Eric told her. "Can I help you?"

The old lady gave it thought. "Perhaps you can," she said. "Mrs. Bulwinkle was to find out if there are any Sherpas now in Kathmandu, and let me know this evening."

"Sherpas, ma'am?"

"Yes. You know what Sherpas are, don't you?"

He nodded. "But I don't think you'll find any here now. They usually just come in the spring, to join up with expeditions."

"There are no expeditions in the fall?"

"Very few. This year, none at all."

"I understood," said the old lady, "that Himalayan weather is good in the fall."

"Clear, yes. But cold—very cold."

"Hmm . . . Well, I have plenty of warm clothing. In New England, in winter, it is often below zero for days on end."

Eric blinked. "You mean—?" He left it hanging. "Would you like a drink, ma'am?" he asked.

She eyed him sharply, almost suspiciously. Then she said, "Why yes, I rather think I would. Do you have a dry sherry?"

256

"I've Domecq's La Ina."

"That will do nicely, thank you."

She did not come to the bar, but seated herself, tall and erect, at one of the small tables along the other wall. Eric brought her drink, returned behind the bar, and poured himself a scotch.

"I hope you don't mind," he said. "This is an informal sort of place."

"So I have noticed," said the lady.

He downed his whisky, and she sipped her sherry.

"Did I understand you to say, ma'am," he asked, "that you are going to the mountains?"

"That is correct," she said.

"It's quite a project, you know."

"I am not going to the top of a mountain. Merely to its base."

"Even so. There's not only height but distance."

"I am aware of that and have made plans accordingly. Through our embassy here I have made arrangements to charter a helicopter that will take me as far as Solu Khumbu."

"*Solu Khumbu?*"

"You know of it?"

"Yes. But not many visitors do."

The old lady ignored this. "You know then, of course," she said, "that it is the Sherpa homeland, and I daresay I could hire porters in the villages. I had hoped, however, to find at least a headman—a sirdar, I believe they are called—here in Kathmandu. Someone who speaks English, preferably, and can help with the provisioning and other preliminaries. That was what I was speaking about this morning to Mrs. Bulwinkle."

There was a silence.

"Would you like another sherry?" asked Eric.

"No thank you," she said.

He poured himself another scotch.

"And from Solu Khumbu—" he said. "When you have your Sherpas, where will you go from there? To look at Everest?"

"No, not Mount Everest. I should be interested to see it, of course, but it is not my destination. I am going to a mountain that is not so well known. It is called Dera Zor."

There was another silence.

A middle-aged couple came into the bar, then two single men, and Eric took their orders and made their drinks.

He drank down his own.

Then Amy came in. Seeing the old lady, she joined her at her table, and Eric, on signal, brought her a Pinch and water.

Amy said, "Have you met Mrs.—er—" For a hotelkeeper, she was weak on names.

"Bigelow," said the lady.

"Yes, Bigelow."

"Mrs. Homer Bigelow," the lady added, "of Cambridge, Massachusetts."

In the night, Amy lay beside him, asleep, snoring lightly. But it was not Amy who was there.

A mountain was there.

"Do you see it?" asked Ken Naylor.

"Do you see it?" asked Larry.

"Do you see it?" asked Mrs. Homer Bigelow.

"Yes, I see it," he said.

Amy still slept as he rose, left the room and went down to the cellar. She was asleep when he returned. She was asleep when, soon after dawn, he rose again, dressed, and went out.

The dining room opened at seven-thirty. At seven thirty-one Mrs. Bigelow entered and sat down, and he joined her.

"You're early," he said.

"I have already been for a walk," she informed him. "Back home, whenever possible, my husband and I would take a pre-breakfast walk along the Charles River Embankment."

"Your husband, I gather, isn't with you now?"

"No, he is not."

A waiter appeared, and she ordered oatmeal, toast and tea with boiled milk.

Then she added, to Eric: "My husband died three months ago."

"Oh. I'm sorry."

258

"There is nothing to be sorry about, really. He was well along and had been ill for some time."

"This is quite a trip for you to be making alone."

"That is what my children think. They even tried to forbid my making it. But my mind was quite made up; I had my reasons."

She fell silent. Eric waited. Then she spoke again.

"My husband was a geologist," she said. "For most of his career he was on the faculty at Harvard. But as a young man, before we were married, he had come to Nepal; to this mountain I spoke of called Dera Zor."

"Yes, I know," Eric said.

"You—know—?"

He took from his lap his mildewed, rat-gnawed copy of *Trek to Nowhere* that he had retrieved that night past from the cellar storeroom. He handed it to her, and she held it, slowly turning its crumbling pages. When she again looked at him, her pale blue eyes and angular face seemed softer, gentler than before.

"It has been out of print a long time," she said.

"I have had it a long time," said Eric.

From his pocket he took Bigelow's scout knife.

"I have this too," he said. "It's for you."

Mrs. Bigelow looked at it, uncomprehending. "What is it?" she asked.

"It was your husband's."

"How do you know?"

"I found it at his old camp at the foot of Dera Zor."

Her eyes changed again. They fixed him. "You mean *you* have been there?" she asked.

"Yes, I've been there." He looked straight back at her. "And I would like to go again—with you."

Mrs. Bigelow said nothing.

"You won't find a Sherpa sirdar in Kathmandu. I can be your sirdar. I can do what has to be done here and hire the porters in Solu Khumbu. From there, I know the way to the mountain."

She was still silent. The waiter brought her breakfast and a cup of coffee for Eric. Then she said:

"All this is most unexpected, of course. What, may I ask, would you expect in payment?"

"You would pay all the expenses. For myself I want no payment."

She showed further surprise. "That is most kind of you, Mr.—"

"Venn. Eric Venn."

"Most kind indeed, Mr. Venn."

She put sugar and milk on her oatmeal and ate a few spoonfuls with an air of disapproval. When she raised her eyes and spoke again, the passing softness was gone, and it was again in her brisk, no-nonsense manner.

"But before accepting," she said, "there is a question I am afraid I must ask you. I trust you will not take offense."

"Yes?" he asked.

"Do you have a drinking problem, Mr. Venn?"

Again their eyes met squarely. He considered his answer.

"I have had, Mrs. Bigelow," he said. "But not now."

Kathmandu was full of camping paraphernalia left behind by expeditions, and in short order he had what was needed. He assembled the requisite food. Two days after his first meeting with Mrs. Bigelow all was ready for takeoff.

Leave-taking from Amy, however, was less simple. To begin with she laughed at him, then she got angry, and finally she settled on a blend of both.

Her last words to him were, "You'll fall flat on your face and freeze your balls off."

Then she was gone. The helicopter roared and rose. The pilot, a Minnesotan called Lundquist who worked for AID, pointed its nose to the northeast, and in a few minutes Kathmandu, too, was gone. Beneath them was the brown and green of terraced fields. To the north, high and white, were the peaks of the Langtang. East from the Langtang, the vast wall of the mountains stretched on and on to the limit of vision.

Mrs. Bigelow sat in one of the forward seats, next to Lundquist; Eric behind, in a welter of duffels and cartons. The old lady—so she had told him—had never before been in a helicopter, yet she seemed wholly at ease as she looked out from the fragile bubble at the wilderness ahead . . . No, *at ease* was wrong, he amended, for one so stiff and erect . . . *Controlled* was the word. Her sharp, seamed face, now topped by a woolen stocking cap, was composed and impassive. Her glasses glinted in the sunlight. On her lap, in gloved hands, she held a sealed metal canister of the sort used in kitchens to hold sugar or flour. On boarding the craft he had offered to take it and store it with the other gear, but she had said no, she would hold it. Why, he didn't know.

Indeed, he knew almost nothing about her. Since that first evening and subsequent morning she had kept her own counsel, and he had learned no more about the motive for her improbable journey. Her husband, as a young man, had stood at the foot of Dera Zor. Now she, as his widow, wished to stand there too. Was this enough of a motive? He didn't know. Along with all the rest, it occurred to him, he didn't even know her first name. She was simply Mrs. Homer Bigelow, widow, of Cambridge, Mass., who took walks before breakfast and had a mind of her own.

He too peered out and down from the plastic bubble. For even a strong expedition, the overland trip from Kathmandu to Solu Khumbu took almost two weeks. By air, in the whirring chopper, it would be an hour and a half, and they seemed barely settled in their seats before they were halfway there. Below, much of the time, he could see the long trail, the old trail, snaking its tortuous way across valley and hill. He could even (he thought) pick out the spot where he had collapsed on his solitary trek in the monsoon of some years past. Beyond it—two days by foot, ten minutes by air—the land began to change, to rise. The terraced fields were gone, and in their place were high pastures, forests, snow-flecked ridges, with prayer flags streaming on the skyline crags. To the north, the skyline leapt upward. The mountains were close now: the real mountains, the High Himalayas, tiering white and incandescent in the clarity of autumn sunlight. Even the nearer, the lower of them were far higher than the helicopter, shutting out the greater ones beyond. But they were close now, moving ever closer, to the realm of Everest—and Dera Zor.

Then the mountains tilted, wheeled. They were coming down.

Or rather, the earth was rising to meet them. Close below were the gorges of the Dudh Khosi, the river artery of Solu Khumbu; above them, on a steep hillside, the houses of Namche Bazar, principal village of the Sherpas; above them, in turn, a small, level patch of alpine meadow—and toward this they were heading. He could see figures standing on the meadow and others moving up to it from the village. The chopper whirred above them. It descended, hovered, touched down. Around the plastic bubble were brown Sherpa faces, staring, grinning. An arm waved, then more arms, then dozens.

It was like coming home.

There was one disappointment, a big one. Tashi was not there. He was out in the back country bringing yaks down from their summer pastures, and no one knew when he would be back. Other men were available, however. Of these, Eric hired six—three of whom he knew from the old days—and with their help set up a first small camp on the outskirts of Namche. Mrs. Bigelow seemed bothered neither by the lack of amenities nor the ten-thousand-foot altitude. That day and the next, with lively interest, she inspected the town and its dwellings, while Eric worked with the Sherpas on sorting and packing for the trip ahead.

How long they would be out from Namche he could only guess. Two weeks? Three? They had food enough for a month, and on return to Namche would send word by the radio at the Government checkpost (which sometimes worked) for Lundquist and his chopper to pick them up. Partly, as on any such venture, the timing would depend on weather; partly on how Mrs. Bigelow did; how far she wanted, and was able, to go. Without telling her, he saw to it that, among their items of equipment, there was a chair-shaped basket of the sort used by the Sherpas to carry the injured and ill. For her age, the Widow Bigelow was a formidable specimen, but the road to Dera Zor was not the Charles River Embankment.

On a cool crystalline morning they started out. The white wave of the peaks loomed high before them, and the trail twisted up and up through the rocky foothills. Leading the brief file, Eric set a leisurely pace, often looking back to see how the old lady was doing. And she was doing all right. At least as well as he, he noted, for the years of Kathmandu and how he had lived there had wreaked their havoc on his own lungs and legs. "Maybe it will be you, not she," he thought sardonically, "who'll be ending up as the basket case."

For ten minutes each hour they stopped and rested, and each time Mrs. Bigelow scanned the heights around them through a pair of binoculars. It was not the mountains she was studying, however. She was searching for birds. "My husband and I were life members of the Massachusetts Audubon Society," she informed Eric. "In season, we went on bird-watching trips every Sunday morning." And even here, on the far side of the earth, she knew her subject. "Ah, a snow pheasant!" she would exclaim. "A Benson's finch . . . a flight of choughs . . ." Then she was on her feet, on the march again, the binoculars sheathed, a pack slung on her back. Despite Eric's protests, she insisted on carrying her own small rucksack, in which she kept a few pieces of clothing and other personal items—among them the kitchen canister she had held on her lap during the flight in the helicopter. What was in the canister Eric still did not know. Cosmetics? For Mrs. Bigelow, hardly. Toiletries? Medicines? More likely. But the container stayed sealed.

Their camps consisted of four tents: two small individual ones for Mrs. B and himself, two larger ones for the six Sherpas. And the first night out from Namche they spent on a shelf of meadow above the Dudh Khosi. On the second day there was more up, always up, past the highest villages, the outpost lamasery, grazing yaks and their herders—but with no sign of Tashi. On the third morning they swung off from the Dudh Khosi to follow the Amun River. The weather held clear. To the northeast, once again as so long before, there was a fleeting glimpse of the snow-plumed crest of Everest.

For Eric, it was a journey through years no less than through miles. Here on the trail was the flat boulder, shaped like a fish, on which Franz Harben had sat to remove a boot and bandage a blistered foot. Beyond it a way, a rock-choked stream flowing down to the Amun, in which Julian Howard had missed his footing and gone in up to the waist. Mile by mile, the memories thronged back. There had been a time, an endless time, when he could not have endured them; when they would have driven him—*had* driven him—to drunkenness, flight, the very brink of self-destruction. Now he could endure them. He did. They were of the past. In the present, the now, Mrs. Bigelow sat on Franz's rock and searched for birds through her binoculars. At the stream where Julian had slipped, he turned, extended his hand to her, and brought her safely across.

His body too, along with his mind, was mending, strengthening. His hand, as he held hers, was firm and steady. Each day, though they moved ever higher, he was able to get more from his legs and lungs.

As for his unlikely client, she continued as she had begun: strong, controlled, imperturbable. By day, on the trail, she kept up the pace, moving slowly but steadily on long bony legs. She ate sparingly but uncomplainingly whatever Pasang, the Sherpa cook, produced at meal times. At night, soon after supper, she disappeared into her tiny tent and was not seen again until morning. The one departure from pattern—abrupt and startling—came on the fourth day, when she emerged from her tent as Pasang was preparing breakfast in the small clearing before it. On previous nights, Eric had noted, she had taken her kitchen canister into her tent, along with her other personal possessions. But on this night past she had apparently neglected to, for now, he saw, Pasang had it and had pried it open. He saw too that he had been wrong in his guess about toiletries or medicines. What it contained, on the contrary, seemed to be what it was designed to contain—flour, a fine yellowish flour—and Pasang, at the moment of Mrs. B's appearance, was about to pour it into a saucepan on his portable stove.

Always her voice, like the rest of her, had been quiet, restrained. But now, suddenly, it was high and piercing—

"No! No!" she cried.

Pasang stared at her.

"No!" It seemed all she could say.

Pasang collected himself. "For pancake, mem sah'b," he explained. "Looks good flour—make good cake."

"No!"

She said nothing more. Almost leaping forward, she snatched the canister from his one hand and its lid from the other. She clamped the lid back on. Then, holding her burden tightly, she rushed back into her tent.

Pasang stood motionless. So did the other Sherpas—and Eric. When a few minutes had passed he went to the flap of the tent and asked, "Are you all right, Mrs. Bigelow?"

Her voice came back low and normal. "Yes, quite all right, thank you. I shall be out presently."

When she reappeared there was no sign of the agitation that had shaken her. Nor any explanation of its cause. Sitting on the campstool that had been provided for her, she quietly ate the substitute breakfast that Pasang had prepared; then made ready with the rest of them for departure from camp. When they set off, the canister, closed and sealed, was in its usual place in her small rucksack.

The mountains drew nearer, closed in, enfolded them. The Amun River roared.

They camped again, moved on again, and each day gained altitude. From Namche's ten thousand feet they climbed to twelve, to thirteen, and it was on the fifth day out, beyond the thirteen mark, that Mrs. Bigelow began to fail. The first symptom was simply shortness of breath. On the trail, for the first time, she had to stop frequently and struggle for air. Then she began to cough, retch, finally vomit. "I shall be all right. I shall acclimatize," she insisted that evening at their campsite. But she had to force herself to eat; that night she was sick again; and in the morning, when she emerged from her tent, her breath came in labored gasps.

Eric spoke to her quietly. "I think we should turn back," he said.

She refused. She could go on, she told him. But after a short time on the trail she was again in distress. This time, after much persuasion, she consented to being carried, riding for the rest of the day on the backs of alternating Sherpas in the basket chair that had been brought along for such a contingency. That night was the same as the previous one. The next day she was again carried. But soon there were new difficulties, for toward midday they entered the gorge of the Amun. The trail narrowed and soared high on precipitous walls; the going underfoot was treacherous; and the rock wall above nudged out against the swaying basket, threatening to topple her and her bearer into the chasm below. About midafternoon, the trail dropped down to a small level shelf near the riverbank, and Eric called a halt. In its deep notch in the earth, the place was sunless and gloomy. But there was nothing for it. Here, he decided, they had reached the end of the line.

While the men pitched camp, Mrs. Bigelow sat motionless, silent. Her angular face was now gaunt, almost skeletal, and her tall, big-boned frame seemed to have shriveled, to have grown small and frail. When Pasang brought her food, she again tried to eat, again retched and threw up. Then weakly, unsteadily, she crept into her tent.

When Eric had finished his own meal, he approached its flap, spoke her name, and went in to her. She was in her sleeping bag, her head propped up against her rucksack, and there was just room enough for him to squat beside her.

"I'm sorry about this. Very sorry," he said.

She drew a deep rasping breath.

"How much farther is it?" she asked.

"To the base of the mountain?"

"To where you can see it."

He told her the truth. "Not far. Another short day's march . . . But we can't make it, Mrs. Bigelow."

"Yes—yes, we can," she said.

He shook his head. "The whole way is through the gorge. The same as today—only worse. The Sherpas can't carry you on such going. I'm responsible for your safety and theirs, and I won't let them try."

"I'll walk then."

"You can't; it's too hard. Tomorrow we'll have to turn back."

"No—no," she protested.

"We must. When you're lower you'll feel well again."

"I don't care about feeling well. I must get to the mountain— see the mountain!" Her voice grated; her chest rose and fell. "I *must*, Mr. Venn. It is terribly important."

Eric was silent.

"You think I'm a crazy old woman. That's what my children think; why they tried to stop me." Mrs. Bigelow's eyes fixed his. Her hand reached out and touched him. "But I'm not," she said. "Believe me, I'm not. Let me tell you why I am here, Mr. Venn, and you will see that—you will understand—"

As she had changed bodily, so too she had now changed in her manner and speech. Her defenses were down, her armor gone. Where there had been briskness, no-nonsense, self-assurance, there was a deep, almost desperate earnestness.

"You know about my husband and Dera Zor," she said.

"It was from him," said Eric, "that I first heard of it."

"From his book, yes. Then you know too how much it meant to him."

Eric nodded.

"I know too—now. But for a long time I didn't. Or pretended I didn't."

The old woman coughed. The cough became a paroxysm, and for a while she sat hunched in her sleeping bag struggling for breath. Then she spoke again. At intervals the coughing and gasping returned, but still, quietly, implacably, she forced the words out.

"I met Mr. Bigelow about a year after he had been out here," she said, "and a year after that we were married. He was then a geology instructor at Harvard, working toward an advanced degree, and when he had it he was planning to return here—to Dera Zor, the whole range of the Himalayas—to make them his special field of investigation. I was a normally romantic girl, I suppose. It seemed to me a grand prospect, and I could hardly wait until we went together . . . Or so I thought. It wasn't really that way at all . . . I had had a secure, settled life, and what I really wanted was for it to continue. I wanted a home, children, and we had them. For a while my husband kept talking, dreaming, of great travels and adventures, but I forced him into the pattern I wanted. He stayed on at Harvard and became a professor. Later, for several years, he was consulting geologist for a mining company, and had trips to the western states, to Canada and Mexico—but no farther. Then we returned to Cambridge to stay."

She drew a few deep rasping breaths and went on:

"For the whole last half of his life he never mentioned the Himalayas—or Dera Zor. I thought he had long since forgotten them. But I was wrong, so terribly wrong. All along they were with him, in his secret thoughts, his dreams; and the frustration poisoned his life. In his middle age he began to drink a lot. It became a problem. So much so that he had to give up his Harvard appointment well before he reached retirement age; and at home things were—well—not good. Perhaps you can understand, Mr. Venn; you said you have had a drinking problem yourself. But at least you are not married, or with a family, I gather. You have had your freedom, done what you wanted."

It was half statement, half question. Eric left it unanswered.

"As my husband grew older," said Mrs. Bigelow, "there was nothing that could have been done in any case. But still I didn't understand what had happened. It wasn't until almost the end that I understood—when he was close to death, in a sort of semi-coma—and then it all came out, it was all he talked of—he was back in the Himalayas, in the high wild places—back at Dera Zor —and he was happy at last."

She paused again. It seemed impossible that she could force more words from her wracked and straining frame. But they came—

"Then he died," she said. "Inside, he had been dead a long time, but now his body died too. And I knew that I had to do something. It was too late, of course. It would be futile, meaningless. But still I had to do it: to make this—this pilgrimage. To show him—or at least myself—that at last I understood. And that I cared—"

With an effort, she moved. Reaching up behind her, she

brought out from her rucksack the kitchen canister she had carried throughout the trip, and from which Pasang the Sherpa, a few mornings before, had been about to pour flour for pancakes.

"These are his ashes," she said. "This is why I came here. To leave them at the foot of the mountain—the place he loved best—"

Exhaustion at last overcame her. Setting the canister down, she lay back in her bag and closed her eyes. Almost instantly she seemed asleep, and Eric zipped the bag up around her and turned to crawl from the tent.

She was not asleep, however. Her voice followed him.

"So I must get there. I must," she murmured. "In the morning we shall go on, Mr. Venn. I shall be stronger, better . . ."

But she was not better.

At daybreak, soon after Eric and the Sherpas had risen, she came out from her tent; but almost at once she was again seized by spasms of retching and had to collapse into her camp chair. Pasang brought her tea, but she could not hold it down. She tried to speak, but the words stuck in her throat.

Eric spoke to her gently. "When we've struck camp," he said gently, "we'll start back and down."

"No—no—"

"We have to."

"We're so close now." Somehow she got the words out. "You said we are close."

"In distance, yes. But it's all through the gorge. It can't be done, Mrs. Bigelow."

She tried to get to her feet. But suddenly she swayed and he caught her. When she was back in the chair he crouched beside her and said, "When we're just a bit lower you'll be all right."

She did not answer. Her old face was drained, blank, with the acknowledgment of defeat. For a while she sat silently looking at the turgid waters of the Amun; then, raising her eyes, at the black rock of the gorge that rose above them like prison walls.

"The ashes—" she murmured.

She was silent again.

"To leave them here—" she said. "It's so dark, dismal. I wanted them close by the mountain with the sun bright on the snow."

She closed her eyes, bowed her head.

Then, a little later, she said, "Mr. Venn—"

"Yes?" said Eric.

"Would you—could you, or the Sherpas perhaps—would it be possible for you to take them on for me—to leave them where you can see the mountain—where it's tall and bright in the sun—?"

It was Eric's turn for silence.

"Please," she said. "Please. It isn't far, you said. And it would mean so much to me. So much—to my husband."

He was still crouching beside her, and with her veined, bony hand she touched his. "I shall be all right here," she said. "I shall rest here and be all right, and then tomorrow we shall go down."

For another few moments he did not move. Then he turned his own hand, took hers, and pressed it gently.

"Very well, I'll take them," he said.

"Oh thank you—thank you—"

He stood up. He ate the breakfast that Pasang brought him. He went into his tent for the few things he needed, then into Mrs. Bigelow's for the kitchen canister. He put the canister into his own rucksack and slung it on. Calling the Sherpas together, he told them that he would be back by midafternoon, and that meanwhile they should take all possible care of Mrs. Bigelow. He should, he knew, be taking at least one of them with him. The trail ahead was steep and rough; he should have a companion. But he did not want a companion.

. . . Unless it could have been Tashi. And there was no Tashi . . .

Mrs. Bigelow still sat in her camp chair, her eyes now closed, breathing deeply but quietly. As if in her sleep she murmured, "—where the mountain is tall and the sun is bright." Then she opened her eyes and said in her usual brisk New England voice, "There is no need to say a prayer, Mr. Venn. And I shall have no further use for the container."

He looked at her. Perhaps he stared at her. Then with a gesture of salute he turned and left. Beyond the campsite, the trail led steeply up from the riverbank along the northern rampart of the gorge, and this he followed for an hour, a second, a third, as it swung up and down, in and out, clinging precariously to the wall above the torrent below. His progress, though scarcely fast, was far less slow than when in caravan with Mrs. Bigelow; and he was able to maintain the pace he first set for himself. Each day on the march he had felt a little stronger, a little more the mountaineer he had once been, and now he neither rested nor felt the need to. Even after the years of shriveling and wastage, he had reserves he could draw on.

From the camp, in the trough of the gorge, the slit of sky far above had been gray and murky with dawnlight. Now, even as the day progressed—even as he climbed higher toward the gorge's rim—it did not brighten perceptibly, and he realized that this day was the first since departure from Namche that was not bright and clear. There was no storm. No wind blew in the canyon, and he could hear none above. But the sky remained gray and heavy. Mist curled on the rims of rock above him, and toward midday a thick damp snow began to fall. The upper end of the gorge was now close—very close. Soon the walls would curve to the north; they would flare out, subside; and beyond would be— what?

Dera Zor? Or a void?

It was a void.

A half hour later he had passed the curve. The gorge had opened, it was behind him, and he stood again where he had stood years before, at the base of the valley fronting the south face of the mountain. In the same place, yet a wholly different place, for all was now different. Then he had been with companions—with Tashi, with Ken and Julian; with Franz Harben, Ted Lassiter, Gil McLeod—and they had stood looking upward in the moment of climax and vision. Now he was alone—and there was nothing. There was snow, mist, grayness. There was a wasteland of boulders. Beyond the boulders, he knew, was the Kalpurtha Glacier; above it the peaks, three peaks, the trinity; to the west, Mount Kalpurtha—to the east, Mount Malu—between them, the south face of Dera Zor tiering skyward. They were there—but not there. What was there was snow, mist and void.

There came a moment, then, when he almost entered the void. He would go on. He would move up through the waste to the snout of the glacier; up the glacier to the icefall; up the icefall to the Gap, and beyond . . . to where he had once climbed and struggled and met shame and defeat . . . to where Julian was, where Franz was, and where he too would now go, with what was left of the man who had first led him to Dera Zor . . . with what was left of himself . . . climbing again, farther, higher, up the soaring west ridge, toward the shoulder, the Wailing Wall, the white dome beyond. For that was why he had come: to go as far as he could, as high as he could: to climb again on this mountain and never come back.

He looked up into nothingness . . .

No.

It was not why he had come.

He had come as the delegate of a widow with no first name called Mrs. Bigelow. He had come for her, not himself. Unslinging his rucksack, he took from it her kitchen canister, opened it, and looked at its yellow-gray floury contents. As she had instructed, he said no prayer. He no longer knew a prayer. He swung the container and scattered the ashes of Homer Bigelow, fellow dreamer and drunkard, on the waste before him, and in a few moments they had sifted down and all but vanished among the stones and snow. Crumpling the canister under his heel, he wedged it tightly under a nearby boulder, so that it would not roll and bang among the rocks when next a wind rose.

The mist was denser now, the snow falling more heavily. Already, there was no sign of the ashes he had scattered—as there was no sign of the mountain that rose above them . . . So be it, he thought. It didn't matter . . . The next day, or the next, the snow would stop, the mist would dissolve, and Dera Zor, as Mrs. Bigelow wanted, would stand tall and shining in sunlight.

Turning, he re-entered the gorge of the Amun River.

Below twelve thousand feet she was all right again, and in four days they were back in inhabited country. As they entered the Sherpa village of Munda there was a sudden shout—"Rick Sah'b!" —and it was Tashi. This was his home town. He had returned the day before from the high pastures, and his monkey face beamed with joy.

The next day he accompanied them to Namche Bazar, and here Eric paid off the other Sherpas and radioed Kathmandu from the Government checkpost. The radio, it developed, was in one of its working moods, and word came back that Lundquist, in the AID helicopter, would fly to Namche the next morning. When, later, Mrs. Bigelow had retired to her tent at their campsite, he and Tashi sat in the darkness outside and talked for much of the night.

At midmorning there was a whirring in the sky, and with Mrs. Bigelow, Tashi and half the population of Namche he ascended the path above the town. To the small level meadow, the waiting chopper . . . And beyond them, to what?

To the Himalayan Palace?

To Amy?

He helped Mrs. Bigelow into the plastic bubble and stowed her gear on the seat behind her.

"You'll be all right with Mr. Lundquist," he told her.

She looked at him uncomprehendingly.

"I've been asked to stay here," he said. "And I'd like to."

"Here?"

She showed her surprise. But there were no more questions, no protest. A woman who made her own decisions, she accepted his right to make his.

"Yes, I shall be quite all right," she said crisply. "I wish you a pleasant stay, Mr. Venn—and I thank you most kindly."

"I thank you too," Eric said.

He kissed her seamed and leathery cheek; then closed the door of the bubble and gestured to Lundquist. The chopper rumbled, roared, rose, angled off. Soon it was a dot over the hills to the southwest, and with Tashi he set off on the walk to the village of Munda.

With Tashi . . .

Thus began the years with Tashi.

But where was he now? . . . He, Pembol, Larry? . . . They had been due to leave the snow hole at dawn. Now they were overdue. The stars, the blackness were now long since gone. The sky was brightening with daylight.

Again (for the tenth time? the twentieth?) he turned and looked downward. And this time, finally, he saw what he hoped to see. Far below, near the base of the dome, there was a tiny movement against the whiteness of snow. Three specks were moving. Moving upward.

They were coming at last.

He forgot his struggle for air, for strength. Raising his ax, he waved it, but he could not tell if they saw him. They were too small, too distant for him to see if they were waving back.

It didn't matter.

They were there. They were coming.

Larry, Pembol, Tashi . . .

18

Back there—back then—it was not a mountain but a hillside on which he stood, and it was Tashi alone who was climbing toward him. Roundabout, the yaks were grazing, snouts bent to the sparse alpine grass. The little Sherpa picked his way among them, joined Eric, and the two sat together on a patch of soft moss.

From their vantage point Tashi counted the animals. "Are all here," he said.

Eric nodded.

As Sherpas went, Tashi was prosperous. This year he owned eighteen yaks, and a few weeks earlier, in mid-June, he and Eric had begun driving them up to their high summer pastures. Sometimes they were together, sometimes they split up; and one of the splits had come three days before, when five yaks had wandered off and they had taken different directions to search for them.

"They'd got up into a gully and were hidden by boulders," said Eric. "It was the birds after their droppings that gave them away."

Tashi grinned. "Are good yakherd," he said. And this was praise from Caesar.

For a while, on the hillside, they rested, with the yaks grazing around them. During the morning there had been a monsoon rainfall, bringing a tinge of new luster to the pale highland grass. But now at midday the sky was blue, the sun was warm, the peaks above them (as Mrs. Bigelow would have wanted) were bright and gleaming. Eric moved his eyes across the immense panorama.

He closed them, half-dozing, and felt the sun on his lids. Then with Tashi he rose and moved on with the yaks.

"You not tired, Rick Sah'b?" Tashi asked.

"No, not tired."

Tashi studied him. His grin was gone and in its place a quiet smile.

"You happy, I think, Rick Sah'b."

"Yes, happy," said Eric.

They moved on and up.

By day they followed the yaks. The nights they spent either in the small tent they carried with them or in the crude shelters of Sherpa "summer villages," built especially for use during the months of high pasturage. In the villages they were usually with other herdsmen. Out beyond them they were alone.

It was a world in which nature was vast, man minute. Looking southward from the slopes, they could see for miles across Solu Khumbu: down the deep gash of Dudh Khosi River (fed by the stream of the Amun and many others), past the Sherpa villages, over ridge and valley, for half the breadth of Nepal. To the north —and as they moved farther, to east and west as well—rose the giants of the High Himalayas, roof of the earth. Nearest were the peaks of Solu Khumbu itself—Khumbila, Taweche, Kangtega— looming overhead in their bristle of rock, their festoon of glacier. Farther back were still greater ones, rank upon rank, culminating in the greatest of all, the triple mass of Nuptse-Lhotse-Everest, called by the Sherpas Chomolungma, Goddess-Mother of the World.

"Because it is there—" Mallory had said of Everest. But it was a sometimes there. The mountains came and went. Monsoon closed in, with rain below, snow above, and they were lost in a weaving sea of cloud and mist. For hours, sometimes days, they were gone. All that penetrated the shroud was the distant rumbling of avalanches. Then the magic happened; the wand was waved; they were *there* again—tall, gigantic in their clarity. One alone among them was not there: Dera Zor. Through night and day, storm and sunlight, it remained forever hidden behind the ramparts of its neighbors.

In the vastness there was also smallness. At sixteen thousand feet, close beneath the sweep of glaciers, the yaks rooted for blades of grass so thin and frail that it seemed a billion of them would not fill one hairy belly. Bordering frozen whiteness, like a myriad winking eyes, were swaths of bright flowers, tiny and tough . . . In the stillness there was life. Here a hare darted, and there a marmot. On a crag above, watching them warily, stood a beardless tahr, the high Himalayan goat. Through silence, suddenly, would come a twittering, a flutter of wings, as a blue-and-gold bird (Mrs. B. would have known its name) spiraled off into space.

For a month and more they moved always upward. Then, as the wheel of summer turned, it was down and down. From whiteness and grayness, they came to greenness, to growth; to silver moss and clumps of juniper; to blooms of gentian, iris, primula, azalea. They returned to broader pastures and other herders, to the summer villages and the world of men. In a high bowl of land above a river's gorge there was a world within the world: an encampment of Tibetans who during the past few years had fled over the mountain passes from their now Red Chinese homeland. Many of the refugees had by now gone on to Kathmandu and beyond; but several hundred had stayed. And though age-old neighbors and racial cousins of the Sherpas, they were, in Solu Khumbu, still aliens, still strangers . . . "More strangers than you, Rick Sah'b," said Tashi, as they passed among them. "It is not how far a man comes but what he brings in his heart."

In man's world now, they descended on trails through the uplands. Along the way stood squat Buddhist chortens and long mani walls ("keep always to the left," said Tashi), and prayer flags flew bright on ridge and hilltop. They came to lamaseries, sounding with horns and gongs, and in their courtyards mingled with red-robed monks with spinning prayer wheels. Then came a zone of terraced hills, bearing crops of potatoes and barley, corn and beans, from which Sherpa women, the sturdy Sherpanis, were gathering the late summer harvest. And still, driving their yaks, they moved on and down, and ahead now, at last, were the permanent villages of Solu Khumbu: the metropolis of Namche Bazar . . . the lesser huddles of houses called Khumjung and Kundi, Millingo and Thami . . . the huddle called Munda . . . and at Munda they stopped, for this was Tashi's home.

And now Eric's, too.

In that autumn that followed it had been his home for a year. Arriving in Munda after Mrs. Bigelow's departure, he had planned to set up his tent close by the village, but Tashi had said, "No, you come my house." And he had gone—and stayed. All Sherpa homes were basically alike: rough two-story structures with thick stone walls and slate roofs, in which the lower level was for animals, the upper for humans. But Tashi's was bigger than most, and upstairs, instead of the usual one room, there were two. The larger was the all-purpose area where he and his family ate, drank, slept—in fact lived totally—in total nonprivacy; the smaller, no more than ten feet by eight, officially a "shrine room" of the Buddhist faith. Like most non-lama Sherpas, however, Tashi was strictly part-time in religious devoutness and, far from showing qualms, enthusiastically insisted that Eric move in among its brass Buddhas, ceremonial scarves and jeweled prayer wheels.

Here he slept, equipped with air mattress and sleeping bag. But the rest of his at-home time was spent largely in the common room—a long, low-ceilinged place, devoid of beds and sparse in other furniture, but filled with household goods and clothes and implements and stored-up food and smoke and noise and adults and children. For Tashi's was no small family, and, except when obscured by gray clouds from the huge but chimneyless fireplace, it was highly visible. At center stage (for, unlike Hindu-Nepalese women, Sherpanis did not retreat into corners) was his wife Ai Lamu, bigger than he, plump of face and midriff, forever busy with the rites of housewifery. And roundabout, now working, now playing, but always there and always audible, were their four daughters, Aila, Pendi, Chanji, Dola, ranging in age from perhaps six to ten.

"No son," said Tashi sadly. "Each time I say it will be son; but no, is girl, four girls." He brooded, then looked at Eric. "Do you have son, Rick Sah'b?" he asked.

It was a question he had not been asked before, and a moment passed before he answered.

"No," he said.

"Is sad to have no son," said Tashi. Then he brightened. "But anyhow is Pembol, who is like a son."

Pembol, the only other male in the household, was a sturdy boy in his early teens whose parents had died, some years before, of smallpox. "I want son, so take him here with me," said Tashi. "Is good boy. I make pretend is mine."

Besides Pembol, there was another adopted family member. This was a girl—or young woman—called Nima, and she too was a waif-and-stray, the widow of a cousin of Tashi's, also a climbing Sherpa, who had been lost two years back in an avalanche on Makalu. She had no children. "My cousin unhappy," said Tashi. "He want, but no come; not even girl." He shrugged. "But now no matter." Like almost all Sherpanis, Nima was short, a scant five feet or so; but whereas most were squat and solid, she was slender, almost frail in appearance, and her face, framed by black braids of hair, was fine-boned, delicate of feature. Her eyes, though Mongoloid, were large, expressive. But she herself was not. In the lively ménage, she was the silent, subservient one, half family member, half domestic slavey. She was fetcher and carrier, nursemaid to the children, charwoman of the premises, including Eric's "shrine room"; and soon after his arrival Tashi asked him if he would not also like her to share it with him at night.

He had declined with thanks.

"She is a nice girl, is clean," Tashi had argued. "And a man needs a woman."

"In Kathmandu," Eric told him, "I had too much woman. I'm taking a holiday."

In the beginning, in his first days in Munda, he had small idea of how long he would stay. His thought, if he could have been said to have one, was that after a while he would take off—for Kathmandu, India, somewhere; but the weeks and then months

279

went by, and there he was, still in Munda. To the degree that he could, he earned his keep. With Tashi, in season, he plowed in the fields. He herded yaks, goats and sheep. He tended to the drafts, leaks and crumblings of the house, and hewed wood for the fires that would keep it warm during the winter. He found satisfaction in what he did. And irony too. For though he had often lived roughly, it had been in the special, even sophisticated world of the mountaineer, not in that of primitive subsistence. He had not even been a country boy, but an urban, or at least suburban one. It had remained until now—until (yes, face it) his early middle age—for him to live as a farmhand; and on a farm not of the present but of the Middle Ages.

What was of the present in Munda derived almost wholly from expeditions. Most of the houses, especially those of climbing Sherpas like Tashi, were storehouses of mountaineering left-overs and loot: canned and processed foods, tents and sleeping bags, pressure cookers and flashlights, even radios and battery razors—and if many of the items were useless, it was still a cachet to possess them. Perhaps half the men dressed habitually in expedition-issue clothing: shirts and knickers, boots and parkas. And the same half were able to talk, in varying degrees, in one or another Western language. Tashi especially, with many British and American expeditions behind him, had notably improved his English since the days on Dera Zor; and it was in English that Eric usually spoke with him, reserving his Nepalese and rudimentary Sherpa for the rest of the family.

Beyond these accretions, however, the ways of Solu Khumbu were as they had been for ages past. The women, without exception, still wore their traditional wrap-around blouses and broad-striped aprons, and even at work in the fields were bright with beads and bangles. The nonclimbing men dressed Tibetan-style in homespun tunics, yak-hide boots, brocaded hats with great earflaps; and some wore pigtails, all carried kukris. Village councils and religious rituals were unchanged from centuries back—as were heating (logs or yak dung), lighting (yak-butter lamps), water supply (from the handiest stream), and sewage (returned to the same stream). Transport was by yak or human foot-power. There were no hospitals or medicines, no schools or books. Contact with the outer world was by a two-week journey (which few ever made) up and down the ancient trail across the saw-toothed miles of Himalayan foothills.

It was a hermetic world: remote, harsh, deprived: a world scarcely touched by the twentieth century. Yet it had in it, too, something that transcended the century, any century; something timeless, eternal. Part of it was a quality inherent anywhere, everywhere, in simple men in a hard environment. But part, too, lay in the special nature of the Sherpas. What made them what they were was a question asked by every outsider who had come among them. Other primitive people lived among high mountains, but did not climb them. Others welcomed strangers (more or less), but did not embrace them. Others lived lives as hard, but did not thrive like Sherpas. They did not play and laugh like Sherpas. No one laughed like Sherpas. No one bore loads as they did, climbed mountains as they did, lived and struggled and made do as they did—undefeated, unbrutalized—with such a will, such a grin, such a total lack of self-pity.

In the village of Munda, Eric watched them. He marveled.

And at first they marveled in return.

Munda was not, like the larger Namche, on the usual route of expeditions. Its people had seen occasional outsiders, but none before had ever stayed there, and in the early days stares had followed him wherever he went. It was the children—Tashi's daughters and others—who started the change. At first frozen with shyness, they soon took to following him around. In fascination, they examined his wristwatch, his shoelaces, the zippers on his parka and trousers. Then, with the novelty past, they took him for granted—and so too, in due time, did their elders. As to Tashi, he became Rick Sah'b to everyone. "No Sah'b, just Rick. My name is Rick," he told them. But it had no effect on them, including Tashi. Rick Sah'b was his name, and so it stayed.

The British Raj had never come to Sherpa-land. There were no overtones in *sahib*, no connotations of servant and master, status or caste; nor were there any such distinctions among the people themselves. As in any community, there were the more prosperous and prestigious ones (such as Tashi), and those who were less so. But the basic equality of all was unquestioned and absolute, the social intermingling complete. The Sherpas loved companionship. They loved a party. They loved to eat and drink and dance and laugh and argue (and sometimes fight) (and then make up), and in Munda, at the slightest excuse, there would be nighttime, often nightlong, gatherings in this home or that. As often as not they would be at Tashi's—with smoke, shouts, and song filling the main room, the children asleep in the midst of the hubbub, and Ai Lamu and Nima serving food and drink. There were great bowls of chang, the Sherpa beer, fat gourds of arak (here called rakshi and made from potatoes), and for the men it was a social obligation to get thoroughly drunk. Eric observed the amenities; he too drank at the parties until he could drink no more. But it was different altogether from what it had been at other times, other places. This was good drinking, happy drinking. It had warmth, laughter, comradeship. At two or three in the morning it would finally end, with half the guests falling down the stairs, the other half asleep on the floor, and Tashi, bedded down with Ai Lamu, shouting to Eric that he should do likewise with Nima.

He didn't. Each night he ended up alone in the shrine room with the brass Buddhas. Each time he thought that perhaps the next time he would take Nima with him. But he didn't.

The parties were most frequent in winter. With the fall crops in and food for the animals provided, there was little to do until the following spring, and for the men of Munda they provided a way of letting off steam. During the day, while the women did the household chores, the men slept or loafed. When work had to be done, no one on earth could work harder than a Sherpa. But he was content to wait for the necessity. While the snow fell on the village and the wind howled down from the mountains, the Mundans idled the hours away in the snugness of their homes.

And Eric idled with them.

Then the day came, in his second winter, when he looked up

from where he was sitting in the main room of Tashi's house, to find the little Sherpa watching him curiously.

"Well?" he asked.

Tashi said nothing.

"You're thinking something. What is it?"

Tashi hesitated. Then he said, "I think—I wonder—you are still happy, Rick Sah'b?"

"Still happy," said Eric.

Tashi nodded, half-smiled. "Am glad." But his monkey face was still puzzled.

"You don't believe me?"

"I believe, yes. But—"

"What?"

"But I not understand. You are sah'b, man from West. But now you live like Sherpa."

"I like the way Sherpas live."

"Yes. But—" Tashi paused, thinking. "But sah'bs different," he said. "Sah'bs know much, do much. I see on expeditions. I see with you on Dera Zor: how much you think, how much you do."

"We were climbing a mountain."

"Even when not climb, when in tent at night—you sit with flashlight and write. You write much then, I remember."

"Yes, I wrote then," said Eric.

"Why you not write now, Rick Sah'b?"

Eric smiled. "Because I have no paper."

"Is paper in monasteries. Can get from lamas."

"No. No, I think not. I'm not writing now, Tashi."

The puzzlement in the wizened face deepened, became a frown. In all their time together—back on the mountain, now in Munda —Tashi had never questioned or disagreed with him. On the whole terrible descent of Dera Zor and the march-out back to Kathmandu, he had made no comment, passed no judgment on what had happened . . . But he passed judgment now.

"I think you should write, Rick Sah'b," he said.

"Why?"

"If man is climber, should climb. If is writer, should write."

Eric shook his head. He rose. "I *was* a writer—but not now."

"And climber?"

"No, not now, either."

Tashi persisted. "Is not good," he said. "Was climber, writer, and now no. Man must be what he is, Rick Sah'b."

"I'm a farmer. A yakherd."

"Is not enough. You are sah'b, can do more. Must do what sah'b can do."

"All right, I'll do more. I've been thinking of something, and I'll start tomorrow."

Tashi grinned. "You be writer again?"

"No, not a writer."

"What, then?"

"A carpenter."

"Car-pen-ter? What is that?"

"A man who make things of wood."

"What kind things, Rick Sah'b?"

"You'll see," said Eric.

That was the winter of the john.

For a long while past he had been telling Tashi and anyone else who would listen that Munda's sanitation system, or lack of it, was a menace, and that the people must stop using as a latrine the same stream from which they drew their water. The climbing Sherpas had heard the same lecture on expeditions. They nodded, they agreed. The village council agreed. But nothing changed; nothing happened. So now the time had come, Eric decided, when he would do something himself. He alone could not build privies for the whole of Munda. But he would at least build one for Tashi's household and hope that the rest would follow along.

Climbing Everest might have been easier. It took a month to assemble the needed lumber, another to fashion it into boards with the primitive tools available. To begin with he set up shop in the lower level of Tashi's house, where the animals had their winter shelter; but nudging bodies, plus the stench, soon drove him out, and in the open he was blue with cold after an hour's work. Further, he was strictly an amateur carpenter. Boards warped and cracked under his hands; joints did not fit; crude tools and rusty nails had plans of their own. Originally he had envisioned his creation as a two-holer, with one seat for adults, one for children. But the cutting of circular patterns defeated him, and he had to settle for a single, roughly triangular aperture abristle with jagged edges.

Still he persevered. At last the structure was finished. It had been his plan to set it up on a patch of level ground behind the house; but the earth there—and everywhere—proved so stony and frozen that no hole could be dug. He therefore fashioned two beams as supports and, with Tashi and the boy Pembol helping, set it up on the rim of a nearby ravine.

The rest of Munda watched and commented.

"Rick Sah'b leaves Tashi," they said.

"He builds his own house."

"Is small."

"He will sleep standing up."

House or outhouse, it was to be all his own. Tashi used it once, emerged with splinters in his buttocks, and returned to the communal stream. Ai Lamu refused to let the four girls use it, for fear they would fall through the hole into the ravine below. And she herself shunned it, as did Pembol and Nima—leaving Eric as sole user. There was of course no toilet paper in Munda. But among Tashi's expedition loot he had found, improbably, several paperback books, which he used both for reading and otherwise; and now, in his clifftop eyrie, his companion was *War and Peace*. The quality of its paper was poor, but there were plenty of pages, and each day he read a half-dozen or so before tearing them out. In them, as Napoleon and his army retreated, raged the Russian winter. Outside, raged the winter of Solu Khumbu. The privy shook in the wind, snow poured through its cracks, and from the ravine below a gale roared up through its saw-edged hole, carrying Tolstoy's discarded pages back with it.

It was not of Tolstoy, though, that Eric thought at these times. It was of Amy Bulwinkle.

"You'll freeze your balls off," had been her farewell words to him.

And the point had been well taken.

He finished *War and Peace*. He began *Moby Dick*. Then at last the long winter began to blow itself out. Ice thawed. Snow receded. On the first springlike day he and Tashi drove the yaks out from their cold-weather pens to the nearby pastures . . . And the day after that came a message from Namche Bazar.

Its bearers were two climbing Sherpas, old friends of Tashi's, and their news was that an American expedition to Everest had arrived in Namche. Many Sherpas, some from Solu Khumbu, some from Darjeeling, had been with it on the march from Kathmandu; but now still more were wanted for the mountain itself. A few—real climbers, Tigers—had been asked for by name, and one of these was Tashi.

Tashi was proud, jubilant. He embraced the messengers. He embraced Eric. Then he told Ai Lamu, and she merely nodded, for she was a Sherpa wife and knew this was the way things were.

An hour later he was ready to go.

Then he stared at Eric.

"But you—" he said. "You not ready, Rick Sah'b."

"I'm not coming," said Eric.

"Yes, you come!"

"They sent for you, not for me."

"But they Americans. Will be your friends. You come, I come, we climb together."

"No, Tashi. They have their team; they won't want me . . . Besides, I've told you, I don't climb anymore."

Tashi argued. He pleaded. But to no avail. In the end, as he turned to take off with his friends on the trail to Namche, he was close to tears.

"Good climbing!" Eric called after him.

Tashi did not turn.

"I'll take care of the yaks."

Tashi trudged on.

He took care of the yaks.

He liked being with the yaks.

They were stupid animals. They were ugly, awkward, dirty. But they were also wonderful. Nothing fazed them. Nothing defeated them. They grazed, munched, grunted, moved uphill, moved downhill, and looked out at the world with brown, gentle, patient eyes. They performed their function, and their function was everything. They were the Sherpa's transport. They were his milk and butter and cheese, and (when he relaxed his Buddhist scruples) his meat. They were his clothing, his boots, his blankets, the oily fat for his lamps, the dried dung for his fires. They were his wealth, his livelihood. They were what enabled man to survive in the harsh world of the High Himalayas.

Spring came on. With the other men of Munda, Eric plowed the fields. Then the women took over for planting, and he returned to the yaks. In the late spring, with the meadows roundabout well grazed over, he began driving them up again to the high pastures, and this time, in Tashi's absence, his companion was young Pembol.

They moved up . . . and up . . .

The sun grew warmer, brighter. The mountains gleamed.

They came to the high lamasery of Thyangboche: to its redrobed monks, its horns and gongs, its flags and wheels. Turning the wheels, the monks chanted the litany of their ancient faith: *"Om mani padme hum . . .* the jewel is in the lotus . . . *om mani padme hum . . ."* And Eric sat beside them, watching, listening. During his years in Nepal he had learned something of Buddhism. Here in Solu Khumbu he had thought of becoming a Buddhist, even of joining a lamasery as an apprentice monk. But it had not come to pass. Nor, he now knew, would it ever. He, like all men (by whatever name they called it), sought the Eightfold Way, the long steep path to Nirvana. But, for him, it was not in the forms and rituals of far Thyangboche—no more than it had been in those of Denver's Claremont Avenue Lutheran Church. With the boy Pembol he moved on from the world of the lamas. Driving the yaks, they climbed on still higher, into stillness and space.

Around them, before them, rose the host of the peaks. And presently, among them, straight ahead, there lay the high white pass called the Nangpa La. This was the gateway of Tibet. Across it had come—and still came—the tide of refugees fleeing their homeland. And beyond it spread the vastness of Red China. If Thyangboche was an avatar of the past, here, perhaps, was the shape of the future; and, as with Buddhism, he had felt its pull, its lure. But to what end? The world beyond was closed, sealed, hostile. If he crossed the Nangpa La, it would be a journey into self-extinction: to border guards, the mouths of guns, arrest, imprisonment. And it was not for this that he had come to the ends of the earth.

He turned away. He faced the mountains. To the east stood Everest, its snow plume streaming in the wild west wind.

"The expedition it should be high now," said Pembol, standing beside him.

Eric nodded. "Yes, high. The weather has been good."

"Au Tashi"—au meant uncle in Sherpa—"he high now too, I think. Maybe he even get to top."

"I hope so."

"When I big," said Pembol, "I get to top. I climb Everest, Dera Zor, all mountains. I climb better than Tenzing, best of all Sherpas."

"Go to it," said Eric.

And he turned away from Everest too.

Spring became summer. They slept in the summer villages. Moving higher, through the flowered meadows beneath the glaciers, they camped on soft moss and built their evening fires of juniper twigs. One night, when the fire had burned low, there was a sound in the darkness beyond it, and Pembol stiffened in fear.

"Is yeti, I think, Rick Sah'b," he said.

"No, no yeti," said Eric.

"This yeti country."

The boy strained, listening. But there was no further sound.

"You have seen yeti?" he asked.

Eric considered. "Yes, once," he said.

"Where?"

"In a mirror."

Pembol did not understand. "He was big?" he asked. "Ugly?"

"Yes. Big and ugly."

"How he look?"

"He had lots of hair," Eric said, "and he smelt. He had red eyes, sort of wild and crazy, and a big tooth that swung loose."

"He scare you?"

"Yes."

"He hurt you?"

"He tried to."

Eric put his arm around Pembol's shoulder. "But there are no yetis here," he reassured him. "The sound you heard was the yaks."

"You are sure, Rick Sah'b?"

"Yes, sure."

Pembol smiled. "I am glad," he said. "Yetis bad, yaks good."

"Yes, yaks are better," said Eric.

They slept, wakened, moved on. Across the meadows. Later, down the meadows. The flowers winked and gleamed; the yaks munched and mooed; and he watched them, followed them, and was content.

Then, in the dark of another night, there was another sound. It was neither of yak nor yeti, but a human voice: a voice he had not heard now, even in dreams, for many years.

"What the hell are you doing with your life?" it asked crisply. And his brother Frank studied him with a cool gray stare.

"What I want to," he said.

No, it was more than that.

"What I must."

"Still the Hillbilly—"

"No," said Eric, "a yakherd."

"Will you spell that, please?"

"Y-a-k-h-e-r-d."

"Hmm." Frank wrote it down. He pressed a buzzer. "Take a memo, Miss Swenson. From the president—" (so he was president now) "—to all department heads. Subject: yakherds. Notice is hereby given that, in its new expansion program, Burden Industries will undertake the herding of yaks. Spelled y-a-k-s. The project will be promptly implemented on all levels, and a time study instituted to insure maximum efficiency."

He switched off and led Eric from the office. Outside, they got into his Cadillac (or Continental? or Imperial?) and drove to his home (that was no longer in Santa Monica but high on a crest above Beverly Hills). The two girls, Joyce and Sheila (now in their late teens: half girls, half women), were there, and Frank said, "This is your Uncle Yakherd," and after wrinkling their noses at his smell, they kissed him dutifully on the cheek. Then Kay was there, slim and glowing (no older, it seemed, than her daughters), bearing dry martinis (or was it chang or rakshi?); but she did not kiss him. (Would she kiss him later?) And Larry was there. (Aged what now? thirteen? fourteen?) But he could not see his face. He had never seen it, did not know it. And Kay said, "This is your uncle—"

"No," said Eric, "not uncle—"

—And Pembol said, "What, Rick Sah'b?" And they rose, drank buttered tea, and moved on with the yaks.

There was only the one dream: no more.

He lived in the world of the yaks. Of the meadows and peaks. Larry—his nephew? his son?—was remote beyond them. Kay was remote. Even Amy. When he thought of a woman now (and after so long without one, such thoughts were increasing), it was of the Sherpani Nima, the waif of Tashi's household: small, shy, silent, with her long black braids and large dark eyes.

Hillbilly . . . Yakherd . . .

All right, it was what he had chosen. He was content.

He recalled the words Tashi had spoken the previous summer while they had herded together: "It is not how far a man comes," he had said, "but what he brings in his heart."

Now the summer was ending.

They moved down . . . down . . .

In the first villages they reached there were climbing Sherpas, and from them they heard about the American expedition to Everest. Though one man had been lost, it had been a great success. The peak had been climbed by two separate routes; six men had reached the summit; and of these, one had been a Sherpa—Nawang Gombu of Darjeeling, a nephew of the great Tenzing.

And the Americans, Eric asked—who had they been?

He was told the names. And they were unfamiliar.

There was no Ken Naylor? No Naylor Sah'b?

No, no Naylor Sah'b.

And Tashi? What of Tashi, from Munda?

Tashi had not gone quite all the way, they said. There had been enough oxygen for only six. But he had gone high, very high—had been a Tiger of Tigers—and as a reward he had been taken, with Gombu and a few others, on a visit to America.

They drank to Tashi: with chang, with rakshi. For Pembol, they were his first man's drinks, and he was proud and happy—and later, sick.

Then they came to Khumjung, to Namche Bazar, at last to Munda. They came to Tashi's house, and he was not yet back, and except for Eric and Pembol it was a house of women. The four girls squealed at them, Ai Lamu cooked for them, and Nima served them. When the meal was over, Eric went into his own room, the shrine room, to the brass Buddhas and scarves and jeweled prayer wheels. He was home again.

He spread his bedding on the floor, removed his boots, prepared for sleep. Then there was a movement at the door, and it was Nima. She held a flickering butter-lamp in her hand, and its light gleamed on the braids of her hair and in her shy dark eyes.

"You have all you want, Rick Sah'b?" she asked.

"Yes," he said.

"You like some more tea? some chang?"

"No, thanks."

Nima turned to go. Then he spoke her name.

"Yes, Rick Sah'b?" she asked.

"Just Rick," he said.

"Yes. Just Rick, Rick Sah'b."
He smiled. He put out his hand to her.
"Stay with me, Nima," he said.
And she stayed.

There had been too much aloneness. Throughout his life, even when surrounded by others, he had been too often, too long alone.

Back there, back then, he had turned to Nima. Now, on the dome of Dera Zor, he turned his eyes downward to the three moving dots on the snow below. The dots that were Tashi, Pembol, Larry. That were coming to join him. They were still far down, but they would move faster than he had. He had done his job, kicked the steps in the snow, and in his steps they were following. In two hours, perhaps less, they would be with him.

Again he rested. He had earned the rest. With the dome intervening, he could not see off to the east; but he knew that the sun had risen. Overhead, the sky shone with its brightness, and the snowy rims of the dome gleamed with pink and gold.

He had earned the sunrise too.

19

Nima had loved the sun. For most Sherpas, weather was simply something to be coped with—for crops, for pasturage, for climbing a mountain. But Nima's moods, the very essence of her, varied with its changes. When days were gray, so too was she: silent, withdrawn, little more than a shadow. When they were bright, she brightened. Her face glowed; her eyes smiled; often she hummed or sang at her work.

She was still a Sherpani, though, and there were limits.

On a summer day as warm and sunlit as any he had known in Solu Khumbu, Eric and she alone, had been following a stream down through the meadows above Munda. He was hot and sweating. The stream ran clear and free; he knew there were no village latrines higher up; and stopping, he stripped and waded in for a bath. Nima stood by, waiting. "You too!" he called, but she didn't move, and, grinning, he came out to get her. "You, my pet," he told her, "are going to have the first bath of your lifetime." And gently, playfully, he began to remove her clothes.

She did not resist him. She had never resisted him in anything. But under his hands he could feel her slight frame stiffen, and when he looked down into her face it was rigid with fear. "You'll like the water. You'll like the sun on your body," he told her. But he knew it was neither of these that she dreaded. In the harsh climate in which they lived, Sherpas, male or female, almost never removed their clothing. In their time together, even when making love, he had not once seen Nima totally bare. Bareness was alien, unthinkable to her; and now, as she stood stripped of blouse and skirt, wearing only her homespun undershift, her whole body began to tremble. He joked, he cajoled, he caressed her. But it was no use. The trembling increased and tears welled in her eyes. To get her bare and into the stream would be nothing less than a rape.

He gave up. He continued his own bath while she got back into her skirt and blouse, and then they moved on down toward Munda. Now that the crisis was past, Nima was no longer trembling, but she walked with head bowed, and her face was still streaked with her tears. Eric raised it and kissed her button of a nose. He kissed her sleek black hair, smelling the rancid yak butter that made it sleek—that he was used to now, and (with no baths in prospect) would grow more used to. "Remind me to order you a bikini from Sears," he told her, smiling. And understanding the smile, if not the words, she smiled shyly back at him; and "What the hell," he thought, "you can't have everything."

Some things he did have (besides Nima). And one, now, was a home of his own. Soon after Tashi's return from America, an old man of the village had died; his widow had gone to live with relatives, leaving their house vacant; and following negotiations with the family, Eric and Nima had moved in. It was a smaller place than Tashi's, but in the same style as all Sherpa homes. On the ground level was the shelter for animals (winter quarters for three yaks, six goats and assorted poultry that he had received from Tashi for services rendered). And up steep ladder-like stairs was the single room (no shrine room here) where he and Nima lived. From her first marriage, Nima still had pots and pans and other household appurtenances, which had been used at Tashi's while she had lived there; and Eric, too, had a few things left from days gone by. Not his air mattress. That had long since flattened out and disintegrated, and they slept on piled-up layers of long-haired yak hide. But his sleeping bag remained, battered but whole, cruddy but warm, and big enough to hold both him and his tiny wife.

Wife—or whatever she was. For there had been no wedding, no formal sanction to their union. Decorous though the Sherpas were about clothing, in most matters of mating they were free and easy, and when Eric had spoken to Tashi about Nima, the reply had been "Take her, take care—she yours." What had concerned him was not marriage but children. "With my cousin Mingma she have none," he reminded Eric. "Maybe none now—is no good." But with Eric's answer he brightened. "You no care? Good, okay then." And with a grin he brought out the rakshi.

Sexually, Nima was no Amy. Though compliant, she was quiet, passive in lovemaking, to the extent that, even after months together, he did not know if she ever reached climax. But he wanted no Amy. No heights and depths, no fire and ashes. No harangues, no fights, no talk-talk-talk; and though most Sherpanis were first-class chatterers, Nima, now as before, was shy and silent. She knew no English, nor did he try to teach her. When they spoke it was in the usual Solu Khumbu mixture of Sherpa and Nepalese, and then only about the whats and hows of daily living. There were no whys. They did not argue. The closest they ever came to an argument was on the day of the bath in the stream—and he had quickly veered off from it.

"No sweat. No sweat at all . . ."

They had been Amy's words. But not life with Amy.

They were his life here, now.

In season, he plowed the fields. He tended the yaks. He chopped wood, fetched water, kept his house in repair. In the evenings he sat in snug, smoky rooms, drinking chang and rakshi with the men of Munda; then returned to his own house, his room, his sleeping bag on the yak hides; and there beside him was Nima, small, warm and his own.

He was content. "I have found a home," he thought.

And so he had, for a while.

It was Tashi who, since his trip to the States, was now discontented in the world he had been born to.

In the beginning, no. Then there had been the excitement of journey and return. At the least excuse—or without one—he put on his blue business suit, white shirt, striped tie and slim black shoes, and paraded the hundred-yard length of the main street of Munda. He talked of New York, Washington, Chicago, San Francisco; of planes in the air and cars on turnpikes; of skyscrapers, hotels, stores, traffic, subways, elevators, Automats, Coca-Cola. Most of all, he talked of television. At night, over the chang and rakshi, he plunked a Tibetan guitar and sang, "Winston tastes good, like cigarette should—"

But then other thoughts had begun to surface.

"In U.S. they make talk about poor," he said. "But no poor like here. There all have shoes, I see them. Have food in can, chang in can, big house, much high, much windows. Have car, road. Have place for sick. Have school."

Of all he had seen, it was schools that had most impressed him. "Yes, schools. For little, big. All kind. Are everywhere," he declared.

In Solu Khumbu, for a few years past, there had been three small schools—in the villages of Khumjung, Thami and Pangboche. They had been built as a gift to the Sherpas by Sir Edmund Hillary, the Man of Everest, and teachers, one for each, had been brought in from Kathmandu and Darjeeling. For Namche Bazar, there had been talk that the Nepalese Government would build a school, but nothing had happened. For Munda, there had not even been talk—until now Tashi, impassioned, talked of little else.

"People here are like yaks, goats, know nothing," he said. "If on expeditions, like me, know maybe a little; from sah'bs, from trips. But cannot read, write. In U.S. they show us paper, say 'is news,' but we shake head. Show us card in restaurant, say is food, we shake head . . . Is time Sherpa stop shake head, go school, learn read and write . . . Not me: too old. But young ones: Pembol here, all boys, girls too. When happens, comes great change for Sherpas. No more like yak, like goat, but live in world and hold up head like sah'bs."

In the village council—the *panchayat*—some listeners nodded, others shook their heads.

"Hillary Sah'b he is gone," said one.

"But is Government," said another.

"Government, faah! They promise school for Namche; nothing happen."

"In Kathmandu is Government by Nepali for Nepali. What they care for Sherpa in Solu Khumbu?"

"I do not think of Government," said Tashi. "I think of Americans."

"Americans? What they do?"

"I speak to men of Everest expedition; also to many in U.S. Have good hearts in U.S. Have money. Say they send teacher, make school for Munda."

"They say, but what they do?" said the village headman.

"Is talk," said someone else.

"No, not talk," said Tashi.

"Why they no come then?"

"Is long time now."

"They never come."

The skeptics won the day, but Tashi kept the faith. "Yes, yes, they come," he said.

The enclosing mountains towered high. Prayer flags streamed. Prayer wheels turned.

. . . And the wheel of the seasons . . .

In yet another spring Eric helped with the plowing. In the early summer, with Pembol, he again drove the yaks to high pasture, and in the late summer drove them down. At the edge of Munda he came to the outhouse, *his* outhouse—still the only one in the village—anticipating a luxury he had not had in two months. But its door was closed. It was occupied. ("That's progress," he thought; perhaps another spin-off of Tashi's visit to the States.) And he waited. Then from within the privy came a voice saying, "Oh dear."

The words were English. The voice was a woman's. What woman's he could not imagine; but he understood the "oh dear," and from his pack he took his current paperback, Faulkner's *Light in August*, of which half was left and pushed it under the door. There was another "oh," a "thank you." Another wait. Then the door opened and a young woman appeared. She was tall, slim and fair-skinned, dressed in a plaid skirt and pullover sweater, and a length of green ribbon was wound tautly around her brown windblown hair.

"This is one way of being introduced," she said, smiling.

Eric simply stared.

"You're Eric Venn, aren't you?"

He nodded.

"We've been expecting you," the girl said. "I'm Carol Flagg. I'm with the Peace Corps."

"The what?"

"The Peace Corps. I'm the new teacher here."

"Oh."

She might have been from Mars, or Betelgeuse. It was almost four years since he had seen a human being who was not a Sherpa or Tibetan.

"I can see *you* weren't expecting *me*," said Carol Flagg. Again she smiled, then held out his book. "I must get back to class. Here—thanks. You were a friend in need."

"Keep it," he told her. He managed a smile himself. "I run a lending library."

She had been in Munda a month and was living at Tashi's, in the little shrine room that had once been his. With three other Peace Corps volunteers assigned to Solu Khumbu, she had trekked overland on the long trail from Kathmandu, and word of their coming was to have preceded them on the Government radio. But this, of course, had not happened. In Munda, she had expected a schoolhouse, or at least a room, to be ready. But there had been no such thing—and without Tashi there might never have been. The little Sherpa, however, had at once become her self-appointed mentor. Besides providing her living quarters, he had cleaned up his ground-floor animal shelter—unused in summer—to serve as temporary classroom; had by cajolery, threat and main force rounded up most of Munda's children; and now, with the help of other villagers, was building a small place for her permanent use.

"Without Tashi," said Carol Flagg, "there'd be no school and no schoolmarm."

"Marm" was hardly the word for her. She was blooming, buoyant and twenty-two: an escapee (in her own word) from one of Philadelphia's glossier suburbs and a graduate of the previous spring from Bryn Mawr College. In spite of parental opposition ("they're Goldwater Republicans, for God's sake"), she had been determined to join the Peace Corps, and Nepal ("so beautiful—and so poor") had been her first choice for service. On her return home she planned to resume studying and go on to a master's degree and doctorate in either education or sociology. "And that's no matter what," she declared. "Marriage, kids, no matter what."

Even now in Solu Khumbu, it developed, there was a candidate for husband. Of the four Peace Corpsmen who had come there, only she was assigned to Munda; the others, two men and a girl, were based in other villages. But one of the men—a tall and lanky young agronomist from Kansas named Bill Hundley—soon proved to have Carol Flagg on his mind no less than seeds and fertilizers. Each week on his day off he hiked across the steep miles from Namche Bazar to see her. He walked with her in the countryside, sat with her in the evenings on a bench in the yard behind Tashi's house. "Each night before he leaves, he proposes," she confided to Eric. "Post-Peace Corps, of course. And I point out gently that we've still got twenty-two months of our two years to go."

"But you like him?"

"Yes, I like him. Bill's a nice boy. But marry him—? move to Kansas—?"

She left the questions hanging. From the valley of Munda her eyes went up to the peaks of the Himalayas, high and gleaming above them. Then she smiled. "Sometimes, here, I think I'm Dorothy in the Land of Oz," she said. "Except that Dorothy kept dreaming of Kansas, and I sure as hell don't."

Eric, too, walked with her, sat with her: the woman from Mars, from Betelgeuse—from the world he had left.

Before her coming he had not heard of the Peace Corps. He had not heard of a man called Goldwater. He had not known that John Kennedy had been killed and that Lyndon Johnson was President of the United States.

"And Vietnam?" Carol asked. Had he heard of Vietnam?

Of the war, did she mean?

Yes, of the war . . . It was over, wasn't it? . . . No, not over. Still going. She told him about it.

She spoke of Negroes—now called blacks. Of marches, of riots. Of a new breed called astronauts and another called hippies.

She looked at him steadily, curiously, with her brown, intelligent eyes and said, "You've *really* been away, haven't you?"

"Yes, really," he said.

Sometimes he looked in at her classroom in Tashi's "downstairs." Though the animals were absent, their smells remained, and the only furnishings were a few benches and a board on two uprights that Carol used as a desk. Teaching materials were equally sparse. A variety of items were to have been supplied by the Peace Corps (or the Nepalese Government, or UNESCO, or someone), but all that was actually on hand were a few primers, pads and pencils that she herself had brought from Kathmandu. For a blackboard, she used stretched pieces of fabric from abandoned expedition tents in Tashi's collection; and for chalk, sticks of charcoal.

Her pupils, some thirty in number, ranged in age from about six to sixteen, and all were in the same grade—the first. Among the oldest was Pembol. At the outset he had protested loudly against both school in general and, in particular, the indignity of being lumped with children half his age and less. But Tashi had been adamant. He had won the day. And Pembol, in an unpredictable reverse, had responded by becoming a prize student.

"Now I read. Soon I write," he announced proudly to Eric. "When I am man and climb mountains, I write books just like sah'bs."

Carol had studied Nepalese in her Peace Corps training. But for the Sherpa language—with no written form, hence no books—she had had no preparation, and now and then, stopping by at the school, Eric helped her out as interpreter. Meanwhile, with Tashi and other men of the village, he worked on the building of the new schoolhouse; and by mid-autumn—with the livestock about to return to Tashi's downstairs—it was ready for use. It was scarcely an edifice. Its single room housed only the barest of furnishings and equipment. But at least it *was* a room, not a stable. It had a floor, a fireplace, even windows (with paper panes). And Munda was proud of it. On the evening of the day on which Carol and her brood moved in, there was party of celebration at Tashi's.

Like all Sherpa parties, it lasted long and late. The women prepared food and chang, the men ate and drank and, when the chang was gone, switched to rakshi. There were toasts to the school, its builders and Memsah'b Flagg. There was singing and dancing, laughter and shouting, until, by midnight, things had reached the traditional state of drunken uproar. Relays of lurching Sherpas seized Carol and whirled her around the room. And presently she too was lurching, barely keeping her balance, gasping for breath in the acrid smoke from the fireplace. But there was no escape for her. The shrine room—theoretically her room—was now occupied by Tashi's wife, their four small daughters and several passed-out revelers; and Tashi himself, thumping his guitar and singing at the top of his voice, was in no condition to conjure order from chaos.

Taking her hand, Eric led her down the stairs. In the cool autumn night, she caught her breath and wiped the tears from her eyes.

"Where now?" he wondered.

She smiled. "A midnight movie?" she asked.

They walked down Munda's dark, empty street, until they came to the new schoolhouse. "Here we are—double feature," he said and, opening the door, they went in. He found a candle and lighted it, made a fire in the fireplace, and, pulling up one of the class benches, they sat together before it.

302

"Don't be upset," he said.

"Upset?"

"About the Sherpas."

"Oh, I'm not. Not at all," said Carol. "A little frazzled maybe, but not upset. They're so dear, so sweet. Even when they're drunk they're sweet, and you can't say that for many men."

They talked of Sherpas. Of Munda and Solu Khumbu. She spoke of what she had expected, what she had found, what she hoped to accomplish; and as she talked her tiredness vanished, her voice grew animated, her eyes, no longer tearing, shone bright in the firelight. "Just to bring something to a single one of these children—to a boy like Pembol," she said, "would be enough to make the whole two years worth while."

There was a pause. Eric watched the fire, and he could feel her watching him.

"You think differently, don't you?" she said.

"Does it matter what I think?"

"I'd like to know."

"For you, yes, it's worth while," he said. "But for Pembol—the Sherpas—?"

"They should go on being illiterate?"

"They're the happiest people I've ever known."

"And will stop being happy if they learn to read and write?"

"If they learn," said Eric, "to want what they haven't."

"They have to live in the world," Carol said.

"They have a world of their own."

"They did have, maybe. But now? In the future? With more expeditions each year—with helicopters, then planes, then tourists—with the Red Chinese Army right up there behind the mountains."

Eric smiled a little. "And better the Peace Corps than the Chinese, is that it?"

Carol Flagg did not smile back. "If you want to put it that way, yes," she said.

The yak dung fire was burning low and he replenished it. In its renewed glow she was again watching him with searching eyes.

"You resent me, don't you?" she said quietly.

"Resent?"

"My coming. My being here."

"Have I seemed to?"

"No, you haven't. You've been kind and good to me . . . But that, I think, is only the surface. Underneath, you feel I'm a threat to you, an intruder in your country."

"Not my country—the Sherpas'."

"You love the Sherpas," said Carol. "I've seen that. I know that. But in wanting everything to stay the same, are you thinking of them or yourself?"

Eric thought it over. "Of both," he answered.

"You came here to find something?"

"Yes."

"And what is it you've found?"

"You're here too," he said. "It's the same as what you've found."

She shook her head. "No, not the same. I'm here with the Peace Corps. To live with the Sherpas, work with the Sherpas— but not to *be* a Sherpa." She paused, watching him; then said, "Don't you see what's happened to you, Eric? You're trying to *be* a Sherpa, and it isn't possible."

He said nothing.

"Herding yaks, plowing fields, carrying firewood—that's not enough to make a life for you, and you know it."

Again he smiled. "I've built an outhouse," he said. "I helped build your school."

"You could keep on building it—more importantly—if you would."

"Keep on?"

"By helping me teach."

He stared at her.

"It would mean so much to the children; especially to the boys —the older ones like Pembol . . . And to you too, Eric, it would mean a lot. Truly. If you'd only give it a try—give yourself a chance to *be* yourself, instead of hiding yourself away."

"I'm not a teacher," he said.

"Neither was I, until I came here."

"I'm not a Bryn Mawr girl, either."

"Very funny."

"I'm what you said before: a yakherd, a plower, a firewood carrier."

"Not a mountaineer any longer?"

"No, no longer."

"Nor a writer?"

He was silent a moment. Then he said, "I was never a writer."

"Tashi said you were."

"Tashi talks too much."

"Even without Tashi," said Carol, "don't you think I have eyes and ears? Don't you think I can tell what sort of man you really are?" Her voice was earnest, almost pleading. "Oh, Eric, come out from your shell; be yourself. If not for your own sake, then for the Sherpas'. You have so much to give them, if you would. As teacher, leader, friend—"

"—and Miss Carol Flagg's special reclamation project—"

She said no more. For a while they sat silently watching the fire; then he put his hand on hers, resting beside him on the bench.

"You're a sweet girl," he said.

He turned and kissed her lightly on the lips. She neither resisted nor responded.

Then he stood up.

"Come on, it's late," he said. "You'll be falling asleep in school this morning."

They rose and put out the fire, and leaving the schoolhouse, they walked down Munda's dark and silent street. Tashi's house, too, was at last dark and silent, and at the foot of the stairs leading up to the living quarters he said good night. Then, alone, he went back along the street to his own house, and climbed the stairs, and there in their room was Nima, lying in the sleeping bag on the pile of yak hides. Removing his outer clothing, he got in beside her, and she lay close against him, small and still.

Several times each day he passed the schoolhouse. Sometimes, looking in, he saw Carol Flagg with her pupils. But he himself did not go in. He went on his way. With winter coming on, there was wood to be chopped and carried and feed for the livestock to be stored in their village pens. If she had her work, he too had his.

In the evenings, though, it was different.

Carol had her supper with Tashi and his family; he with Nima in their own home; and usually, in the past, he had stayed home afterward, doing odd jobs while Nima finished up the household chores. There was little talk between them. Often a whole evening would pass without a word. But it was a gentle, not a strained silence. He was content with it . . . Or had been . . . But now no longer. Now the silence had grown oppressive, the walls were a prison, and breaking out from them, leaving Nima, he would go down the street to Tashi's. There he would visit with Tashi. He would perhaps drink a bowl of chang or a dram of rakshi. But this was not why he came. He came because Carol Flagg was there. And often, as Tashi and his family prepared for sleep, he and Carol together would go down the stairs and out into the night. The first few times they walked: through the village, along the trails beyond. Then as winter came on it grew too cold for walking, and they went again to the schoolhouse. Each time, as on the first time, they built a fire, and sat before it and talked.

She made no further attempt at "reclamation." When she spoke of her work it was of *her* school, *her* pupils, and that was it. Ranging off from them, she spoke of the other Sherpas, of Tashi and his family, of the old and young, of the herders, farmers, housewives, climbers, lamas, and of what she had learned of them since she came to Munda. She asked questions of Eric, and he told her of his years in Solu Khumbu. They veered off, in time and place, to Kathmandu, to India, to the world beyond; to America and what had happened there in the years since he had left. They talked of events, ideas, people. They talked of themselves. She spoke of her home, her schools, Bryn Mawr, her Peace Corps training. And then it was he who was speaking: of Denver, Seattle, Italy, White Valley. He talked of skiing—even of climbing. He talked of writing. He talked of reading (pointing out that when they had finished their current paperback, Steinbeck's *East of Eden*, they would be out of both reading matter and toilet paper). And with that they were back in Munda. They were talking of the outhouse and its drafts, of Tashi's house and its smoke, of the prayer room where Carol slept . . . of its bowls and tapers and guardian Buddhas . . . of many Buddhas, the One Buddha, the Buddhist faith . . . and Carol said, "Back in college, for a while, I studied Zen. I used to go to bed listening for the sound of one hand clapping." They had now left the schoolhouse, and Eric was walking her toward Tashi's along the empty night-time street. Suddenly she stopped. Raising her head, she looked up at the wave of the Himalayas rising white and gigantic against the stars. She whispered, "Listen. You can hear it clapping now."

There was no plan to their talk. It was something that simply happened. Night after night they sat in the schoolhouse, and the words came—the thoughts, the memories, the associations—and it was they themselves, the act, the fact of talking, that held the magic for Eric. He was starved for talk, for communication, and what it was *about* did not matter; it was enough that the communication existed. Carol talked, and he listened. He talked, and she listened. Through the hours they talked, as he had not talked in years—since the long-gone days with his sister-in-law Kay. Then at last they would rise and leave the schoolhouse and walk to Tashi's. At the foot of the stairs he would say good night. But he did not kiss her again. Her face was close, her eyes were raised to his. She would have let him kiss her, but still he didn't. They stood there quietly, the yakherd and the school-teacher, the grizzled man of forty-plus, smelling of earth and live-stock; the college girl of twenty-two with fresh face and green hairband. Then he turned and walked on down the street to his own house, his sleeping bag, Nima. As on the first night, so on all nights, Nima did not speak. Usually he could not tell if she was awake or asleep. But then came a night that was different; when, though her face was hidden and, as always, she was silent, her small body beside him was taut and trembling; and he knew she was awake, and he knew she was crying.

The next night he stayed home.

And the next.

Nima worked silently at her chores, and he at his. When they got into the sleeping bag and lay side by side, she was not trembling, not crying. He took her in his arms, and after a while, still in silence, they made love.

On the third night, an hour or so after supper, he put down the old pressure cooker—a relic from a French expedition—he had been trying to repair, and for a while paced about the room. Then he went down the stairs and out and along the street to Tashi's. The whole family was there: Tashi himself, his wife Ai Lamu, the four girls, Pembol—and Carol Flagg. Carol, in jeans and sweater, was sitting cross-legged on a mat, knitting, and she continued knitting while Eric shared a bowl of chang with Tashi. The little man was excited. The previous day a message had come through —from New Delhi to Kathmandu to Namche Bazar to Munda— that an Indian expedition was going to Everest in the spring, and that he, Tashi, was wanted as a high-climbing Sherpa. As he talked, the grin on his monkey face gave way to a frown of determination. "And this time I get to top," he declared. "If Tenzing, Gombu can do, so can me too. Am no more old than Tenzing when get to top. Am still strong, still good. Yes, I make it . . ."

When he had finished and the chang was gone, Eric rose. Carol, still at her knitting, raised her head; their eyes met; on other nights this had been the signal between them, and she too had risen and they had left together. But now he looked away. "Good night," he said to the room. Then, alone, he went down the stairs, along the street, to his own house. Nima was already in the sleeping bag, small and silent, and he got in beside her, and again they made love.

Later, however, as Nima slept, he lay wakeful in the darkness . . . thinking of her . . . thinking of Carol Flagg. And what he should do, he did not know.

Then came the next day. And he did know.

It was Sunday, and Sunday was Bill Hundley's usual day in Munda. As from the beginning of Carol's stay there, the tall young

Kansan, once every week, came over the hills from Namche to spend the day—and presumably propose to her. On many of his visits, Eric, busy elsewhere, did not see him at all. When he did, it was usually for no more than a casual hello on the street. This time, however, on a gray morning in December, Hundley sought him out—appearing alone while Eric was storing animal fodder in the lower level of his house.

"I want to talk to you," he said.

His lank body was tense, his voice edged and rasping.

Eric looked at him curiously. "Sure," he said. "Go ahead."

"About Carol," said Hundley.

Eric had been bent over, removing the cordage from a bale of hay. But now he straightened and faced his visitor. "What about Carol?" he asked evenly.

"You know damn well what."

"Do I?"

"—And so does every Sherpa in Solu Khumbu." Hundley took a step forward, chin jutting, hands clenched. "You keep away from her, do you hear me?"

"Is that an order?" asked Eric.

"It's what I'm telling you."

"And suppose I tell you—"

"You're not telling me anything. You're laying off her. She's my girl, my fiancée, understand?—and you stick to your Sherpa woman and keep your hands off her!"

He was close to Eric now, his face contorted, almost beside himself with rage.

"Look, son—" said Eric quietly.

"Don't call me son, you cruddy old bum."

Eric's eyes narrowed. "You prefer sonny, maybe?"

"Why, God damn you—"

Hundley swung at him. It was a long wild swing and Eric caught it on the forearm. "Stop it, you fool," he said. But the boy closed in, swinging with both arms, and again he parried. Instinctively his own hands had balled into fists, but he did not hit back. Instead, opening his hands, he pushed the boy on the chest. He

309

pushed hard. Hundley's lank frame went spinning back, and he fell. Getting up, he charged again; Eric pushed again; he fell again, sprawling in the mud, hay and yak dung that covered the floor of the stock pen. Again he started to rise, thought better of it, and lay glaring at Eric.

Eric pointed to a corner. "There's a brush; you can clean the shit off," he said. He went to the door of the pen. "Both outside and inside," he added.

Going out, he walked slowly down the village street. He listened for the sound of Hundley coming after him; but there was no sound, no Hundley. At the end of the village he turned and walked back to his house and into the stock pen, and the boy was gone.

The next day it was he, Eric, who walked across the hills: not to Namche Bazar, but about five miles in another direction to a village called Dhamu. There he asked questions, found an empty house, made the necessary arrangements. And a few days later, driving their yaks and goats before them, and with four young men helping to carry their household possessions, he and Nima moved from Munda to Dhamu.

It was full daylight now. Ablaze in whiteness, the snow dome of Dera Zor stretched above and below him, and below, tiny but clear against it, were the three moving dots that were his companions.

He was still resting. He let his gaze move still farther, to the rim of the dome and the gulf of space beyond. In the maw of the gulf, two miles down, was the Kalpurtha Glacier, and his eyes crossed it; then rose again up the mountains on its farther side. Though their summit ridges were now far below him, he could see only sky beyond them. Nepal, the whole earth to the south, was hidden. But he knew that on that earth, close beyond them, on their very skirts, was the land of Solu Khumbu which for so long had been home.

Down there were the Dudh Khosi and Amun rivers, Namche and Thyangboche, Munda and Dhamu. There they still were, unchanged, as they had always been; but no longer his home, nor Nima's. There was no more Nima . . . No Carol . . . There had been times when he wondered about Carol. Was she long since Mrs. William Hundley of Somewhere, Kansas? He rather doubted it.

20

It was the Year of the Snake.

Then the Year of the Horse.

The house in Dhamu was almost indistinguishable from the one in Munda. The village was much the same, his life the same —or at least the same as it had been before Carol Flagg came to Munda.

There were the seasons. There were plowing, firewood, yaks. There were chang and rakshi and snug smoky rooms on winter nights. There were the peaks, the stars. There was Nima. Nima cooking, cleaning, weaving, fetching, carrying. Nima small and silent in the sleeping bag beside him . . . But no longer trembling. No longer crying.

In Dhamu, as in Munda, there was no outhouse, and again he built one: this time a better one, for after his years in Solu Khumbu he was a better carpenter. By now, however, he was out of toilet paper—and reading matter. In the outhouse he simply sat; then made do with leaves or grass and a bucket of water. But as compensation of sorts, Nima had at last been persuaded to use it. In another few years, he mused hopefully, he might get her to take off her clothes for a bath.

Now and then Tashi came over from Munda, and twice he returned the visits. Both were on weekdays, in the daytime, and all he saw of Carol was through the window of her schoolhouse. One of the times she didn't see him. On the other she waved, he waved back, and that was all. Before school was out he was on his way back along the trail to Dhamu.

Winter passed.

Spring came.

Tashi took off to join the Indian expedition to Everest, and Eric went no more to Munda. He had his work, which now in spring was mostly plowing. The Dhamu Sherpas, like all Sherpas, were friendly and sociable; they had their gatherings, their parties; and when there was no party there was his home, and Nima. Again, he was content. Or almost content. There were times in the evenings, in the long silences with Nima, when he hungered for the talk, the communication he had had with Carol. But he swallowed his hunger. Alone, in the castle of his outhouse, he yearned for the vanished companionship of Steinbeck, Faulkner, Melville—even Agatha Christie. But he did without it. He used his leaves, grass and bucket of water, and went back to his plow, his yaks, his house, Nima.

Yes, he was content with Nima.

Then more than content. Then happy . . .

This came with the summer; with the yearly trek of the yaks to high pasture. In mid-June, as before, he made ready to go, and this year, with no Tashi, no Pembol (for Pembol was still at school), it was to be alone. But when the time came it was not alone. Nima went with him. It was not unknown for Sherpanis to accompany their men on the summer tour; but it was rare, and at first he was dubious. But it was Nima who asked to go. She pleaded, persisted. For the first time in their marriage (yes, marriage: what else was it?) she took a stand, she pressed him. In the end he agreed.

And it was not a mistake.

Up, up they went, driving their herd, on the immemorial journey. Up valleys, slopes, ridges, past the last towns, the lamaseries, to the summer villages and beyond. Nima had no troubles. She moved at the normal pace of the grazing yaks, became adept at rounding up laggards and strays, and with no seeming effort carried two-thirds her own weight in the pack on her back. Though she wore the same clothing as at home—including the long striped Sherpani apron—she easily managed hill and hollow, crag and boulder. Her one concession to the rigors of life was in the style in which she wore her hair. Instead of carrying it atop her head, coiled in complex braids and held with combs and pins, she let it fall in two lustrous pigtails, framing her large dark eyes and the brown button of her nose.

The monsoon was late this year. Day after day the sun beamed on the green of meadows, the white of snowfields, and in its brightness Nima smiled and laughed, her small face blooming like a mountain flower. Even toward summer's end, when the clouds came with rain and mist, she remained happy and gay: chasing and prodding the yaks on their downward journey; talking brightly, almost chattering, as she prepared their suppers over evening cook fires; warm and loving as they lay close in their sleeping bag in the mountain night.

Then they were home again, in Dhamu. Summer passed into fall. And still she was happy. No longer silent, she hummed or sang at her work, and on her face, increasingly, there was now a soft and gentle smile: a Sherpani Mona Lisa smile, Eric thought, as if she were carrying a secret.

—Which she was, he soon discovered.

She was pregnant.

In the nights, with her asleep beside him, he lay wakeful in the darkness. In the afternoons, with the day's work done, he walked along the trails near Dhamu and sat alone on a stump or tuft of grass. He thought of the child that was coming. And the thought was new and bewildering. Nima had had no child by her first husband, and he had assumed from the beginning that it would be the same with him . . . Now it was not the same. A child was coming. Boy or girl. Son or daughter . . . And when it came, then what? What would its coloring be? Its hair? Its eyes? Would it be an Eric or a Tashi? A Nima or a Mary? . . . At first, in Dhamu, it would live like any village child (meaning Tashi, Nima). But when it was older? Would he, the father, then take it by the hand and lead it across the hills to Munda, to the school, to the successor—or successor's successor—of Carol Flagg? What

314

would he say? "Good morning, Memsah'b, this is my son (daughter) Eric-Tashi (or Nima-Mary). Will you please prepare him (her) for entrance into Harvard (or Bryn Mawr)—or do you suggest, rather, a course in elementary yakherding?"

Tashi—the original Tashi—had still other thoughts. On his first appearance in Dhamu after his return from Everest, he had been in low spirits, for once again he had fallen short of the top. But once he heard the news of Nima he brightened with excitement. "It will be a son, Rick Sah'b," he declared. "Yes, a son, am sure. A sah'b-Sherpa son—smart like sah'b, strong like Sherpa—and when is grown he will be greatest climber in whole world!"

He drank toasts in chang, toasts in rakshi; then, unsteady but happy, took the trail back toward Munda, while Eric's thoughts returned to a lesser trajectory . . . So, a child was coming. A son or daughter. A sah'b-Sherpa. It was a fact: so be it . . . At night, in their sleeping bag, he felt the soft roundness of Nima's belly. And as the weeks, the months passed, the roundness grew and swelled; her whole slight body, her tiny face, grew soft and round, and the face was glowing; for now she was full of child, and full of happiness.

Through the winter she grew.

Then it was almost spring. It was a night in March, and she was six months gone; and in the night he awoke, and all was different.

At first it seemed to him the same as on the night, a year before, when he had come home from hours with Carol Flagg to find Nima crying in the sleeping bag . . . But it was not the same . . . She was not crying now, but moaning; not stiff and trembling, but hunched up, knees high against belly and breasts, and her face, when he touched it, was sleek with sweat . . . She was in pain. In labor . . . Rising quickly, he lighted a lamp. He wiped the sweat from her forehead. Kneeling, he held her hands and spoke to her, but her only reply was a deeper moaning. Her eyes rolled away from his, and she clung to his hands, her nails digging at the flesh.

Moments passed. He too was now sweating.

Then, releasing himself, he left the room, ran down the stairs and into the village street. In a neighboring house lived an old

315

Sherpani called Ayma, who was the village midwife; and going there, he roused her, and she said she would come. Returning home, he brought out such clean cloths as he could find, built a fire, and put a kettle on to heat water. (Crazily, for a moment then, he was back in his boyhood, back in a Denver movie house watching a Western; and ol' Doc Whosis, reaching the ranch house, was briskly ordering "lots of hot water.") By the time the kettle was simmering the midwife Ayma had appeared, bringing with her another old woman. He opened the sleeping bag, in which Nima still lay hunched and moaning, and they brought her out and straightened her, and the crones lifted her nightshift. They fingered her belly. They put their ears to it and listened. Ayma produced a pouch, poured out a palmful of green powder and rubbed it on Nima's flesh. Her companion chanted softly. With one hand Eric held a lamp for them, and with the other again wiped the sweat from Nima's forehead.

How much time passed he could not have said. Nima's contractions came and passed; her moaning rose and fell, and for a while she would lie limp and spent. But now each new spasm came more quickly than the last, and was more intense, more enduring. Her body arched; it too was rising, falling. Her legs were spread. One of the old women had seized her knees and was holding them high and far apart, and the other, Ayma, was now crouched between them, hands extended. In the light of the lamp Eric could see the hands clearly: old, bony, dirt-streaked, the broken nails rimmed with grime—

"Wait!" he said.

He had forgotten the water. Now he remembered. "Wait—wash your hands!" he commanded.

Ayma seemed not to have heard him. Going quickly to the fireplace, he poured water from the kettle into a basin, brought it back and set it beside her. "Wash," he repeated. "Wash your hands, do you understand?"

She looked at him briefly, blankly, and turned back to Nima. Between the spread thighs, in the bush of hair, a patch of pink had appeared—was growing swiftly larger—and she was reaching out to it with grimy fingers.

316

"Stop!"

Then he had moved again. Grasping her shoulder, he was pulling her away . . . and she was resisting, she was chattering angrily; the other woman was chattering . . . but still he pulled, then pushed, at Ayma, the other, then the two together, until he had them away from Nima, across the room, near the head of the stairs. And whether they left or not he didn't know, whether there was chattering or silence he didn't know; for he was back with Nima; he was himself washing, scouring his hands in the basin, then spreading a cloth, kneeling, leaning forward . . . and now (he thought wildly) he was ol' Doc Whosis in person (only this part wasn't shown in the movie), as the pink spot in the hair still grew, emerging toward him, as what had been inside came out at last from Nima's womb.

There was not much for him to do, for the head was small, the rest smaller. There was a tiny red and wizened face, a tiny body, part red, part mottled yellow, and legs curled under it like the legs of a frog. There was the cord—the placenta—and no need to cut the cord. In a few minutes it was all out, all there, a red and yellow viscous blob on the spread cloth between Nima's legs; and he closed up the cloth and tied its corners and put it in a sack and put the sack in a corner.

The two old women were now gone. Back with Nima, he wedged another cloth between her thighs to stem her bleeding, then sat beside her, again holding her hand. She did not dig at him with her nails, nor did she writhe or moan, but lay quietly, eyes closed, breathing slowly and deeply; and when at last he released her hand she did not seem to notice. A little later, sure that she was asleep, he rose and got the sack from the corner. Then, going down the stairs, he got a shovel and pick. Outside, the night was ending; a band of grayness hid the stars to the east. But there was no one yet about as he moved along the village street and onto a trail beyond.

He did not go far: perhaps two hundred yards past the end of the village. Then, turning off the path, he went another short distance through bushes and brush, until he came to a small space that was open and level. There was still snow on the ground, so first he shoveled. Then, with the pick, he broke the frozen earth below, and again shoveled until he had dug a small round hole. He put the sack in the hole, shoveled back earth and snow, and walked slowly back to the village. On the way, it occurred to him that he had not noticed if the baby was a boy or a girl. But it didn't matter.

March passed. Spring came. The snows receded and the sun shone bright.

But it brought no brightness to Nima.

It was not, Eric knew, that she was mourning for the child. She had wanted it, yes. It would have been her first, and she had wanted it greatly. But she was, after all, a Sherpani, herself the child of a world in which life was cheap, death always close, and the very essence of her nature was quiet acceptance of fate. From the moment of the stillbirth, she did not speak of the baby. She did not ask what he had done with it. Within an hour after his return from the burial she was up and about her household duties, as if nothing had happened.

Yet something *had* happened—to her, as well as to the child. Something had been wrong with her, causing the miscarriage. And now the wrongness grew worse.

It had first shown itself, he realized in retrospect, while she was in labor. Else, why had she had so hard a time of it? Most Sherpa women had babies, full-grown babies, almost as casually as bowel movements; but with only a tiny thing, a stunted embryo, Nima had suffered agonies. True, she had later seemed the normal Sherpani, taking the blow of fate uncomplainingly and quickly returning to her daily work. But he soon noted that she tired more quickly than before. Her quietness became listlessness. The spring sun came and shone, but though he urged her she did not go out. Her work done, she sat passively in a corner or lay on the sleeping bag, eyes open and fixed on the ceiling.

April came.

And she was ill: that was now obvious. Though he had no

318

thermometer, Eric could tell that she was increasingly feverish. She ate little, was often nauseated, and had recurrent pain in her lower abdomen. But what was the cause of the symptoms he didn't know. The ailments endemic to Solu Khumbu were legion: smallpox, typhus, cholera, the dysenteries, hepatitis, worms, other parasites, deficiencies—the list was almost endless. And though it was soon apparent that she did not have one of the infectious plagues, which of the others she had he could not determine. He did what he could: keeping her clean, making her eat, drink and rest. But the poison—whatever it was—had hold of her. Her face grew pinched, her eyes dull, her thin body even thinner. Presently she was too weak to do her household chores, and Eric took over the cooking and cleaning.

Word of her illness, of course, spread quickly through the village. One of its old women—not Ayma, another—took to coming daily to see her, and she too chanted and spread powders—this time, red ones—on Nima's belly. Then two lamas came from the nearest monastery. Who had summoned them Eric did not know; but suddenly, one day, there they were, also with chants and powders, plus spinning prayer wheels, with which they paced the room. During his years in Solu Khumbu he had learned to respect, even cherish, Himalayan Buddhism. Now, with this visitation, he loathed it; indeed could barely refrain from throwing the lamas out. But he did refrain, sitting by in impotent silence. Grotesque though their performance was, they—and the old woman—seemed able, at least briefly, to bring Nima comfort, and he let them stay until, in their own time, they took their leave.

She showed no real improvement, however. On the contrary, she grew weaker, sicker. By the time April passed into May she was unable to get up from the sleeping bag; and in the evenings, home from work in the fields, he sat beside her holding her hand as she murmured and tossed in fever.

What was he going to do? *Sit there until she died?*

For years he had lived the life of a Sherpa. It had been his choice, his decision, the replacement of a life that had become intolerable by another that, however crude and primitive, possessed dignity and meaning. With the coming of Carol Flagg he

had briefly wavered. The world beyond Solu Khumbu had beckoned again; the Westerner in him had begun to surface. But he
had again renounced that world, pushed the Westerner down.
He had left Munda, come with Nima to Dhamu, still to live as a
Sherpa.

—Until now—

But now what? Now Carol's words had caught up with him.
"You can't *be* a Sherpa," she had told him. And here, now, at
last, she was right. He could not sit forever in this room at world's
end, while crones spread powders, lamas spun prayer wheels, and
Nima died by inches before his eyes. He had to act, to get her to
medical help, to go back with her, because of her, into the twentieth century . . .

He was no longer holding her hand. He was pacing the room.
But how? *How?*

It was now the expedition season. Some half-dozen climbing
teams were on mountains roundabout, and one or two, at least,
would have doctors along. But they could not be reached. If
reached, they could not come. Even if one came, what could he
do but dispense a few pills from a meager supply . . . What
Nima needed was total care, hospitalization. And the nearest
hospital was in Kathmandu . . . It was no great institution, to be
sure: neither when he had been there nor, probably, now. But at
least it *was* a hospital: with physicians, nurses, medicines, surgery.
It was there.

He must get her there . . .

Again, how?

There was the helicopter—the one he had flown in (five? ten?
a hundred years ago?) with Mrs. Bigelow. There might be more
now. But helicopters cost money, and he had no money. That
left the overland trail: the two-week, two-hundred-mile trail: there
was no other alternative. But on this he would need companionship, help. And who was there? His first and foremost choice, of
course, would have been Tashi, but Tashi was again off on an expedition; and this year, Pembol—second choice—had, at age eighteen, gone along with him as an apprentice porter. Almost all the
young men of Dhamu and Munda were with one expedition or

another, leaving women, children, oldsters—and these were largely busy in the fields.

Still, he had to find helpers. And he did. Canvassing the two villages the next day, he came up with one elderly man, two fairly sturdy women, a twelve-year-old boy, and an older but feeble-minded youngster: five in all, to help carry Nima and the needed supplies. For money to pay them (and this much he could manage) he sold half of his yaks; then arranged for a neighbor to take care of the rest, and spent a day assembling food and gear. Nima, he believed, would be better off lying down through the journey than sitting in a Sherpa basket chair such as he used for Mrs. Bigelow; and to this end he made a litter with poles and yak hide. On the morning of the third day after he had reached his decision, all was ready. Food and gear, in its sacks and packs, was out in front of the house. His little troop stood ready. Carrying Nima down the stairs, he laid her on the litter, tied her in with leather thongs, and gave the signal to hoist burdens. The spring sun was shining bright and warm: but Nima, eyes open but blank, seemed neither to see nor feel it.

On the first day they reached Namche Bazar. From the second through the fourth they moved southward, following the twisting trail along the gorges of the Dudh Khosi River. As with Mrs. Bigelow in her basket, there were times when it was difficult to get Nima, on her stretcher, up and down steep pitches and around projections of rock. But they managed. They had to manage. Through each day's march Eric was one of its bearers, directing its handling, while the old man and two boys took turns at the other end and at joining the two women in load-carrying. There were no accidents, no mishaps. On the second day out from Namche, the sun withdrew, there was mist, then rain, and Eric covered Nima with an old expedition tarpaulin. But she did not seem to notice the rain any more than the sun.

On the fourth night they camped near a village called Khari-khola, at the point where the Kathmandu trail bore off to the west. And there they had their first defection. In the evening, the older of the two boys, the not-so-bright one, went to sleep, as usual, in the tent he shared with the other boy and the old man. But in the morning he was gone. There had been no explanation; he had not even asked for his wages. He was simply not there. In Kharikhola, Eric searched for a replacement and came up with a boy of about the same age, who seemed mentally normal, thus an improvement. And so he was, for a day.

Along the river, the trail, though with rises and falls, had been predominantly downhill. But now, leading west, it was across the grain of the land, forever up and down between valley and ridge. On the ridges there was still snow, with knee-high drifts and a battering wind. In the crotch of the valleys were streams, now spring torrents, spanned by spidery, swaying bridges. For their crossing, Eric lifted Nima from the litter, strapped her onto his back (for she was too weak to hold on), and thus bore her across, while others carried the litter. Then it was up again, down again, to the next snow, the next torrent.

The new boy did well. But no sooner had they reached their night's campsite than he announced he was going home. Again, there was no explanation (though this one *did* ask for his day's pay)—and no persuading him. In the morning, he left. They were down to five, plus Nima, and at this stop there was no nearby village in which to recruit a replacement. By now, however, they had consumed about a third of their food supply, and with a redistribution of loads they managed as they were.

In the next few days the land changed again. The ridges were lower and snowless, the valleys warmer, greener, more humid. To the south, a band of purple-gray clouds was steadily building up on the horizon (it was obvious that this year, unlike the last, the monsoon would be early), and both mornings and evenings there were showers of rain. For most of the time, however, the sun still shone; and one day, as they rested at noon, a thing happened that brought a great lift to Eric's spirits. Nima stirred on her litter. Raising her head, she looked at him and murmured, "Sun nice." It was the first time she had spoken in days, and he smiled, took her hand and kissed her. "Nice—nice," she repeated, smiling back at him weakly. And as they moved on he allowed himself the hope that the worst was over, that she had turned a corner.

She hadn't, though. That night, in their tent, fever gripped her again, and for hours she tossed and gibbered in delirium. The next day she lay limp, barely conscious, through the hours on the trail . . . And on this day, too, more misfortune struck. Earlier on the journey, Norbu, the twelve-year-old, had cut his leg in a briar patch; and while it had not, at the time, seemed much of an injury, it had grown gradually worse. Now it was badly infected, the whole leg was swollen, and he could barely walk. Eric had done what he could, cleaning and bandaging the wound, but it had not helped. There was nothing further he could do now; nor, because of Nima, was he willing to delay the march until Norbu was better. They left him, crippled and tearful, with a Sherpa family in a wayside village—to be sent back to Munda, when well enough, with another party of travelers. He had been a good boy, a good helper. Eric paid him his wages, plus half again as much as bonus. Then—with again no replacement available—loads were once more reapportioned, and the dwindling caravan moved on.

Four, now, they were—plus Nima. And the old had outlasted the young. The two Sherpanis, squat, stolid, middle-aged, plodded on through the miles without sign of fatigue; and the old man, Lobsang, despite his frailness of appearance, was doing no less well—though he now shared with Eric full-time duty as stretcher bearer. Up and down they went; down and up. Through sun and rain. Through dust and mud. Each day, as the monsoon clouds moved closer, there was less sun and dust, more rain and mud . . . But it was neither terrain nor weather that brought on the next misfortune.

About halfway in their journey they crossed a human frontier. Through the first part, in the highlands, they had still been in largely Sherpa country, a land of Mongoloid Buddhists; but now, in the lowlands, they were in the realm of Hindu Tamangs. Faces, clothing, language were different. The villages were different. In place of stone houses were houses of wood. In place of chortens, mani walls and prayer flags were carved temples, images of Siva

323

and Vishnu. On the trail, instead of Sherpa-to-Sherpa greetings between Eric's troop and passing travelers, there were stares, blank glances, as between aliens or enemies.

On the evening of their second day in this country the two Sherpanis spoke to Eric. "We will not go on, sah'b," they told him.

"Why? You've done well. The rest of the trail is easy."

"Is not the trail, sah'b. Is the people here. They are strange people—bad. We see it in their faces, their eyes, and are afraid for our lives."

Eric argued, cajoled. He offered extra wages. He pointed out that if there was any danger—which there wasn't—there would be more of it for them traveling alone on the return trip than in going on with him and Lobsang. But they would not be moved. "Is bad place; we go home," they said. In the morning, reluctantly, he gave them their pay and watched them trudge off on the trail back to Solu Khumbu.

Lobsang had sat by, saying nothing. Until the last moment Eric had thought he might decide to join them. But he didn't. He stayed. With the women gone, the two men would have both loads and stretcher to contend with; but the burden of foodstuffs was now greatly diminished, and there remained only another four or five days to Kathmandu. They started off again. They still managed.

At least for a while.

But now the monsoon closed in. For days its main cloud mass had stayed to the south, with only outriders of storm blowing in above them. But now the whole of it came. It enveloped them. Hour upon hour they moved through a dim world of mist and rain; and when occasionally the rain stopped, it was only to give way to gray stillness, hot and sodden, that was even more oppressive. In this season the Tamangs stayed in their villages and adjoining fields, and the trail was almost deserted. On the ups and downs they slipped and stumbled in its morass of mud, going ever more slowly, stopping often to rest. Eric's thoughts moved back through time. It had been during a monsoon, long past—and at almost this point on the trail—that he had slipped and stumbled, then collapsed in the mud, on his futile flight from Kathmandu toward the mountains. But then he had been alone; his collapse had affected no one but himself. There had been no stretcher, no Nima. And no matter what, they must keep on with Nima. They must hold the stretcher tight, keep it level; not jar her, not spill her.

In the rain, he pulled the tarpaulin up so that it covered all of her, including her head, and the downpour drummed on its hard, stiff fabric. It did not keep her dry, however. When the rain stopped and he pulled it down, she was as wet as if she had not been covered at all, lying drenched in the sweat of heat and fever. In the tent, at day's end, he tried to dry her, but there was nothing dry with which to do it. He forced a little food and liquid between her flaccid lips. Under the tarpaulin, her long black hair had come undone from its combs and pins, and now hung heavy and dank over her cheeks and shoulders. Clumsily, as best he could, he twined it into two pigtails—as she had worn it that past summer in the high pastures—in the hope that this would give her more air, a little coolness. As he finished, she opened her eyes, and for a moment he thought she was going to smile—as she had that day on the trail when she had opened them to the sunshine. But there was no smile this time. Her eyes looked through him, unseeing. During the night, as usual, her fever soared, and in the morning she showed no sign of consciousness as he strapped her into the litter.

They moved on. There was rain, then mist and swelter, then rain again. And always mud. In the mud, on a steep downhill, the old man, Lobsang, slipped and fell; his end of the litter fell with him, twisted, turned over; and Nima, still tied to it, also lay in the mud. Eric righted the litter, wiped the worst of the mud from her face, and turned to Lobsang, who was getting slowly to his feet. He did not berate the old man. He knew he had fallen not from carelessness but exhaustion. "We'll rest," he said. And they rested. Then lifted the litter, went on again. And again Lobsang fell. This time he did not drop the litter; he somehow got his end down gently, then fell, and when he tried to rise he couldn't. Eric lowered his own end of the litter, helped him up and to the side of the trail and they sat there together on a hummock of grass. The rain had stopped now; the earth around them was steaming with damp jungle heat. But Lobsang's frail body shook, as if he were shivering with cold.

After a while Eric said, "Look—Nima is very sick. I must get her to Kathmandu as soon as I can."

The old man nodded. "Yes, sah'b."

"You can't carry the stretcher anymore. I'll carry her myself, on my back, and go as fast as I can. You rest here today. Eat, drink, sleep. Without the stretcher to carry, you'll be all right tomorrow. Then come on at your own pace and meet me at the hospital in Kathmandu."

"Yes, sah'b." Lobsang nodded again . . . "Am sorry, sah'b," he said.

Eric gave him money. He left him a tent and half the remaining food and slung his own now-light pack on his chest, like a paratrooper. Lifting Nima from the litter, he got her onto his back and, with Lobsang's help, tied her securely. She seemed to weigh almost nothing. Ready, he shook hands with Lobsang. "Come tomorrow," he said. "Go slow, take it easy, and you'll be all right." Then he turned and set off down the trail.

Without the litter and the exhausted Sherpa, he moved faster than before. From where he was now, he judged, he could reach Kathmandu in three days; no, less than that, even—in the rest of this day and two more. Nor would he have to walk all the way into the city. Some miles this side of it he would reach the Valley of Nepal, where there were roads and cars, and he would find a car, a truck, something, that would take them on to the hospital. As his thoughts moved ahead, he trudged on through the mud. One of his boots had a loose sole that was flapping, and he tore the flapping part off. The path went steeply down, then steeply up. It began to rain again—first lightly, then hard—and he put the tarpaulin that had been used on the stretcher over his head, so that it hung down his back and covered Nima. "Hang on, girl, we're getting there," he said. He expected no answer, and got none.

That evening in the tent she did not seem to have so high a fever as before. When now and then she opened her eyes she neither spoke nor smiled, but by the light of the lamp he thought he saw in them at least a flicker of recognition. Their camp was near a stream, and bringing cups of water he washed her face and hands. Her hair, in the pigtails he had fashioned, had come loose again, and again he braided and tied them, a little less clumsily than before. Framed by them, her face seemed as small and pinched as that of their stillborn child. Now her eyes were closed again. Her breathing was shallow but steady as he turned down the lamp and lay beside her.

Then it was morning. Securing her on his back was more difficult without Lobsang's help; but he managed it. He slung his pack on his chest. He started off again. And again there were the hills, the rain, the mud, the miles. He walked through the miles, as it seemed to him now he had walked through the whole of his life . . . through Colorado, Washington, Utah; through Alaska, Apennines, Alps; through Los Angeles, Paris, Calcutta, Hong Kong; through Kathmandu, Solu Khumbu, the Himalayas beyond them . . . now through the miles of Nepal, with his wife on his back . . . after all the miles and the years, still walking, still moving on . . . He could still do it . . . He was tired, bone-tired, but not, like Lobsang, exhausted. He slipped and stumbled, but did not fall. It was raining again, and he put the tarpaulin over himself and Nima. He trudged on. Though she was a tiny thing, now tinier than ever, her ninety-odd pounds were a load for a man's back. Yet carrying her thus was less awkward, in a way easier, than carrying the stretcher. As the hours passed, he grew used to his load, was scarcely aware of it.

It was toward midday that there came a change. Suddenly— or perhaps gradually—he *was* aware of it: it seemed somehow to feel differently, to have shifted position, lost its balance. Groping behind him under the tarpaulin, he tried to adjust the straps that held Nima to him, but his manipulations had no effect. To get things straight he would have to untie her, see what was wrong, then tie her on again. Stopping, he loosened the bindings and let her down; and as his hands felt her body under the tarpaulin he knew it was not the straps that had caused the change of balance. He laid her down on a strip of grass beside the trail and pulled back the section of canvas that covered her face. Her eyes were open, her mouth was open, and the rain fell into them. Pulling the canvas back over them, he sat beside her and covered his own face with his hands.

He sat there a long time.

The rain stopped, resumed, stopped again. No one came along the trail.

The last village he had passed through was about three miles back. The next, at a guess, should be the same distance ahead. Their inhabitants were Tamangs, Hindus, whose strangeness and hostile stares had frightened the two older Sherpanis back to Solu Khumbu. If, an alien himself, he carried a dead Buddhist Sherpa to a Hindu-Tamang cremation ghat, he would be driven away in outrage.

Except for children—and embryos not yet children—the Sherpas, too, cremated their dead. But they were far from lamas, prayer wheels, the burning grounds high in the uplands beneath the streaming flags. He looked at the dank and dripping world around him. A big enough fire could not be built from it; and even if it could, he could not have done it.

Still he sat for a while.

Then, leaving Nima, he rose and moved away. As he had done two months before, carrying their child out from Dhamu, he cut off from the trail into the land that bordered it. Here there were trees as well as brush and bushes, and coming to a clearing among them, he stopped. This time he had no pick and shovel; but when he bent to feel the earth, it was soft—half earth, half mud. Finding a fallen branch, he brought out his knife, pared one end of the branch into a wedgelike shape, and began to dig.

Nima was small, but not so small as the child, and it took some time. But using branch and hands, he kept at it until he had made a shallow but, he thought, adequate grave. Returning to the trail, he picked up Nima in the tarpaulin and brought her to it; and yes, it was big enough. Again, now, he lifted the top of the canvas, exposing her face. He closed her eyes and her mouth, kissed them quickly and lightly, and re-covered her face with the canvas. Her two black pigtails protruded, one on either side, and he tucked them in. Then with his hands—for the branch was no good for this—he refilled the grave and tamped the earth flat above it. On a nearby bush grew bright yellow flowers whose name he did not know, and plucking a few, he strewed them on the earth.

He said, "*Om mani padme hum.*"

Then he turned away.

He came back to the trail, slung on his pack (now once more on his back) and moved on toward the west. It had begun to rain again, but he neither saw nor felt it. What he felt was a void. What he saw was Nima's pigtails sticking out from the tarpaulin; then other pigtails—not Nima's, not black but brown—spinning, dwindling in the void.

He had no luck at all with pigtails.

He saw them now, again: spinning . . . spinning . . . He saw the face of Robin, the face of Nima, dwindling, receding, engulfed in darkness.

He too was engulfed. It was around him, within him. Where breath should have been there was void and darkness, and he had half-blacked out for lack of air, of oxygen. He was struggling for them . . . and slowly winning. He was struggling for light, and light was returning: at first dim and gray, then stronger, brighter . . . still brighter . . . There was an explosion of light, as blinding as darkness, as the morning sun blazed on the high snows of Dera Zor.

He flipped down his dark goggles, and he could see again. Oxygen was trickling through to blood and brain; he was fully conscious again. Down below were the three dots, ascending. Above was the peak, the sky, a shining sky. It would be a day of glory.

He had been resting, motionless, too long. At this height that was as bad as overstraining, and when now he stood up he was cold and stiff. He thumped his feet and hands. He breathed slowly, deeply, and faced the slope above.

Nima was gone now—Robin was gone—both gone with the darkness, as he started to climb.

"No sweat, baby," said Amy Bulwinkle. "Remember that always —no sweat at all."

21

The barroom of the Himalayan Palace had been redecorated. There were new tables and chairs, new lighting fixtures (that sometimes worked), red instead of green curtains at the windows. But the bar itself was the same. The Haig Pinch was in its familiar niche. When he came in, Amy was sitting alone on her favored stool at the end of the bar.

"For God's sake, take a bath," she said.

"First things first," he replied, pouring a tumbler of Pinch.

There had been some changes in Amy too. She had put on a few pounds—not many, but a few—and her hair was no longer platinumed but a sort of streaked reddish blond. But otherwise —and fundamentally—she was still Amy.

"Even letting you stick your nose in here, I should have my head examined," she told him. "But what the hell—" She poured a drink for herself. "Here we go again."

It was June, July, August. The monsoon rains still poured down. Tourists were few. They drank almost alone at the bar.

Then it was fall, winter, "the season." The bar was crowded, and he worked behind it. On Saturday nights there was the entertainment, the dance troupe, the yeti, with Dorje the waiter still prancing inside the ape skin.

"We once had a yeti who climbed to the roof," Amy informed her customers. "But he retired on Social Security."

Some things were the same.

Some were different.

Ashkar the clerk was still behind the desk in the lobby, dispensing keys, bills—and, in off hours, hashish. The boy Babul, whom he had once brought to Eric's room, was now a young man, a head bearer, slim and elegant; but he did not again appear to offer his services. The venerable Osmun Shumsher Jung Bahadur Rana was dead, his three wives had moved elsewhere, and Amy—though presumably still not the owner—now held total sovereignty at the Himalayan Palace. The style of operation, however, was unchanged from before. She still prowled the corridors, stormed through kitchen and pantries, shouted for absentee bearers as if through a bullhorn. "No sweat, baby," Eric reminded her. At which she swore, then grinned, then reached for a drink.

"Who's sweating?" she asked.

Amy was still Amy; the Palace, the Palace; Kathmandu, Kathmandu. There were the teeming streets, the bazaars, the pagodas and temples. There were the soldiers, merchants, beggars, holy men, cows, dogs, monkeys, dirt, smells. But the city, too, had seen changes; it had further opened up to the world. The airport was enlarged, planes bigger and more frequent, the tourist tide—in season—far greater. Added to the Palace, Royal and Snowview, there were now two new hotels, the Annapurna and Soaltee, in which it was said—to Amy's aggravation—that the toilets flushed and the cockroaches stayed out of sight. Also, in the outskirts of town, there was now an encampment: not a succession of seasonal camps, as expeditions came and went, but a year-round establishment, tenanted not by mountaineers but by hippies.

Carol Flagg had talked of hippies. She herself, she had said, had been a semi-hippie during her "Zen phase" while in college. But at the time of her arrival in Solu Khumbu they had not yet come to Nepal. Now they had. Kathmandu was full of them —bearded, bangled, barefoot—from New York, Los Angeles, Zanesville, Ohio; from London, Paris, Hamburg, Stockholm. They had come, they declared, in quest of the Asian mystique. Of Zen, yin and yang, yoga; of gurus and sadhus, Nirvana and Karma.

"—Of cosmic consciousness," Eric was told by a freckled, snub-nosed girl who, with a bath, change of clothes and megaphone, could have passed for a cheerleader at Hughes High School in Denver. And he wished her good hunting.

What they sought most of all, however, was hashish. And Ashkar, the Palace room clerk, did a booming business. For a while, a large part of it was conducted over the desk in the lobby. Then Amy cracked down ("get those creeps the hell out of here") and Ashkar moved his nonclerical headquarters to a shed on the hotel grounds. It was the same shed in which Eric, in days past, had had his own first bouts with hashish. But he did not go there now. Sometimes he talked with the youngsters as they came and went. As something of his past became known, he was recognized by them as a non-square, as even a guru emeritus. But for "his own thing," in these later days, he went not to the shed but the bar.

On the trail from Solu Khumbu he had thought back through the miles and years of his walking. Now, sometimes, he thought back to the years of bars (and there were perhaps miles there too, if laid end to end). To—which was first? He couldn't remember. Yes, he could. It had been a sleazy place in downtown Seattle in his freshman year at the U of W. To—what came next? It didn't matter. To—in more-or-less order—the Cloche in Paris, White Valley's Sitzmark, Calcutta's Palm Club, Hong Kong's Blue Dragon, San Francisco's Phriendly Phoenix (where there had been hippies too, but then called beats). To others, dozens, hundreds of others, in the States, Europe, Asia, Australia. (Somehow he had missed out on South America, Africa, Antarctica.) But still there had been hundreds; there had been miles of them all right; miles leading to *here*—to Nepal, Kathmandu, the bar of the Himalayan Palace Hotel—where it now seemed he had been for years (as indeed he had), with one long interruption and now back again.

—Back on one side of the bar, then the other. Making drinks for the guests, and when the guests were gone, for himself and Amy. Usually these were Pinch; occasionally, for old time's sake, arak (not rakshi here—arak); and when the night was late they went to her rooms—now, again, *their* rooms—but not the same as before; now the apartment formerly occupied by the late departed O.S.J.B. Rana and his wives. And there they were home. Sometimes they fought, sometimes made love, sometimes both, almost simultaneously. And if neither fighting nor loving was quite so intense as in earlier days, performance was not negligible either; for long practice—despite interruption—had made them expert at both.

"Did your Sherpa babes have the old girl's pizazz?" Amy asked him.

—And grinned, knowing the answer.

The world of the Sherpas was gone, lost—as if it had never been. The last Sherpa he had seen had been Lobsang, his porter, who had reached Kathmandu two days after himself and waited for him at the hospital. He had seen to it (thanks to Amy's financing) that the old man had been fed, reclothed and given the medical attention he needed. He had told him of Nima's death and burial and asked him, on his return to Solu Khumbu, to tell the story to Tashi. After a week's rest in the city Lobsang had left on the journey home.

He was gone.

Nima was gone.

Since then, the months had passed . . . A year . . . A second year. And now it was she, Solu Khumbu, his life in Munda and Dhamu, that seemed as remote as Betelgeuse.

The reason no Sherpas came to Kathmandu was that something else, too, was gone. There were no expeditions. Red China, a scant few miles to the north, beyond the Himalayas, had complained about "spies" being allowed to approach, even cross, her frontiers; and Nepal, wary and fearful, had responded by closing its gates to mountaineers. In late winter and late spring, there was no longer the familiar bustle of climbers coming and going. There was no thump of boots in the hotel hallways, no piles of food

334

and gear in the courtyard. In the camps in the city's outskirts there were only hippies.

Eric wondered about the Sherpas. For years, almost all their cash income had been from expeditions. Even more importantly —at least for the men—the meaning, the joy, of their lives had come from them; from doing that which, of all things, they did and loved best. What, for instance, was Tashi doing, after his years of climbing—and now no climbing? What of Pembol, who had waited so eagerly until he would be old enough for it—and now was old enough—and there was nothing? Was he still, at nineteen or twenty, in Carol Flagg's school? Learning what? To what purpose?

Then, thinking of Carol, he realized that she would no longer be there. Her Peace Corps service over, she would long since have come back and passed through Kathmandu . . . When? he wondered. Where had she stayed? Had they perhaps passed in the street without seeing each other? . . . In any case, she was surely gone. By now there was someone else at the schoolhouse in Munda, and she was back—where? On Philadelphia's Main Line? In Kansas? (No, not Kansas.)

Carol—
Nima—
Both gone.
And before them, others.
Sometimes—not often, but once in a while, when someone or something nudged his memory—he found himself remembering other women he had known; and like the miles he had walked and the bars he had drunk at, there had been quite a few. The hippie who had looked like a Hughes High School cheerleader had stirred memories of Denver; Denver had led to Winton Academy (there was Kansas again), Winton to the university at Seattle; and in Seattle—and on the ski slopes of Rainier—there had been Doris Flanner. He had not thought of her for years. He could scarcely recall what she had looked like. But had it not been for the war he would probably have married her.

After that—also thanks to the war—there had been Nicole . . . Nicole what? Nicole Vaudrier . . . There had been no thoughts of marriage there. Just Paris, pernod, existentialism, love in an attic—and Julian Howard coming down the boulevard carrying a bottle of *le vrai absinthe*. Back home, there had been White Valley; the girls on the slopes, in the Sitzmark, in bed. Later (and here the order was hazy) Thalia of the Phoenix, Lily of the Dragon, Charlotte—no, Charlayne no less—of the Big Bend Motel, Cisco, Cal. And others, now nameless, faceless, in bars and beds around the world.

They, too, were gone, lost.

—Leaving one more: not nameless, not faceless. And one night, very late at night, she came and joined him at the Palace bar. Amy had gone upstairs; he was alone and had been drinking for hours. Then, "one more drink," he thought, and went behind the bar to get it. But this time it was not scotch or arak that he poured. He took down the gin, the dry vermouth, and for the first time in all his years in Kathmandu he made a martini. He made enough not for one drink but two, filled two glasses, added the lemon peels, and across the bar Kay raised her glass and smiled. They had come from skiing, her face was fresh and glowing; and they drank their drinks, had a second round, then drove down to the roadhouse to dine and dance. They did not talk—it was enough to dance, to hold each other close—and when the dancing was over they returned to the inn. They walked in the night and the snow. They came back indoors, but not to the bar (the bar was closed now, the lights out); and they went upstairs, down a hall, to a closed door, and Kay opened the door. For the first time, she spoke. "I'm going to be the mother of your son," she said. Then they were in the room, and there was Frank . . . then no more Frank . . . and no more Kay. He had pulled off his clothes, tumbled onto the bed, and Amy, half-awake, said, "Well, here's old Gin Rummy himself."

The past would emerge, flicker briefly, recede.

By now, there was plenty of past just with Amy.

Almost twenty years had gone by since he had first met her; since he had come, beaten and broken, from Dera Zor to the Government guesthouse, and the others had left, and she had come to his room with a bottle of arak. For about half that time, of course, he had been elsewhere; first around the world, back home; then in Solu Khumbu. But that still left ten years with her—and the overall twenty. They were now both in their mid-forties. ("The Geriatric Kids," she said). They had not considered marriage ("Once was too often," she said), and she had made carefully sure she would not become pregnant. But still they were as much a pair, a couple, as man and woman could be. They lived together; ate, drank, fought, bedded down together; then rose and started over again.

He stayed away from hashish. It was hashish that had, literally, once driven him up the wall. And though he drank every night, often half through the night, he had not, like the ghostly old Cess Bulwinkle, become a true alcoholic. Like Amy—she of the two hollow legs—he could now manage his drinks. He could do his day's work, such as it was: making drinks for others, doing odd jobs around the hotel, occasionally conducting tours (pornographic or otherwise) around Kathmandu. Drinking no longer led him to depression or desperation. In the first days after his return from Solu Khumbu, he had grieved for Nima—but neither as long nor as deeply as he would have in earlier days. Perhaps it was that, by now, he had known too many losses to suffer greatly from another; perhaps that, after so long in Asia, he had acquired the Asian acceptance of karma, of fate. In any case, drunk or sober, he found that, as time went on, he accepted it ever more fully.

This was the hippies' creed, too: "Keep your cool," they said. And Amy's: "No sweat. No sweat at all."

One day he went down to the cellar. Not drunkenly running. Not by night but by day. Going to the storage bin, he found his old rat-gnawed suitcase and lifted it out. He did not open it, nor reach in through the rents in its sides, but simply carried it out to the dump in the courtyard and threw it away. Then he went back upstairs and washed his hands.

Not long after, he bought some pads and pencils in the bazaar. At the hotel, he found an unoccupied room, sat down at its table and began to write. He did not write a story; merely notes. One pad he labeled *Sherpas—General,* a second *Villages,* a third *Women & Children,* a fourth *Yaks,* and in each he set down the thoughts and memories that came to him. He had no specific purpose in mind; no book; no *Esquire* or *True* or *Saturday Evening Post.* He wrote the notes because he wanted, somehow needed to; because, after all the years, he was still enough of a writer so that thoughts and memories had more meaning for him if they were written down.

On the first day he stayed at it for about an hour. On later days he returned for more hours. When it came time for the bar to open he left the room and went to work.

Then something new—and old—was added. There were mountaineers again.

In the fall of the year past, for reasons unspecified, the Nepalese Government had decreed that expeditions would again be permitted; and in the late winter following they began to appear. To the Himalayan Palace came a Japanese Everest party and a French team bound for Dhaulagiri. There were others in the other hotels and camped in the fields roundabout, and, again as in former times, there were Sherpas in from Solu Khumbu to join them. Not a few were from Munda and Dhamu, and known to Eric; but Tashi was not among them. He had, the others said, been hired as sirdar by one of the expeditions; but back in Munda his wife, Ai Lamu, was sick, and he had had to stay with her.

The climbers came and went. To some, Eric served drinks. Then came an evening when he returned from an errand in town, entered the bar, and there was Amy on her usual stool. "There's a kid been here looking for you," she told him.

"A kid? A hippie?"

"No, a mountain type. He said he'd be back."

338

He made drinks for a tourist couple, then for Amy and himself. Then a boy—a young man—appeared in the door, and Amy gestured to him, pointing to Eric. The boy—or man—approached him. At a guess he was about twenty, an American, and he was wearing khakis and a sweater. His height was roughly the same as Eric's, but his build more slender. His face, though young, had strong lines, framed by touseled brown hair and a thin growth of beard. His eyes, brownish green—but more green than brown— seemed not merely to be looking but staring at Eric, as he came up to the bar and faced him.

"You're"—he hesitated slightly—"you're Mr. Venn?" he asked.

Eric nodded.

"That's my name too," the boy said.

There was a pause.

"I'm Larry Venn," he said. "Your nephew."

There had been—how many?—hundreds, thousands, call it three-thousand-and-one nights in the bar of the Himalayan Palace. The nights of tourists, whisky, arak, Amy. And though this and that had happened and many had come and gone, they had all been, in essence, the same—except two. On the first, long past, an old lady wearing steel-rimmed glasses had appeared and said, "I am Mrs. Homer Bigelow." Now a boy with a scrubby beard and greenish eyes appeared and said, "I'm Larry Venn, your nephew."

The old lady had had a sherry.

The boy had a beer.

She had been alone.

He was not.

He was a member of the American Dera Zor Expedition that had arrived in Kathmandu that morning and was quartered at the Royal Hotel. It was a team of seven, of whom he was the youngest. The oldest, and expedition leader, was an eminent mining engineer, past president of the American Alpine Club, and one of the top mountaineers of his generation—by name, Kenneth Naylor.

"I've just phoned Ken and told him I've found you," said Larry. "He's coming right over."

He started to speak again, stopped, and took a sip of his beer. Eric started to speak, stopped, and finished his whisky. "This is Larry Venn," he said to Amy. And to Larry, "This is Amy Bulwinkle."

"Hi again," said Amy.

"Hello," said Larry.

"Nice night out," said Amy.

"Yes, very," said Larry.

Two more guests came in and Eric made their drinks. Then he poured himself another scotch.

"Hey, how about me?" said Amy.

He poured one for her too.

"Like another beer?" Amy asked Larry.

"No thanks," said Larry.

Two more tourists came in.

Then Ken came in.

There he was, first in the doorway, half-staring, half-smiling; then shaking, clasping Eric's hand in both of his. And he was older, of course—now middle-aged, almost bald—but with his face still brown and square-cut, his body broad but solid, the old football lineman, the powerhouse of Rainier and the Tetons, after all the years still the warhorse fit and ready for the fray.

All the years . . .

Ken was struggling back across them. "My God, it's twenty!" he said. "Twenty damn years, Rick, since we've laid eyes on each other."

Eric let it pass. It was not twenty years but—what?—nine, ten, since he had last seen Ken Naylor; since Ken, unknowing, had last seen him, Eric the yeti, in his ape suit, prancing, whirling, climbing the wall, in the glare of a bonfire, the mist of hashish—and had left for him, with Amy, ten rupees and a Polaroid snapshot.

"This is Ken Naylor," he said to Amy. "This is Amy Bulwinkle," he said to Ken.

And the two said hello without recognition.

Then Ken, over a whisky, was saying: "I was back here once, you know. Nine years ago. We had another try at DZ and wanted you; I wrote you. Your sister-in-law—Larry's mother—said you were back in Nepal, and I wrote, but no answer. When we got here, I looked for you, but no luck."

With Larry, they had moved to one of the tables. Amy was now behind the bar, serving the other customers, and between servings she drank her own drink and watched them.

Ken said: "Then a few years later I tried to find you again. I'd heard from Kay that Larry—he was still a kid then—had written you, and you'd answered; and when the American Everest Expedition came out I asked them to keep an eye open. But no deal. No sign of you, they said. So this time—now—I figured you were gone for good."

"Or even dead," said Larry. "Mother especially: she began to think you were dead."

"But Larry here wasn't buying that," Ken said. "We weren't in Kathmandu ten minutes before he was looking around for you—and, by God, he was right!" He pressed Eric's shoulder and grinned. "It's a wise child that knows its own uncle," he added.

The bar was filling up, getting noisy. A tourist, glass in hand, came over and said to Ken and Larry, "I hear you're going to Everest."

"No, not Everest," Ken told him.

"Well, the Matterhorn then. Good luck to you. But watch out for those Abominable Snowmen."

He laughed and, uninvited, sat down with them. Soon others joined him. The bar was now full of talk, laughter, the clinking of glassware, and Amy, to top it off, had turned on the tape recorder with rock music. Presently, two other members of Ken's expedition appeared and squeezed in beside them. They were introduced as Paul Loring and Arne Norstad, and like Larry and Ken, they too stared at Eric; but between rock and interruptions there was small chance for talk. "They're both good men—damn good," Ken managed to tell Eric. And later: "Larry's good too. He's our baby, of course, but quite a baby—a real mountaineer. You'll be proud of him." But that was the end of the conversa-

341

tion. Amy was called away by a crisis elsewhere in the hotel, and
Eric had to go back behind the bar. Then a phone message came
for Ken from the Royal that some of the expedition Sherpas were
complaining about their sleeping quarters. "If it's not this, it's
that," he said, sighing. "And tomorrow—customs, no less."

He rose to go, and the others followed.

"I'll call you as soon as I'm free," he told Eric.

"Me too," said Larry. (He and the boy, thought Eric, had barely
exchanged ten words.)

Then they were gone.

He would have liked to leave too. Not to go with them to the
Royal. Not to go anywhere, but simply to be by himself, to walk
for a while, to breathe slowly and deeply. But the bar was too busy.
Even when Amy returned, she needed help. For the next two
hours he made drinks—including some for himself—and it was,
as always, past midnight, when he and Amy went up to bed.

"The old-home-week kid himself," she said to him as they un-
dressed. "I thought you were the guy who knew *nobody*."

"Almost, but not quite," he said.

"—And had no family. You've never let out a peep about a
family."

"I have a brother," Eric said. "This boy is his son."

"And the old one—who's he?"

"You've met him before. Twenty years ago." He left out the
nine-years-ago: the yeti snapshot, the ten rupees. "We were together on the expedition when you and I first met."

"Jesus, back then! I can't remember any more what happened
night before last." She had her clothes off now and was slipping
on her nightgown. "And after twenty years—as old as us, for godsake—he's still out chasing mountains?"

"The same one," said Eric.

"He must be some kind of nut."

He didn't argue the point. She got into bed, and he followed
and turned out the light. There was no lovemaking; no contact
of their bodies. He lay in the darkness, unmoving, eyes open,
and she too was motionless and presently, he thought, asleep.

But she wasn't asleep. "You know," she said after a while,

342

"that nephew of yours—when he first came in—*he's* the one gave me that funny feeling I'd seen him before. At first I couldn't figure it out; then I did. It was *you* he looked like . . . Not now, for godsake. Way back where you were just talking about, when you first came here . . . A dead ringer, I thought—except for the eyes, those green eyes of his. Then you came in and he said nephew and I got it. Nephew-shmephew: hell, he could be your own kid . . ."

Ken phoned the next day in the midafternoon. The Sherpas, he reported, were pacified, and customs could have been worse. Now they were sorting loads in the Royal courtyard; and could Eric come over? No, he couldn't, said Eric. Why not? Because he was working. That could wait, couldn't it? No, unfortunately not. Ken persuaded, argued, then took no for an answer. "I'll come over this evening, then," he said finally.

But he was there in an hour.

Eric was in the vacant room he used for writing, seated at the table with pads and pencils, when there was a knock and one of the bearers showed Ken in. "Sorry to bust in," he said. "But I want to talk to you: here, now."

Eric had risen. Ken sat down. He looked at the table. "So this is the work," he said. "You're writing."

"I'm making notes," said Eric.

"You've been writing all along?"

"No, not for years. Not now. I'm just making notes."

"May I ask what about?"

"About the Sherpas."

"Oh?"

"For a few years," said Eric, "I lived with the Sherpas."

"So that's where you were when—"

"Yes."

"You climbed with the Sherpas?"

"No."

"I don't believe it. There in Solu Khumbu, right under the mountains—with Dera Zor just next door—"

343

"I went to Dera Zor once. To near its base, that's all. There was snow and mist and I couldn't see it."

Ken seemed not to have heard this last. "So it's twice for each of us," he said. "Once together, once separately. And now—"

Here it comes, thought Eric.

But it didn't. Ken veered off. "On that second go we thought we had it," he said. "Everything went right—men, weather, logistics—right up through Camp Five to the foot of the Wailing Wall. Then it all fell through. The wall was iced solid, impossible. We made one try and it was hopeless, and that was the end of it."

Eric had sat down again. Ken leaned forward a little. "This time ice won't stop us," he said.

"Ice is ice, isn't it?"

"Yes, but other things have changed. Since we climbed together—even since that last go—there's all sorts of new and better gear. New skills and techniques. What the best of these youngsters can do on steep ice and rock is enough to make your eyes pop."

"What about the not-so-youngsters?"

"You mean me?" said Ken. "Good God, man, I'm not going for the wall, or the top. I'll be happy if I can get to Camp Three at the Gap; at best, to the top of the ridge. To put the show on the road; to guide and direct it and see the young ones come through—that's what DZ means to me now, and it's as good as climbing it myself would have been in the old days."

He paused, then went on: "Besides, there are a couple of other things to sweeten the pot. Do you know that DZ is now the highest unclimbed mountain in the world?"

No, Eric hadn't known.

"Well, it is. Everest, K2, Kanch, Lhotse, Makalu—the bigger ones—they've all been had. That leaves DZ, the only twenty-seven-thousander that's still a virgin."

There was another pause.

"That's Item One," said Ken. "Then there's Item Two, that's not a bad one either."

344

He was leaning forward again, hands spread on the table. Here it comes, thought Eric again, and this time he was right.

"—That we'll be going together again," Ken said.

There it was.

Eric shook his head.

"Yes," said Ken. "Yes, you're coming."

"No . . . I knew what you wanted when you asked me to come to the Royal. I knew still better when you walked into this room." Eric's voice was quiet, almost gentle. "And the answer, Ken," he said, "is no."

"Why? Why no?" Ken demanded.

"For one thing, I'm too old."

"I'm two years older."

"And I haven't climbed a mountain in twenty years."

"So what? You still know how. You lived a rugged life with the Sherpas. And no one's expecting you to go to the top, any more than myself."

Eric smiled thinly. "You mean we'd go along as a pair of senior scoutmasters?"

"We'd go along as co-leaders, that's what. As the two men who know more about Dera Zor than anyone on earth." Ken leaned still farther forward. The whole of him, every ounce of him, was in his words. "—Who *care* more about it," he said. "Who started the whole thing—dreamt it, lived it—you even more than I." Eric started to speak, but he overrode him. "Do you remember that book, *Trek to Nowhere*, you used to carry around with you? In Seattle, Hale, Italy, everywhere. That was your Bible, Rick, your Song of Songs. DZ was yours, remember? If it was the last thing in the world you did, you were by God going to make it yours!"

"That was a lifetime ago," said Eric.

"Lifetime, hell. You're still Rick Venn. Dera Zor's still there . . . I'll tell you what's a lifetime ago. Julian Howard and Franz Harben, that's what. They've been dead twenty years. They're gone. But you won't let them go . . . That's it, isn't it. *Isn't it?* For twenty goddamn years you've been living with their ghosts."

Eric got up. He walked away.

But Ken kept on:

345

"When we came back here from the mountain and I left with the others, I wasn't walking out on you. I was leaving you alone because I knew you had to be alone, to sweat it out. But I didn't know you'd be sweating it out for the rest of your life."

Eric stood at the window. "There's no sweat any more," he said quietly. No sweat at all. (He heard the echo.) "Back then when you knew me, I was living one life. Now I'm living another."

"Tending a bar—"

"Yes."

"Getting drunk every night—"

"Yes."

"Servicing a crummy old bag who—"

"Careful," said Eric.

But Ken was angry now. His voice grew louder, harsher.

"For God's sake, can't you see what I'm offering? A chance to live again, be yourself again . . . I didn't come here this afternoon because the expedition needs you. I came because you need *us*. For your own stupid sake—"

Ken, too, got up.

"And for Larry's—"

Eric turned from the window.

"What do you mean," he said, "Larry's—?"

"Can't you figure it out?"

"No."

"You have no idea what it means to the kid that you come along on this thing?"

Eric said nothing.

"You don't remember a letter he once wrote you—and one you wrote him back? . . . Well, he does. I do . . . You wrote him, *When you're grown up, you come here, Larry, and we'll climb together.*"

"That was years ago," said Eric.

"That's right, years ago. And all those years he's remembered. You've been his hero. It's because of you that he started climbing in the first place. To be like his great Uncle Rick. He told you, his mother had given you up for dead. Some of the rest of us had too. But not Larry. Never. Great Uncle Rick was still out there in the bush somewhere, waiting for him, and when he was grown they were going together to climb Dera Zor."

Ken paused. "Well, now he's grown," he said. "Any comment?"

Eric was silent.

"All right, I'll tell him his hero's too busy tending bar," said Ken.

He waited, still got no answer, then turned and went out.

That was Ken.

Then came Larry.

He had called; Eric had suggested meeting at the Annapurna Hotel, where there was neither expedition nor Amy; and now there they were. They had a beer, the two of them (no whisky, no arak), and went in to dinner. On either side of the table they sat awkward, constrained, taking care to look anywhere except at each other's faces. "A dead ringer," Amy had said, but of that Eric wasn't sure; his image of his own long-ago self was too dim and remote. What was not dim or remote were the boy's eyes— his green eyes—the eyes of his mother.

Then he spoke of his mother.

"I cabled her," he said.

"Cabled?"

"I knew how much it would mean to her to know I've found you." The boy smiled shyly. "I promised her a rundown later."

There was a pause.

"How is she?" asked Eric.

"She's fine," Larry said. "Mostly busy being a grandmother."

"A what?"

Larry's smile became a grin. "She doesn't look it, but she is. Joyce, my older sister, has been married two years now, and last fall she had a baby."

Eric shook his head. "And"—he fumbled—"your other sister?"

"Sheila. She graduated from UCLA. She's decided to be a doctor, and now she's at medical school."

"Hmm—" Whether in Nepal or California, Eric thought, time passed, things happened. But the California sort of things were different.

347

"How about your father?" he asked.

"Dad's all right, I think. I haven't seen much of him, though, since he moved East."

"Moved East?"

"Oh—you don't know, of course. He and Mother were divorced about three years ago. Soon after, he switched from Burden to another company and went to New York."

Eric stared at him, then looked away. A bearer came and went.

"It had been coming a long time," Larry said. "As far back as I can remember they didn't really get along, but they were waiting for the girls and me to grow up."

"Has he remarried?"

"No."

"And your mother?"

"No." The boy considered a moment. "I think she should," he said. "She still seems so young—grandma and all; but she hasn't and says she won't . . . About Dad's plans I don't know. Even before he moved East, we weren't very close."

Larry thought again. "It's funny—" he said.

"What's funny?"

"How things line up. Most of my trouble with Dad has been about climbing. There were you, his brother, one of the world's great mountaineers, but he wanted no part of it—not just for himself, but for me. All through my teens, when I was starting in, we used to fight about it. Not Mother, that's the strange part. Mothers are supposed to get upset about things like climbing, but she didn't at all; she encouraged me. It was Dad who was rough. First he tried straight out to forbid me to climb, and then, when that didn't work, he made fun of me."

Eric smiled, a little grimly. "Did he call you Hillbilly?" he asked.

The boy looked surprised. "You too?" he said.

"Me too," said Eric.

"As I say, it's funny—but it figures. From the beginning, I felt it was because of you that he was against my climbing. And because of you, too, that Mother was for it. She did some worrying, of course, and was always begging me to be careful. But deep down she was for it. She understood what mountaineering was all about, and I knew it was from you that she'd got it."

"Has she kept up her skiing?" asked Eric.

Again Larry showed surprise. "Skiing? I never knew she skied; she's never talked of it . . . But of mountains, yes. She's always asked me about my climbs—and told me about yours. Especially about Dera Zor and how much it meant to you. And it meant a lot to her too—I could see that—almost as if she'd been part of the thing herself. Or part of you." The boy paused, reflecting. Then his eyes—the green eyes—fixed on Eric. "Maybe I shouldn't say this," he added, "but I've often had the feeling that Mother felt closer to you than to Dad—even that it was you rather than he that she wished she'd married—"

The bearer took away some plates and brought some others.

"It looks like beef," said Eric, "but it's water buffalo."

They ate for a while in silence.

Then—"Let's hear about your own climbing," he said.

"That began with you, too," said Larry. "With what Mother told me about you. You remember that letter I wrote you years ago? And you wrote me back? Well, that was the starting gun, I guess. Pretty soon I was reading everything in sight about mountains—Alps, Andes, Himalayas, the works—best of all, that old book on Dera Zor that Mother remembered your carrying around for so long; and meanwhile I got in some kid sort of climbing of my own, with the Scouts and at school. Then I went to Stanford . . ."

He talked of Stanford. There had, he said, been more than one reason for his going there, but not the least was that it had perhaps the best mountaineering club of any university in the country. Starting in freshman year, he had learned cragsmanship on the walls of Yosemite. He had climbed on snow and ice on Rainier and the other Cascades. During his post-freshman summer he had been on a small expedition in British Columbia, and after sophomore year on a more ambitious one to Mount Logan in the Yukon.

"That was just last summer," he said. "Then back at Stanford in the fall I heard that Ken Naylor was organizing a third go at

Dera Zor. I'd known Ken for years, of course; he and Mother kept in touch, hoping they'd hear something about you. So I went after him full blast. He said I was too young, and I argued. I reminded him that Sandy Irvine was only twenty when he went with Mallory to Everest. And he said yes, and look what happened to him. Then he said what about college?—I'd miss half junior year—and I said I could make it up later. Then it was back to too young again, and I said we'd find you out here and you'd come along as my nursemaid."

Larry grinned again. "At last I wore him down," he said.

The grin faded. "But now no nursemaid," he added. "Ken says you won't come."

Here it is again, thought Eric.

"I can't," he said.

"Because—"

"Because I'm too old. Because I'm not a climber anymore."

"That's what Ken said you said."

"Well?"

"He didn't believe you."

"What Ken thinks is his own business."

"But he's sorry he got angry," said Larry. "He asked me to tell you that."

"It doesn't matter," said Eric.

"He also asked me to give you this."

The boy took from his pocket a piece of note paper and handed it across the table. Eric unfolded it and read:

Rick—

I said we didn't need you, but now I'll take that back. A tricky situation has developed and you could help us a lot.

You remember Tashi of course—your old Sherpa? Well, this time Tashi was to be our head Sherpa—our sirdar—I signed him up from back home. And so he will be when we're on DZ. But he hasn't come to Kathmandu. I have a message from him that his wife is sick and he can't join us until we reach Solu Khumbu —which means that for the approach march we're minus a sirdar, a man who knows the Sherpas and Tamangs and their languages and can handle them effectively.

Would you therefore consider taking over as far as Namche Bazar? You'd of course be welcome to go farther, but I won't pressure you. For you just to do that much would be of great help to us, not to mention meaning a lot personally to me and to Larry.

Hopefully—

Ken

Eric refolded the note. Across the table, Larry was watching him.

Now he's going to speak his piece, thought Eric. But he didn't.

"Ken says to think it over," Larry said.

They went separate ways from the Annapurna: Larry back to the expedition at the Royal, and Eric toward the Himalayan Palace. He did not, however, turn in at the gate. He kept walking. For an hour, a second, a third, he walked on through the city, as he had so often before over so many years.

When he returned to the Palace it was after midnight. Amy and guests had gone to their rooms, and in the lobby there was only the night clerk (not Ashkar—his relief man) asleep in a chair behind the desk. He went to the bar, and it was dark and empty. He went behind the counter, but did not put on a light, nor did he turn to the shelves where the liquor was kept. He simply stood at the bar, leaning his elbows on it, and for another hour or more he remained there—alone—alone with Ken, with Larry, with Kay—with the years of his life—with the image that loomed behind them, high and distant, white and gleaming in the night.

At last he left. He went up to the apartment, to Amy. And Amy was in bed. Undressing, he got in beside her; but he could not sleep, nor even lie still, and soon he was up again. He prowled the apartment. Opening the door, he started down toward the bar, changed his mind, and returned. Back in the bedroom, he sat in a chair by the window and looked out at the stars.

Then Amy spoke from the bed.

"Are you crocked?" she asked.

"No," he said.

"Not hopped up, for godsake?"

"No."

"What's spooking you, then?"

"Nothing."

"Nothing, hell." Amy turned up the bed lamp and peered at him with sleep-bleared eyes. "After five hundred years," she said, "don't you think I know the symptoms when you're going nuts?"

The symptom of going nuts, he thought, was being where he was now. Age: middle forties. Altitude: 27,000 feet. Alone. No air, no oxygen. With each step upward, the snow was steeper, deeper.

He kicked, stepped. Kicked, stepped. Stopped, breathed. Kicked, stepped. When the others, using his steps, caught up with him, they should damn well carry him on their shoulders the rest of the way.

He looked down at the three dots, and they were no longer dots but human figures. At his pace and theirs, they should be with him within an hour.

He looked up. Then what? Then, say, another two hours to the top.

He kicked, stepped.

Nuts or not, he had come a fur piece, as they used to say in the Westerns back in the movie houses of Denver. Two hours to the top. Thirteen weeks from Kathmandu . . .

22

They had left in the second week of March—about three weeks earlier than on what Ken called DZ 1. "It will make it colder in the early stages, when we're still low down," he said. "But at the end we'll have more leeway with the monsoon."

Men and gear were to go in trucks to the edge of the Valley of Nepal, and on the morning of departure one of them picked Eric up at the entrance of the Himalayan Palace. Amy was there. Long ago, she had stood at the entrance of the Government guesthouse while he boarded another truck and said, "How about me too?" She didn't say that now. Less long ago—but long enough —when he took off with Mrs. Bigelow, her farewell had been "You'll freeze your balls off." But now she didn't say that, either. She simply stood there, and he kissed her lightly, and she said, "Well, here we go again." And with something close to astonishment he thought, "My God, the old girl's mellowing."

Then she was gone.

Again, gone.

Kathmandu was gone.

There was the rattling truck, the rutted road, the fields and paddies of the valley. There was the field at road's end, filled with climbers, Sherpas, Tamang porters; with disgorging trucks and stacks of gear and dust and shouting; and presently he, in his role of sahib-sirdar, was shouting too. There was the sorting of loads, the heaving on of loads, the milling of men as they funneled from the open field into single file on the trail. With pad and pencil he checked them off as they passed: seven team members (plus himself), fifteen Sherpas (to whom Tashi would be added) and 192 Tamangs. Then he followed behind. As leader of DZ 1 he had usually, on the march-in, been at the head of the column. Now, as sirdar pro-tem of DZ 3, his place was at the end, to watch for stragglers and deserters.

There was the rest of the first day: up and down, down and up.

There was the first night. The tents. The cookfires.

There was the second day, and again he was at the rear of the column, and as morning moved on toward noon he dropped gradually behind. He was not tired. He was watching for landmarks, studying the trailside, and presently he found what he was seeking. There was a steep pitch in the path, a leveling off, then a large rock to the right, a stand of trees to the left; and turning off from the path, he picked his way through brush and branches. After some twenty yards straight on, he estimated, he should come to a clearing. But he didn't. He went on farther, and didn't. He bore to the right, then to the left, and still there was no clearing, and at last he beat his way back through brush and branches to the path. There beside it was the strip of grass where he had once sat in the rain, with Nima, under her tarpaulin, lying quiet beside him. Now, again, he sat there for a while, under a gentle sun; then rose, moved on, and resumed his duties as sirdar of DZ 3.

The mountains gleamed to the north. The trail dipped, curved, climbed. They passed through the villages of Chaubas, Chitare, Risingo, Kirantichap. At each of them a few Tamangs quit and were replaced by others, and along the way, in spite of vigilance, there were occasional defections and petty thefts. Overall, however, things went well; progress was steady. As always, the Sherpas formed a nucleus of strength among the rank-and-file porters and acted as NCOs on the march and in camp.

Two of the fifteen were from Munda, one from Dhamu, and several of the others were also known to Eric from his days in Solu Khumbu. In age and experience they were the usual mixture: some veterans, some novices, some in-between. But as with the world at large, so with Sherpas: there had been changes with the years. Most of the young ones had had a year or two of schooling (one with Carol Flagg in Munda), and all, young and old, had had more experience of the non-Sherpa world than the generations before them. They had a climbers' union now. There were fixed rates of wages and conditions of work, and a few of them tended to be what had become known as "expedition lawyers." But they were still Sherpas. They still found it easier to grin than frown. They shouldered their loads, trudged through the days, did their evening work at the camps, not because they were paid to but because they wanted to. In the mornings there were the brown, smiling faces in the tent flaps saying, "Coffee, sah'b—tea, sah'b."

As transport officer, Eric soon became familiar with the loads as well as their bearers. And they were both the same and not the same as twenty years before. There were, of course, all the basic essentials: food, tents, clothing, climbing gear, assorted utensils. But within each category were many differences. The food was more effectively processed and packaged; tents were lighter but stronger; clothes lighter but warmer. Ropes—miles of them, neatly coiled—were made of new synthetics, and pitons and other hardware were in a profusion and variety that Eric had never before encountered. One thing there was not was oxygen—excepting a few cylinders for medical use. ("I still think we can take DZ without it," said Ken. And if they did, it would be earth's highest peak on which this had been done.) But as a new feature, there were walkie-talkies for communication between camps. Messages to and from the outside world would go back and forth in old style: by Sherpa couriers shuttling at three-week intervals between their Base Camp and Kathmandu.

"On Everest in '63," said Ken, "they had a base radio that could reach the outside. But Dera Zor—well, it's a more private sort of mountain." He smiled. "And besides, we hadn't the dough."

As before, he and Eric shared a tent on the march; and it was astonishing, thought Eric, how, now that they were again together, the twenty-year interval tended to vanish. Perhaps it was because they spoke so little of those years. He had learned that Ken now lived in Phoenix, Arizona; that he had a wife, Phyllis, and three children, aged seventeen to twelve; that he had long since left Cerro de Pasco and now headed his own firm of consulting mining engineers. But that was almost all. As on every expedition, talk was not of what lay behind but what lay ahead—of the mountain, only the mountain—and Ken's enthusiasm and determination were undimmed by time and age. As in his youth, he was not demonstrative. If anything, he was quieter, more thoughtful, more deliberate in speech. But beneath the middle-aged corporate executive there was still the old linesman, the bulldog—who had growled angrily at Eric in the Himalayan Palace—who still thrust out his stubbled chin when he talked, after all the years, of Dera Zor.

"—So it's my third crack now—and my last," he said. "This time it's three strikes and up or three strikes and out." His chin was in its DZ position, but his eyes were smiling. "Me, I'm voting for up, Rick," he added. "I've a hunch we're going to get the bastard at last."

There they were again: tentmates, the two of them.

With them, before, had been Franz Harben, Gil McLeod, Ted Lassiter, Julian Howard.

With them, now, were Willard Meach, George Barr, Arne Norstad, Paul Loring, Victor Kellerman.

—And Lawrence Venn.

Will Meach, aged thirty-five, was second-in-command to Ken. Tall, lean and bespectacled, he looked like a Ph.D. who had mistakenly got into mountaineer's clothing. And a Ph.D. he was—a biochemist from Berkeley—but also a climber, one of the best, a companion of Ken's on the second Dera Zor climb and a member of the 1963 American expedition to Everest. He was quiet, contemplative, by reputation tireless and unflappable in times of stress, and it was in Ken's scheme of things that he would take over the leadership on the upper mountain.

357

Of about the same age, and third of the "seniors" (or fourth, with Eric), was George Barr, a surgeon from Hartford, Connecticut. Short, stocky and puckish, he too was a mountain veteran, with a record that included Alaska and the Andes. But he had not before been to Himalayan heights, and his expected role on DZ was to share the backup position with Ken.

Of the younger men—in their twenties—Eric had briefly met two, Arne Norstad and Paul Loring, in the bar of the Himalayan Palace. Norstad, blond and ruddy, was both mountaineer (once before to the Himalayas) and ski professional (Aspen)—the Franz Harben of the expedition, except that he was Scandinavian, not Austrian, and both more powerful and more phlegmatic . . . Or perhaps the latter, thought Eric, simply came from the fact that, unlike Franz, he had no new and abandoned bride on his conscience . . . He was the team's snow-and-ice expert, whereas Loring, said Ken, was primarily a rock man: a dark, lithe and almost excessively handsome youngster who, by way of Dartmouth, geological field work and several expeditions (though not before to the Himalayas), had become a mountaineer of the first rank. In Ken's book, both he and Norstad, along with Meach, were prime prospects for DZ's heights, and hopefully for its summit.

The number one man, however, was unquestionably Vic Kellerman. Scarcely taller than the Sherpas, thin to scrawniness and with a sharp, lopsided face, he looked the very antithesis—as Loring and Norstad were the models—of an outdoorsman-athlete. Even more unlikely was his background of Nebraska farm, spotty education and odd jobs around the country. Yet something in his body, his mind, his genes had made him a climber, and one of fabulous talent. He had, said Ken, made ascents on the walls of Yosemite that had set new standards of cragsmanship. He had led in the pioneering of a new and sensational route on McKinley, and had twice distinguished himself on successful climbs in the western Himalayas. In the language of the new breed of mountaineers, he was "a hard man": a technician, fighter, all-outer—and a genius of the vertical. "Know how good he is?" said Ken to Eric. "As good as you, twenty years ago . . . No, better.

They're all better now than then. And he's the best . . . Wait and see: Vic's going to make mincemeat of that Wailing Wall."

Meach and Kellerman, Norstad and Loring: these, if the planning held, would be the summit teams.

And Venn? Lawrence Venn, junior class, Leland Stanford University?

Larry, of course, was The Baby. Hence the question mark. He might go high or he might have trouble, said Ken; there was no telling. (When you came down to it, there was no telling with anyone.) "But I'll tell you this," he added, "Venn or no Venn, I wouldn't have signed him on if I didn't think he has what it takes."

Certainly he looked no baby, with his growing beard, his strong stride, as he moved along the miles of rugged trail. But from day to day Eric saw little of him on the march; for his own place was at the rear of the column, while Larry's drive and excitement kept him up at its head.

"I've been meaning to stay back with you," he told Eric apologetically. Then he smiled. "But it just doesn't seem to happen."

"Go at your own pace," Eric said.

"You don't mind, Uncle Eric?"

"I'd mind if you didn't . . . And for God's sake, my name's Rick."

The boy hesitated. "It's sort of hard to—"

"Ken's Ken, isn't he?"

"Yes, but—"

"Try it."

"Rick."

"Good, practice it," said Eric. "It's not hard to pronounce."

It was all right with him that he did not see too much of Larry. When they were together—however hard he resisted—he could not keep his eyes from studying him, his mind from speculating. Nor was speculation decreased when George Barr, the doctor, spoke to him one evening at the campfire.

"I thought I was seeing double today," said Barr. "I knew you were back at the end of the column, but then suddenly there you were on the trail up ahead. When I got closer I saw it was Larry, of course, but for a minute I could have sworn it was you. The way he walked, the way he held his head—"

Barr looked across the fire to where the boy sat on its farther side. Then his eyes returned to Eric. "In your faces, no," he said. "There's a resemblance, of course, but not all that much. On the trail, from a distance, though, it was really remarkable."

"Things work out that way in some families," said Eric.

"Is he a brother's son or a sister's?" asked Barr.

"A brother's."

"A twin brother's?"

"No, not a twin."

The trail wound on. They climbed higher. It grew colder. On the passes and ridges winter snow still covered the ground and their pace was slowed, but not too greatly. At column's end Eric kept the pace in a series of stops and forced marches: dropping behind to help a porter with broken sandals or an off-balance load, then moving on again to close the gap. And it went all right. During the first days of the march he had had trouble with the spare pair of expedition boots he had been issued, and his feet had blistered on both toes and heels. But now the blisters had calloused. His legs and wind held out. He was again what he had been for so much of his life: a man moving on through the hours and the miles.

They left Hindu country. They came to Buddhist country. To lamaseries and mani walls and chortens and prayer flags high on the ridges. Out of the past, one day, lines came to him, lines of his own, long forgotten. "Here is a magical world, a secret world," he had written on the first of his journeys. "Some day, if I am lucky, I may learn a few of its secrets."

Well, now it was some day. It was twenty years later. And what had he learned?

A porter dropped back, complaining that he was tired and lame and could carry his load no farther; but after some conversation he persuaded him to continue.

Item one: He had learned to speak Nepalese and Sherpa.

What else?

360

He had learned that the Year of the Pig followed the Year of the Dog, and that the Year of the Hare followed the Year of the Tiger.

He had learned about plowing fields and brewing chang and building privies.

He had learned about yaks.

My God, had he learned about yaks!

They came to forests. To small streams and spidery bridges. They heard a roar ahead and came to the big stream, the Dudh Khosi River, and followed it north along its sounding gorges. They camped for a night, then a second night, beside it, and on the fourteenth day out of Kathmandu angled up from the river, from the gorges and forests, to the open uplands and the town of Namche Bazar. At the town's edge, as they approached, were the Sherpas of Namche—men, women, children—some to greet their kinsmen now arriving from their journey, some simply in excitement at the first mountaineering expedition to appear in Solu Khumbu since the Government ban of a few years past. There were shouts, laughter, embraces. It was a Sherpa festival. The Tamangs, unknown, unhailed, trudged stolidly past to deposit their loads at the nearby campground; the Americans stood by, smiling and awkward . . . Until, at the end of the line, came Eric, and for him, as for the Sherpas, there was recognition and welcome . . . There was a crowd around him. There were handclasps, more shouts; then above them, through them, one shout louder than all the others. There was a darting figure, a tiny figure, small as a child, but not a child, with a wizened face, a monkey face; and the figure seized him, the figure held him— Tashi held him—his face grinning, weeping—

And Tashi cried, "Rick Sah'b! Oh, Rick Sah'b! You come back! You come back!"

The camp was pitched. The Tamangs were paid off. The Sherpas got drunk on chang and rakshi.

Except for Tashi. Tashi sat with Eric before his tent in the waning daylight, and Eric asked, "How is Ai Lamu?"

"She is dead, Rick Sah'b."

"I'm sorry, Tashi."

"Is few days now," said the little Sherpa. "She was fat, so fat, you remember? Then was thin, so thin. Then was gone." He was silent a moment. "Your Nima, she is gone too, Rick Sah'b."

"Lobsang told you."

"Yes, Lobsang tell."

"How are your four girls?" asked Eric.

"Are not four now—are six. The four you know, two more, but still no son. When Ai Lamu die I leave them with my sister. They all right; I come here." Tashi paused again. "With good is bad, with bad good," he said. "If Ai Lamu still live, still sick, I cannot go with expedition."

He brightened a little.

"Now can go," he said.

Then he brightened more. He pointed across the campground. "And he go too." He gestured, beckoned, and a young man, tall and broad for a Sherpa, came across the camp and stood before them. "You remember, Rick Sah'b?" said Tashi. "Is Pembol here."

Eric rose, shook hands, embraced him. As if at a stranger, he looked at the powerful, square-faced youngster who when he had last seen him had been a half-grown adolescent.

"Is big, yes?" said Tashi, smiling. "Is smart too, from school, and good climber. Already I speak to Ken Sah'b, and he say yes, he can come along."

"I am happy to come," Pembol said in Carol Flagg's best English. "I hope to go high on the mountain."

"Yes, high. Most high of all porters." Tashi's smile became a grin. His grief for Ai Lamu could not hold its own with his excitement at the prospect ahead. "He will carry our packs for us, Rick Sah'b, when we go to top of Dera Zor."

Then there was no more time for past or future. Ken appeared with a problem. There were the other team members to be introduced. As of the time of his reporting, Tashi was expedition sirdar, and for the rest of the evening, with Eric helping, he was involved in his manifold duties—with tentage, food, loads, departing Tamangs, drunken Sherpas.

The next day's schedule called for rising at five, being on the trail by six, but it was past eleven when Eric crept into his tent. Ken was already in his sleeping bag, busy with his notebook in the beam of a flashlight. On Eric's bag was a pile of expedition clothing for colder weather: heavy trousers and sweater, long johns, mittens, a down-filled parka with hood.

"Try them for size," Ken said.

He went on with his notes. Eric sat down on his bag.

"No, Ken," he said. "No."

Ken said nothing.

"I told you I'd come here to Namche—no farther."

"Yes, you told me."

There was silence again.

"You won't have long with Tashi," said Ken.

Silence.

"Have you said goodbye to him?"

"No."

"To Larry?"

"No."

Eric pulled off his boots and outer clothing, moved the stack of new clothing aside, and unzipped his sleeping bag. After a while he said:

"Tashi is sirdar now."

"Yes," said Ken.

"So what's there for me to do?"

"I've already told you. You can be co-leader with me."

"No."

"You can be what you want then. Climber, porter, bottle washer, Larry's valet." Ken put away his notebook. "Or if, as you said, you're too old to climb," he went on, "you can stay at Base Camp. We're planning to leave a couple of Sherps there anyhow, to keep the place going and relay mail; and you could free one of them for the mountain."

Ken warmed to the idea.

"That's it," he said, "you could be camp mother. No crummy icefall, no hairy ridge. Just snug as a bug at base, with some fine big tents, plenty to eat, lots of nice warm clothes."

He pushed the pile of new clothing toward Eric.

"Here, try them for size, Rick Sah'b."

"You're a cute one, aren't you?" Eric said.

In the gray of dawn the cook fires crackled. At sunrise the next march began. Soon, as for two weeks past, the long file was strung along the trail; but now the Tamangs were gone and all the porters were Sherpas—the core of "high" ones (now mostly hung over) who would go onto the mountain, plus a newly hired brigade of "low" ones who would carry only to base. As they moved out from Namche, Tashi and Eric checked their numbers and loads; then swung onto the trail at the end of the line.

Ken had long since set off. That morning he had already been out of the tent when Eric wakened, and at breakfast had merely eyed his clothing and said, "They seem to fit all right." The other team members, apparently, took it for granted that he was coming farther—including Larry, who, with a wave of the hand, had left, as usual, with the head of the column.

. . . And now the column moved on . . .

To the American climbers new to the eastern Himalayas, here and now was the entry into the ends of the earth. But for Eric, what lay about him was the landscape of home. Roundabout were the familiar peaks of Taweche, Kangtega, Khumbila; below them, their skirts of glaciers; still farther down, the mountain meadows, just beginning to emerge from beneath the winter snows. On a steep hillside, they passed a herd of yaks, moving slowly across a quilted pattern of white and brown. Beyond the hill, in an upland valley, was the fork in the trail where a path bore off eastward toward Munda and Dhamu.

But their own path led on north, then west. And Tashi said, "Is long since we have been this way, Rick Sah'b."

"Yes, long," said Eric.

"Then we are young," said Tashi. "Now not so young." He thought it over. "But still we walk good," he added. "I think we climb good. Go high, most highest."

They walked on a way.

"And if cannot do," said the little Sherpa, "are young ones. Young now—and strong—like Larry Sah'b who is your—"

He groped for the word.

"Nephew," said Eric.

"Yes, nephew. He go high, I think . . . And Pembol too. He young and strong, go high . . . Sometimes I think: I have now no wife, no sons, only daughters. But no—Pembol, I say, *he* is my son. When I am old, can climb no more, he climb instead—to top of mountains, top of Dera Zor—and I am happy, proud; is like I climb myself."

Tashi thought again.

"For you maybe is same," he said, "with Larry Sah'b who is your nephew. You too have no wife, no son. But he is like son, yes? Like for me Pembol. Maybe they climb high, all way to top, and you and I we watch; it is our sons we watch and we are happy."

A new thought came. The monkey face grinned.

"Or maybe is other way," said Tashi. "Maybe it is they watch us, Rick Sah'b, and we are happy too."

They left the Dudh Khosi River and followed the Amun. On the second evening out from Namche they camped beside the river, and during the night the wind rose, snow fell. In the morning it was blowing a blizzard and they stayed where they were. During the next day and the next the storm continued, and still they stayed. "No harm done," said Ken Naylor, for somewhere along the line a storm was inevitable. Here they were already at more than fourteen thousand feet and needed time for acclimatization.

There was the usual crop of ailments: headaches, muscle aches, nausea, insomnia. For a while, Ken himself and George Barr, the doctor, were the worst off, unable to keep down any food at all. But by the third day they were all right again. Larry, Will Meach and Paul Loring had hacking coughs, and Arne Norstad, with the most severe of the headaches, had also recurrent spells of double vision. Among the basic team members, only Vic Kellerman, small and tough—the "hard man"—was unaffected by the altitude.

—Along with the Sherpas, of course.

And Eric.

"But you too are now Sherpa," Tashi told him.

The storm blew out. They moved on again. And their ailments, if not cured, were at least under control. They came to the gorge of the Amun, threaded it, and toward midday stopped to rest at the broad shelf beside the river where, long before, Eric had pitched the final camp for Mrs. Homer Bigelow . . . Bigelow: the name that had been so much a part of his life, then no part at all. Until Ken had appeared, exhuming the past, it had been years since he had thought of the Bigelows: or of the book, *Trek to Nowhere*, that had first led him along this trail . . . Where was it now: that book, that Bible, that Song of Songs? He didn't know. Yes, he did. It had been, what was left of it, in the rat-gnawed suitcase he had dug out of the cellar of the Himalayan Palace and thrown away. Part of the past that he had thrown away. And that had now returned . . .

In the gorge, the waters roared. The high cliffs shut out the light, and they sat in grayness. After a short rest Ken rose and said, "It's gloomy here. Let's go."

Then again the long file uncoiled. Below was the torrent, above, a strip of sky, and between, on the wall of the gorge, the path rose, humped and twisted, rising higher and higher. Progress was slow now. Footing was precarious, and at the narrower places, with thin air beneath them, the porters bunched and waited while those ahead inched across with swaying loads. Midday became afternoon. Afternoon waned toward evening. Then at last the change came. The gorge bent; its walls flared, fell away; and for the third time in his life Eric Venn, still with Tashi at the end of the column, emerged from the gorge into the valley beyond.

Here was the unforgotten, the eternal . . .

Here was the waste of boulders; beyond it, the Kalpurtha Glacier, in its long trough, angling upward. At the glacier's head, to the west, rose Mount Kalpurtha; to the east, Mount Meru. And between, straight ahead: there it was—Dera Zor. Twice before Eric had been where he was now, but only on the first of those times had he seen the mountain: on that long-gone day, twenty years past, when he had come, young, bedazzled, to the place of his dream. Then, in the brilliance of midafternoon, of the soaring within him, it had been a crash of music, an explosion of light. The second time, the Mrs. Bigelow time, it had been—nothing: a phantom hidden behind snow and mist. Now it was there again—but again different. Now there was no snow or mist, but also no afternoon brilliance. It was early evening, and the vast south face rose through a gulf of shadow. Its battlements of rock gleamed black in space and stillness; its snow and ice were a metallic blue. Only at its extreme top, beyond the black of the Wailing Wall, at the crest of its snow dome, was there a last quick dazzle of brightness—of pink and gold, then of burning magenta —as it caught the last high rays of the setting sun. Then the sun was gone; the gray gulf rose and deepened. The mountain tiered into dusk, locked in ice and iron.

As before—long before—the file of low-level porters had emerged from the gorge without pausing, and were now moving on toward the appointed campsite in the waste of boulders beyond. But—as before, too—climbers and "high" Sherpas had stopped to stare at what lay before them, and they were all still there when, at column's end, Eric and Tashi appeared. Seeing them, Ken Naylor detached himself from the others and came to stand beside Eric. In that same place, once, he had said, "So there's the bastard." But he did not say it now. He said nothing. He simply put a hand on Eric's shoulder and let it rest there.

Eric looked at the mountain.

He looked at the boulder field—at one of the nearest boulders —at the scrap of rusted metal, the flattened canister, that lay wedged beneath it.

He looked at Larry. And Larry's face was raised, his eyes were bright.

They camped.
They moved on.
They came up from the boulders onto the snout of the glacier,

and ascended the glacier, westward, upward. Ahead, a two-day march from the gorge, was the icefall leading to the saddle—the Gap—between Dera Zor and Kalpurtha. To their right, sheathed in ice, spewing avalanches, rose the immensity of Dera Zor's south face.

Then the face vanished. Everything vanished. Again the wind rose, snow lashed through the valley, and they lay over in their second camp, halfway up the glacier. This storm, however, lasted only a day. On the next they were moving again, and toward evening reached the site for Base Camp. It was in the same place as on DZ 1 (and on DZ 2 as well, said Ken): on a medial moraine in the glacier close to the foot of the icefall. There was the setting up, the digging in, the payment and departure of the "low" Sherpas. Twenty-five men were left now: the seven team members, the fifteen original "high" Sherpas, plus Tashi and Pembol. Plus Eric—whatever he was. It was the first week of April, with a probable two months at hand before the coming of the monsoon.

Two of the "low" Sherpas had been held over as mail runners, and a day was spent writing letters. Ken and George Barr had wives and children. Willard Meach had a wife. The others, girls, families, friends . . . What did Eric have? Amy . . . He had never written to Amy. He tried. *Dear Amy,* he wrote, *they're not frozen off yet. Or at least I don't think they are. It's hard to be sure with so many clothes on.*

He threw the scrap of paper away. The mail runners took off. After three days of shakedown and acclimatization, the vanguard of DZ 3 entered the icefall.

It had, of course, changed with the years. Old towers and chasms had long since moved, toppled, crumbled, with new ones taking their places, so that a whole new route had to be forged through the labyrinth. For the work, the team split into subteams of twos and threes: some as the spearhead, reconnoitering, probing; others as follow-up, hacking steps, stringing ropes. The long unpredictable process of acclimatization was still going on. Alternately, the various men had their good and bad days, and on the worst of the bad ones they took the day off. But little time was lost. Slowly, but on schedule, the thin thread of their route wound farther and higher.

Besides the struggle with height, there were also the icefall's own special defenses. Avalanches plunged down from the ramparts of both Dera Zor and Kalpurtha, forcing them to keep to the middle of the slot, regardless of obstacles. Ice towers swayed and crashed. Snow broke off from cliffs and piled in drifts in the hollows, obscuring the network of crevasses. It was a crevasse that caused the first accident, when its snow covering broke and one of the Sherpas—a youngster named Gyaltsen—fell through. He did not fall far. He was roped, and the rope held him, but in the process he broke an arm. George Barr quickly splinted it; eventually it would mend. But for the time Gyaltsen became, of necessity, a custodian of Base Camp.

Eric, too, stayed largely at base, or close to it. ("A camp mother's duty," he told Ken.) On some days he worked with the backup teams, maintaining and improving the trail in the lower icefall; but only once did he go farther, to where the route's high point was being pushed ahead. This was with Arne Norstad and Larry—for he wanted at least once to see Larry at work. And though Arne, as the more experienced, did most of the leading, Larry did well; indeed, better than well. His handling of rope, hammer and pitons was deft and expert. On the steep ice, clinging with ax and crampon, he moved with balance and ease.

Ken had known what he was talking about when he had said, "Venn or no Venn . . ."

The weather held, cold but clear. At first, all hands came down to Base Camp every night. But at the end of a week Camp Two was established, halfway up the icefall; loads began going up with processions of Sherpas; and Two became the nightly base for those out front. Will Meach had moved up to take charge there, and with him were Norstad, Paul Loring and Vic Kellerman. Ken, for the time, remained quartered at the lower camp, as did George Barr and the impatient Larry. ("Seniors and freshmen," Ken told him, "should make haste slowly.") Together with Tashi, they took turns leading the Sherpa caravans back and forth on their daily shuttles.

Then word came down through the walkie-talkies that the ice-fall route was complete. The advance guard had reached the Gap, two tents were already in place there, and it was time for the carrying of loads to build up Camp Three. On the morning of April 20, Ken, George and Larry (Tashi was already gone) made ready for final departure for the higher camps.

Eric did not make ready.

He had made his decision.

Late into the previous night, Ken had urged him to come; argued, pleaded with him to come. ("Just to the Gap," he had said. "I probably won't be going much farther myself.") But Eric had stuck to his refusal. Two men were needed to man Base Camp, and he and Gyaltsen would be the two. Of the other Sherpas, there was not one who would not be of more use than he on the mountain.

In the dim light of their tent Ken had studied him carefully.

"Do you expect me to buy that?" he asked.

"You can buy what you want," said Eric.

"Will you, for Christ's sake, stop thinking about twenty years ago!"

Eric did not answer. Finally Ken fell silent. Through the night, the shadow of the past loomed, huge as the mountain, between them.

—And in the morning Ken did not press further. Larry had never pressed; nor did he now. Eric shook hands with them and George and said, "Good luck. Go get it." Then they roped up, hefted packs and axes, moved out across the glacier to the foot of the icefall; and he watched them—watched the figure of Larry —until they were out of sight.

Days passed.

He and Gyaltsen kept house. They readied the final consignment of loads, which a final Sherpa convoy, soon to descend, would then carry up to the Gap. Three times a day, at appointed hours, he received news on the Base walkie-talkie from the climbers above. On the first day, Ken, George and Larry reached Camp Two; on the second, Camp Three at the Gap. During the next two days all were busy at Three, with Sherpa shuttles carrying up from Two. On the fifth day it stormed, and the radio brought only the roar of static. But by the next morning it had cleared, Ken's voice came through again, and the word was that the final shuttle was descending to Base. Toward midday, with happy timing, two mail runners appeared, trudging up the glacier. There were letters for every team member except Eric (if he was a team member), and he put them in one of the loads that was awaiting the shuttle.

The afternoon was fair, almost mild, and he sat out on a flat rock near the cook tent, watching for its appearance . . . Or at least he watched at intervals . . . On the day the last of the others had left he had taken a pad and pencil from the expedition stores, and since then, in his spare time (which was much of the time), had been making notes. They were not notes about Sherpas. Those were back in the Himalayan Palace Hotel. What he was writing now was about the expedition: its men, its journey, its arrival at the base of the mountain. The page on which he was now was headed *View from the Bottom*. And beneath this he had written:

> Distortion: looking up
>   "   "   down
>   "   "   forward
>   "   "   back

He looked back, and there were Julian Howard, Franz Harben. He looked up: there was Dera Zor. And yes, it was distorted, foreshortened, its lower reaches vast and looming, its heights remote, recessive, dwindled by distance. He looked at the icefall, thrusting upward, white, frozen, immobile; but he knew that this too was illusion, that within its maw it forever lived and moved. He looked at its base, and there was movement there, not of ice but of specks, then not of specks but of figures. And the figures came closer, grew larger, became a column of Sherpas, roped and goggled, crossing the glacier, approaching the camp. Rising, he put away his pad and pencil, called Gyaltsen and went out to meet them. And at their head was Tashi.

It was that night, the cook fires burned, and Tashi's head was bowed, his face was sorrowful.

"You do not come, Rick Sah'b," he said. "At Camp Two, Camp Three, I wait, I watch, but no, you no come with others. Then Ken Sah'b he tell me you no come at all."

It was morning. The Sherpas swung on their loads, and Tashi looked at him, his face the same. Then, turning, he looked at one of the men who had dropped his load.

"Why do you do that?" he asked in Sherpa.

"I am sick," said the man.

"No, not sick—lazy. Pick up your load."

Then Eric spoke.

"If Mingma doesn't feel well," he said to Tashi, "let him stay here with Gyaltsen."

"But his load, Rick Sah'b—"

"I'll carry his load."

He picked it up. He slung it on. Tashi stared at him.

"You mean—you come?" he said.

"Yes, I'll come. To the Gap."

Tashi's stare became a grin. The grin exploded in a shout. "You come, you come!" he cried. "We climb together, Rick Sah'b!"

Erick tied onto a rope.

"You go first," said Tashi.

"No, you first; you know the way. I last."

They started off. There were nine of them, on three ropes, with Tashi leading the first one and himself third on the last. They crossed the strip of glacier. They entered the icefall. On a knob of ice, ahead, Tashi turned, waved and shouted, but he could not hear what he said.

What he heard was Tashi speaking, years before, in his house in Munda. "If man is climber, should climb," he had said.

Eric waved back. He swung his ax.

He climbed.

He climbed . . .

Since that day he had been climbing for five weeks, for nine thousand vertical feet. Now all but the very tip of Dera Zor was below him.

Closest below were the three figures who were following him. Again he looked down, and there they were: the three in a file, unroped, plodding upward in his steps; and though goggled and helmeted, they were now identifiable by their size and bearing. Larry came first, Pembol second, Tashi third.

Tashi, it was apparent, was having trouble. When the three stopped, he did not look up like the others, but bent motionless, heaving, over his ice ax. When they moved again, he moved more slowly, so that the others had to stop and wait for him to catch up.

But still he moved. Still the three of them came on . . .

They were now, Eric judged, about a hundred feet below. He would go on just a little farther, then let them come up to him. Not far above him was a flatness, a shelf, in the white ramp of the summit dome, and there he would stop and rest.

He turned back to the slope. He kicked a step.

He climbed . . .

23

In the icefall he was truly climbing for the first time in twenty years. In Solu Khumbu and elsewhere—many elsewheres—he had been high on slope and pass, ridge and hilltop. But that had been walking. This was climbing. On his feet were crampons, in his hand an ax, around his waist a rope.

Under their heavy loads, the Sherpas moved slowly. And he was used to loads; he kept the pace. In six hours, on the first day, they reached Camp Two, in the heart of the icefall, where they spent the rest of the day and the night. And on the next morning they moved on toward the Gap. For him, it was both an old and a new journey: new in its detailed route, in its leads and windings; old in its changed yet changeless pattern of hump and hollow, tower and chasm. It was a closed and sinister world, sunless and windless, hunched and twisted. A silent world—until an avalanche spumed, a tower toppled—and when the roaring faded, the silence returned, thicker, deeper than before.

By midafternoon of the second day they were nearing the top. Ahead lay only the final ice cliff—the cliff up which he and Ken and Franz Harben had once hacked and clawed their way through one of their hardest days on the mountain. But there was no struggle now. As before—once the lead parties had passed—the wall was pocked with steps, festooned with guidelines, and their ascent, if slow, was steady and secure. At the top they emerged into wind and the glare of sunlight. They had reached the Gap. Ahead, framed by the soaring ridges of Dera Zor and Kalpurtha, were its level waste of rubble, the nest of tents that was Camp Three. And roundabout, then converging to meet them, were Ken, George Barr and the other Sherpas.

Ken came to Eric. He said, "Dr. Livingstone, I presume?" Then he crept into one of the tents, with Eric following, and showed him the empty space beside his own sleeping bag.

"It's been waiting for you," he said.

Something else was waiting, too . . . And later, in the westering sun, Eric walked alone across the desolation of the Gap to where a pile of stones marked Franz Harben's grave. He had not seen it before. Franz had died of his embolism here at Camp Three while he, Eric, was still being helped down the upper mountain by Tashi and the others. He had presumably already been buried when Eric reached the Gap. But he had not asked or been told about it; Franz was dead—as Julian was dead—that was enough to know; and he had stumbled on, numbly, blindly, down the icefall to Base . . . Now, after twenty years, he stood at the grave. A stone had fallen from near the top of the cairn, and he replaced it. There were stones all around—stones and snow and frozen rubble—and he wondered how it had been possible to dig a grave at all.

He thought of another grave: one he himself had dug. Nima lay in mud. Franz in stones . . . Franz too, he thought, had had a woman, a wife. What had her name been? Jill. Jill Something, then Jill Harben (briefly), now long since, probably, Jill Some-thing-else. By now, like Kay, she might have grown children, by another man. Or might one of them, the eldest, be Franz's?

He turned away. The sun was low and it was getting colder. Above, a file of men was descending the gully that led down to the Gap from Dera Zor's west ridge.

Five of them—all the team except Ken and George Barr—had gone up that morning for the first day's work on the ridge. Ken had expected them back between four and five, but now it was close on six, and they were moving slowly. To the watchers below it was obvious that something had not gone as it should have.

But what it had been was not clear until they trudged into camp —Kellerman and Larry on the first rope; Meach, Loring and Norstad on the second—when it became apparent that Loring was in trouble. There had been no accident, it developed. He had had altitude problems. On the way up, said Will Meach, he had done as well as anyone; but once at their highest point, about fifteen hundred feet above the Gap's twenty-one thousand, he had suffered acute weakness and nausea. Neither rest nor the subsequent descent had seemed to help him; and they had all kept together at his own slow pace, so that, if he collapsed, there would be enough manpower on hand to carry him.

It had not come to that. He reached Camp Three on his own and was able, with the others, to greet Eric. Then Barr took him into his tent to administer pills and oxygen, and Meach went on with his account of the day's reconnaissance. Loring's illness, he reported, had not been the only problem. Dera Zor, too, had posed one of its own.

"You remember the tower on the ridge," he asked Ken, "where we had trouble last time?"

Ken nodded . . . And Eric, too, recalled that tower. It was the bastion of cliff, half-vertical, half-overhanging, which had blocked the ridge below the eventual site of Camp Four, on DZ 1, and which he and Ken had bypassed on a snow slope to the right . . . Apparently the procedure on DZ 2 had been the same, for now Meach went on:

"Well, the snow on the south face is gone. Some of the rock underneath has obviously peeled off too, and what's left is sheer wall—as bad as the tower head on."

"Did you give either a try?" Ken asked.

"No. With Paul's trouble, there wasn't time. Besides, we'll need more hardware than we had today."

"Which do you think it should be: straight up or around the corner?"

"It needs more study," said Meach.

Ken looked at the others.

Arne Norstad nodded.

Larry, the freshman, said nothing.

"Straight up," said Vic Kellerman.

"It looks like a bitch," Norstad said.

"It'll go," said Kellerman coolly. "Take my word for it, it'll go." He was DZ 3's prize cragsman. His opinion bore weight.

"We'll have another look tomorrow," said Ken, "with lots of hardware."

It was growing dark now on the Gap. Dera Zor faded. Kalpurtha faded. Pressure cookers were primed, food was warmed, supper eaten. Later, in the tents, by the beams of flashlights, the men read the mail that had been brought up that day from Base Camp.

—Except Eric and the Sherpas.

The Sherpas talked, joked, laughed, fell asleep. Eric took out the pad and pencil he had brought up in his pack, turned to a fresh page, and wrote *Icefall Revisited*. Then Larry appeared, holding a letter.

"It's from Mother," he said.

"Oh?"

"And Mother's still Mother." He gave Eric the letter and pointed. "Begin there. The early part's about home and the girls and stuff, and how glad she is I found you. Then comes the end. Read it."

Eric held the letter. He read:

Now comes a surprise I've saved for last, and please, sweetheart, don't be angry. Anyhow, you're going to see me a little sooner than you thought, because, believe it or not, I'm going to fly out there. Have reservations already, first to India (always wanted to see Taj, Benares, etc.), then to Katmandu (sp?), arriving just before you're due back . . . Yes, I know mothers aren't supposed to follow sons around; it's a gas chamber offense. But—now read this carefully—I am not following you. I am following your long-lost Uncle Eric, the Mad Mahatma of the Mountains. I will, I promise, do no more than say hello to you politely. Then your uncle and I will go off by ourselves to drink the coldest, driest martinis to be found in Nepal . . .

Eric handed back the letter.

"So—get ready," said Larry.

Eric said nothing.

"Martinis with the Mad Mahatma," said Larry.

Eric still said nothing.

Ken put down a letter of his own he had been reading and said, "Vic's probably right about straight up for the tower. He's awfully damn sure of himself, that hard-nosed baby, but the payoff is that he's usually right."

It was another clear morning when they set off for the ridge. On the previous day's push there had been five men. On this there were eight.

Paul Loring, still unwell, stayed at camp, with George Barr looking after him. But the others of the first group were back for more.

Also, Ken went.

Eric went.

"This may be the last lap for us old crocks," Ken said to him. "But at least we'll give it a whirl."

Two Sherpas, it had been decided, were needed to help carry the hardware and extra ropes for the tower, and Tashi, as sirdar, had picked himself as one of them. Young Pembol had pleaded to be the other (just as Tashi himself, thought Eric, used to plead to go higher, higher); but Tashi had said no, he must wait his turn, and selected instead a steady older man named Phutar. Pembol and the other Sherpas would keep house at the Gap and sort out the loads that had come up the previous day from Base.

On the first climb up the ridge there had been two ropes. On this there were three, with Meach and Kellerman, in tandem, leading, Ken-Norstad-Phutar second, and Larry-Tashi-Eric third. Like Tashi in the icefall, Larry had urged Eric to go first on their own rope; but he had refused. On DZ 1 he had been leader. On DZ 3 his place was last and he would keep it. And besides, from last, he could watch Larry climb.

As in the icefall, he climbed well. True, there were no great difficulties in the slanting gully that cut up from the Gap to the spine of the west ridge. But still he moved easily, surely, pushing neither too hard nor too little. Even when they reached the ridge, where the going was narrower and steeper, he showed no perceptible change. Though they were now close to the twenty-two-thousand-foot level, he kept the pace, stopping only when those ahead stopped, at preset intervals, to rest and breathe deep.

Tashi, behind him, and Phutar, last on the second rope, moved steadily, trudgingly, neither with grace nor with show of effort. For grace, one had to look beyond them to Arne Norstad, the golden Swede, the ski professional, moving even at this height with fluid rhythm; for effort, to Ken Naylor, bulky, dogged, raising each foot, advancing, planting it, as if to the beat of a metronome. Still farther ahead, Will Meach and Vic Kellerman were too distant for detailed observation. But in outline against snow or sky, they made a striking contrast: the one (Meach) long, loose-limbed, seeming almost to be ambling; the other (Kellerman) small and controlled, compact and driving. For some time now, Kellerman had reminded Eric of someone he had known and climbed with before; but who it was had escaped him. Now, suddenly, he knew. It was Uli Brandel, the German ex-mountain-trooper, on the north face of the Matterhorn. "Do I go too fast?" Brandel had asked coolly. "Take my word for it, it'll go," said Kellerman coolly. They did not look alike. They spoke different languages, came from different worlds; but they were brothers. Both were "hard men," skilled and proud men, tough as rope, cold as steel.

Those were the seven ahead.

And the eighth—himself—Venn the Elder: how was he doing? He faced the fact: he was doing all right.

Why, he didn't know . . . He was forty-seven. Behind him were the years of Kathmandu: of Haig Pinch, arak, hashish, of waste and sloth, of bar and bed, of life with Amy—scarcely a training program for a mountaineer. But there had also been the time of Solu Khumbu, with its rugged life and high altitudes, and perhaps this had been the counterbalance. In any case, altitude, so far, had not bothered him; and in the icefall the climbing itself had gone routinely—though there, of course, he had been spared the heavy work. Most important of all, he had passed the test he had most dreaded: not a physical test, more than that. He had stood at the grave of Franz Harben, and thought of Franz, and

379

endured it. He had looked beyond, toward the heights, where lay whatever was left of Julian Howard. And that, too, he had endured.

Now, on this morning, he was moving up toward those heights. Ken had spoken of "old crocks" and "a whirl" and handed him a coil of rope. "Tie on with Larry and Tashi," Ken had said. And he had done so. They had started off. They had climbed. Through the hours they had climbed: beyond the maw of the icefall, from the desolation of the Gap, through the confines of the gully, to the crest of the ridge. And now they were *on* the ridge, on the real, the true mountain, moving up its thin catwalk between the gulfs of space. There was no wind. The sun shone. On another shining day, long past, he and Ken, the first of all men, had climbed together up this ramp in the sky, and it had been one of the best of all days he had known on a mountain. In the vastness there had been glory; in the stillness, music; and the lift and joy of his youth had burst from him in music of his own, in a high wild exultant yodel . . . Well, that was then. This was now . . . He did not yodel now. He climbed on in silence behind the others—behind Larry and Tashi—as foot by foot, pitch by pitch, the ridge soared on skyward.

He could no longer yodel.

But he still could climb.

Then, ahead, the ridge changed. It was blocked. There was the tower. By the time he reached its base, the others, their packs unslung, were staring upward, and now he too was craning at what lay ahead. The tower, head-on, was as he remembered it: a wall of some two hundred feet, part vertical, part overhanging, its smoothness broken at intervals by only the faintest of cracks and bulges. Then he looked off to the right, toward the bypass he and Ken had once taken, and there it was not the same. As Will Meach had reported, there was no more snow slope. It had fallen away, along with its underlying support of rock, and all that was left was the south face of the mountain, even steeper and smoother than the wall facing the ridge. He turned back to this. Ken and Meach were talking and pointing. Norstad and Larry were still silently staring. Tashi and Phutar were standing by. Only Vic Kellerman was in action, selecting pitons from an open pack and hanging them from a sling around his waist. That done, he put two coils of thin rappel rope over his shoulders and slipped the thong of a piton hammer over his right arm. Then he approached the foot of the wall.

The others were watching him now.

Ken said, "Remember we're high, Vic. Rest as much as you can."

That was all he said. The others said nothing. Kellerman said nothing. After a brief look upward he began to climb.

. . . And for the next two hours, his neck craning until it ached, Eric watched a performance of cragsmanship such as he had never before seen. Ken had told him of the so-called Yosemite School of rockcraft that had developed back home in recent years, and he knew that all the other younger team members, Larry included, had been schooled in its techniques. But here was the master, the champion. Kellerman did not move quickly. Draped in his ropes and hardware, it was remarkable that he could move at all, let alone keep balance. But move he did, balance he did, in an exquisite blend of control and timing. For the first part of the ascent, Meach, below, had him on belay, with Kellerman hammering pitons, then passing the rope through attached carabiners, so that Meach could hold him if he slipped or fell. But he did not slip or fall. Watching, one *knew* that he wouldn't. However long it took him to negotiate a pitch, there was no unsureness, no fumbling. Each movement he made was precisely right for what it was designed to accomplish.

Part of the time he was climbing "free": using pitons only for protection, effecting his progress by what his fingers and toes could find in the rock of the wall. Then came stretches where they could find nothing, and he climbed "artificially"; using pitons as direct support for hand and foot, or hanging *étriers*—loops of rope hung from the pitons—in which he stood while hammering a yet higher spike. By angling and traversing he succeeded in avoiding the worst of the overhangs. But now and then he came to places with no crack for even the thinnest of pitons, and here he had to drill holes and insert expansion bolts.

Nowhere was there a ledge or other resting spot. Such rests as he had were on verticality. Yet as he reached the tower's midpoint, his progress continued as at the outset. Here, after an hour or more, he spoke for the first time. "Unroping," he called; and untying the line that joined him to Meach, he tied it to a piton and went on above it. Perhaps a quarter of its 125-foot length remained unused; but its protection, he had apparently decided, was no longer worth the drag of its ever-increasing, dangling weight. From now on to the top he would be on his own, without lifeline.

The one word was all he spoke. Before and thereafter, the only sound in the stillness was the clink of hammer and piton; and for those below, as for him, it was a game of "true or false," as the tone of the clink identified a sound crack or a false one. By the time he was on the upper third of the wall it was hard for the others to see what he was doing. Then he swung around past an overhang and was gone entirely. Only the clinking came down —more faintly—and at the foot of the cliff the others listened, waited. They did not expect a shout when he reached the top: Kellerman was not the shouting type. In time he would simply reappear . . . And so it happened . . . Suddenly one of his rappel lines spun out from beyond the overhang, and a few moments later he himself followed, roping swiftly downward. The doubled line reached only about halfway down the tower, where its ends dangled in air. A lesser climber would soon have been dangling too. But as he neared the danger point Kellerman dextrously swung himself in toward the wall and found a stance on two of his previously placed pitons. There he released himself from his first line, secured and threw down his second, and descended on it to the base of the tower. As against some two hours going up, he had taken ten minutes to come down.

No one asked if he had made it all the way. It was taken for granted. The others wrung his hand, clapped his back, gave him a hero's welcome. But Kellerman simply rested for a bit and drank from a flask of fruit juice, seeming scarcely more tired than those who had watched him. Above, on the precipice, were the visible fruits of his labor: the climbing rope and two rappel lines he had

382

left there, and the stairway of pitons extending from base to top. The barrier had been mastered. The framework for a general advance was in place. But it was growing late now; that would be for another day. In the waning midafternoon light they began the descent to the Gap.

There was the long arc of the ridge. Then the gash of the gully. And though still roped for protection they moved quickly and easily. In the gully the going was particularly easy, little more than a steep downhill walk; and Eric, again at the end of the file, watched the tents of Camp Three growing larger and clearer. Then, in the file below, there was a sudden breaking of rhythm. Someone shouted. The moving figures had stopped. Following Larry and Tashi, he continued the descent until they caught up with the others; and there were the five of them close together, four standing and one—Vic Kellerman—sitting in the trough of the gully. If all the gully was easy going, this particular section was especially so—neither narrow nor steep. But a few moments before, Kellerman had stepped on a loose stone, the stone had slipped, and he had fallen. Now, when he rose and tried to take a step, he could not do it.

He sat down again. He had come through his conquest of the tower with no sign of strain or distress; but now his body was tense and hunched, his thin face suddenly pale and haggard. Ken had kneeled and was unlacing, then removing, the boot from his left foot, and then he felt the foot gently, while the others watched.

Kellerman watched. "Shit," he said quietly.

"We'll get you down to George," said Ken.

He eased Kellerman's pack from his back. At a signal from him, the Sherpa Phutar also unslung his load, and Ken and Meach hoisted Kellerman onto his back.

"Got him tight?" Ken asked.

"Yes, sah'b," said Phutar.

Two of the others took the discarded packs, and the file continued the descent, more slowly. On Phutar's back, Kellerman repeated softly, at intervals, "Shit . . . shit . . . shit . . ."

383

He had, said George Barr, broken two of the bones of his metatarsus. The doctor manipulated and taped the foot, and the next morning Kellerman hobbled to breakfast with an ice ax as crutch. He said nothing. His sharp, lopsided face seemed frozen. When breakfast was over he hobbled back to his tent.

On this day, too, there was a change of weather. The sun withdrew. Wind rose. No snow fell, but hour by hour the wind grew higher, wilder, and the cold was savage. All hands stayed in camp.

The next day was the same. Again they stayed in camp. George Barr, who at first had tried for a show of optimism, now reported that Kellerman's fractures were no hairline affairs, but bad ones; and that while there was no need to get him off the mountain (he could mend as well at Camp Three as at Base), he was through for the duration as a high climber. Faces were grim; Kellerman's grimmest of all. In partial compensation, however, Paul Loring, after several days at the Gap, was feeling far better and declared himself ready for action. During the following night the wind dropped, the sky cleared. In the morning there was again a setting off for the ridge.

This time it was in a party of seven. No Sherpas were taken, for enough climbing gear had already been deposited at the foot of the wall. But of the team members there were all of the previous group, minus Kellerman, but plus Loring, and also Barr. Soon after sunrise, with Kellerman watching them gloomily, they filed out of camp; then followed the gully to the ridge, and the ridge toward the tower.

Then again trouble struck. Again Loring took sick. For the first part of the ascent he had seemed in fine form: a handsome, almost debonair figure, as he moved strongly, easily upward. But as before, when he came to about the twenty-two-thousand-foot level, there was a sudden collapse. He began to retch, then to vomit. When he had nothing left to vomit, he still went on retching; he coughed, and the coughs became paroxysms, and weakly, miserably, he sat down on the ridge. Barr gave him liquids and tablets, but these too he vomited. "I'll take you down, Paul," Barr said. Loring shook his head. He was crying. But there was nothing for it; his strength was gone. Watching him, Eric thought of Ted Lassiter, twenty years earlier, and the tears that had streaked his face as he was led down toward Base Camp. Ted's ceiling had been lower. He had collapsed at the Gap, whereas Paul was all right at the Gap. His limit was a thousand feet higher. But limit it was; he could go no farther. As the others—now down to five—moved on again, he and Barr began a slow descent, and another of its prospective top men had been lost to DZ 3.

Still, for long hours that day there was work on the tower. (Vic's Tower, they now called it.) With Meach and Norstad leading, Ken, Larry and Eric following, they moved up Kellerman's sketchy rope-and-piton route and elaborated it into what was in effect a ladder from bottom to top. For the night they went down to the Gap. The next day they returned, and with them now came Barr (this time the whole way) and a train of Sherpas (led by Tashi and including Pembol), laden with provisions for Camp Four. The loads were not carried up the tower, but hauled on lines by men at the tops; and the Sherpas, unburdened, were roped to team members and led up the "ladder." Even without loads, two refused to make the ascent. The climbers coaxed; Tashi, tiny but formidable, swore and threatened; but still they refused. In the hauling there was also a setback, when a load of foodstuff, badly tied to its line, fell first to the ridge, then on to the Kalpurtha Glacier, a mile below. But finally all the other loads were up. All the Sherpas, less the two defectors, were up. Above the tower the procession continued, and Camp Four was established at above twenty-three thousand in the same hollow on the ridge that had been its site on DZ 1 and DZ 2.

In the revised table of organization, Meach and Norstad were now the number one team. While the others—climbers and Sherpas—returned to the Gap, they dug in at Four, and the next day reconnoitered along the upper ridge toward the broad shoulder at its crest. On return to Four they radioed down to Three that all had gone well, and that they were ready to go for the shoulder as soon as reinforcements appeared. While they rested for a day, the reinforcements went up. Again there were

Ken, Larry, Eric and Barr, along with—this time—ten Sherpas. The two who had refused to climb the wall, plus three others who had not done well, were left at the Gap as custodians, together with the disconsolate Loring and Kellerman.

On the night of May 3, therefore, there were sixteen men at Camp Four, and, in spite of losses, things seemed set for a massive push. It was not to be, however, for in the morning there was again Sherpa trouble—on a larger scale. This, recalled Eric, was nothing new for Camp Four. It had been here, on DZ 1, that Sherpas had become fearful of the "godwind," and during the night—a still one on the ridge—he had again heard its organ-sound on the Wailing Wall, high above. But that was not the issue this time. As he had noted on the approach march, there had been some changes over the years, among Sherpas as elsewhere, and what they were concerned about now was not godwinds but oxygen. For going on to Camp Five they must have oxygen.

"But there is no oxygen," Ken told them.

"Yes, is."

"You know there isn't."

"Have seen oxygen. Loring Sah'b he use oxygen."

"He was sick," said Ken. "There's only a very little, for the sick."

"We sick," said the Sherpas.

The argument ground on. Ken reasoned, pleaded. Eric and Meach joined in. Tashi stormed again. Again to no avail. Besides Tashi and Pembol, only Phutar and one other Sherpa, a youngster named Nawang, were willing to go on. The other six would not budge without the nonexistent oxygen.

"Sonofabitch," said someone.

But sonofabitching didn't help.

All right, said Ken at last: if they wouldn't, they wouldn't. The six would go down to the Gap, shepherded by Barr, who was descending anyhow, leaving nine—five climbers and four Sherpas—to make the carry to Five. In the past there had been only one tent on the shoulder; this time it had been planned to have two. But now that was out. All that could be managed was one tent, big enough for three men, and enough food and gear for those three for a few days on the heights. The other six, with their loads deposited, would turn around and come back to Four. Then when the top men made their summit bid, they would go up again in support.

Two of the top three would of course be Will Meach and Arne Norstad.

And the other?

"Larry," said Ken to Eric. "He's damn well earned it."

But it was decided not to tell him until they arrived at the shoulder.

Barr shook hands, wished them luck. The six defecting Sherpas stood about looking glumly shamefaced, but did not change their minds; and when Barr gave the signal they roped and started down. The others started up. Meach, Norstad and Larry went on the first rope; Ken, Phutar and Pembol on a second; Eric, Tashi and Nawang on a third. Through the morning and into midday they moved up the jagged spine of the upper ridge.

Here there were no major obstacles, such as the tower below. On the stretch where the ridge narrowed to a knife-edge they were able, as on the earlier expeditions, to proceed on a series of ledges beneath it; and in the steep flange of the chimney beyond them they found, brown with rust but still secure, the line of pitons that Eric and Franz Harben had placed there during DZ 1. Still higher, and back on the ridge, they came in view of the shoulder, looming tall and broad in the sky above them. And here, for Eric, was another, darker reminder of Franz: the place where his thrombotic leg had first lamed him and they had had to turn back from their try for the shoulder.

This time, no one went lame. But now they were nearing the twenty-five-thousand-foot level, and altitude was taking its toll. Meach and Norstad seemed still all right, and Pembol—young Pembol—even better than that, appearing, remarkably, to become stronger the higher he went. But the rest were having trouble. Eric himself was breathing in labored gasps, and his feet were leaden. Ken, from all visible signs, was no better off; nor were Tashi, Phutar and Nawang. And Larry, who until now on the mountain had kept up with the best of them, was presently in the worst shape of all: coughing, retching, then vomiting, as had Paul Loring, farther down on the ridge. On their lead rope, Meach and Norstad had to stop for ever longer and more frequent pauses, while Larry hunched over his ax, struggling for strength and control. On the rope behind, Eric and Ken rested, breathing hard and fast, while Pembol waited restlessly and threw stones into the abysses on either side of them.

Still, they all kept on. Slowly the shoulder came nearer. And at last, in the early afternoon, they were there, on its airy platform. They dumped their loads; again they rested. Then it was time for those descending to be on their way, if they were to get back to Camp Four before dark. Ken looked at Larry, still coughing and retching, his young face drawn and strained under its half mask of beard and goggles. He looked at Pembol, whistling, smoking a cigarette, as he cleared ground for the tent. He spoke with Meach and Norstad. Then with Eric. Then he said to Pembol, "You'll stay here with sah'bs Will and Arne."

The boy grinned. "Yes, sah'b," he said. "Thank you, sah'b. I am happy."

Larry did not seem to be listening. At least, thought Eric, he had not been told that, as of that morning, it had been he who was to stay. Now he got up slowly. The six who were leaving re-roped. There were again goodbyes, good lucks. Then they started down.

They reached Camp Four before sundown.

And Larry—like Loring, when he had reached Camp Three—was quickly all right again.

"I'll do better," he said grimly. "Next time up I'll do better."

"Sure you will," said Eric.

"You've done damn well already," said Ken.

At seven, by prearrangement, they talked by radio with both Three and Five. All was well below. All was well above. Plans were reviewed. On the next day everyone would rest. On the day after that, if the weather held, Meach and Norstad would go for the top, with Pembol helping as far as the base of the Wailing

Wall. Simultaneously, those at Four would again go up to Five, in support, and Barr would again lead a squad of Sherpas from the Gap to Four. Thus there would be manpower in all three camps on the upper mountain, ready either to help the top men down, if they had been successful, or to mount a second try, if they had not.

"Over and out."

They signed off. They would talk again in the morning.

At Camp Four, the six men occupied two three-man tents: Ken, Larry and Eric in one; Tashi, Phutar and Nawang in the other. Bone-tired, Eric was soon asleep. But later he wakened. It was dark and still, and in the stillness he could again hear the sound of the wind on the Wailing Wall, high above.

Then he slept again.

Again wakened.

And the darkness was different. There was still wind, but no longer the godwind. It was closer now, blowing over the camp, against the walls of the tent; and after listening a while he crept from his bag and looked out at the night. There had been stars before, but they were gone. Instead of stars there was scud. A blast of wind struck his face and shook the fabric of the tent, and, going out, he checked its guy ropes and the ropes of the other tents in the camp. Then he returned to his sleeping bag. Again he lay listening, dropping off toward sleep His bag was the middle one in the tent, and on either side of him were his two companions: Franz Harben on the right, Julian Howard on the left.

He tried to rise, but couldn't.

He tried to speak, but couldn't.

It was Julian who spoke. "I'm all right, Rick," he said.

It had been the hallucination of height, of hypoxia. It struck unpredictably.

It struck again now.

For there they were again, just behind him, in full sunlight on the snow dome. Julian, Franz—and beside them, Robin in her pigtails.

This time it was Robin who spoke. "I'm all right, Ricky," she said.

He put out his arms to embrace them . . . No, to push them away . . . He pushed, and they were gone, but he himself almost fell; and now he was clinging to the slope with ax and crampon while a white glare whirled around him.

Breath came back. Sight came back.

You've gone far enough alone, he thought.

Above, only a few steps above, was the ledge, the flatness in the slope, he had been making for, and he took the steps and was there.

He sat down.

He looked down.

Below were the others: not the dead but the living. They were close now. He waited.

24

"Rick—"

Was it Julian again?

No. It was Ken.

As he surfaced from sleep, Ken was half-sitting, half-kneeling on him, grappling with the loose wall of the tent close by his feet. Larry, sitting up in his bag, was holding the wall on the far side. The beam of a flashlight was sawing the darkness, and the tent walls flapped and crackled in the battering of the wind.

"Hold it here," Ken yelled through the din. "I'm going outside."

Pulling on his boots, he crept out through the sleeve. Eric and Larry hung on to the loose walls and tilting tent frame until he had done the needed job on guy ropes and pitons; and then they still had to hold on, though not quite so desperately. Some time passed, while Ken was presumably checking the other tents. Then his bearded face, plastered with snow, reappeared from the sleeve in the gleam of a flashlight, and now they were three again, in a tangle of bodies and gear.

"How are the Sherps?" asked Eric.

"Still there," said Ken.

He rejoined them in holding on. The storm roared. The tent shook.

"I guess we're overdue for it," he said.

"Never mind the philosphy," Eric told him.

There was no more sleep that night. There was the holding of walls. There was the roaring and crackling, and though there seemed no opening in the tent's fabric, the snow still came in, covering them and their possessions with its icy powder. At last the darkness began to thin. They could see the shambles about them, and out of the shambles, slowly, fumblingly, they assembled the things needed to make food and drink. For a half hour Eric worked on the pressure cooker, and at last elicited a small blue flame. Larry filled a pot with snow. They waited for it to melt, then to reach a tepid boil, and poured in packets of dehydrated soup. The result was lumps and glue, but they got it down. They had brought out bread and jam, but the bread was like slabs of rock and they dumped it in the soup, making more lumps. When they had half-finished eating, a blast of wind, stronger than any before, rocked the tent, and again they had to lunge to hold its walls. Someone's foot knocked over the stove, it went out, and what was left of the soup spilled on Eric's bag.

"At least we didn't have a fire," said Ken.

"You," said Eric, "are looking for a punch in the nose."

They began all over again.

Then there was a movement in the tent sleeve. Another snowy head appeared, and beneath the snow was the face of Tashi.

"The sah'bs are all right?" he asked.

"Just dandy," said Eric.

With the three already there, even so small a man as Tashi could not fit in the tent. He had to remain on hands and knees in the sleeve, head and shoulders inside, his rump protruding into the storm.

"Get back into your tent," Ken told him.

"I go bring sah'bs tea."

"No, we've eaten, we're all right. Get back in your tent—in your bag. Keep warm, that's the main thing."

"Yes, sah'b. But if something you want, you call please."

"Tell Phutar and Nawang to keep warm too. And watch your tent ropes."

"Yes, sah'b."

Tashi backed out.

Through eating, the three in the tent got back into their own bags. They lay in them as if in pockets within the larger pocket of the tent.

Eric closed his eyes. He listened to the tumult beyond the thin screen of nylon fabric.

Then he swore. His bowels were signaling.

They had with them in the tent a bottle for urinating, but for this there was only paper. He unzipped his bag and sat up. He got into his boots and pulled the hood of his parka over his head. Then he crept out through the sleeve into the storm. This was not a storm of wind alone, but of wind with snow, and the snow was already deep in the hollow of the ridge that was the site of Camp Four. All rock was hidden. The five tents were no more than dark smudges in the drifts, and around and above them the storm blew in a horizontal tide. He breasted the tide for only a few steps. Then turning his back to it, he began the long fumble with layers of clothing. At last he was ready, squatting. Like Tashi's in the tent sleeve, his rump jutted into the blizzard, but Tashi's had at least been covered; his was bare. He did what he had to do. Paper streamed, whipped and vanished, and in the snow now there was another, smaller smudge, dark, steaming, strangely alive in the sterile whiteness. It was a neat symbol, he thought—of something. Then he was standing, struggling again with layers of trousers. As long as he was out, there were other jobs to do. He went to the Sherpas' tent and checked its guys and holding pitons. He checked the three empty tents. Returning to his own, he stopped before entering and raised his head, trying to see beyond the hollow of the campsite. But there was only the snow, the wind, the storm, the boiling whiteness.

He thought, "Dera Zor, the big white whore—"

He crept back into the tent, dripping snow. Ken, in his bag, was holding the walkie-talkie, calling Camps Three and Five. In the storm, of course, he couldn't reach them, and knew it. "But it's something to do," he said. Static squealed and crackled for a while, and then he turned it off. Eric got back into his bag. The snow he brought in with him condensed and enveloped him in a steaming mist, and his private parts, he realized, had gone numb with cold. Somewhere, a long way off, someone seemed to be grinning. "I told you so, you jerk," said Amy Bulwinkle.

In the sack, now, he sought warmth. He rested. With the snow outside drifting ever higher against the tent, its walls had increasing protection, and there was no longer need to hold them against the blasts of wind. Also, the din of the storm was somewhat muffled. He drifted into sleep.

When he awoke, the other two were asleep. Ken, on one side of him, was breathing stertorously, half-snoring, half-gasping, as he labored for air. But Larry, who had had such trouble the day before on the climb to Camp Five, lay quietly, his breath coming and going in steady rhythm. His face was no more than two feet from Eric's, bearded and thinner—as was everyone's—than when the expedition began. And now, for the first time since that beginning, Eric looked at it close-up, carefully, for several minutes . . . Was this boy beside him, all but a stranger, his nephew or his son? . . . Amy had spoken of a "dead ringer." George Barr, one day on the trail, had mistaken Larry for himself. But uncle and nephew could look alike, no less than father and son . . . Did Larry also look like Frank? He had never been conscious of resemblance between himself and his brother, and now, after all the years, it was hard to bring him into clear focus. All he could see were the cool eyes, the glasses; but then the glasses became Will Meach's, the face became Meach's, and the image was gone . . . Larry remained. He remained. There they lay side by side, almost touching, in a tiny tent on a savage mountain: uncle and nephew, or father and son. Which, he didn't know. Kay didn't know. They would never know.

He thought of Kay.

Now comes a surprise, she had written. She was coming to Kathmandu. She would be there when they returned to greet her son and her . . . what?

He had turned away from Larry. Now he turned back. And what had happened before now happened again: it was not Larry who was there, but Julian . . . Julian had been young too. Not so young as Larry, but still young, young enough to have a mother; a mother with money who could have come to Kathmandu to

394

meet him. What would he, Eric, have said to her when they met? "I'm sorry, ma'am—so sorry—but you see, there's been a slight mishap—"

The beginning of the end for Julian had been in a tent in a mountain storm. That had been at Camp Five, on the shoulder, and Julian, like Larry, had been lying beside him. "I'm all right, Rick," he had said. But he had not been all right. The next day he would go on up to his death—and Eric had put him in the position to do so. He had thought of himself, not of Julian (let alone of Franz), and Julian had followed him, and he had died . . . He was gone again. It was Larry in the bag beside him. Larry his nephew. Larry his son . . . And what was in store for this nephew-son, this youngster, this boy of twenty, who was now beside him, high on the same murderous mountain? Dera Zor was roaring at them. Up higher, it could roar still louder. Up higher were the corniced ridge, the Wailing Wall . . . He made his resolve. There would be no corniced ridge, no Wailing Wall for Larry; no "I'm sorry—so sorry" to Kay in Kathmandu . . . Larry had already had trouble on the mountain, on the climb to Five. He would not let him compound that trouble by going on farther, or even to Five again. When the storm ended and it was time for the ascent to the high camp, he would stay here at Four with one of the Sherpas. Then he would descend with the rest of them to the Gap and below.

Again he watched the sleeping boy. He was not Julian Howard but Larry Venn. He was the son of Kay Burden and one of two brothers named Venn—and whatever else happened on the mountain, he was, by God, coming off it alive.

The day dragged by. The wind howled, fell for a bit, then rose and howled again; but their tent was now well buttressed by the drifts of snow, and they did not again have to grapple with its walls and struts. At intervals, one or another of them went out to inspect the other tents—now looking less like tents than igloos —and they were all right too. The Sherpas were all right. Toward midafternoon, as they were about to prepare another meal of sorts, Tashi appeared again, this time carrying a pot of simmering stew. They blessed him, and he returned to his own tent. No sooner had they finished the stew than Ken gagged, retched and vomited on his sleeping bag before he could get out of the tent. They cleaned up the vomit as best they could.

Later, they again tried the radio—but again, as expected, with no result. They were not unduly concerned about Camp Three, at the Gap; it was lower than their own camp and at least partially protected. But Camp Five was another matter—two thousand feet up on the jutting shoulder—and what Meach, Norstad and Pembol must now be enduring was not a happy thought. Once the radio was off, however, they did not speak of them again. There was nothing they could do. Until the storm ended, they were as cut off from them as if they had been on the other side of the earth.

Dusk came. Then night. And it stormed through the night. They dozed, wakened, coughed, sucked deep for air, and for an hour or more, toward midnight, Ken suffered an attack of convulsive Cheyne-Stokes breathing. Later, Larry's bowels signaled him out into the snow. Eric's—and he was grateful—did not again. He lay through the hours, half-awake, half-asleep, while dreams and half dreams flickered in the darkness. Julian did not return. Nor did Franz. For a while, in the distance, Amy grinned again. Then someone seemed to be crying, sobbing. (Kay? How could it be Kay, if Larry was coming back safely?) But this turned out to be Ken, in his bag, again gasping for breath.

At last it was dawn. It was daylight: a brown, subterranean sort of daylight beneath the layers of tent and snow. Once more they prepared a meal, checked on the Sherpas and empty tents, and struggled to bring a semblance of order out of the chaos of their own. Ken brought out the radio again (everything, now, was *again*—and *again*), still with the same nonresult. Still the storm kept on. It would keep on forever, thought Eric. There had been a change in the world, in the cosmos, and storm no longer came and went but was the natural, permanent, eternal state of things.

It was morning . . . noon . . . afternoon.

It still stormed.

From his pack beside his sleeping bag Eric took pad and pencil. He wrote: *big white whore*. He wrote: *turd in snow*. He wrote: *Tashi and stew . . . Ken and radio . . . three without words . . . time turned inside out (better than tent doing same)* . . .

Looking up, he saw that Larry was watching him. And Larry said, "Wow!"

"Wow, what?"

"Writing a letter. Here—now."

"It's not a letter," Eric said. "Just notes."

"For a book, you mean?"

Eric looked at him curiously. "What makes you think that?" he said.

"Mother's told me about your writing."

"Oh?"

"She said you used to write stories for magazines. And that you had a contract for a book on—"

He broke off.

Eric said it. "On DZ 1." He paused. "That never got done."

"But you'll do one now?"

"Maybe."

"It would make Mother happy, I can tell you that. She's always had a great thing about you as a writer."

Eric smiled a little. "I'll see what I can do for her," he said.

That was the longest conversation of the days in the tent. They went back to silence—a few words when necessary—then silence again. They waited. And waited. There was another meal (and Ken held it down). There was the radio (with static). There were the storm, the sack, darkness. There was fitful sleep. Out of the last of the sleeps, late in the night, Eric awoke to what seemed an explosion of sound.

But it was not sound that he heard. It was stillness. There was no wind; not a whisper. Almost lunging from his bag, he crawled through the tent sleeve into the open—into a world reborn. The storm was gone. The stars were out. In their frosty light, above and below, the vastness of Dera Zor stretched white and gleaming. The big white whore had gone in the night and left in her place the Faery Queene.

397

In moments, Ken and Larry were out of the tent beside him. Then the Sherpas came. There was a thumping of feet, a stretching of long-cramped bodies. There was a lifting of eyes, of hearts; there were voices raised; and Tashi grinned and shouted, "Is gone! Is gone!" In the few remaining hours of the night there was no more sleep. They ate, cleaned up, made ready to move. At six, as the sun rose, Ken was on the radio, and now at last there was an answer. George Barr came on almost at once. Camp Three was all right, he reported. Vic Kellerman and Paul Loring were all right, though, in their different ways, still immobile. The Sherpas were all right, with only a few minor ailments, and within half an hour he would be starting up with six of them for Camp Four . . . "Good. Good," said Ken. But that was all that was good. For there were just the two of them on the air . . . "Calling Camp Five—calling Five," Ken said over and over. "Calling Five—calling Five," said Barr from below. But Five didn't answer. They stayed on the air for ten minutes, but still with no answer. "We'll keep trying them on the way up," said Ken at last. "Come on every hour on the hour." Then he added: "We'll take two of the tents from here, in case"—he chose his words—"in case they're needed up there."

His face was grim as he stowed the walkie-talkie in his pack. The others were quiet and somber as they dug two of the spare tents out of the snow, collapsed and folded them, and added them to their loads. While they worked, Eric kept his eye on Ken. Physically, he had had a bad time of it during their stormbound two days. But this past night he had done better than earlier; he had held down his breakfast; his breathing was almost normal. Besides, Eric well knew that nothing short of total breakdown could keep him from going up on their mission to Camp Five.

"I'll tie on with Phutar and Nawang," he said now to Eric. "You go with Larry and Tashi."

Eric uncoiled a rope, handed an end to Larry . . . Then he remembered: he had resolved that Larry must not come . . . He started to speak—but couldn't. To withdraw the rope—but couldn't . . . Larry had had hard going on the way to Five the last time, but here at Four he had made a good comeback. He seemed strong, controlled, ready and eager to be off . . . And besides . . . Besides, how could he forbid him to go, any more than he could Ken? He was not the leader here. Even if he were, how could he keep a man, ready and able, from going up to help companions in trouble? For all they knew, this was a rescue party. Everyone who could *had* to go . . .

Larry was tying on to the rope, and he watched him in silence . . . As he had watched Julian Howard tie on, in this same place, years before.

Larry was a better climber than Julian. Younger but better.

But he was also—

The hell with that.

"You lead the rope," he told him, as he tied on too. He indicated Tashi and himself. "We two old birds may need some hauling."

The sun beamed; the mountain glittered. But once they were out of the hollow the snow was not too deep. On the exposed spine of the ridge the wind had swept much of it away, and the going was little different than on the earlier ascent. The Larry-Eric-Tashi rope went first; the Ken-Phutar-Nawang rope followed. "I've an idea I may be the slow one today," Ken had said as they started. "Go at your own rate. Don't wait. We've got to get someone to Five as soon as we can."

Leading the first rope, Larry set a normal pace: a slow, steady upward grind, broken at intervals by stops for rest and the catching of breath. Here and there snow had to be cleared from hand- and footholds, but it was soft and powdery, requiring no blows of an ax. In its following position, Ken's rope maintained the pace, but, for himself at least, with much effort. At eight o'clock the procession halted and he brought out the walkie-talkie; but now it was Eric who did the calling, to save him breath. Again, George Barr came on at once. With his six Sherpas, he too was on the way up, some two thousand feet below. But as before, there was no answer from above, and after five futile minutes they resumed the climb.

At nine, they stopped for the same procedure. And the same result.

Then they came to the knife-edged section of the ridge, and again detoured it by a traverse of the ledges below and the ascent of the steep and narrow chimney that rose beyond them. Choked by new snow, the chimney was a formidable obstacle. But Larry patiently dislodged the drifts and, using the old fixed pitons, heaved his way upward. Eric, in his second position on the rope, belayed him carefully. But there were no slips; Larry climbed impeccably. Further, he had acclimatized remarkably during the lay-over at Camp Four, and there was none of the coughing and retching that had plagued him three days before.

Ken, however, was now having his troubles, and it was here in the chimney that his rope started dropping behind. As for any companion in distress, it was Eric's impulse to stop and wait for him. But it had been agreed, and rightly, that the first rope should move as quickly as it could. Whether, strictly speaking, they were on a rescue mission, no one knew. But the odds were high that there was also distress—perhaps far more serious distress—above.

They came up out of the chimney, regained the ridge; and here they rested. But the second rope did not catch up. Peering down, Eric could see it at about the chimney's halfway point: still moving, but slowly. He called down, and a call came back, but whether from Ken or one of the Sherpas he could not tell.

He looked at Larry and Tashi.

"Ready?"

"Ready."

They moved on.

They passed Franz Harben's high point. The ridge dipped and rose, and at the top of the rise they would be at the lowest point from which they could see the shoulder. The dip was short. The rise was steep. They were now well past the twenty-four-thousand-foot mark—perhaps halfway on to twenty-five thousand—and with each new pitch legs grew heavier, breathing harder. But still they were making progress, good progress: better and faster than on their previous climb to Camp Five.

During a rest Tashi said to Eric: "When we start, you say we are birds, Rick Sah'b."

"I said old birds."

"Yes, is right. Larry Sah'b he is young bird. You, me, old birds." Tashi smiled his monkey smile. "But some old birds they fly O.K.," he said.

That was the only smile on the ascent. The sun still beamed, the mountain shone; they were moving up through a world of magic and glory. But they were not thinking of such things. They were thinking of the next step, the next breath. Of Meach, Norstad, Pembol. Of Camp Five, wrapped in silence, in mystery—through the storm, and now the calm—

Then they came to the top of the rise, and there ahead was the shoulder: white with snow now, broad and clear against the shining sky. But whether the camp, the lone tent, still stood, they could not tell. It was not a matter of distance but of angle. The tent, they knew, would have been pitched as far back from the shoulder's rim as possible; and between them and shoulder the ridge was so steep that they could not see past the rim. They rested, bent over axes, fighting for breath. When they had the breath, they shouted. There was no answer. Even if the others were there, it was too far for an answer.

They climbed on. About halfway up they stopped, shouted again. There was still no answer.

Then they reached the shoulder. And the camp—the tent—was there. It was battered, drunkenly tilted; a long rent showed in one of its walls. But still it was there. No one was in sight. Dropping his pack and unroping, Eric crept through the sleeve. Inside was snow, wild disorder, and two empty sleeping bags. In a third bag was a muffled figure. Eric spoke and touched the figure; and it stirred, a head was raised, it was Arne Norstad; and Norstad, bearded and haggard, stared at Eric as if at a ghost.

Larry crawled into the tent. Tashi's head appeared in the sleeve, but as at Camp Four, in the crowded tent, that was all of him that could get in.

"Are you all right, Arne?" Eric asked.

Norstad still stared. He nodded vaguely.

"Where are Will and Pembol?"

"Up."

"Up? You mean they've gone for the top?"

Norstad nodded again. He half-sat up in his bag and made a strong effort to think and speak clearly. "Left at first light," he said. "Will knew wasn't much chance but wanted to try. Knew it had to be today or not at all."

"And you? Why didn't you go?"

"Feet bad. Spent a lot of time out in storm, holding the tent, and they began to freeze. Thought they might thaw out if I spent the day in the sack."

"How are they now?"

"I don't know. Can't feel them."

"We've been trying all morning to get you on the radio," said Larry.

"That froze too," Norstad said. "I've had it in the sack here, trying to warm it. But it won't work."

There was a pause.

"Christ, it's good to see you guys!" he said hoarsely.

Then there were other voices outside. Tashi backed out of the sleeve, Larry and Eric followed, and there was the second rope of Ken-Phutar-Nawang. They were dropping their packs. As he dropped his, Ken swayed with it, stumbled, and half-sat, half-fell among the snow-covered rocks. He remained there, head bent to his knees, heaving, gasping.

"There's room in the tent," Eric said to him. "Come in and rest there."

Ken fought for control. At last he raised his head. "Who's here?" he whispered.

"Arne."

"He's all right?"

"Half and half."

"Will and Pembol?"

"They've gone up."

Ken began coughing, choking. When the spasms had eased a little, Eric helped him up, got him to the tent and through the

402

sleeve. Then he followed him in. There was room for only three, and Larry and the Sherpas stayed outside.

"We make food, tea now," Tashi called.

Ken lay on one of the empty bags. Eric sat on another.

"Christ, it's good to see you!" Norstad repeated.

Companionship was obviously having a good effect on him. He was now fully sitting himself, and his speech came more easily as he told briefly what had happened at Five during the storm . . . On the exposed shoulder, it had of course been a terror. For two days and three nights, he, Meach and Pembol had had to spend at least half the time outside the tent, struggling with guy ropes and pitons, and after one of the walls had ripped, there was little more protection inside than out . . . Had they eaten? Yes, some. But only cold things—their stove wouldn't light—and their only liquid had been snow melted in their mouths . . . Still, Will had had the strength to go up that morning? "I didn't think so," said Norstad, "but he was set on trying" . . . And Pembol? He had been great, incredible, strong as a yak. "You'd have thought he's been spending his whole life in a mess like that."

Eric opened Norstad's bag, pulled off his layers of socks and examined his feet. They were hard, cold, dead white. When he tapped them, Norstad did not feel it.

"When did you last have your boots on?" Eric asked him.

"This morning."

"Could you walk?"

"Sort of."

Tashi's head appeared in the rip in the tent. "Tea, sah'bs," he said, and passed in three mugs.

A while later he appeared with slabs of half-thawed bread and jam.

"Shall we set up tent?" he asked.

"Is there room for another?" asked Eric.

"For one, yes. Two, no."

"Better do it, then."

How or if it would be needed, he didn't know. Who, if anyone, would spend that night at Five, he didn't know—except that it could not be more than six of them. It depended on many things, not yet clear. On how Norstad was. How Ken was. Most of all on Meach and Pembol: if they reached the top . . . how they were when they came down . . .

. . . *if* they came down . . .

Norstad himself was examining his feet. Ken had so far managed to hold down his tea and bread, but was still heaving for breath. Eric called to the tent sleeve.

"Larry and I'll go up a bit," he said, "and see what we can see."

But there was to be no need for it. There was a shout from outside.

"They come!" cried Tashi.

Eric left the tent. And there, above, were two figures emerging from among the ice towers on the upper ridge. The first was long and lean—Meach; the second shorter and compact—Pembol; and Pembol had Meach on a length of rope, holding him, while he lurched and stumbled toward the camp. With Larry and the Sherpas following, Eric went up to meet them and help them down.

There was no need to ask if they had reached the summit. Leaving at dawn, they would have taken all day, perhaps into the night, to get there and back. And now it was only early afternoon . . . At the campsite they dropped their packs and sat down heavily, wearily; but Meach was obviously far more done in then Pembol. There was something about his face, too, that appeared strange to Eric—and then he recognized what it was: he was wearing neither goggles nor glasses. His eyes seemed somehow glazed, unseeing. When they were open. Mostly he kept them shut.

Ken had come from the tent, and Norstad followed, hobbling stiffly in unlaced boots. They stood with the others around Meach and Pembol, but Meach did not seem aware of them. Every few moments his face contracted in a grimace of pain.

"Will—" said Eric.

Meach looked at him blankly.

"You're snowblind—"

Meach nodded. "I'm afraid so."

"Can you see at all?"

"A little."

404

"Does it hurt?"

"Yes."

Tashi had brought tea for the new arrivals. Eric went to a pack, brought out a first aid kit and put a capsule in Meach's hand. "Take this with the tea," he told him. "It will help the pain."

"Thanks." Meach drank and swallowed. "Stupid—stupid," he said.

"What's stupid?"

"Me . . . What happened."

What had happened?

He told them. He and Pembol had started up the ridge toward the base of the Wailing Wall. Considering the storm, the going wasn't bad. "But I was bad," he said. "Not Pembol here—he was fine. But I was slow—slow. Until then, I hadn't realized how much the storm had taken out of me."

He paused for breath; then to sip his tea. At intervals he pressed a hand against his eyes.

It had taken them three hours, he continued, to reach the point where they could see the top of the mountain: the wall, the corniced ridge, the dome of snow.

"The ridge is still corniced, then?" Eric asked.

"Yes, still corniced. Impossible . . . It's the wall or nothing."

By now he had already known they couldn't make the top. He was too slow. But he had decided to try at least the lower part of the wall. So they had gone on to its base, started up—and the very first pitch had been the end of it. "I wasn't just slow, but unsteady," Meach said. "I missed a hold and slipped." It had not been a bad slip; he had caught it in an instant. But in that instant he had struck his face against a projection of rock, and the rock had shattered the prescription lenses of his goggles. That had been it, and he knew it. To go on would have been madness, and he called to Pembol and backed down. They had begun the descent of the ridge, and for a while had moved normally. But then the glare of sun on snow had begun to stab into his unprotected eyes. "Like swords," he said. And he had begun to slip again. Once he fell. Coming down, he had been second on the rope, in the belaying position, but now he told Pembol to change with him. With Pembol holding him, and vision getting worse and worse, he had groped down the rest of the way.

The recital exhausted him. Like Ken, a short while before, he sat heaving and gasping.

From a pack, Eric again brought something: an extra pair of goggles, of plain glass but dark, and lowering the hood of Meach's parka, he slipped them over his eyes.

"Is the pain less?" he asked.

"Yes," said Meach.

"Can you see?"

"Some."

There was another silence.

The silence stretched.

The sun shone in a cloudless sky.

What now?

Ken was the leader. Ken spoke.

"You can see a little," he said to Meach. "Arne can walk a little. George is coming up from the Gap to Four today, and he'll have his medical kits with him. We'll have you down to him by dark."

He was still breathing hard, and speech was an obvious effort. But he rose to the effort. His voice was low but clear.

"Take an hour's rest here, Will," he told Meach. He looked at his watch. "That'll bring it to about two, and there'll still be time to get to Four before dark. I'll take you on one rope. Phutar and Nawang will take Arne."

That was five men.

There were nine, now, on the shoulder of the mountain.

"And the rest of us?" said Eric.

"The rest of you stay here."

"You mean—?"

That was Larry. Eric was silent. Tashi and Pembol were busy setting up the new tent.

"We brought up two good tents," Ken said. "There's enough food for at least three days. The weather's perfect, and will probably hold."

"We're not licked yet!" said Larry. He almost yelled it.

"No, we're not licked yet."

Tashi and Pembol heard this. They turned from their work, faces beaming.

"Pembol and me, we go up?" Tashi asked.

"That's up to Rick Sah'b," Ken said. "He'll be in charge here." The Sherpas looked at Eric.

He said nothing.

Ken turned back to Meach. "Rest now," he said. "Lie down in the tent." As Eric had done with him a while before, he helped Meach up and led him to it. "You too, Arne," he said to Norstad. "And me." He smiled wryly. "The walking wounded—"

The three crawled through the sleeve. Tashi and Pembol rejoined Phutar and Nawang in setting up the new tent. Then Eric and Larry also joined them. In half an hour the tent was up and secured, and though it tilted a bit, it was the best that could be done. They rested, sitting on rocks in the sun, and another half hour passed. Then Ken, Meach and Norstad appeared from their tent.

"Last time it took us three hours down," said Ken. "We should make it in five."

His breathing, if not yet right, seemed better. Norstad, his boots now laced, stumped experimentally around the campsite. Meach, wearing the dark goggles, also moved about, and could apparently see at least a little.

Ken took his walkie-talkie from his pack and gave it to Eric. "I'm taking the broken one," he said. "Maybe we can fix it. But anyhow, there'll be George's we can use." They agreed to go on the air at seven, by which time Barr would surely be at Camp Four, and Ken hoped to be.

There were few other words. The five who were descending roped up. Hands were shaken. And the last hand that Eric shook was Ken's. Like Meach—like everyone—they were wearing dark goggles, and they could not see each other's eyes.

It was just as well, Eric thought.

He sat, now, high on the snow dome.

He watched the others, close now: Larry, Tashi, Pembol.

But no Ken.

That was the bitter pill: no Ken. Ken, who had wanted this so much, who had tried so hard . . . So had Meach and Norstad, of course. And Loring and Kellerman . . . But not for so long. For so many years.

The three below had stopped to rest—their last rest, probably, before they reached him. Larry and Pembol looked up and waved their axes. But Tashi's ax remained fixed in the slope; his head was bent to it, his shoulders were heaving.

They rested for perhaps a minute. Then they came on. Tashi came on. His head was still bent, his small form swayed, his legs seemed ready to buckle. But still he came on with the others—slowly—slowly—

If there was no Ken, at least there was Tashi.

25

There was the rest of that day . . .

They took down the old Camp Five tent, with its torn side, loosened its guy ropes, and pushed it down the mountainside. In its place they set up the second of the new tents. On the now windless shoulder, the old one would have served all right as a shelter, but they wanted as sound a camp as possible for when they returned the following night.

They?

And who was *they?*

Eric had reached his decision. And as they sat out between the tents in the afternoon sunlight, he told the others what it was.

"The four of us will go," he said.

Tashi and Pembol beamed.

"Is fine—fine—Rick Sah'b," said Tashi. Beam became grin. "Two old birds and two young birds, we go to top."

"We go good. You will see," said Pembol.

Larry did not speak. When Ken, a while before, had chosen him as one of those to stay at Five, he had all but shouted in his joy. But from that he had known he would be one of the top team, whether it was two, three or four. Of all of them who had come up that day, he had done the best. He had earned his place, and knew it . . . As Eric knew it . . . Whatever his previous thoughts—of Julian, of Kay, of risk and hazard—he could not now deny the boy his chance at the top.

It was the way the cards were dealt, he had thought. Ken had dropped out of the running. Meach and Norstad, Loring and Kellerman had dropped out. Larry had not dropped out. He had earned the chance. Pembol and Tashi had earned it: Pembol on his tremendous performance of the past few days; Tashi on the record of years—because he *was* Tashi.

And himself?

Ah yes, himself . . .

What had *he* earned?

For him, it was not a matter of earning. It was a situation, a set of facts. He alone had been before on the heights of the mountain—on the Wailing Wall. The Sherpas were strong, eager, devoted, but no masters of rockcraft. Larry had proven himself as a climber, but he was a boy of twenty—his nephew—or his son— and it was inconceivable that he could let him go and stay behind. So, that was it. Whether he himself *wanted* to go, he didn't know. It didn't matter. He had to go. It was the way the cards were dealt.

They assembled their gear, readied their packs. Of food, they would take little: a few tins of meat, raisins, chocolate, some juices. But their climbing equipment would of necessity be bulky: several coils of rope, pitons (though there would probably be some old ones left on the Wailing Wall), axes and crampons for the summit snow dome. Into his own pack, finally, Eric slipped pad and pencil, and Larry, watching him, smiled.

"Notes from topside?" he asked.

"To read to your mother," said Eric, "over those martinis."

They ate an early supper, again sitting in the open between the tents. Then came the shadow moving up the mountainside. And soon after, dusk. At seven Eric turned up the radio, and George Barr came on. He was at Camp Four, and said that Ken and the others had arrived there about a half hour before. They were all right. Norstad's feet had begun to thaw on the way down (he was giving him librium for the pain), and Meach's vision was improving. On arrival, Ken had been the most done in, and had fallen asleep almost the moment he entered his tent. But he would be on the air in the morning. They would keep their radio open all through the next day, so that those above could call whenever they wanted.

"All four of us are going," Eric told him.

"Good," said Barr.

"We'll be leaving early. I'll call about sunrise."

"We'll be ready."

"That's it for now, I guess."

"Go get it," said Barr.

There was night . . .

The stars blazed.

And at eight they were in their tents.

Now there were only two instead of three of them in each, and consequently more room. But Eric and Larry were in the tent that tilted, and Larry, on the higher side, kept sliding down. Once, Eric awoke from sleep to a touch on his shoulder, and again, in that moment, Julian Howard came back. It had been here, in a tent at this place twenty years ago, that Julian, in the dark, had touched his shoulder and murmured, "Thanks, Rick." But this was not Julian. It was Larry. And he was asleep. Eric eased him back upslope to his own side of the tent, and still he didn't waken; he didn't speak. In the tent and beyond there was only stillness—and through the stillness, faint and distant, the sound of the wind on the Wailing Wall high above.

There was morning . . .

And it was still dark, still night, but his watch, in the beam of a torch, showed a few minutes past three-thirty. He wakened Larry. He called to the Sherpas, and they answered. Inside the tents, they pulled on their boots and outer clothing. Outside, they roped up, slung on their extra ropes and packs and hardware. Eric tied on with Tashi, Larry with Pembol. And Eric led off. As they moved up from the camp it was just short of four, and the starlight glittered on the snow of the ridge.

They wound between the ice spires—the tall stalagmites—and emerged on the open ridge above. The snow was deep in places, but not too deep for steady trudging, and before them, on and up, stretched the track made by Meach and Pembol the day before. Eric followed the track, stepping in each footprint to make the going easier. You did not climb a mountain alone, he thought, but in the tracks—on the backs—of others. It was Vic Kellerman who had mastered the great tower on the lower ridge. Will Meach and Pembol had been the pioneers here. Ken and Arne Norstad, George Barr and Paul Loring, Phutar, Nawang, the other Sherpas —all had done their share, lugged their loads, driven bone and flesh, to bring these two ropes of two to where they were now.

Thanks, and we'll be seeing you. We hope.

Even in the night, the starlight, he could recognize features of the ridge from his climbs of long ago. He had ascended this stretch twice on DZ 1: once with Julian on reconnaissance, once alone—with Julian following. Pembol had been on it yesterday. For Larry and Tashi, on the other hand, this was the first . . . No, not the first, he realized: not for Tashi . . . Tashi had climbed here, alone, in the night, on his rescue mission to the foot of the Wailing Wall. To find him, bring him down, save his life . . .

He wrenched his mind from the past. He looked back at the others: Tashi—Larry—Pembol. They were doing all right.

He was doing all right.

Now as they moved on, the stars were fading. Where there had been blackness there was grayness, and through the grayness, slowly, appeared the world around them. There were the ridge ahead, the abysses below. In the abysses were glaciers; beyond the glaciers, Kalpurtha, Malu, other mountains; a host, an ocean of mountains sweeping off through the miles. Already they were higher than most. By day's end, they might be higher than all. In the eastern Himalayas, only four summits—Everest, Kangchenjunga, Lhotse, Makalu—were higher than Dera Zor; and these all lay to the east, still hidden by the mass of Dera Zor itself.

To the west, behind them as they climbed, seen only when they turned, the mountain sea stretched out past the end of vision. To either side, they could see beyond it: on the north, to the plateau of Tibet; on the south, across the hills of Nepal to the plains of India. Above the plains, banding the morning sky, was a rack of clouds, dark and purplish—the same as had been there twenty years past—the clouds of the summer monsoon . . . The same, yet not the same. For they were more distant now . . . Then, on DZ 1, the climbers had not come to the heights until early June. Now it was just past mid-May; the monsoon was weeks off. Above the Himalayas the sky of dawn hung pure, translucent.

The mountains could make their own storms, of course. They already had. They could again, without warning. More than anything else, including man himself, weather, on a mountain, was the difference between success and failure. Between life and death. A storm had taken the summit away from Meach and Norstad. If it had caught them still higher, on the Wailing Wall or above, it would have taken their lives. Now it was gone. The world shone. Meach and Norstad were down, four others were up, and how long it would shine for them no one knew.

It was how the cards were dealt.

An hour had passed now since they left the camp. They were on the rise leading to the crest of the ridge from which they would be able to see the top of the mountain . . . Then they were there. And there it was . . . It was the dome that caught the eye first: high, white, gleaming in dawnlight. Down from it, toward them, swept the graceful arc of the upper ridge—also white, shining— and yes, it was still corniced; drifts of snow, like curved wings, projected from it above a two-mile depth of space; as beautiful, as murderous as ever. To its right—the south—beauty vanished. There was the wall, the Wailing Wall, dark and looming; so steep that it was barely flecked with snow; the core of Dera Zor, its bones laid bare. There were its columns, its fissures, its vast organ pipes, and the pipes sent down the wail of the fingering wind.

They stopped. They stared. For three of them, it was again; for Larry, the first time. He looked at the ridge, but he did not, like Julian, say, "It'll go." He was a mountaineer. He knew it would not go. He looked at the wall, studied it, was silent.

They moved on again.

And in less than an hour they reached the point where ridge met wall. Here, for Eric, was the haunted place, the place on all the mountain which he dreaded most—where Tashi had found him and Julian in the hollow in the snow—where he had said of Julian, "Cannot bring. Cannot help." Tashi said nothing now. Eric glanced down the snowy slope beneath the ridge, and there were many hollows. They were white, empty. There was no grave, like Franz's . . . Where was Julian now? He had never learned what Tashi had done on that morning . . . Was he lying close by, beneath the snow?—or had the years carried him down the mountain? halfway? to its base?—wherever he was, intact and frozen, unchanged in face and body from the day of death.

This was all in a moment, in a flick of seconds. Then he was no longer looking down but up: at the wall, the dome above, the brightening sky. Here on the ridge the sun had not yet risen, but its rays, streaming horizontal from the east, now lighted the summit snows with pink and orange fire.

They had stopped, he had unlimbered his radio, and there was Ken.

How were things? Ken asked.

All right . . . And below?

All right too. Meach's eyes and Norstad's feet were better— Meach to the point where he was ready to go back up to Camp Five. George Barr was in good shape too; he felt he could make it to Five. And Ken himself was ready to try. With two or three Sherpas, they would soon take off to meet the high team that evening on their descent.

"—from the top," said Ken.

"We'll try," said Eric.

"Go get it."

Then the radio was stowed. Eric turned to the wall. His eyes moved up its lower pitches: from point A (where they were), to crack B, to ledge C, to bulge D. It was all as if he had last looked at it a week before.

He glanced at Larry.

"You lead," Larry said. "You know it."

He nodded; then spoke to Tashi and Pembol. "On each rope," he said, "we'll move one man at a time. Larry and I will belay you as you come up. Watch where we put our feet and hands, and do the same."

414

The Sherpas nodded.

Eric moved out on the wall.

And yes, he thought, it had been a week ago. There was crack, ledge, bulge—another ledge, a narrow chimney—and he worked his way up almost mechanically. Progress was slow, however, for he himself was climbing less than half the time. As he had instructed, Tashi waited on each pitch while he went up for a rope's length and found a belaying point; then, at a signal, came after, with Eric securing him from above. Tashi did not slip. His small body was agile, and he seemed not to be bothered by the exposure on the precipice. But he was not, as Eric knew, an expert cragsman. Sometimes, with his short reach, he was unable to gain holds that Eric had used, and his search for others tended to be long and fumbling. Each time he came up to Eric's level, he looked at him for approval, and Eric nodded encouragement. Then Tashi waited, watching, while Eric went on again. What with his diminutive size and the almost vertical wall, a belay from below would have been useless. It was up to Eric himself not to slip or fall.

At the belaying points he looked down past Tashi, and the second rope was following the same procedure. Larry, in the lead, was climbing strongly and well; and Pembol, with a longer reach, seemed to be moving faster than Tashi. But their overall pace was, of necessity, set by that of the rope above them.

They came to the "wailing" part of the wall—the soaring pillars, the organ pipes, with the fissures between them. The wind keened, eddying around them. But it was not too strong, not too cold; the weather still smiled. Here and there on the smoother surfaces, Eric found, as expected, his old pitons still embedded in cracks; and these he used gratefully. One, however, came off in his hand as he tested it. Another—at a point where he knew he had driven one—was gone entirely. And here he hammered in new ones. As on the ascent years before, the main difficulty in climbing came from the pack and ax and other gear that hung bulkily from his shoulders and waist. But he made do with them. He edged and shifted, wormed and swung—and kept his balance.

There were the breaks in the organ pipes—the platforms and

embrasures—and here, as before, there was a place for rest. There were not, however, any big enough for all, or even two of them, and they spread themselves on four perches, hunched and small in the vastness . . . Like gargoyles, thought Eric, on the high eaves of a cathedral.

He looked out at the vastness: now even deeper, broader, than from the ridge below. At the Kalpurtha Glacier, ten thousand feet straight down between his dangling legs. At the mountains beyond, and those beyond them; at the hills and plains, at Nepal and India (Tibet was gone now, behind the wall), sweeping on and still on to the curve of earth's sphere. Only twice before in his life had he known such immensity: once, twenty years past, from this very place; once—for yes, there *had* been another time, even more remote—from the top of the Lookout in the Front Range of the Rockies. He had been with his father then. His father had pointed and said, "There's Denver." And he had seen Denver, and past it—all the way across Colorado, across America, to the Atlantic Ocean—with the eyes and mind of a boy of ten. He had not then been a gargoyle on a cathedral, but a king on a castle. And Robin had said, "Where there's a king there must be a queen."

In the gulf below there was a flash of movement, a spinning of pigtails. Then another voice spoke, a voice unheard now for many years. "I don't want you to do things," his mother said, "that are foolish and can hurt you."

Dera Zor returned. The gargoyles returned. On their perches, the others had taken food from their packs, and now Eric opened his, and ate and drank a little. He looked at his watch, and it was going on ten—almost an hour later than when he had been at this point on DZ 1. Almost two thirds of the Wailing Wall remained above them. He rose, called to the others, and again started to climb.

He had thought of telling Larry to take over the lead. Because of Tashi's troubles, he and Pembol were unquestionably the faster rope. But even out ahead, they could not move at their own pace; after each pitch they would have to wait for Eric and Tashi. For such climbing as they were now doing, it would be the height of imprudence to separate; too many things could happen in which one rope might need the other . . . Nothing did happen. They were just slow. Still slow . . . Some hundred feet above the resting place they came to the end of the organ pipes, and on the steep but rough slabs above them the going was somewhat easier. But even now there was small increase in speed, as Eric carefully scaled each successive pitch and brought Tashi up after him.

Further, he knew that the "easiness" would not last long; that, not far above, the slabs buckled out into the bulge, the overhang, that on DZ 1 had been the worst of all obstacles. As he moved up, he tried repeatedly to angle off to one side or the other; to avoid, to circumvent it. But there was no way out and around; only blank walls, sheer and holdless. He had to keep on, straight up, until he was directly beneath the bulge. Here was a ledge, small, sloping, but big enough for four, and at his signal the others came up beside him.

They scanned the rock above. One of the two pitons he had knocked in—the lower one—was still there, within arm's reach from the ledge. The second, higher piton was gone. Above the crack which had held it, the overhang flared out to its farthest point, crackless, holdless, then curved back above, out of sight.

"Is there a hold up beyond?" asked Larry.

"A few wrinkles," Eric said.

"May I lead it?"

Eric hesitated—but for only a moment. In the days past, Larry had earned the right to come. In the hours past, he had earned the right to lead. They were not Number 1 and Number 2 here. They were fellow climbers, equals.

"Go to it," he said.

In plain fact, the passage of the bulge was neither as hard nor as dangerous as it had been before. A second ascent is always simpler than a first. For several, there is less risk than for one alone. The first needed piton was already in place, and, with Eric tying into his rope and belaying from below, Larry moved up to it, tested it, used it as a handhold, then a foothold. He hammered in a second piton where the old one had been. Into it he slipped a carabiner, and passed his rope through the carabiner, so that

417

there would be a new and higher point of belay if he slipped up above. Now came the snout of the overhang, jutting and holdless, and standing on the higher piton, Larry inched up against its outward thrust. His right arm was extended, his hand searching above the snout for the hidden wrinkles on its upper side. Unlike Eric on his lone ascent, he at least knew they were there; but still it required the utmost in stretch and balance to reach them. There was a long wait. His body seemed half-pinioned against the rock, half-arched in space. Only his arm moved. Then a foot moved. One foot, then the other, left the piton below, and obviously he had the wrinkles, he was holding, gripping them, for now the whole of his body was moving slowly up. On the ledge below, Eric readied himself for a slip. If Larry fell, it would at least be for only part of the rope's length, not for ten thousand feet. But he did not fall. He had got his left hand up over the bulge; he was now pulling with both hands. His head was past the bulge; then his shoulders, trunk, thighs. He was up, over, out of sight. He had made it.

With the first man up, the worst was over, for now an anchorage above could hold a slip to a matter of inches. There was a wait while Larry rested. Then his call came down—"On belay"—and Pembol started up. He lost his footing momentarily on the second piton and had to be steadied. At the crux of the climb he could not quite grasp the wrinkles; the rope tightened and pulled him. But in a few minutes he too was up and over. Then Eric went. And he made the pitons. He maneuvered, stretched, found the wrinkles, then pulled—and whether he cleared the bulge on his own, or was held by the taut rope, he could not for the life of him have told. Nor did it matter. Soon he too was up. And now he took over from Larry for the belaying of Tashi.

He knew that Tashi would have trouble—and he did. He was not tall enough to reach from piton to piton, let alone around the bulge to the wrinkles, and had to be hauled almost all the way. His weight was negligible. Eric did not even need the help that Larry and Pembol gave him at the crucial point. But for the better part of five minutes Tashi was half-scrabbling, half-dangling over two miles of space, and when at last he appeared he was spent and shaken. They all rested again. At twenty-six thousand feet plus, after such exertion, they needed all the rest they could get. But it was Tashi, unmistakably, who was going to continue to be the problem. Apart from his smallness and slowness, he was now visibly losing strength and, for the first time on the mountain, was breathing in gasps and shudders. He should not have taken him, thought Eric; he should have left him at Camp Five. But even as he thought it, he knew he could not have done so. The defeat, the pain in that monkey face would have been more than he could have borne.

So what now? They couldn't leave him on the wall. The moment they had begun to climb the wall they had committed themselves as a team. They must all go up or all go down together.

Tashi read his thoughts. "Am bad—am sorry," he murmured.

Eric touched his shoulder. "No, you're all right. Easy does it. You'll get your breath back."

"Yes, will get." Tashi fought for control. "Am getting now. Will be O.K., Rick Sah'b."

A little later he rose.

"Am O.K. now. We go," he said.

The others rose too. They hauled up the packs and hardware that they had left, tied to ropes, beneath the overhang. They coiled the ropes, reslung loads, and were ready.

"Keep the lead," Eric said to Larry. "But don't get too far ahead of us."

Larry and Pembol started up. He and Tashi followed. Above the overhang the going was not too severe, and Tashi, behind him, moved slowly but steadily. After each rope's length of climbing, Larry and Pembol found stances and waited for them to come up. For another hundred-or-so vertical feet the wall was still familiar to him, still trodden ground, but he gave no directions to Larry as to which way to go. Larry needed none. He moved from hold to hold, from crack to knob, buttress to chimney, with the sound, sure instinct of a mountaineer.

Even his rope, however, was now slower than before. They had come to a height at which no man could climb except slowly, slowly, with pauses every few steps to suck in airless air. This was the stretch of wall—his next-to-highest stretch—where, before, Eric had felt his legs turn to rubber and lead; where hypoxia had seized him, with illusion, hallucination, and the rock of the mountain had seemed to heave like the sea . . . He looked up. It did not heave now. He felt the mountain, and its rock was rock . . . Hallucination came more readily to a man alone than to one with others: perhaps that was the answer. But eyes and mind were one thing, legs and lungs something else. Lead and rubber had returned; he was barely able to raise one foot above the other; he was breathing as convulsively as Tashi had breathed on the roof of the overhang.

Above, Larry and Pembol had stopped to rest. He rested too . . . Was it he, rather than Tashi, who was giving out? Even without injuries, others had reached their limits. Paul Loring at the Gap. Ken at Five. Was he reaching his now? What, for God's sake, *was* the limit for a man of forty-seven who hadn't climbed a mountain in twenty years? . . . What was he doing here anyhow? Was he mad? A sound came from him, half gasp, half laugh. Kay had had the name for him: the Mad Mahatma of the Mountains.

Steady, he thought. Steady . . .

Other "old birds" had gone as high as this—and higher. Dyhrenfurth, leader of the American expedition to Everest, had been forty-five when he climbed to within a few hundred feet of the top of the world. Hunt and Tenzing, with the British, had been no youngsters either . . . But they had not (presumably) spent years of their life swilling arak and Haig Pinch in the bar of a crumbbum hotel. And they had had oxygen . . . That was what he needed: oxygen. What sort of nonsense, of inane hubris, had it been to challenge a twenty-seven-thousand-foot mountain without oxygen? His lungs cried for it. Flesh, blood, bones cried for it. He could not go on without it.

Steady . . .

Above, Larry and Pembol had started climbing again. Below, Tashi was on his feet, ready. Larry and Tashi, too, had had their troubles, and here they still were. Here he still was. He stood up. ("God damn you, breathe!") He breathed. ("God damn you, move!") He moved. He climbed.

From the rocks above, his father looked down at him.

"—And not to yield," he said.

It had been a little past noon when they topped the overhang. Then it was one . . . Then two . . .

And now they came to his former high point on the wall, the place where he had turned off toward the ridge—and Julian. He looked at the ridge, and there was no movement now; it rose white, bare, frozen against the sky. He looked back at the wall— up the wall—and Larry and Pembol were still climbing. But slowly —slowly. From here on, as he had noted before, the angle of the rock eased off; all technically difficult going seemed to be behind them. The rim of the summit snow dome gleamed not far above: no more than two hundred vertical feet. But at their present rate, their best possible rate, it would take them two hours to reach it. It was now going on three. Larry and Pembol had stopped again. He signaled them to stay where they were, and he and Tashi came slowly up and sat beside them.

"We can't make it today," he said.

The others were silent.

"The dome won't be hard, I think. We could do it in the dark— reach the top. But coming down—no. Not the wall in the dark."

He stopped, breathing hard.

The three others were breathing hard.

"We must either go down now—"

"No," said Larry.

"—or get to the dome and find some shelter for the night."

"A snow hole," Larry said.

"Yes, a snow hole. There'll be lots of snow, from the storm. It should still be soft, not frozen."

"And in the morning," said Larry, "we go for the top."

There was another silence.

Eric looked at the Sherpas, and they nodded.

"Can you make the dome?" he asked Tashi.

"Yes, Rick Sah'b, I make it—if go slow."

"We'll go slow all right."

They rested. They breathed. Then Eric remembered the radio. All the way up the wall he had not used the radio; he had forgotten it; there had been too much else. Now he asked Tashi to take it from the pack on his pack, and, holding it in mittened hands, he turned it up.

There was a crackle of static—then Ken. Ken faintly but audibly.

"Can you read me? Over," said Eric.

"Roger. We've been worried. Over," said Ken.

Eric told him where they were, and paused to breathe. He told them their plan, and paused to breathe. "We won't be down until tomorrow. Late tomorrow," he said.

"Roger, late tomorrow," Ken replied.

He was at Camp Five, he said. He, Meach and Barr, with two Sherpas, had come up that day from Four, and would now spend the night there. In the morning, if they were able—and they were all in fair shape now—they would come up to meet the descending top team at the foot of the Wailing Wall.

"With wheelchairs," said Eric.

"No, champagne."

They agreed to talk again that evening when the snow hole had been built. They signed off. Eric handed the radio back to Tashi to stow in his pack, and between their mittened hands it slipped and fell. Both snatched for it, but too late. It hit a rock a few feet down the wall, bounced out into space, and was gone.

"Oh, Rick Sah'b—" Tashi's face was desolate.

"It's all right, Tashi. We both dropped it. Anyhow, they know the main thing—that we won't be down until tomorrow."

Tashi did not say, "Tomorrow it go bang." No one said anything more. The thing had happened, and breath was for climbing. Feet were for climbing, and they got to their feet, and were climbing again. Eric and Tashi resumed their place in the lead. There was no tactical reason for it; simply that they had been sitting in slightly higher positions during the stop. Whoever led, they would do no more than creep.

But Eric had been right in his judgment from below. The wall was easing—easing. Indeed, it was now less a wall than the steep slope of a roof, and though hands were still needed for balance and leverage, there was no call for delicate maneuvering or for belaying the Sherpas. At least, as they crept, it was all four at a time, with pauses only for rests.

It was four o'clock . . .

Four-thirty . . .

The base of the snow dome was very close now—no more than fifty feet above—its whiteness shining in late-afternoon sunlight. But peering up, Eric saw that in its final reach the wall flared up again, almost to verticality, and that there would be one more bit of tricky rock work before the snow was reached. There would be nothing as bad as the overhang, however. Below, there had been no choice of routes, but here there was, and, making his choice, he bore to the right, then straight up a pitch that, though steep, had adequate holds. For a way, at least. Then the holds gave out; the rock rose sheer and seamless. But it was no dead end he had come to, for to the side, projecting from the wall, was a buttress, and the buttress was climbable. For the first ten feet there were holds, for the next ten or so a crack wide and deep enough for jamming with knee and elbow. Finally, toward the top, the crack narrowed; there could be no jamming there. But at least it did not end. It continued. It could take a piton. With a single piton hammered in, first to secure his rope, then for hand- and foothold, he would be at the top of the buttress, above the sheer wall—above the whole of the Wailing Wall on the rim of the snow dome.

It took him fifteen minutes. There was no single move all the way that was not plain to him, that would not have been almost routine on a lesser mountain. But here, the making of the moves, the mere lifting of hand or foot, was a monstrous effort. From somewhere—God knows where, he thought—within him, he called up the reserves of breath and strength that were needed. With Larry now belaying from below, he climbed the section with holds. He clung, resting. He jammed up the ensuing crack as far as it was wide enough to hold him; then clung again, but not resting now—there was no way to rest—holding himself to the rock with his hands pressed to smoothness and one deeply wedged knee. Above was the place for the piton, and he needed both hands to get it in. He lifted them from the rock, first tentatively, then wholly, and his knee alone held him. It quivered and ached, it was rubber and lead, but still it held him, and his hands, moving quickly now, loosened the needed hardware from his waist. Then he raised his arms. And still his knee held. His balance held. He got the nose of the piton into the crack above, and swung the hammer, and there was the clank of metal on rock as the thin spike went in, true and deep. With the last of the strokes he was breathing so hard that he feared the thrust of his chest against the wall would at any moment push him off. But he got a hand down and stowed the hammer in a parka pocket. He brought out a carabiner. He snapped his rope through the carabiner, and the carabiner into the piton. Now he had his support from above. He tested the piton, grasped it, pulled himself up. He was kneeling, then standing on it. Before his eyes now there was no longer rock but snow; no longer steepness but a gentle white slope.

He stepped up onto it. He sank down into it. For a while he simply breathed, while, below, the others waited. Then, slowly, he did what next had to be done: finding a secure position in the snow and passing the rope in anchoring position around his shoulder and waist.

"On belay," he called down.

It was dusk . . .

The sun had flamed and set. The sky and snow had gleamed with rainbow color, then drained into a sweep of gray and white. With axes and hands they had dug a hole in a drift at the base of the dome, and now they huddled within it. Protected on three sides by walls of whiteness, they looked out to the south.

They were directly above the Wailing Wall, but the wall was invisible, tucked beneath the rim of the dome. There was only space, distance. Nepal, India. Above India, the horizon was banded by the clouds of the monsoon, but the Himalayan sky was still clear. In the distance, now below them, they could hear the familiar keening in the organ of the wall. But the wind on the dome was negligible, and the cold was not too bad.

"Whoever's in charge is still with us," said Larry.

In the fading light they left the hole and looked at what was left of Dera Zor above them. It was all snow, all billowing slope. The underlying ice, as they had discovered while digging, was deeply covered, and they would not need crampons, only axes. But the snow would be deep in many places, and there would be many steps to kick. At the top of the dome its curving sides met in a final point of whiteness against the darkening sky; but whether this was the summit they could not tell. It might be. Or it might be a false summit, with the true one behind it. But it did not greatly matter, for it would not be far behind. At the best reachable estimate, they had some five hundred vertical feet still to go. With the deep snow, the altitude, and their physical depletion, they might need as much as an hour for each hundred. If they left their bivouac at first light—about five o'clock—they should reach the summit by ten, leaving the rest of the day for the descent of the dome and the Wailing Wall.

Back in the snow hole, they ate a supper of sorts. They had no stove, of course, but again munched raisins and chocolate, opened two tins of pressed beef, and sucked at half-frozen juices. Tashi said he wanted no food, but Eric made him eat some, and he did not throw it up. Instead, he fell asleep with a chocolate bar still in his hands.

Tashi was tired, very tired. So were they all, but Tashi most so.

It was night . . .

Again stars blazed.

In the hole they half-sat, half-lay on coils of rope between the snowy walls, their breath hanging in clouds of steam around them. They kept their mittened hands in their parka pockets and shoved their booted feet into their packs, for an extra layer of protection against the cold. From his own pack, Eric's writing pad spilled out, and Larry, seeing it, grinned.

"No notes for Mother?" he asked.

"That's for the top," said Eric.

Tashi still slept. Soon Larry and Pembol slept. But tired as he was, he himself could not sleep. He willed to, but still could not. He lay watching the stars.

When he looked at his watch it was a little past ten.

The next time it was not quite midnight.

Then almost two.

Avoiding the others, he crept from the hole. Below was a sea of blackness, on which the snow dome rested like a floating island. Above were the dome, the stars; the point where the dome ended and there were only stars. For a long time he looked up, then returned to the bivouac.

The others still slept. Crawling past Larry and Tashi, he touched Pembol on the shoulder, spoke his name. And Pembol opened his eyes.

"Yes, Rick Sah'b?"

"I'm going to start up now," Eric told him.

He could not have said this to Larry or Tashi. They would have protested—or insisted on coming. Pembol would do as he was told.

"The snow is deep," Eric said. "I'm going to make steps in it. When the rest of you start up it will be better going."

Pembol's small eyes blinked. He nodded. He was still half-asleep.

"Understand?" Eric asked.

"Yes, Rick Sah'b."

"You leave at five. You'll catch me halfway up."

"Yes, Rick Sah'b."

Eric turned away. He needed no pack, no rope, no crampons. He was already fully clothed. He took his ax and left the snow hole. Again he looked up through the night. Then he kicked a step. And another . . .

Once before, he had started up alone from the highest camp toward the top of the mountain.

But this was different. Very different.

426

26

In the beginning was the mountain. In the end was the mountain.
In the beginning was the Lookout.

In the end was Dera Zor. Through dark and dawn and sunrise
he had climbed alone up its summit dome. But now he was no
longer alone. There were Larry, Tashi, Pembol. They had climbed
after, in his steps; they had caught up, reached him, and now
they sat beside him on his perch in the sky.

At first, no one spoke. The three sat in the familiar position
of rest: heads bent over axes, bodies heaving for breath. Then
Larry raised his bearded and goggled face.

"You're out of your mind," he said. "But thanks for the staircase."

"I needed exercise," said Eric.

There was silence again, except for the breathing. Presently
Pembol, too, raised his head; but Tashi remained bent over his
ax, his small frame shuddering in its struggle for air.

"He's had it rough," Eric said.

Larry nodded. "Otherwise, we'd have caught up sooner. I kept
asking if he didn't want to stop and wait for us, or go back to the
snow hole. But each time he said no. He begged to go on."

The effort of so many words left Larry, too, gasping. When he
was able to speak again, he said, "He kept saying, 'If Rick Sah'b
can, then I can too.'"

There was another pause.

"So what could I do?" said Larry.

"What you did," said Eric.

They looked down the white slope, to its rim, to space beyond. Then, turning, Larry looked up toward the summit.

"I'd say about two hundred more feet," he said.

"About that."

Larry glanced at his watch. "Eight-thirty," he said.

He breathed a few more times—slowly, deeply—and stood up. Pembol stood up. Tashi at last lifted his head; he looked at them; he tried to rise too. But his legs would not hold him, and he swayed and fell. When he tried a second time to get up, he again could not do it, and Eric, sitting beside him, put an arm around his shoulder. Even with Tashi's bulky clothing, it was like putting an arm around a child.

"Rest now," Eric said.

Tashi struggled. "No rest," he gasped. "Must climb."

"You can't climb anymore. You'll stay here."

"No—"

"Yes, stay here," said Eric softly. "You and I—we're going to stay here together."

Tashi seemed not to hear him.

But Larry did.

"What?" he said hoarsely.

Eric looked up at him. "Tashi and I will stay here," he said. "You and Pembol go on."

Larry stared. His goggles stared.

"But—but the rest is easy—nothing—"

"Still I'm staying," said Eric.

Tashi at last understood what was happening. "No—no, Rick Sah'b," he protested. "You not stay for me—no."

"It's not just for you," Eric said. "I've climbed enough."

"Enough?" That was Larry. "With the top just a walk—"

Tashi tried to rise again. He fell again. Eric turned to Larry.

"It's true, son," he said. "I've been climbing this mountain for twenty-five years. That's enough."

Larry stood wordless.

Now it was Eric who looked at his watch.

"Go on," he said. "You and Pembol. You'll be on top in two hours. Spend, say, fifteen minutes there. You'll be back here in three hours. That will give us time to get down the wall before dark."

Larry still stood there.

"Go on. Please go. Now."

The goggles stared. Larry made one more try. "But Dera Zor is yours," he said. "It belongs to you."

"No—to you now. You and Pembol. Go get it."

Larry shook his head. "I called you crazy before. But now—*now* —I don't understand—"

Eric smiled a little. "Maybe you will when you're forty-seven," he said.

A long moment passed.

Then Larry breathed deep. He hefted his ax. Nodding to Pembol, he faced upslope and began to climb. A sound, half cry and half moan, came from Tashi and again he tried to rise, but Eric held him gently. Larry, kicking steps, moved slowly up the snow above them, and Pembol followed.

Eric watched them a while.

When he turned away, Tashi was crying. Tears slipped out from under the rim of his goggles and froze on his cheeks.

Eric pressed his shoulder. "None of that," he said.

"Am sorry—sorry. Am no good," said Tashi.

"You've been tremendous."

"Is not for myself I cry, Rick Sah'b. Is for you. That for me you stop here—not go to top."

"I told you it's not just for you," Eric said. "I don't want to go any farther."

"But Rick Sah'b—"

"It's a good spot here. Rest. You're breathing better already. We'll have three hours' rest and going down will be easy."

He leaned back against the snow of the slope. Though it was cold (the frozen drops still glinted on Tashi's cheeks), there was no wind, and the beaming sun gave the illusion of warmth. It was like one of those spring days, he thought, on the slopes of White Valley, in Utah—except that from White Valley you could

429

not see half the Himalayas plus Nepal and India. Barring the distant monsoon clouds, all was radiantly clear; and he was aware, too, of an inner clarity, a calm and peace within himself. They were at almost twenty-seven thousand feet on the dome, but his breathing, at rest, was slow and even. There was no hint of hypoxia, of hallucination; no dead men—or a long-dead girl—beside him, but only Tashi.

Tashi seemed better now. He was no longer crying, and his breathing, too, was easier. But he did not suggest going on, nor again try to get up. He had accepted the fact that they were going no farther. He was a Sherpa. An Asian. He took what came and made the best of it.

"It's nice here, Tashi," said Eric.

"Yes, nice, Rick Sah'b."

"Good view."

Tashi managed a smile. "Like from Empire State House in New York," he said.

Eric turned, looked up.

Larry and Pembol were smaller now—much smaller—no more than specks again. They were moving faster than when they had been with Tashi, and seemed to be almost halfway to where the two skyline arcs of the dome met at a white point in the sky. In another hour or so they would reach the point . . . And have another view, Eric thought. A view in full circuit, with all Dera Zor below . . . And Everest beyond, rising higher . . .

Tashi was looking up too.

"The young birds they go whoosh," he said.

"Yes, whoosh," said Eric.

"They get there soon."

"Soon."

"When you speak before to Larry Sah'b, you call him son," said Tashi.

"Did I?"

"—And I think that is like what I say when we leave Namche Bazar." Tashi paused, sorting out his thoughts. Then he said, "Larry Sah'b he your nephew, but like son. So for me, Pembol

like son. You, me, we have no sons. But yes, we have"—he pointed
—"they are there. They are our sons, Rick Sah'b, they climb the
mountain for us, and it is like we climb ourselves."

They watched the specks—ever smaller, higher. Then Eric
turned away. Again he leaned back comfortably against the slope.

"—And so to yield," he said.

"What, Rick Sah'b?" said Tashi.

"I said the young birds climb, the old birds rest."

"Yes. Is good to rest."

Eric was looking out and down again. Now it was he who
pointed.

"There's Denver," he said.

"What, Rick Sah'b?"

"I was thinking of another time, another mountain. The whole
world there. Us here. Fathers and sons. Not climbing now; just
resting, looking. With no sweat—no sweat at all."

That wasn't his father, though, thought the dentist's son from
Desmond Street.

That was Amy.

He thought of Amy.

He thought of Kay.

It was the first time he had ever thought of Amy and Kay simultaneously, and it produced an improbable image. He had returned
to Kathmandu and was in the bar of the Himalayan Palace Hotel.
He had entered the bar with Kay, and there was Amy behind the
counter, and he and Kay sat down on adjoining stools. "Two
martinis, please," he said to Amy. "Very dry, on the rocks, with
a twist." And Amy looked at him. At Kay, beside him. And Amy
said—

He made a sound, and Tashi looked at him.

"You laugh, Rick Sah'b."

Eric nodded.

"You think of something funny?"

"Yes."

"You have much to think of. Much funny, much sad. Much
things have happened with you, have they not, Rick Sah'b?"

Through his brush of beard Eric smiled. From his pack he took his small pad and stub of pencil and clumsily made a note with his mittened hand.

"I could write a book," he said.